BENEATH THE SHATTER

T.A. REILLY

Editor: Taylor Robinson (Instagram: @tayloredtext) & Caitlin Lengerich (Instagram: @chronicledbycait)

Proofreader: Brittany Corley (Instagram: @thisbitchreads_)

Cover Designer: Moonpress (Instagram: @moonpressdesign)

H&B's: V. Domino (Instagram: @author.v.dom)

Hand Art: Mikki (Instagram: @art.bymikki)

Map Frame: Amanda Hawkins (Instagram: @eternalgeekery)

Character Art: Angelika Nidua Buergo (Instagram: @colouranomaly)

 Formatted with Vellum

Author's Note

As a reader, I love reading about adventure, romance, and anything fantasy. About being swept off my feet and dragged into a world of my own imagination. When I wrote this, I wanted to make it precisely the type of book *I* would pick up and read. I could see the story written in my mind, a story I had on repeat over the years, a story that just had to be shared.

This is a new adult fantasy book, and is not recommended for minors. Please consider all trigger warnings before starting the book.

This book may include triggers such as: violence, bloodshed, on-page death, profanity, torture, kidnapping, alcohol, murder, and explicit scenes (please refer to the Spice Rack for specific chapters).

Reggeon
Sea of Avyz
Estaire
Avyon
Caperdov
Calante
Saltridge Point
Nytestarr
Krymson Forest
Arcelya
Verastarr
Château Co

East Engles
Hallyus
VANAIYER REALM
Dyfinn
Nordak
Kyllios
Vytley Inn

Playlist

◄   ▶   ►

Power - Isak Danielson

Secrets and Lies - Ruelle

Monsters - Ruelle

Downfall - Neoni

Fallout - Unsecret & Neoni

Fangs - Neoni

A Little Wicked - Valerie Broussard

Waves of Grey - Ruelle

Love into a Weapon - Madalen Duke

Prisoner - Raphael Lake

Darkside - Neoni

Vanaiyer Magic Guide

ELEMENTAL MAGIC

Elemental magic is the magic a citizen of
Vanaiyer is born with, gifted from The God.

Shadow Wielder   **Fire Wielder**

Mist Wielder   **Air Wielder**

Water Wielder   **Land Wielder**

POWERS OF THE REALM

Powers only naturally appear in royals. Any
others who possess these abilities have sworn
loyalty to the ruler of their land.

Wolvyn Shifters
the power of Verastarr
they have the ability to shift into a larger than life wolf and can
communicate down a bond to other wolvyn

Vamprys
the power of Avyon
they have the ability to move swiftly, their fangs can inject
venom, and their blood heals (though this is not a widely
known fact)

Tidesworn Syrens
the power of the East Engles
they can breathe underwater and feel the call of the sea

Fae
the power of Reggeon
they have the ability to fly and their power allows them to fly
unseen

Gryffins
the power of Nordak
they have the ability to shift into a part lion, part winged
creature

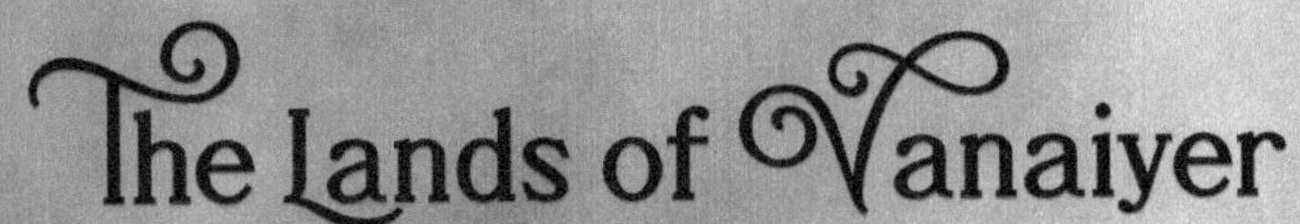

The Lands of Vanaiyer

The Vanaiyer Realm consists of five unique
lands, all connected by the Sea of Avyz

VERASTARR

Home to the Wolvyn
King: Adrastan Capetian
(claimed throne by default after his father)

AVYON

Home to the Vamprys
King: Kodrayn Deverell
*(claimed throne after his father's passing by
fighting to claim the title)*

EAST ENGLES

Home to the Tidesworn Syrens
King: Carawn de Caude
*(claimed throne by murdering his brother
and marrying his brother's wife)*

REGGEON

Home to the Fae
King: Ryker
*(claimed throne when his father relinquished
the title)*

NORDAK

Home to the Gryffins
King: Dathrian Demira
(claimed throne by default after his father)

Pronunciation Guide

Cassandra: Cuh-sahn-drah
Sébastien: Seh-bast-e-ahn
Capetian: Cap-eh-tea-ahn
Kateya: Cat-e-ah
Dravyn: Dray-vin
Emalyee: Emma-lee
Eryx: Air-icks
Kodrayn: Code-drahn
Aerilyn: Air-ill-in
Ryker: Rye-ker
Adrastan: Ah-drast-ahn
Kairon: Kai-ron
Vanaiyer: Van-air
Avyz: Ah-ve-zuh
Caperdov: Cap-er-dove
Nytestarr: Night-star

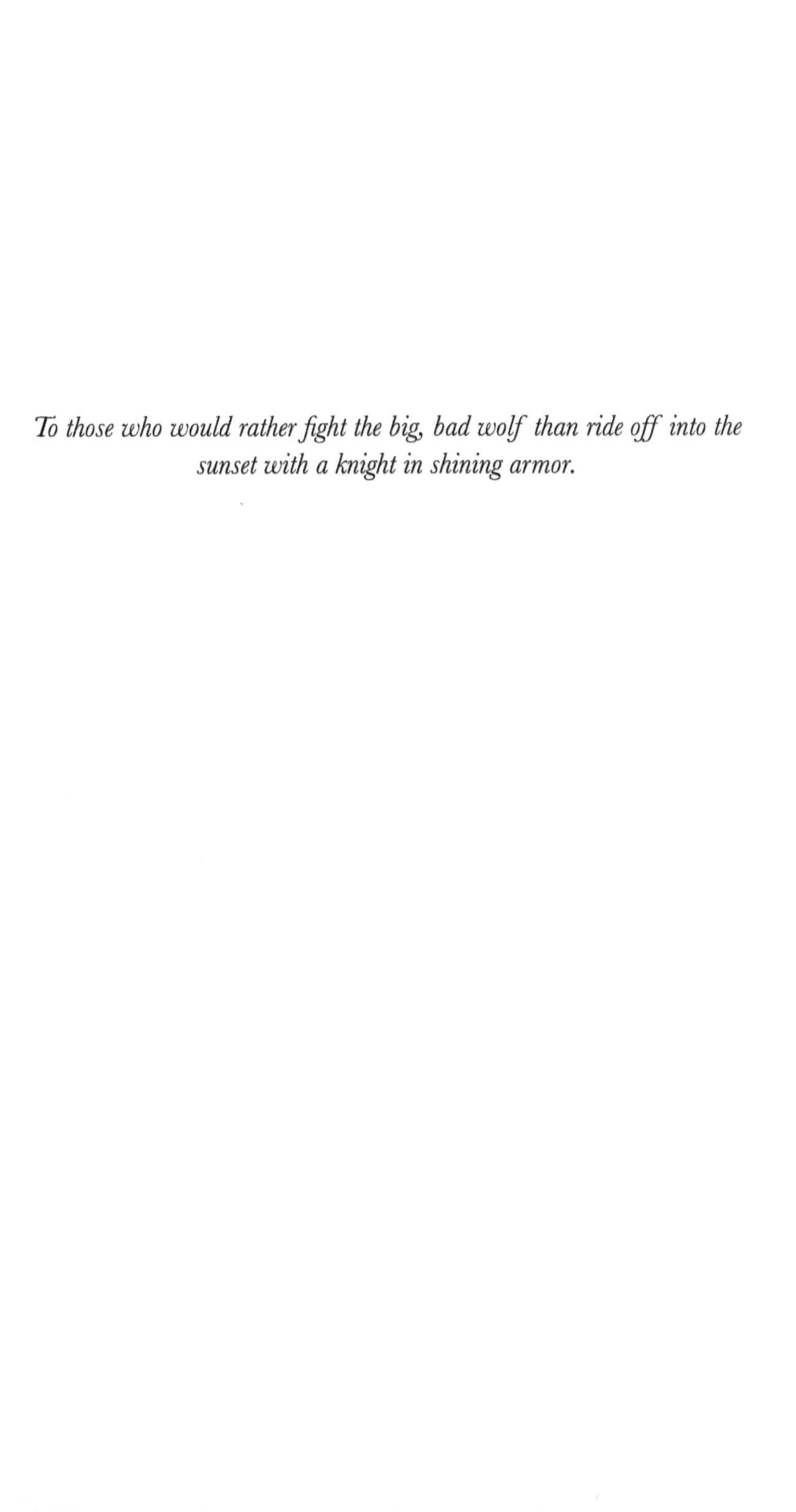

To those who would rather fight the big, bad wolf than ride off into the sunset with a knight in shining armor.

VERASTARR

I PAUSED, grimacing as the rough edge of the stone sharply dug into the palm of my hand, pain coursing through me. Glancing upward, I watched my sister, perched on a foothold an arm's distance from me, as she placed her hand in the stone's crevasse and lowered herself down.

The golden-orange sunset was at our backs as we carefully eased our way down the tower's ruins. As the rough stone gave way to the soft grass, I stepped back, leaving room for Kateya to jump down. Once she had landed, we looked at each other, grinning. Even as we began to feel exhausted from the strenuous climb, we were not entirely over the surreal feeling we had felt when sitting on top of the tower, overlooking the land.

Our mother's voice calling for dinner shook us from our adrenaline high, sending our thoughts scattering as we hurried over toward our picnic spot—a patch of grass a mere two meters from a circular pond that held the sun's reflection. We sat by the water's edge—Kateya, our parents, and I—with our backs facing away from the tower ruins, looking over the pond and the setting sun, and I felt a welcoming peace. As if all was right in the realm.

That blanket of happiness lasted through the night as we

laughed and talked by the fire's light, reminiscing over our adventures and memories, wishing the day could last forever.

While we sat on the grass, the pinks and oranges in the sky faded to blues and blacks, and my parents decided it was time to make our way back to town. We walked the bustling, Verastarr streets for the last time, taking in all the unique smells and sensations. The summer breeze was gently tugging my long, brownish-blonde hair, making it dance in the night air. Smells of rich cuisine and chocolate pastries drifted by, alluding to a magical night.

I stopped by a fountain with a statue in the center of an angel flying off the water—head looking up—eyes focused on The Void. Slowly, my gaze lifted toward the sky, mimicking the carved angel, and skimmed over the full moon—the stars.

I closed my eyes and prayed to The God, wishing I never had to leave this land.

Turning away, a wrinkled, cracked hand urgently snatched my wrist. Clean, painted nails dug into my skin as I whirled around. My eyes widened as my breath caught in my throat, my voice momentarily escaping me. I cautiously took in the appearance of the person grabbing my wrist. She was an elderly woman who appeared close to ninety years old, with fine, white hair, wearing a simple, silky dress with a lightweight shawl hanging off her shoulders. She looked at me with a fierce, determined gaze, her eyes a deep purple with a mysterious silver swirl.

"Take this." she croaked. "And when the time comes, you must be ready!" She fumbled to open my closed hand.

"Take what? Ready for what?" I questioned, concern laced in my tone. My voice was heavy with suspicion as I regarded the stranger. I could feel a small object with sharp edges being pushed between my fingers before I could reject it.

"An artifact. A memory." she replied, placing the smooth

object in my palm and curling her fingers over mine. "For when you desire it the most."

She released my hand, then pushed me away, vanishing into thin air right in front of my eyes. Pushing me from the fountain and from Verastarr itself. I made my way toward my family, barely processing my surroundings, wondering why the elderly woman gave me this object. I pondered her last statement: *For when you desire it the most.*

I unfolded my tightly closed palm to reveal a red, rectangular pendant on a simple, gold chain. The pendant itself was a ruby-red gemstone with swirls of gold, and a few more intricate designs trapped within it. I gazed at the pendant, wondering what I was to do with it, before shoving the necklace into my pocket. I planned to look at it further in the morning.

Looking up, I focused on being present with my family and noticed how the streetlights left patterns of light and shadow on the road before me.

A sense of peace settled over me as I walked home that night, away from Verastarr, the place that I loved so dearly.

I knew then that I would find my way back, somehow, sometime, should The God allow me to . . .

"LADIES AND GENTLEMEN, we will begin boarding Flight 253 to Nytestarr in Verastarr in 30 minutes."

The announcement blared from the overhead speakers, shaking the darkened thoughts from my mind. I stood by the security checkpoint at Estaire International Airport, saying goodbye.

It was still a shock to me that I was returning—after twelve years away—to my childhood home.

I remembered the stories my parents whispered when I was younger in our childhood home, stories about the ancient times. Times when the regions were at peace. When The God was pleased with the rulers of the regions, magic flowed naturally from the land, and power thrummed in our veins. When the hues of The Vanaiyer Realm were brighter and mystic waterfalls and star-showers filled the regions.

The Nordak disturbed that peace hundreds of years ago as they hunted and stole the magic of the regions, harvesting it in darkened channels, which led to what was whispered of as the Great War.

All that was known was that the Great War was a war of the five regions, during which, a dark magic was cast and shattered the boundaries, releasing the Seefers, and forcing those with magic and power in their veins to hide.

I often wondered what truly occurred.

I wished we had more than tales passed down, yet most of the records in the Archives had been destroyed when the Nordak took control of our lands to keep us from learning our own history, from learning of the magic that had flowed throughout our land.

Fresh out of university, I had secured a job as a journalist, working for Madelyn Leroy, the CEO of *Destined Magazine*. It was the leading magazine for all things travel and news, and working there had been my dream since I was in my first term of university, sitting in a lecture hall for an Intro to Journalism course. I couldn't believe my luck when I got the phone call. Sure, it was a smaller section, covering news, but I said yes with no hesitation. My university roommate, Aerilyn, had gotten a call two months later with an offer for an intern position. We made it our goal to take *Destined Magazine* by storm, outranking each other and those around us whenever we could manage.

Three years later, I had risen in rank at the magazine. At twenty-four, I was the youngest journalist, with my own column, focusing on the latest travel trends and hotspots. Travel was still limited, as the Nordak controlled every aspect of our lives, including air travel and the approvals to visit other lands, which could take months to be granted.

Aerilyn had also excelled in her department and now held an artistic designer position—calling all the shots on photography for the magazine.

Three months into starting my own column, Madelyn Leroy herself called me into her downtown Estaire office, one of three main offices in our land, to discuss a new story. She had received an invitation from the royal family of Verastarr inviting *Destined Magazine* to the royal coronation ceremony.

Madelyn had gone on and on in the office, talking about

how just because she was the CEO of a leading magazine, did not mean she had all the time in the realm to travel for "just another story." I was not currently attached to any stories of high importance, and the piece would fit nicely into my column; therefore, she decided I was the perfect candidate to travel to Verastarr for the coronation.

I was unsure why *this* royal coronation was more important than the one in Reggeon two months ago, or Avyon a year before that. Yet, I nodded excitedly at the prospect of travel and took the piece—happy she recognized my worth as a journalist.

It seemed that royal coronation ceremonies had graced the headlines of every newspaper for the past three years, and they didn't appear to be stopping anytime soon. The East Engles were bound to have a coronation a few years from now, once the Seefer attacks settled down, but I was content to avoid the flock of citizens that would arrive on the sandy shores of Estaire, where our Capital was located.

Which is what led me to this moment, at the entrance to the security checkpoint, saying goodbye to my sister Kateya as I headed off to Verastarr for the next week and a half.

Kateya and I had always been close, but we had gotten closer after I headed off to university. No longer sharing a room and stealing each other's clothes (and then denying it) seemed to have been a turning point for our relationship. While we weren't always the best of friends, we frequently met up for dinner and drinks, sharing stories and laughing at the stupid things we had fought over growing up.

Two years younger, Kateya was finishing up her fourth term at a university forty-five-minutes south of me, and was my complete opposite. While I had spent my time focusing on journalism and completed multiple internships, Kateya was on the executive board at her university and participated in various events daily, while still unsure of what she wanted to do after college.

Shifting my purse, I glanced over at my sister. "If I don't go now, I'm going to miss my flight and will never hear the end of it at work," I said with a slight laugh.

"Yeah, yeah. I know. Go off and be the big-time journalist that you are," my sister joked back. "I hope you know, I tried a million different ways to fit myself inside your suitcase. I still can't believe that you get to go back. It's been *so* long since we were last in Verastarr. I miss it."

"I've missed it too," I responded softly. My fingers unconsciously reached for the necklace I had worn nearly every day since the night I left Verastarr—the necklace that had strangely become a part of me. "I sometimes wish we had never left. Don't get me wrong, I love it here in Estaire, and I know we had to move back home at some point. But there was just something about it, wasn't there?"

"Yes. I don't know how to explain it, though. It just had a certain feel to it. I wonder if it will still feel the same now, after . . . you know, *The Fall*," the whisper came out.

Darkness clouded my mind as I thought about The Fall and how it still haunted our lives seven years later. The Fall of the Cordial shook The Vanaiyer Realm in a way I had never thought possible. The Nordak encased the realm in despair as they rained terror down on the four other lands of The Vanaiyer Realm. Reggeon fell first, with Avyon and Verastarr close behind. We were lucky, but not by much. The East Engles were across the Avyz Sea, which meant that the full force of the Nordak didn't hit at once.

When it did, no one stood a chance.

The first to be hunted by the Nordaks were those with ancient ties to magic, and once their magic had been harvested, the Seefers were released to feed on us mortals. I often wondered why The God would allow our land's magic and power to be drained, our realm to be shredded to pieces by the clutches of darkened magic. Why would The God establish the realm, only to allow its inhabitants' lifelines to be swallowed back into The Void much too early?

"It felt like home," I answered my sister. "But like, a peaceful, calming sense of home. *The Fall* took so much away, and we've lost too many souls to The Void. I wish we could just go back to before that time."

Kateya nodded in agreement. "I wish I could come with you. I know I have final exams, but what I wouldn't give to trade places with you right now and jet off to Verastarr and live on chocolate pastries, bread and good drinks every day."

Laughing, I thought about the delicious smell of freshly baked bread and how good a warmed pastry would taste.

A vibration in my pocket pulled me from the thoughts. I took my phone out of my back pocket to check my notifications.

> Aerilyn: Girlll. Where are you?! The flight boards soon, and I've got dibs on any hot men in first class. I don't plan to share!

I couldn't help but laugh. Of course my best friend had managed to work her way onto this trip as well. I mean, who would miss the opportunity to go to a royal coronation? Aerilyn would live and breathe gossip and luxury if given the chance.

Turning my attention back to Kateya, I responded with, "I can promise you I will eat more than enough pastries for the both of us! But if I don't make it through security, neither of us will be getting any pastries for a long time."

"I *know*. Fly safe, okay? And maybe bring me back a fresh load of bread, if possible. I promise I will love you forever if you do!" Kateya grinned as she said her goodbye.

"Can't promise anything, there's a good chance I will eat it before it makes its way back here, but I'll see what I can do for you." Grabbing my bags, I turned away, my hand nervously reaching for my necklace once again, as I did out of habit so often. There was practically no one in line at security, as was typically the case at EEI, since it was such a small airport. But just as I was about to enter the gated line, a hug tackled me from behind.

"Bye, Cass. I wish I was coming with you," Kateya muttered, her eyes tearing up slightly.

"I'll only be gone a little over a week, but I wish that you were coming with me, too, Kat." My eyes teared up as I glanced at my little sister. I realized that deep down, I truly wished that my sister was traveling back to Verastarr with me.

No sooner had I thought that than a burning sensation began at the base of my neck. "OW! What the hell?" I yelped, clawing at my necklace as a searing heat spread over my chest.

Kateya regarded me with a curious expression.

"My necklace! Feel it. It feels like it's burning up," I heard myself saying as my hand was scalded in my attempt to take the necklace off.

Soon Kateya's hand was next to mine, feeling the pendant that was somehow overheating. "*Okay*, that's not normal. Just take it off. Where did you say you got it from again?"

"It's not coming off," I snapped, yanking roughly at the gold. The clasp felt as though it was locked around my neck.

"Okay, let's both try pulling and just break the chain," she said, as her hand wrapped around mine—over the pendant. "One . . . Two . . . Three . . . PULL."

Neither of us felt the chain break, yet the pendant flew through the air, before crashing to the floor, creating sparks of shimmering gold energy as it spun in a circle then settled. The sparks ricocheted off one another before gaining speed and swirling into the air, as though drawn in by an unseen energetic force field.

Then, they vanished.

Looking at Kateya, I noticed the confusion in her eyes, most likely a reflection of what was in mine, wondering if we had truly seen the gold shimmers or just imagined it.

The panic set in a few seconds later as a chill began twisting its way around my body, snaking up my limbs, until I was entangled by a powerful, freezing force, my senses heightening while my strength diminished—as though sucked from my limbs. An ominous mist of gold-flecked black encased my body until I could not tell where I ended and the mist began.

I heard a screech in the far distance and then a, "What the fuck!" coming from my sister. As if time had frozen, I stood in a trance-like state, unable to move, to breathe, to process a coherent thought. My eyes closed of their own accord as an arctic breeze chilled my bones, surrounded my body, and forced me into submission.

My vision went black.

VERASTARR

MY EYES FLUTTERED OPEN, my mind embracing the peace my heart felt.

"Cassandra . . ." I heard my name being called in a quivering voice that could only belong to my younger sister. My sister called out again, and I instantly snapped out of whatever feeling I had to focus on her.

"Where are we? What just happened?" Kateya questioned as her voice squeaked. "There were sparks and mist, and then *poof*, you just disappeared. *We* disappeared."

I began to look around and fully take in my surroundings for the first time. We lay in what appeared to be a field, where wheat softly swayed with the wind. A few aged oak trees huddled a little way off, the sun's light reflecting on their leaves. The vibrancy of the hues distracted me as a few sparrows flittered by, singing with glee. A fleeting smile graced my lips. I glanced around Kateya, trying to get a feel for my surroundings, only to do a double-take as my mind caught up.

This wasn't right. What had happened? How had we arrived here?

It all slammed back into me. The burning pain of my necklace, the chilling feel as the mist had surrounded me at the airport, the unsettling peace I had felt right before the realm went dark. Something had occurred because as I looked around, the land we were sitting on was not familiar in the slightest, and it certainly did not look like the sandy shores of Estaire. *Had we been kidnapped? Was this an attack from the Nordak? What had just happened and how? How on Vanaiyer were we in a field in the middle of I don't know where . . . they don't even have fields like this in Estaire.*

"Hello! Cassandra!" Kateya called out, her hands waving in front of my face. "Any idea what the heck just happened?"

"Honestly. I've got no clue. I just . . . it really doesn't . . . I don't understand," I stuttered in response as a knot of panic began to rise. "One minute we're at EEI saying goodbye and now we're in the middle of a glittering field? There's got to be some sort of logical explanation."

"*Yeah.* Sparks flying and dark mist appearing out of nowhere in the airport . . . that totally sounds like logic to me, Cass," she mocked in a higher pitch than usual. "Maybe we got kidnapped? Or drugged?"

"I thought the same thing." I paused, my mind racing through a multitude of scenarios, none of which calmed me in the slightest. "But how could we have been drugged? And if we were kidnapped, then why are we all alone in a field? I mean, you've got to admit that doesn't add up at all. Who would kidnap someone and leave them unattended, not tied up, and in a field, of all places?"

I froze, my hand shooting up to my neck. *My necklace.* I felt for the golden chain that so often weighed heavily around my neck, but in its place was a void—an emptiness—as though a part of me was missing. "I didn't *buy* the necklace. Remember, Kat? I got it in Verastarr that night before we left. Some old lady with glowing eyes handed it to me by the fountain." My mind drifted to that night. How strange it had been. The feel of her cracked hands over mine made me shudder once more as the memory flashed by. But what was it she had said that night?

Come on, Cassandra. Think. You've got to remember what she said to you. Something about when you desire it the most. But desire what?

"Do you think your pendant had something to do with where we are? Maybe that lady was in some sort of cult or part of a secret society that plays pranks on people? She couldn't have been a Cordial, but could she have been a Nordak? Did we use magic? Are the Seefers going to hunt us now?" I could hear the worry in my sister's voice as she tried to think of an explanation, and to be honest, I had no idea.

I thought back to that night in Verastarr. Life had an air of freedom back then, with the Cordial ruling together as a unit from four of the realms. Even then, the Nordak had sought power, subdued as it was.

Trying to keep fear out of my voice, I responded with, "Yeah, it probably had something to do with the pendant on my necklace because whatever happened definitely should not have happened. It felt ancient, powerful. We yanked on my necklace and the pendant hit the ground, remember?"

"*Yeah?*"

"Well, it hit the ground near us, so maybe it's around here somewhere."

"You really want us to look for a stupid necklace when we don't even know where we are?"

"Unless you have a better idea? Huh, Kat?" I snapped, frustrated at the circumstance, my lack of answers, and the unknowns.

"Of course," she huffed, pushing off the ground as she began looking. "My sister would be the one to wear a necklace given to her by a stranger. Wearing it like a prized possession given to her by someone who cares. Now we are in the Void-damned middle of nowhere. Sure, Cass . . . I'll drive you to the airport. No problem at all," Kateya mumbled to herself.

"Where even are we?!" The frustrated scream escaped her lips as she stared hopelessly at the sky.

Standing up, I took in more of our surroundings. It really was a beautiful field. Beyond the wheat that surrounded us, I could see green grass swaying in the warm breeze and the oak trees lining the field, almost as if it led into a forest. There were so many trees; it honestly surprised me as the East Engles were bare, scarcely a tree insight. These trees were dense, many had thick trunks and full branches of emerald green leaves reflecting in the glimmering sunlight, with luscious bushes and thickets surrounding them. The land felt alive. Had the situation we were in not been so stressful, the forest would have appeared quite peaceful. I focused then on the task at hand and started looking where we had been laying for any sign of that red glass pendant typically around my neck.

After scouring the ground for another half hour, a groan made me glance up. "Can we try to find the closest town to see where we are? Do you think we're even still in Estaire?"

"I've got no clue, Kat. I mean . . . Estaire doesn't have fields like this." My mind drifted back to our home, the Capital of the East Engles. The island was expansive compared to Reggeon, one of the four kingdoms surrounding us. Yet our city-state of Estaire was the picture of the coastal East Engles. Sandy dunes faded into golden coastlines, and the waters were opaque as they silently lapped at the shorelines. Our home, our land, was a coastline that ebbed into urban cities of gray skyscrapers. "Yeah, let's try to find the closest town, give Mum and Father a call and figure out where to go from there."

We decided to head toward the large oak trees in hopes of spotting a road that would lead us into town, or better yet, a highway sign that would tell us where the fuck we were. I still couldn't quite wrap my mind around the fact that my pendant had produced sparks—a mist—and seemed as if it had trans-ported us somewhere. It was almost as if we were living in a fantasy book or dreaming. Except fantasy books were just that, fantasy. And what we had seen looked way more like actual magic. Magic that had been banished during The Fall. Magic that was punishable by death for using if the Nordak patrols found out.

I kept pinching myself, for the pain the sole reminder that this was not a dream. It was our reality. My mind flitted to a childhood folktale, one that parents shared at bedtime to keep us in our rooms. A tale of elemental magic that once graced the five lands before a pursuit of darkness shattered the realm in the Great War and the Nordak created the Seefers. Magic had still existed, in lesser quantities up until The Fall of the Cordial seven years ago, when the last remaining leaders with any drops of magic flowing in their veins had been hunted by the Nordak, and magic no longer flowed in our lands.

I'm such a terrible person, I thought. *I mean, what sort of person takes a necklace from an unknown wanderer late at night?*

Great. Just great.

Kateya and I slowed ourselves to a dawdling walk as we approached the trees. My body was on full alert as I scanned the perimeter. Peaceful as nature should be, it held the unknown dangers of ancient creatures. The Seefers lurked in every region of The Vanaiyer Realm now. The mangled beasts with battered gray fur and venom soaked fangs prowled through the realm, attacking mortals and hunting those who had elemental magic flowing through their veins.

The harrowing experience we encountered with one of the beasts in our home during The Fall would be forever etched in my mind and written across my skin. A shudder coursed through me as we took in the oaks' towering heights, their majestic, smooth trunks, and their full canopies of emerald-green leaves that hung from the branches like gleaming gems. We searched for some sign of civilization, but the closest we got was a beaten-down path, if you could call it that. Since in all reality, it appeared to be little more than grass rubbed bare from people walking on it.

"So much for that idea," Kateya muttered under her breath. "What now?"

"We can sit and wait for someone to drive by, I guess."

"And what, wait a couple of months? You've seen this path . . . it hardly looks used, let alone used by cars. No thanks! Why don't we pick a direction and just start walking?"

"Fine." The word cut from my mouth in annoyance. "Any thoughts on which way to head?"

After deciding to follow the worn-down dirt path north, we set off walking. "We should call the emergency patrol once we make it to town. Maybe they could help, or at least track down the crazy lady that gave you the necklace. I guess you missed your flight too. What's gonna happen with your job?"

The truth was, I had no idea. But one thing I knew for sure was that Madelyn Leroy did not take too kindly to journalists not showing up promptly to flights and events. "Yeah, Kat." I laughed. "I'm sure the emergency patrol will be able to track down the lady who gave me a necklace twelve years ago in Verastarr. Not to mention that if the pendant was indeed magic, we can't even tell them about it or we will be punished."

We were so focused on what to do next that we didn't hear the rumbling that pulsed through the ground until it was two or three hundred meters out. I urgently yanked Kateya back, pulling us back into the thick bushes and crouching. Branches clawed at exposed skin as I pressed us into the darkness.

"What are you doing?" Kateya hissed, attempting to go back out into the open.

She hadn't seen what I had. While I had been excited to see other people, my excitement had soon faded to terror as I had seen them approach. There appeared to be ten horses riding at breakneck speed, their riders covered in full armor as they headed straight toward where we happened to be standing. Taking chances wasn't an option, not with Nordak and Seefers lurking in every region, not without any form of protection. A silent curse left my lips as I wished I could have brought my knife with me to the airport. Leaving my apartment without it was rare, as one never knew if a Seefer would show up.

The thunder of hooves shook the ground as they sped by, oblivious to the fact that we were hidden behind the trees.

I softly breathed a singular sigh of relief that the rapid rush of horses had not trampled us. Rising, I began to tell Kateya that I believed we ought to head in the direction the men had come from when I heard the sound of hooves again. Only this time, the returning noise was not quite as loud; it was more like a dull roar than the deafening one from before. As I shoved her back into the cover of the trees, I shot Kateya the same glance I gave her when we often got in trouble with our parents, telling her to be quiet. I could hear the horses' hooves clopping against the dusty path at a slow canter before stopping no more than five meters from where we stood. I felt Kateya stiffen beside me and grew suspicious myself. They'd stopped much too close to us, which led me to believe that the fully armed riders had indeed spotted us as they passed by.

"Show yourself!" an authoritative male voice stated with a hard tone that lacked enthusiasm.

I remained in place, frozen in fear as the deep voice sent a jolt of fear through me.

"I said show yourself." The voice stated again, using the same tone my father did when he was slightly agitated. Glancing at my sister, I realized she wasn't moving. A look of pure terror had crossed her face, freezing her. I hesitantly rose from where I was squatting and stepped out from under the cover of the trees on shaky legs. Clearly, whoever they were expecting to appear from under the cover of the trees, had not been a woman.

"Who are you?" the voice growled in question. "Where do you live?"

I realized then that I was standing before a tight group of ten warhorses, each carrying an imposing male dressed in deep red and gold tunics beneath black armor, weapons poised and at the ready, pointed in our direction. I swiveled my head in the direction of the voice, settling my gaze on the speaker. I took in the man in front of me, who clearly seemed to be in charge, based on the air of authority in his voice and the deference the riders seemed to show him.

My breath caught; heat rushed over me as my eyes widened. Seated upon a horse, he towered over me. I could tell he was not the type of man who took jokes lightly as he held his lips together in a pale line. He seemed to be in his late twenties, give or take a year. An outline of bunched muscles hid behind a thick wall of chain mail and armor, and his luscious, black hair had the kind of slight wave that had always made my heart drop. But his eyes. They had me frozen in place, forgetting the existence of the realm around me. Those deep blue eyes looked me over with a gaze that seemed to perceive every single detail, one that I knew meant I couldn't keep any secrets hidden from him.

What I couldn't quite get past was the fact that he was covered in what appeared to be a form of armor and was riding atop a chestnut mare. He gave me a quizzical glance that instantly reminded me of the question he had posed not a moment before.

"I'm Cassandra," I replied, mustering confidence I didn't have, "and where I live is not of importance. But what I find to be important is who you are."

"I am Commander Sébastien Capetian, second son of Adrastan Capetian, King of Verastarr," he said back crisply, showing an air of authority as he spoke to me. "And it is of importance as to where you reside, for that determines where your loyalties lie."

"Very well," I forced out, while struggling to appear calm. "And what year is it?"

The Commander's eyes narrowed at my question, probing to discern why I wanted to know. Even as he responded, "578."

I nearly fainted at the words 578. If we are indeed in 578, that would mean . . . No. It was not possible. They must be part of some reenactment group. *Didn't people still do those? Yeah, that would make sense. Should we just go along with it—they had to end their reenactment at some point, right?*

I searched through my mind, urgently trying to think of a story to tell the commander that would make sense in the timeframe they were reenacting. My mind traveled back to my history classes, trying to remember what happened in the 500s. As much as I loved learning the history of The Vanaiyer Realm as a young child, there wasn't expansive detail in the Archives anymore. Once the Nordak seized control after The Fall, the access to our own history was banned. The records detailing the wars, the use of magic, our origins, all vanished. It was harder than it would seem to come up with something right on the spot, especially with my knowledge of the 500's being so limited.

At that moment, my sister cautiously crept up behind me since she was as hesitant as I was about the group of armed men standing around me. "We are just passing through Verastarr; we live in the East Engles."

"The East Engles, truly? Why are you here, in Verastarr, clearly without any male relatives or guards? It's dangerous for two young women to be traveling unaccompanied, especially two foreign females," Sébastien's deadly voice answered me.

Dang, this commander was good. I grimaced. But my dad had taught us well. As the father of two girls, he taught us to imply that we were not alone, even if we were, for safety. "What makes you think we are unaccompanied?"

He casually glanced around the perimeter, then back at me. He definitely knew we were alone.

"How do I know that my sister and I can trust you and your men?" I retorted.

Commander Sébastien Capetian's eyes narrowed slightly. Anger flared in his icy blue eyes, matching the mood with his voice. "Perhaps you do not understand the circumstances. *I am Prince Sébastien Capetian, Commander* of the wolvyn guard, second son of Adrastan Capetian, *King* of Verastarr. Presently, your *only* option is to trust my men and I."

"We were accompanied," I began. "Yet we ran into some complications. My father is a wealthy man in the East Engles, and my parents decided to go on a trip. My sister and I, along with our guards, were to go stay with our uncle, who resides here, in Verastarr. Upon arriving, we soon learned it would be unsuitable to remain with our uncle and so ventured to return home. Two nights into our trip, our guards took off at twilight with our belongings. The following morning we noticed the missing items, and yet no one had returned. So, as you can understand, we were accompanied, just not at this moment," I finished, smirking. Relieved to have thought of something that quickly, yet still hoping he believed my story.

Sébastien's eyes narrowed as he studied me. "We shall speak more on the subject later. These are dangerous times for anyone. You will come with us; we will do what we can to see you returned to your parents or relatives as soon as The God allows," he said in a way that let me know the offer was non-negotiable.

I looked over my shoulder at Kateya to see her opinion. She whispered, "What other choice do we have? Maybe these reenactors will *take* us to town and then we can call Father." She then walked away to sit on a patch of grass nearby.

Sighing, I cautiously turned around and replied to the armed men on alert, "Very well, we shall accept your offer, thank you."

Sébastien signaled with his hand, at which point two men galloped off in the direction they had been heading. His gaze returned to mine before stating, "Two of my men are returning to Château Comptal. They shall return shortly with two day dresses so that you may make yourselves presentable."

"Thank you," I replied, sensing I was *dismissed*. I turned to comfort my sister, glancing down at my designer, white-washed blue jeans and casual yet oversized olive-green t-shirt. I wondered why the reenactors wanted us to change into dresses. What I wore was casual for my time, as I was supposed to catch a flight shortly. But yet, here I was, *supposedly* in the 500s. They must have considered my clothes to be odd-looking in comparison to their outfits.

As I glanced at Kateya, I found her eyes were watching the eight men in front of us with fascination. As she heard me approach, she looked over in my direction with a worried look on her face.

I reached her and settled down on the soft grass beside her. "It seems that we have stumbled upon some weird group of reenactors, who think they live in the 500s. That or the pendant around my neck somehow brought us back in time to 578 in Verastarr." Kateya chuckled slightly beside me. "What I don't get is why the reenactors care about us changing into less modern clothing."

"Wait . . . did you say Verastarr?" she inquired softly.

"Yeah. Kind of an odd time and land to choose, right?"

"It is. I mean, I thought most reenactments were of, like, The Vanquishing, but that is still a few years off, right? I mean, there weren't any major battles at this point in history, were there?"

I paused for a moment, trying to draw on all the history lessons I had half paid attention to in class. "Not that I know of. I mean, there was the Great War, but that happened before the 500's I thought. But again, the Archives don't have much in terms of our wars, so it may not be accurate for all we know."

"You don't think it's possible that . . ." She didn't finish her sentence, but she didn't have to. I knew what she was getting at. *Time travel.* But no, that wasn't possible. I mean maybe, but no magic ever documented spoke of time travel. Healing, strength, speed, some shapeshifting was mentioned, but never time travel. "I mean, you must admit, Cass, the whole sparks flying and mist circling following a pendant hitting the floor is kind of crazy. It has no explanation other than magic. Magic that, need I remind you, hasn't existed since The Fall a few years ago."

I eyed my sister then, her light green eyes staring back at me with concern. "*Okay.* Let's say that hypothetically, we traveled back in time, which somehow happened because of the pendant. Why did it happen? And why did we end up here . . . in what, according to Commander Sébastien, is the year 578 in Verastarr?"

"I dunno," she whispered. "I mean, right before the pendant burned you, what happened? Did you say anything crazy?"

I stared at the grass and played with it between my fingers as I thought back to those moments, the burning sensation that happened, trying to replay this morning in my head. "I don't think so, Kat, I remember holding my necklace, you know how I typically do when I'm anxious, and then you saying you wished you were coming with. I think I responded by saying I wished we were both going back to Verastarr, and I remember really meaning it. Then you hugged me, and my necklace grew hot."

"Maybe it's like a magic lamp. You know, you rub it and make a wish. Except you touched it and made one?" Kateya said inquiringly.

Laughing slightly, I looked at her again. "Yeah, Kat, because a magic genie necklace is totally a thing."

"Well, I don't have any other explanation. It's either some crazy reenactors content to pretend they lived in the past, or time travel. Either way, you've got to admit they are a pretty hot group of guys. I mean, they've got to work out at least every day to get muscles like that. They don't even compare to the unwashed barbarians on campus, do they?"

Glancing back over, I stared at the eight men a little way off from us on the path. I had to agree with my sister. No matter what odd situation we had gotten ourselves into, these guys had it going for them. Tall, muscular arms were visible underneath dark chainmail, and an air of authority and control surrounded them. They could easily take any of the half-drunk boys we frequently encountered at bars down in a fight.

"Sooo," I drew out. "I'm thinking that since neither of us has any clue where we are, no cell phones, and it's quite evident that there is no way we can outrun these guys, we should go along with this act until we make it into town. And then we need to call an emergency patrol as soon as we can. It's probably best that we share as little about ourselves as possible, since we don't really know who they are."

"And what if this isn't a reenactment? What then, Cass? We don't have that necklace anymore."

"I don't want to think about that," was all I replied, because at that moment, the two riders who had gone off rode back up. After speaking with Sébastien for a moment, they unlatched a saddle pack and handed it to us. I automatically accepted the worn leather sack and politely replied, "thank you," before returning to my sister's side.

We headed off in search of a concealed location to get dressed. Once out of view, we cautiously opened the sack and peered inside. On the top, there were two dresses with thin straps. The garments were made entirely from soft, sheer white silk, with lace edges that would fall to mid-calf. I could see that this was some form of underdress, and the beauty of it was lovely, yet nothing compared to the "casual" day dresses we had been given.

Mine was an evergreen gown with gold intertwined. The seams were cross-stitched by hand, and the material was softer than any I had ever felt before. I marveled for a minute at the intricate design and wondered how this reenactment group had managed to get dresses that, as far as I could tell, were so well designed, they could have been made in 578.

The design of the dress was complex compared to any zip-up dress or sundress I had ever worn, so I took my best guess on how to button it up. I finished dressing, and, remembering reading that it was considered proper to wear your hair up, quickly braided my hair off to the side. May as well play the part if it meant getting back to civilization and a phone. After helping Kateya with her hair, we slowly trekked our way back to where we had started.

Chapter Three

VERASTARR

UPON ARRIVING BACK to where the men were waiting, we thanked Commander Sébastien Capetian for the gowns and for patiently waiting. The men had already decided how we would proceed to the château, because when I turned toward my sister, I realized that a dusty, brown-haired guy, possibly a few years older than her, was escorting her to his mare. After ensuring that she was adequately seated, I returned my gaze to the commander, about to inquire which of his guards I would be riding with. However, there was no need to ask, for as soon as I faced him, his deep voice questioned, "Ready?"

After assuring him that I was ready, he gestured toward his chestnut destrier. Hesitantly approaching the destrier (because I am not fond of horses, especially huge horses), I stopped and stared at it, wondering how on Vanaiyer I was supposed to mount it. I felt large hands press in on the sides of my waist, a slight heat spreading through me at the touch as I glanced up and realized it was the commander. He lifted me up and set me on the horse easily, as if he did it every day, before mounting behind me, a slight space forming between our bodies. I was still wondering how on Vanaiyer this man had lifted me up as if I weighed absolutely nothing, so I did not pick up on the command he gave. Caught completely unaware as his horse leapt into a trot, I was instantly jerked back against Sébastien, my body flush against the armor on his chest.

I heard a low chuckling noise, presumably at my shock at the departure, before the noises of the forest drowned it out. Having only ridden a horse once before, I was slightly terrified at the idea of falling off as the horse gained speed, covering the distance of the forest. I noticed that two of the men from the group had a head start on us, and were maybe 300 meters away, making me think that they were possibly scouting ahead as the men journeyed on. Opening my mouth to inquire as to why the whole group didn't just ride next to each other, a loud gasp escaped me as I watched what appeared to be an arrow hit one of the men, who then fell to the ground.

My mind could barely process the next few moments as Sébastien's destrier came to a swift stop on command, throwing me roughly against the armor on his chest, the metal digging into my skin in a way I knew would leave a bruise. Men scrambled into a defensive position as Sébastien shouted commands. Glancing back at Kateya, I almost laughed, realizing we were amid an actual historical reenactment, and these guys were committed to their roles. Sébastien roughly helped me down off his horse, still commanding his men, some of whom had split off and headed toward the fallen reenactor, while others circled around my sister in a protective stance.

Black arrows rained from the sky, and a swirling purple mist trailed in their wake as an electric static filled the air above us, pelting down toward the two men in the distance. *Magic.* My eyes narrowed, then widened in fear as an unsettling feeling sunk in. My stomach sank as the amethyst hues of the mist faded into the obsidian, creating an ominous fog, the chill from within it spreading to reach us.

There was a sharp yank on my wrist, and I felt Sébastien leading me over to my sister, as two men moved to the side, leading me into the inner barrier before closing the circle back up. I noticed Sébastien turned, remounting his destrier in one swift movement and charging off in the direction of his other men.

"Cass," Kateya whispered, "I'm starting to think this isn't part of the reenactment . . ." She gasped as the chill sunk into our bones, ten times stronger than it had in Estaire. "How—it couldn't possibly be . . . you know . . . real life?"

A brief manic chuckle escaped my lips. "I wish I could say we are going to have a really good reenactment sto—" The word *story* died on my lips as a bloodcurdling scream pierced in the air and the sounds of swords clashing reverberated. I noticed the men getting closer together, raising their weapons, an unspeakable tension circling them as they stood their ground; their shadows still visible as the mystical fog settled.

"Cass," my sister whimpered as her small hand gripped mine, her knuckles turning white from her fear as the metallic smell of blood drifted past us. A smell that had coated the coastlines of the East Engles during The Fall. One we were all too familiar with. I once again cursed myself for not attempting to bring my knife with me on my flight to Verastarr, as I stood defenseless during an onslaught.

Fear bolted through my body as the realization hit. The battle happening in front of us was very much real. "Void-damned . . ." A whisper slipped through the crack of my voice as I pushed my sister down and behind me, praying to The God that nothing happened to us as childhood tales of ancient magic and deadly reigns flooded my mind.

"Cass, if this is real. Does that mean . . ." A sob broke through her words. "Does that mean we aren't in Estaire anymore, or even the East Engles?"

My eyes glazed over and a million thoughts rushed in, my mind churning in vicious circles of thoughts until it hurt as I tried to process what exactly happened to us. "I'm beginning to think we aren't, Kat. And if that's the case . . . This is really, really bad." A gasp for air emerged as an unseen weight pressed in around my neck, suffocating me.

A somber feeling reached us before the men did, as the coppery scent of blood filled my nostrils, edging me closer to heaving the slight breakfast I had wolfed down prior to riding with Kateya to the airport. Shifting my gaze between the men, I took in the lone body draped across the back of an ominous black destrier, four darkened arrows protruding from his form, a dark byzantium color surrounding each one. A fallen soldier. Another soul.

We had grown up with far too many souls being lost to The Void and yet each time, I wondered what it meant. What it was like in The Void, the place The God resided and one's eternal fate was determined. The men made no mention of the arrows, or the trails of shadowy darkness that had followed, a precursor to certain death.

A single flick of his hand and Sébastien's men wordlessly leapt into action, the silence unsettling and the mood darkened. Sébastien's destrier curved up beside me as his hand stretched down, clasping my forearm with an effortless lift. After an abrupt landing, I found myself between the horse and the armor of Sébastien's chest. His hand was a tight, firm presence across my middle as the horse leapt into a swift movement, lurching down the path.

I felt his body then, between the strides, covering mine, his fingers a steady pressure on my side, pressing into me and pushing me closer toward him—his armor shielding me. My body betrayed me as it inched closer, despite my apprehension toward the day's events, and a grim, low chuckle rumbled from behind me.

As we slowed, I began to see an extensive gate of black iron with elaborate gold spokes decorating the fence's top train. I strained to look beyond the guarded gates, and I could make out a white cobblestone courtyard filled with soldiers and servants, all bustling with work. The actual château was an enormous gray building, multiple stories high and quite wide. Bushes of lavender surrounded the planes of the château, the lilac color creating a serene pop against the darkness that encased the day. I spotted a stable way off in the distance, the large wooden pane opened for our arriving party, and a few other structures attached to the château, though I wasn't quite sure what they were for. The central part of the château was onyx black, with plated gold around the windows, and a large crest near the roof caught my eye. A grand staircase led up to large double doors; the stairs were made of pristine, pale gray marble with beautiful, jade-colored bushes on either side.

The gates slowly opened as we neared, the scent of lavender and lemon verbena flooded my senses, washing away the lingering copper scent of blood. The laughter and jesting of the men surrounding me grew louder as we passed through the towering bars into the relatively safe château. The stares of those inside the gates had a heavy presence as the men rode in, streaked with blood and sweat—Kateya and me in tow. Fear rose, a black din cresting the corners of my eyes as the horses slowed to a stop and more men armed with sharp, jagged daggers approached. We didn't even know these men. How could I trust that we were any safer here with them than on the dirt path where they found us? So many things could go wrong. So many things had *already* gone wrong. What would happen if we couldn't even make it home? If I couldn't find that pendant, which I knew held the answers I was looking for? What if someone else found my pendant before I could?

The horses came to a stop, and the men dismounted. Sharp commands and urgent whispers laced the air, detailing the events of the ride. Kateya and I sat helplessly atop the horses, uncertain whether moving was the right action. Sturdy hands once again wrapped around my waist and lowered me to the ground. My feet stumbled as I tried to get my bearings, and a steady arm held me upright. Red tinted my cheeks, as if my luck couldn't get any worse, before I glanced again at the powerful man towering over me. Thankful to be in what I prayed was a safe place. A whisper of embarrassed thanks fell from my lips at his gesture and he gave a singular nod of his head at my comment while he focused on what his right-hand man was saying to him.

As his man walked away, Sébastien turned to me and crisply retorted, "Stay here, understand."

"That's it?" My voice squeaked as I voiced my unbridled thoughts aloud. "*Stay here*? Aren't you going to tell us what just happened? Someone died!" My voice rose as the shock began wearing off. "*Died*, Commander."

The commander's icy blue eyes met mine, a fire burning inside them at my outburst, before he walked away, leaving Kateya and me in the middle of the courtyard, alone. We stood there, glancing at each other hesitantly, trying to determine whether we should flee right then, or proceed to get help from these people. The memory of purple-hued bruises and protruding, onyx arrows kept my feet firmly planted where they were.

Shortly, Sébastien returned, a fierce, towering soldier and a pristine, uptight woman trailed behind him. Stopping a few feet away, Sébastien introduced them as his right-hand man and Captain of the Guard, Dravyn de Cauda, and then to his left, Emalyee. Emalyee wore a detailed, golden tunic that fell mid-thigh accentuating her deeply bronzed skin, paired with dark leggings and a long dagger attached to her left thigh. Her chestnut hair was draped in a plait over one shoulder and her emerald eyes, identical to my sister's, gazed at us with intrigue.

As I nodded in greeting toward the couple, the

commander spoke once more. "You shall stay here at Château Comptal for the remainder of the week. While you are here, you both will be under our protection. As we are in warring times, you are not under any circumstance permitted to leave the château grounds." As he finished speaking, he turned and walked across the courtyard, Dravyn by his side.

"If you follow me, I shall lead you to your rooms, and you may freshen up, for I am sure you are exhausted from your travels," Emalyee said as she led the way.

We followed a few steps behind, and my gaze drifted up the charcoal marble staircase and through the grand double doors. I was in awe of my surroundings—the mystical appearance of the building, the lure of the lemon verbena, and the tingling calm of the lavender drifting by as we entered. Emalyee chattered on about the design and art in Château Comptal as she guided us to our rooms up three flights of the spiraling staircase to the side, each turn closing in as the staircase got narrower. We came to a stop in a hallway with doors on either side, where Emalyee declared we could choose whichever room we wanted and informed us that a maid would be coming up to assist us. We thanked her, and as she left, I turned to face my sister, concerned about how she was processing this whole situation.

I could tell with one look at her face that she was shaken from our circumstances, from the brutal attack we witnessed. Wrapping my arms around her, I encased her in a hug as though I could squeeze our problems away, and whispered, "I will fix this, I promise." My sister had been so young when The Fall happened, yet I knew that the memories of the Seefers breaking through our front doors haunted her sleep most nights, as they did mine. The screamed shrill snarls of the Seefers were a sound feared by all. The memory tugged me under, shrouding me in flashes of my past.

My parents had known they were coming. How, I didn't know. Urgency filled our home as my mother guided Kateya and me into the underground shelter, slamming the trap door shut with a lock. Growls and screams shattered the air. Those growls were deep, guttural, and ancient, and flooded our home just as they now flooded my nightmares. We heard scraping and clawing on the floors above us, the floor quaking as I shoved Kateya into the shadowy depths of the corner, holding the knife my mother had urgently pressed into my palm in front of me. The door broke, an ominous, dark gray face gleaming in the light, amber eyes meeting mine.

A heavy thud of a door brought my memory to a halt. I felt as if I had failed my sister as her body trembled slightly while I held her. Taking a deep breath, I released her, opened the door to the right, and walked in. The first thing I noticed was an enchanting bed with a shimmering jade canopy covering the bed frame. I softly padded over to it, feeling the soft, feather-down bedding against the tips of my fingers before gently sitting down, afraid of breaking something in a room more decadent than any I had seen. I felt for a fleeting moment as if I had strolled into a magical fairytale as I laid down on the bed, relishing the momentary security I felt. Pushing up onto my elbows, my eyes darted around, admiring the tapestries that hung from the walls depicting scenes from nature, creatures I'd never dreamed of seeing, then glancing over the remaining furniture in the room. I noticed a rustic, chestnut armoire in one corner of the room and spotted a second door off the wall across from the bed.

A knock sounded from the opposite door, and when I did not reply at first, the door slowly opened. A maid walked through and curtsied. "Good evening, I'm Rosalie." She hesitated for a moment, before continuing, "I hope you don't mind; I knocked, but when I didn't hear a reply, thought it was best if I just came in. Would you like me to draw a bath for you? Perhaps bring up some food? No doubt you are exhausted from traveling and would appreciate a change of garments . . . oh dear, forgive me, I see you have no travel trunks. I shall have some dresses brought up until we can get you measured for a variety of your own."

I felt a strange sense of calm wash over me as Rosalie rambled on. Perhaps because we appeared relatively close in age, her incessant chatter made me feel welcome.

I sat on the edge of my bed, unsure of what to do or what to believe. The bath had provided momentary relief from the circumstances, as jasmine and vanilla mixed and lulled me into a tranquil state. But now, as I sat down, my mind began racing—sprinting—with scenarios of what happened from the airport, to the scalding pendant, to the brutal death I had witnessed. The thoughts just kept coming as a silent, frustrated scream escaped my lips. I was attempting to answer a million questions at a time. My breathing stilled as I willed my mind to ease, a prayer slipping from my lips as I forced my anger and fear aside, mentally locking it away for good.

My head rested against the silken fabric of the bedcover as I focused on breathing in and out, in and out. Freeing my mind from the questions swarming around thought by thought. A knock startled me from my escape, pulling me back into the present. With a glance up and another resounding knock, I remembered Rosalie's statement that I hadn't replied to her knock, and hastily replied.

"A moment, please." I raked my hands through my hair, attempting to gain any semblance of composure, while also confident I had single-handedly destroyed Rosalie's delicate efforts to style my hair. Wiping my eyes, I turned and forced a smile as the door opened. Emalyee stood patiently waiting on the other side, all smiles, yet the moment she took in my face, my pale blue eyes gave me away. She gently grabbed my hand and asked me what the matter was. Pasting a smile across my face and borrowing some calmness I couldn't seem to find, I simply replied in the most ladylike voice I could muster as I went along with the lie we had told the commander. "I'm simply concerned about my parent's wellbeing. It is quite troubling to be without them in an unknown land."

Emalyee smiled sympathetically in return and nodded her head before requesting, "I am sure you are still exhausted, however, won't you both join us for dinner?"

I replied with a yes, knowing there was no way I could refuse, seeing as they were graciously allowing us to stay here.

Dinner passed by in a flurry. I was too exhausted to focus on conversation, and while I could tell that our presence intrigued many of the soldiers and subjects there, no one asked for an explanation, and we gave none. As the meal neared an end, Kateya and I slipped out, going to our rooms to sleep off the nightmare of a day. Hugging my sister, I turned to my room and found Rosalie there waiting for me. She simply smiled, noting the half-present gaze I must have been displaying and helped me prepare for bed, which was slightly strange, seeing as I was quite capable of getting ready for bed myself.

However, when I voiced to Rosalie that I could dress myself, she *tsked* before responding with, "Oh no, miss, it's quite alright." Exhaustion crept over me, and I was in no position to put up with a fight, so I allowed her to help me. I resolved to decline her offer for help tomorrow, seeing as I managed to get ready each day at home myself.

Climbing into the large bed, I sunk into the comfort of the feathered bedding, wishing for it to distract me from the struggles that danced across my mind on repeat. The bed, however, did no such thing. I laid there, attempting to fall asleep for quite some time before exhaustion finally overcame me, shutting down my wandering mind, and a distant darkness allowed me to drift into a fitful sleep.

Chapter Four

VERASTARR

SUNLIGHT DANCED ACROSS MY CHEEK, warming my skin, rousing me from a restless sleep. I shifted up, glancing around the bedroom, foggy confusion building as I took in my surroundings. Not a second too soon, my memories came flooding back, bringing with them a throbbing headache, as the pressure and difficulties of the previous day returned, an ever-present nightmare I couldn't escape. I sighed, wishing I could return to sleep and magically awaken in my loft bedroom in Estaire.

A soft knock on the door drew me from my thoughts as Rosalie entered the room. I inwardly groaned, not at Rosalie, but at the reality that I must drag myself out of bed and find a way to get home, which involved leaving this castle to search for the pendant that I prayed to The God was still somewhere in the field we woke up in.

Rosalie helped braid my golden brown locks into an intricately woven design that flowed loosely down my back—a custom in Château Comptal, I discovered. Afterwards, I slipped on a dusty cobalt-colored tunic and paired it with a pair of black leggings that seemed to fit well.

Dressed and ready, I headed over to Kateya's room. I

knocked on the door several times before opening it slightly and discovering my sister sprawled upside down across the bed; passed out in her usual manner. A slight laugh slipped through my lips at the simple act of normalcy amidst our circumstances. Not having it in me to wake her up and bring this nightmare into reality for her, I turned and went to search for some food.

Wandering around the hallways in search of the kitchen should be an excellent way to clear one's thoughts and draft plans to depart. Yet all thoughts froze as I meandered around a corner and Emalyee's voice broke the silence. "Searching for the dining hall?" she prompted, ever chirpy and the picture of the demure hostess with a slight air of a cautious warrior.

Smiling softly, a "yes" flowed from my lips in response. "I woke up and realized that barely touching one's dinner only results in being hungry the next morning," I finished with a slight chuckle.

"Well, you're in luck. No one does breakfast quite like the cook here at Château Comptal . . . in my opinion, at least. I would quite literally kill Dravyn if he made me miss it. If you couldn't tell, I'm quite serious about my breakfast food."

I laughed while she led the way to the dining hall, where she swore I would taste the most delicious, delicate pastries. We chatted along the way, and she told me of her family back home. Her two brothers were training as guards in a neighboring city, and she told me about her relationship with Dravyn. I learned that Dravyn grew up with Sébastien Capetian and their bond went beyond Commander and Captain of the Guard. I began to tell her about myself. I told her of Kateya, and of my mum and my father, and our misfortunes with our imaginary guards who had abandoned us. The story flowed so easily through me that I thanked The God I was a journalist, and was used to crafting stories for a living.

Emalyee paused every so often, pointing toward various

rooms that crossed our path. I noted that we were in one wing of the château—one that appeared to be for everyday life. The west wing, she briefly mentioned, held the war rooms; a location I tucked into my mind for if I ever found an opportunity to attempt to leave. Before I knew it, we were approaching the dining hall, and it crossed my mind as I realized that I had only known Emalyee for a day, but it felt as if we had been lifelong friends.

The dining hall was crowded with soldiers meandering about, talking to one another rambunctiously and preparing for the day ahead as laughter and scents of freshly baked bread filled the air. A long, birch wood table lay alongside a wall, piled with plates of food for breakfast. I ogled the table, hunger gnawing at my insides after walking the hallways. Silence spread table by table as I followed Emalyee, the men eyeing me with suspicion and something else as I walked by, before resuming their conversations. Settling down on a long wooden bench, we ate oatmeal with milk and raisins and fluffed pie bread—a local bread I learned that was crisp on the outside but flaked with a buttery softness inside that warmed you.

We traded stories, speaking of our lives and laughing over similar moments shared with siblings. We had been talking fondly of our childhood moments when I noticed Emalyee's attention fading off. A brief glance up and I understood why as Sébastien and Dravyn approached our end of the lengthy table. They appeared deep in heated conversation, yet abruptly dismissed the topic as they stopped in front of us and sat down. Sébastien swiftly glanced over at us and gave a curt, uninterested nod, while Dravyn grinned at us before inquiring in a flirtatious tone, "Sleep well, ladies?"

We replied that we indeed had, and Emalyee then began to speak with Dravyn further. Picking up my pie bread, I listened to the jokes being passed around the tables, until I froze, listening intently as my sister and I were mentioned.

"Pity that they were found on Sébastien's patrol, *no?*" A voice drifted past my ears. Laughter fluttered as raunchy jokes of what they wished to do with my sister and me filled the air. Ducking my head, I noted the hardened looks on the commander and his captain's faces as jokes continued to drift by.

Grateful for a moment free of questions and conversation, I let my thoughts drift off to my life back home. My parents would have noticed by now that we hadn't called, and Madelyn Leroy would be furious I'd missed my flight to Verastarr even though I'd ironically made it to Verastarr . . . just centuries early. My worry grew as I realized how much was at stake. A burning feeling rose within me as the need to find that pendant, to discover how we had gotten dumped here, and to make it back grew with each passing minute. My entire future, everything I had worked for, could be lost. My sister's dreams, our parents. This situation wouldn't solve itself. I knew then that we needed to try even harder to return to our time, no matter the cost. There was too much at stake not to make it home to Estaire.

Amidst the bustle of the morning preparations, I quickly excused myself, not even bothering to wait for a reply as I turned and exited the hall. I started down the lengthy hallway, completely lost, unsure of where I was in the château. All I knew was that I desperately needed to get out and try to locate the pendant. If I could find the pendant in the field before anyone noticed I was missing, I could bring it back and Kateya and I could wish ourselves home. At least, I hoped that's what would happen.

My mind thought back to the dangers of yesterday and the memory of Seefers from my childhood haunted me, matted faces and amber eyes that pierced through me reminded me that I needed protection. I needed a weapon.

I wandered in the direction I prayed was west, searching the wing for the armory. The first two levels proved to be empty chambers, possibly for councils and entertainment like in our Capital building. Space after space, door upon door, yielded nothing. A hidden door in the distance drew my attention as three men exited, strapping onyx swords across broad backs. A smile curved on my lips. The armory. I slipped into the shadows of the corridor, certain that while they might consider me a guest, stealing weapons was not how one thanked a host.

I found the door still ajar from the guards who had exited, and noticing no one inside, I slipped through the crack, my feet unmoving once I entered. The armory held more weapons than I had dreamt; swords and javelins lined the stone walls from floor to ceiling. Lengthy tables were scattered in an organized manner throughout the room with various lengths of daggers, spikes, bows, arrows, and other weapons I was unfamiliar with. A shudder coursed through me as I imagined what they might do in battle. Lit black torches rested on the walls, their flames dancing in the chilled room as their shadows cast an ominous glow over the multitude of weapons before me.

Knowing that the chances of this particular room remaining empty were unlikely, I willed my body to move, glancing over the various throwing daggers across the smooth tables before settling on one smaller than the length of my forearm, its bone handle wrapped in a dark leather. Tucking it into the holder on my leggings, I turned to find a way out, the weight of the dagger against my thigh providing the first sense of comfort I had felt since being thrown into the past.

Searching the hallways for an exit took time, more so than I had wished. The halls wrapped and tangled until I was lost in a maze of doors and barricades. A small, wooden door, lower in height than the others, finally caught my eye. The handle went undetected, a simple carved hollow in the frame. Silently leaning my weight into the oak, I gave a hard nudge, and the door slipped open, leading out the back of the château directly into an emerald forest of pines.

With a silent breath, I quickly took off toward the trees in hopes of returning to the field we'd arrived in. My footsteps stayed soft and cautious, even as I hurried across the open expanses, striving to remain silent and unseen. Fear of the Seefers or other unknown creatures replaced worry for my sister as I made my way deeper into the tangles of the forest. Branches and vines clawed at my skin as I carried on. The scent of pine and nightshade blended as the trees drew closer and their leaves blanketed the sky, casting a shadow on the terrain they protected. The woods grew darker, the emerald of the leaves fading to a darkened green, as though they wished to be black. The sunlight cast distanced beams of light from small gaps in the leaves high above as the forest took on an eerie lure. I began to wonder if I was actually heading in the right direction, but there was nothing I could do now. I had committed to finding the pendant, and now, I couldn't return empty handed.

Intently focused on escaping, on mastering the art of silence, I paid no attention to my surroundings until I glanced up and noticed a lone rider on a horse facing me, the rider's outline a dark shadow in the distance. Stumbling to a stop, I surveyed the surrounding woods, willing myself to blend into the trees and brambles that pressed against my body in protest. The rider was alone.

I had to find my pendant. I had no other way out of this land where magic killed and time travel was possible. If not for my sake, for my sister.

I took off sprinting in a new direction, even though I could hear the horses' thundering hooves behind me as it gained on me. I bolted as quickly as I could, crossing my tracks in an attempt to distract the rider. Branches scratched my arms and thorny bushes clawing at my legs as I willed them to move faster, *faster*.

A glance behind me indicated the rider was approaching and a tawdry curse slipped through my lips. My hand slipped to my thigh, to the weapon secured there, gauging the distance, wondering if my throw would fly true. No sooner had I glanced back than a sickening smack filled my ears . . .

I felt myself sail through the air before my mind knew what had hit me. I threw my hands out in front in an attempt to break my fall as a searing pain met me when I hit the ground. Glancing behind me, I had failed to notice a protruding fallen pine tree directly in my path. The silence of the forest told me the rider had caught up before I could even rise from the ground. Wincing in pain, I twisted, one hand firmly on my dagger before meeting the smoldering gaze of Sébastien's captain, Dravyn de Caude.

"Why don't you get on my horse, and we will return to the château and talk this over; hopefully before Sébastien notices your *small* escape charade." His piercing voice rang in the forest as he towered over on his horse.

I looked up at him, an enraged "no" on the tip of my tongue.

"*Or* perhaps I should leave you here. The Seefers would welcome the offering, and Sébastien would certainly thank me," he finished. My eyes met his with disdain when a searing pain in my arm demanded I begrudgingly follow his demand.

The warm trickle on my left side told me everything I needed to know: I had a gash that no doubt would require attention. Slipping the dagger in the folds of my tunic, I took his outstretched hand. Dravyn assisted me onto his horse before mounting behind me to maneuver us toward the place that I just sought to escape. The trees opened as we headed away from my chance to get us home; the sunlight peeking through despite the dimness surrounding me. Wondering why he came after me, or how he knew I even left, I probed.

Dravyn was silent a moment before responding. "I'm Sébastien's Captain of the Guard. My sole duty is to track, to hunt, to kill. No one, and I mean *no one,* slips through our walls without my knowledge." He paused for a moment before adding in a softer voice. "I am also aware of the weight of sacrifice an elder sibling holds, the drive to do unthinkable things for those we love."

I fell silent for a moment, reflecting on what Dravyn said, the heaviness in his tone, as the castle approached. I wondered yet again, if returning had been right, if maybe I should have bitten back the sting of my arm, the warning of the Seefers, and carried on.

Dravyn's voice broke the silence. "If we have good fortune, Sébastien will not be waiting for your return, otherwise, I fear there is nothing I can do to assist you."

Chapter Five

VERASTARR

AS LUCK WOULD HAVE IT, we did not have good fortune. Somber, iron-colored clouds hovered as we approached the gates, where the commander's brooding form was rigidly awaiting my return. I groaned inwardly as the gates opened, and I was led through on Dravyn's mare as though I was a conquest to be delivered. A few guards approached, before scurrying away at the threatening growl coming from their leader. I grimaced as my feet touched the ground, every muscle in my body protesting from the pain it had endured. My face, an impassive mask, met the fury of those arctic blue eyes and the strong face I pasted on began to fade as Sébastien paced, dismissing Dravyn.

I remained frozen in place, trembling on the inside while attempting a façade of confidence and control that had all but run away. He stopped before me, no words, as his gaze crashed into mine, as though he could peer into my very soul and see my secrets, my lies. The air around us seemed as though it had dropped ten degrees in his presence.

There he was, analyzing my every breath, before motioning for me to follow him, turning on his heel, and storming off. I stood motionless, refusing to be summoned by a mere flick of a hand. I was aware of the customary etiquette due to him being the son of a king, and the results one might face for defiance. However, a mere hand flick was not a way to command, and he could stand to be brought down a peg if he thought I would respond. Sébastien was halfway across the marbled courtyard before he realized I was not behind him. With another flick of his hand, two soldiers flanked me, an unyielding grip on each arm forcing me to follow after their commander.

Apparently, someone isn't too fond of people not following his every command. I smirked, making a mental note even as a gnawing fear rose in my chest and my breathing strained in my lungs.

We entered the château through yet another unseen door that blended into the pavers. This one led, not to an escape, a chance of freedom, an opportunity home, but toward certain fear. A dampened chill settled into my bones as we quickly walked through the cavernous hallway; a darkened gloom seemed to soak into the very walls. I shivered at the thought of where we might be headed.

My mind echoed my body's shivering state as it recalled the stories—the legends—passed down over the years of dark magic wielded throughout the lands, of unspeakable powers and evil that roamed free. The tales my parents scared us into behaving with. Stories of what happened to those who dared defy or anger the reigning rulers of the lands. Terror coursed through my body only to clash with the arctic chill that surrounded the corridor. I had heard of the battles that happened in my own land, of the power that had ripped the East Engles apart, shattering its beauty and peace. A part of me wanted to believe that the commander wouldn't hurt me because I was a woman. The other part toyed with the idea that you only become a commander by earning the title.

Approaching a heavy, worn, oak door with an iron barricade across it, Sébastien thrust it open before gesturing for me to enter before him. My breath caught as I hesitated, unsure of what lay behind the door, when I heard a voice snarl, *"Now,"* and my body betrayed me, nearly racing into the unknown at the sharp command.

Taking in the surroundings, I noticed two lanterns hanging on the polished stone wall, dimly lighting the room with an orange sheen while casting the darkness into corners. An uncomfortable looking couch was against one wall and a wooden chair rested against another. A glance around told me that the chamber was windowless, creating a forlorn atmosphere of despair that my heart echoed.

Lost in thought as I noted my surroundings, a resounding thud reverberated across the room, distracting me. Whirling on my heel, I saw that the door had closed, leaving me trapped alone in the room. With the commander. His powerful frame stood tall, and the room felt two sizes smaller. I glared at him with such a fierce look that if looks could kill, mine would have been his demise. My fingers tightened on the handle of my dagger, prepared to strike.

I studied him for a moment under the low light of the room, taking in the bronzed skin speckled from hours outdoors, the light dusting of freckles spreading across defined cheekbones, and the five o'clock shadow. I noticed the way his tunic pulled taut as muscles stretched the seams, and how his dark hair didn't quite touch the tips of those broad shoulders. A smug smirk rested on his rugged face as he leaned against the wall, crossing his arms across his chest, and my breath caught in betrayal as his muscles strained. Even then, my mind screamed with fury, as I realized he'd locked me into the room with him as though he had the right to do so.

"First, I find you wandering around my lands without any authority to do so. Then you rudely disrespect me in front of all my men. Even so, I offer you shelter and protection in my land during warring times. Still, you take advantage of me, of the protection I offered to you and your sister, and attempt to run away. Without your sister, no less." Sébastien scowls, frustrated even as I glare defiantly at him. "But no, that wasn't all, was it? You lied to me as well. That pathetic story you told me, you remember the one, *no?* About your guards abandoning you on a trip to see relatives? That's not true in the slightest. Do you truly think I would be in my position if I couldn't tell who lies to me?"

I tried not to shift my gaze, matching his, as he watched me like a predator stalking their prey. His look, piercing and cold, made me squirm.

I can't let him know, though. Heaven knows what he would do if he found out the truth. I mean, you can't just blatantly tell someone that you are from the future. Ha, even I wouldn't believe it, and it happened to me. I knew the control old magic had on our region in the future, but here, in the past, magic . . . Magic was what people murdered for. Any small grasp of power; it was the force that controlled the regions and that pendant, that was pure magic.

I just stood there, staring back at him, building up a defensive wall in my mind, not quite sure what I could say to make him believe my lie.

An annoyed grunt had me focusing my attention on Sébastien, who had pushed off the wall and was now striding toward me with fury written across those sharp features. Angry swirls of black mist began circling the air between us as I started to back away from him. *Elemental magic.* My grip tightened on the weapon at my side as I realized he could control mist, even as I looked at him with cold defiance. I winced as I backed right into the cold stone, with nowhere to go. The chill seeped into my bones, freezing me with terror as the black mist inched closer, surrounding my body with dangerous precision.

Sébastien stopped, inches from my face, his body casting a shadow over mine as he towered above me, his arms caging me in without so much as touching me. I knew then that this look was what captives received. That numbed feeling of terror as they stared back into the eyes of the man who controlled their next breath, and my lungs wheezed for air. Looking at me with such a deep stare, his voice rumbled, dripping control. "We both know you're withholding the truth, and I can assure you that you won't be leaving this room—you won't see the light of day—until I have found the truth."

I studied him and then risked a quick glance over his shoulder to the door on the opposite side of the room. Sadly, I wasn't as subtle as I had hoped, because when I looked Sébastien in the eye again, his ice-blue eyes were dancing with dark amusement before he voiced with a chuckle, "Go ahead. Try to escape."

I brushed past him, my arm shoving against his shoulder which only resulted in pain flaring up on my left side as I stalked over to the barred door. I grabbed a hold of the splintered, wooden jab that barricaded me in and lifted . . . or at least I tried.

This thing is way heavier than I thought it would be. Who in Vanaiyer would make a door lock that heavy? I mean, Void-damned, it shouldn't be this hard to unlock a door. It's not like I'm weak or anything. I've been going to the gym a few times a week and have some muscle . . .

His low chuckle sounded again from behind me at my failed attempt to exit the room he'd trapped us in. Fuming, I spun back toward Sébastien, glaring at him as my hand launched the dagger I had kept hidden. Time slowed as I revealed my hand; the dagger pierced the air between us, cutting through it as it sped toward its intended target. Slight surprise, tinted with amusement, lit in his eyes before he caught it, midair, inches from his heart. He simply chuckled, blood staining his hand as he stalked toward me, twirling the blade.

His hard body pressed mine into the door. Arctic, onyx mist circled my wrists, holding them in place. He lifted the dagger, leveling the blade under my chin as he forced my gaze to meet his, the sharp edge of the blade pricking against my skin. I froze, unable to breathe, to move as his hand, now tinted with crimson, trailed along my jawline, before tucking my unruly, blonde-streaked hair behind my ear and he leaned in.

"Next time you do that, *princesse,* make sure to hit your target." He breathed into my ear; a scent of spice and pine filled the air between us as I attempted to control the shiver of terrified delight that coursed down my middle. Spinning me around, he lifted the bar with ease as if it weighed nothing before glancing back toward me. "Don't forget, you only get out once you tell me the truth." And with that, he left, locking the door from the outside, trapping me in.

I stood there at a loss, my body tingling where his hands had been.

How? How had he caught that dagger? And the mist? The same mist that had been at the battle. That had showed up when we traveled back in time. The commander had elemental magic. How was I supposed to tell him the full story and make it out of here alive? The truth might very well be a death sentence.

I tried pulling on the door a few times before giving up and sitting on the floor. My head rested against the stone wall, and I tried to think about what to do.

What will I tell him when he comes next? If I tell him the truth, well, he would probably use me to find the pendant for his own power gain. A pendant that allows you to travel through time had to be more than worth it to a commander. And my death would be a mere afterthought once he had the power he wanted. But lying wouldn't work either because he saw right through that the first time.

I did the only thing I could think of at the moment; I prayed. I prayed that we would get out of this mess with our lives still intact. I prayed that my sister was okay, and nobody touched her after I had run away and thrown a dagger at Sébastien. I prayed that we made it home, to Estaire, to the East Engles.

At some point, I must have drifted off because I woke up to the sound of the door slamming open and Sébastien storming in. I sat up, wincing and groggy, my body on fire. My side protested in pain as a blanket fell off my shoulder. Confused, I looked around before realizing that someone must have put me on the strange-looking couch when I fell asleep and wrapped me in a wool blanket. Glancing up, I noticed that Sébastien's muscular frame filled the doorway as he watched my every move like a hawk and yet, the urge to utterly ignore his presence filled my body.

"Well," Sébastien voiced, breaking the silence in the room. "Would you care to inform me why you lied?"

I shifted my gaze, black spots lining my vision as I struggled to push off the couch. A searing pain and a familiar warmth stopped me, a whispered curse sliding from my lips. Sébastien studied me, taking in my frozen position, the look of shock and pain etched across my features as his eyes traced up and down my figure, focusing in on my arm.

"You're injured."

It was not a concern or worry, just a mere statement, the same as one would say, "I'm hungry." Before I could nod or agree, he left the prison of a room, locking me in once more.

The return was quicker this time, yet it was not Sébastien's smoldering gaze that met mine, but the worn, wisdom-filled eyes of a shorter male in his fifties. He held a leather bag at his side as he walked in. "I hear our *escapee* has been injured?" he prompted with a softened tone, much like the voice my father spoke to me with.

A healer, I realized. He eased up the left sleeve of my tunic, where crimson blood trickled down my forearm from a gash curving down in a crescent shape. The elderly man knelt beside me, cleaning the wound. Not a single word slipped out of our mouths as he bandaged my arm tightly, the pain lessening already.

He handed me a vial. "Drink this. It will reduce the chance of infection."

My hand reached out, then paused, doubting if it was safe to accept the unknown liquid before me.

A chuckle met my ears as I glanced up. "I have no reason to poison you, girl. If you wish to risk infection, to learn of your eternal fate in The Void, be my guest," he muttered, withdrawing his hand as I grasped the vial he offered.

I downed it like a shot, holding back a rising cough as a cinnamon heat coated my throat. The door locked yet again, my eyes drifting as a warming calm mixed with a slight tingle settled over me, lulling me to sleep even as my mind protested the behavior.

I awoke with a start, the shadows on the wall creeping over the room as the torches cast a dull shine from their dying embers. A faded pain in my forearm and a slight ache in my head were the only reminders of waking up earlier.

Struggling, I pushed myself into a seated position, a dampness settling into my clothing as I leaned against the stone wall, willing my head to clear. A slight shift from the corner of the chamber alerted me that I was not alone, my arm sweeping to the side only to be met with air, a reminder of my prior attempt to injure the commander.

Eyes adjusting to the settling heaviness of the dark, I focused in on the outline of the man, knowing instantly who it was.

"Morning, *princesse*," came the husky drawl in the corner. "Tell me, are you planning to be cooperative today? Or do you simply wish to live out your existence in this drab space?"

My silence greeted him, contempt sparking in my eyes as I rudely glared at him.

"I don't have all day, *Cassandra*," he stated, irritation rising as smoky words filled the room. "Let me tell you how this works. You have two options. You can be a good little girl and tell me the truth, or you can fade away in here, forgotten and alone."

I shifted my gaze, attempting to avoid looking him in the eye as anger flared deep in me. Briefly glancing at him, I asked, "Do I have any other options? After all, I *do* have a sister and she will be searching for me."

The response was not entirely encouraging; he just chuckled before stating, "If I were you, I wouldn't want to find out. Your sister is safe, so long as you cooperate and provide me with the truth."

"Are you threatening my sister's safety, commander?" I spat.

"I'm not threatening anything." His voice cut through the air. "I'm simply informing you that our sisters' stay here is dependent on your cooperation."

Glaring at Sébastien in disdain, I muttered, "Fine."

Taking a deep, shaky breath, I prepared to recount the crazy strand of events that had occurred. Staring at Sébastien with contempt, I sighed. "Alright, but it's not my fault if you don't believe me." I began to speak, praying that he would. "We are from a time where those with magic have been hunted and killed off. A time where the King of Nordak rules with terror and Seefers are used to control the citizens of the realm. We live in a time where magic has been banished from the realm."

"A time?" he prompted, interrupting me.

"Yes. A time hundreds of years in the future. A time when—"

"Enough with the lies, Cassandra. Truly, you don't expect me to believe that," he growled as his fists tightened in anger.

Black mists swirled violently around his ankles at his frustration and I pressed myself against the wall, watching him.

"We *are* from the future. When I was younger, this elderly woman gave me a ruby red pendant when I visited Verastarr. I have worn that pendant every day, yet one day, when wishing for my sister to travel with me for my job, the pendant grew warm around my neck. Mist and sparks flew out of nowhere, before circling us in a cold mist. And then our vision went black."

"And you arrived here?" he sarcastically inquired.

Nodding, I continued on about how we thought we were in a reenactment from a time before the Cordial ruled over the regions. A time before the Nordak hunted, seeking power and their dark magic spread across the Vanaiyer Realm. Not sure how much he truly needed to know, my voice rambled on for a few minutes as the words Kateya and I had not voiced to others flowed from my lips.

When I finished recounting most of the story, I looked at him. "I am aware of how outlandish my story seems, trust me." I scoffed, laughing. "If I were you, I wouldn't believe me either. But you said you wanted the truth, and this is all I can tell you."

I hadn't told him my true thoughts though, the ones where I believed that if I found the pendant that Kateya and I could return home. I didn't tell him that's why I ran off; that the pendant was what I had been searching for since we arrived in the damned past. I refused to tell it all when I hardly knew if I could trust this commander. As I spoke, I noticed his eyes began to soften with consideration before morphing back to a familiar ice-cold stare.

"What elemental magic do you possess? You claim to be from the East Engles, are you a syren?" His eyes tracked my face as he questioned me further.

"I don't—I'm just a mortal. I have no elemental magic, I'm unable to shift. And anyone from our time who would be able to use elemental magic has long since been hunted down."

"Yet the pendant you claim you possessed has magic?"

"It's the only explanation I can think of." I paused as I held the commander's gaze, wondering if he did indeed believe my story.

He glanced at me once more, as if discerning whether I was stating the truth, and then strode out of the room, leaving me for the third time, alone and clueless.

I'm confused. He demands that I quit lying and tell him the truth, but when I tell the truth, excluding certain pieces of the story, nothing changes. I'm still stuck in this cell of a room, with no idea whether my sister is okay or if we will ever be able to search for the pendant again.

I didn't even bother to check the door, knowing it would be locked. I just sank down the wall to the cold, barren, marble floor, hopeless defeat rising within me.

I didn't know how long I sat there; at some point I lost track of the time, counting the cracks on the gray marbled floor. I hadn't eaten anything since the morning I ran away after breakfast, and time slipped by at an unknown speed in the abyss of the room. Drained and famished, a dull throb pounding in my arm, I couldn't even think properly. I simply sat there, staring at the wall, before drifting in and out of sleep.

The door was thrown open sometime later, reverberating throughout the room, and Sébastien's foreboding presence filled the door frame as his gaze swept over me, and stated, "Let's go, we're leaving soon."

He turned on his heel and stomped out the way he came in. The guards glanced at me sympathetically as I slowly stood up and walked out the door. *Go where?* I thought as we walked through yet another dimly lit hallway with various axes and swords displayed on the walls.

The front guard pulled open a door before walking through, with me trailing behind him. Sunlight caressed my cheeks, melting the chill which had sunk into my skin as we walked out onto a dirt path in the back garden close to the stables. All around me, horses were being saddled up as soldiers rushed about finalizing preparations. But for what?

Dravyn approached me as the guards who had retrieved me stopped, motioning for me to follow him. I didn't necessarily want to, but for some reason, I trusted Dravyn in a way I didn't with many others in this château. Perhaps because he had a lightness about him, or the kindness he showed me the other day. Either way, I hurried to catch up to him, taking in the growing group of men assembling. He walked over to a beautiful chestnut gelding, which was saddled and ready.

As I hesitantly stroked the gelding, Dravyn handed me a small roll of bread before saddling up his onyx destrier, which huffed impatiently next to the gelding. The horse seemed to be taken with me, which was an unusual turn of events, as I was still wary of them. Turning to Dravyn, my voice cut the silence, as I asked, "What's his name?"

He glanced at me for a few moments as though hesitant to speak with me or share more than necessary before responding. "Eldyor."

I smiled as I looked at the horse standing before me, my fingers trailing its nose as I leaned in and whispered in his ear, "Eldyor, I like it. Although, I think I will call you *El* for short."

Chapter Six

VERASTARR

DRAVYN ASSISTED EMALYEE and me onto our mounts before approaching his destrier, and I was still as lost as ever about where we were going with the procession of horses formed in front of my eyes. At Sébastien's command, soldiers began to draw their horses into motion. I smiled briefly as Kateya rode up beside me and breathed a sigh of relief that my sister was safe in one piece. A soldier I vaguely recognized rode past, nodding toward my sister, who informed me that the soldier's name was Eryx.

Confused as to where we were headed, we looked around for someone to ask. Emalyee and Dravyn rode in front of me, deep in conversation, and I felt it rude to interrupt them. Glancing to the sides of me, I noticed there were soldiers all around us. Everyone was in a procession of sorts with four horses side by side, with the soldiers on the outer edges. Turning to the soldier to my right, I sweetly questioned, "Excuse me, could you tell me where we are headed?"

Continuing to scan the horizon, he distantly responded without so much as a glance in my direction. "Not my place to tell, miss." I sighed before reluctantly giving up and chatting with my sister as we rode.

The truth was, even as bizarre as this entire circumstance happened to be, this place was truly beautiful. Vibrant green trees proudly filled the grassy meadows, towering overhead as they surrounded us. The sun had come up a few hours ago and was now filling the meadows, dancing off the tips of everything it touched with a peaceful enchantment. The birds were singing to each other, and the wind was gently floating through my hair as our horses walked along. For a moment, I let myself forget the stress and fear of everything. I only thought about the nature around me, and I felt free. We continued our journey for the remainder of the day, pausing occasionally for the horses to drink and to eat.

As night approached, I noticed we began slowing down, my legs screaming in protest from the long day of horseback riding, even as I noticed that there didn't appear to be any towns or signs of life nearby. We turned off the path we'd traveled along before stopping at a clear patch of land circled by trees that towered overhead, creating a shield of protection. I could not figure out what we were planning on doing here with this many guards and people.

I was just about to ask when a strong voice spoke out, breaking through the crisp night air. "We'll stop here for the night, set up camp."

I nearly laughed out loud at the absurdity of the idea, as my parents always warned us not to camp outside—*not that I willingly would have with Seefers wandering the region*—before I realized that they were serious.

Kateya glanced toward me, bubbling with excitement at the idea of camping out in the forest. "Hear me out, Cass. I know we need to find a way home quickly. And as much as I'm worried about making it back, we've never gotten to camp outside. Like ever."

I smiled toward my younger sister, loving her ability to make the most of the situation as I replied, "maybe Seefers aren't as big of an issue here as they are at home."

"Imagine the stories we will have to tell," she sing-songed as she headed off to watch the camp be set up.

Before I knew it, tents had been set up, and a fire was slowly heating the surrounding area, a warm layer drifting into the tents. When I stopped to think about it, it was quite astonishing how quickly Sébastien's men could set up a campsite. The sun swiftly faded into the night, and dinner had been prepared. Dinner, as I learned, lacked delicacies, consisting of salted venison and warmed barley bread. A simple meal that somehow managed to lull one into feeling safe, cozy, and even relaxed.

As the meal ended, Kateya and I headed off to our assigned tent and began preparing for bed. Exhaustion coursed through my body after the day of traveling, and the little food and sleep I'd had in the past two days began to catch up to me. I resolved that come morning, I would figure out how we would make it back to where we first arrived. I needed to find my pendant before it was too late. I still didn't know whether we would be able to travel through time to get back home. Whether the pendant made it into the past with us, or if it was still in one piece. The only thing I knew for certain was that the pendant held the answers we so desperately needed and we were currently traveling in the opposite direction.

My mind was running in circles as I laid down on the hard ground, sharp little jabs pricking through the mat from the stones underneath, and felt myself drifting off to sleep on the roughly woven bed mat. As I shifted to get comfortable, I rolled over before finding myself off the mat and lying with my face in the grass. Glancing to my right, I noticed Kateya was sound asleep beside me, snoring lightly. Rolling back onto the mat, I attempted to once again get comfortable.

After a multitude of restless turns, and more exhausted than I previously was from the day's ride, I decided to go and walk around for a few minutes. Gently pushing the woven fabric of the tent to the side, I slipped out into the night air, a welcoming chill settling against the bare skin of my arms. Dew-covered grass met my toes as I silently walked through the campsite toward the trees, praying I hadn't woken anyone. I felt safe as I wandered through the dark shadows of the trees before approaching the shoreline of a lake in the distance. The lake wasn't big in size, but it was enchanting, reflecting the dancing moonlight off its surface; it drew me in and reminded me of home.

Settling into the patch of dirt by the base of a large tree by the lake, my mind went back to a summer's day years ago. My parents had taken us on an adventure a short drive inland from Estaire. We stayed a while, laughing and swimming in the river before having a picnic dinner by the river's edge. The moon was slowly rising in the sky and stars were appearing, a rare sight for us living in the Capital. The moonlight's reflection on the water drew us in for a midnight swim. That memory was one of the last peaceful times we had in nature, before The Fall and the unknown creatures that began to roam the woods.

As I focused my thoughts back on the lake, I felt unwanted tears stream down my cheeks. I didn't recall when I started crying. The peace of the lake entwined with childhood memories brought them to the surface, but the longer I stared at the lake, the more tears appeared to violently stain my cheeks. Wrapping my arms around my legs, I hugged them close to me, shivering slightly from the nighttime chill as I took in the beauty and calm before me. It was a stark contrast to the overwhelming fear and concern that was the turmoil inside me.

Recognizing the risk I was taking by being outside the campsite border, a sigh broke my lips as I began to push myself off the ground to head back to the campsite, when a husky voice broke through the silence. "Can't sleep?"

I froze, every muscle in my body tensing in recognition before turning around at the sound of the commander's voice and murmuring, "No, not really. Don't worry. I'm not planning to escape. I was about to head back, I promise."

He closed the distance between us with unspeakable speed, lowering himself to the ground beside me. His long limbs stretched out in front of him as he settled against the tree trunk next to me. I tensed as his knee brushed against my leg, and silence once again took over the lake. After a few moments of deafening silence from the form to my right, I couldn't take it anymore.

Slowly, I glanced over toward Sébastien, wondering why he was here, only to find him intently gazing at me, those icy blue eyes filled with a look of concern I hadn't known he could feel. My breathing silently hitched, caught in my throat as I wondered why he was looking at me in such a way. My eyes traced the angles of his chiseled jaw before getting hooked on his lips.

I hated that my mind drifted as I briefly imagined what those freckled lips would feel like controlling my own, covering them in a passionate kiss. As I imagined what else he was capable of doing with those lips when he broke the silence. A concerned note in his voice as he stated, "You've been crying."

The words *no shit* flew to the tip of my tongue even as I ducked my head, upset he could so easily observe I'd been crying. I had no intention of admitting I had been; even if it was obvious, I wouldn't give him the satisfaction of being right. I'd started to get up off the ground again rather than answer when a strong hand clamped around my arm, tugging me back down to the ground and holding me firmly in place. I couldn't help but wonder what those hands could do; what they would feel like wrapped around my neck, even as frustration rose in me.

I glared up at him in frustration, as I attempted to pry my arm from his sturdy grasp, to no avail. "What would you like now?" I angrily mocked. "I don't answer to you. Especially not after you locked me in a *cell* and once I actually give you the truth, you don't even inform me of where we are going."

Sébastien simply chuckled, looking at me with those ice-blue eyes that danced with amusement as he replied, "An explanation. Preferably now."

Angered by the fact that he thought he had the power to force me to answer him, I held my glare, my eyes narrowing at him in defiance. I could have told him what was wrong, but the truth is, I only know the reason why I started crying, not the reason I continued for so long.

Sébastien seemed unfazed by my glower, however, as he made himself comfortable, settling his long body further against the tree bark and said, "Well, *princesse*, we have all night."

A deep groan slipped from my lips before I muttered under my breath, "Arrogant men," as I resolved to remain silent, even if that meant sitting here in awkward silence for hours. I was angry. I was angry about the fact I was here; at the fact he was making me sit and talk to him when I didn't want to; at the fact that my younger sister had been roped into all of this. To make matters worse, I was in some serious need of a solid night's sleep at this point.

Apparently, the mixture of those feelings didn't go well together because, before I knew it, hot tears were streaming down my face again. I heard him mutter a curse under his breath before two muscular arms wrapped around me, guiding me into a solid chest. His grip tightened as my body shook, the scent of spice and pine lulling me into safety. A low voice whispered in my ear as my sobs began to fade. "Tell me what's wrong Cassandra."

I hiccupped as I realized I had completely drenched the front of his charcoal gray tunic with my sob fest. Slowly looking up, my gaze met Sébastien's as he watched me, concern laced across his face. I got lost for a moment, those crystal blue eyes gently holding mine, the freckles splattered across high cheekbones scrunching, a wave of darkened hair draping past his eye. I noticed a tiny scar marring his skin, running from his forehead into his left eyebrow, making me wonder what had happened. The intensity of his gaze sweeping over my facial features sent a burst of heat coursing through me.

How could I tell him what was wrong? How could I tell him my entire life felt as if it was falling apart, and I couldn't do anything to stop it? How could I tell him I felt like such an awful sister for still not being able to protect her, much like I hadn't been able to the night the Seefers ransacked our house in the East Engles? How?

His dark gaze searched my face as though trying to uncover the questions I had on repeat through my mind. I honestly didn't know what to do, so I did the only thing I could think to do. "Can we just forget about this and go back to the camp . . . please?" I quietly asked, nearly begging him to drop this. To forget this entire night.

I felt Sébastien stiffen, every muscle in his chest and abdomen rippled in frustration, even when he let out a sarcastic laugh. "You attempt to sneak out of *my* camp, avoid answering *my* questions, then cry all over *my* shirt, and have the audacity to ask *me* to drop it."

Cringing at his words—because they made me come across as rude and shallow—I swallowed any remaining pride within me and begrudgingly mumbled, "Yes . . . *please.*"

His eyes swept over my face once more before he spoke. "Very well, we shall drop this topic. *For tonight.* However, in the morning, we *will* continue this conversation, and I *will* demand an answer by then, whether you feel it in you to give me one or not, *understand?*"

Why does this man always need an answer? Doesn't he have anything better to do with his life? And why did he insist on calling me "princesse"?

I managed to pull off a weak smile as he helped me up and escorted me back to the campsite. Crawling back into my tent silently so as not to wake my sister, I felt sleep reaching out to me once more, this time drifting over and taking me.

Sunlight peeked through the flaps of the cloth tent, tickling my cheek as it floated by, softly waking me up. As I sat up in the tent, I glanced over at Kateya and laughter bubbled, bursting through my lips. My sister was sprawled out on the grass, her blanket tangled around her feet and her bed mat lying on top of her stomach. She had her mouth half open with a patch of grass attempting to enter her mouth and a dandelion stuck on her forehead, leaving a yellow imprint.

As I began laughing at my sister's morning appearance, Emalyee stepped into the tent, took in my sisters' appearance and was soon laughing alongside me. Kateya woke up at that exact moment to find us both nearly dying of laughter. She stood up and stretched, unaware of her sleep-enabled appearance, before asking, "What's so funny?"

Sucking in air, struggling to regain breathing, neither Emalyee nor myself could respond, so we simply pointed toward the flower still stuck to her face. Kateya reached up, slowly pulled the dandelion off while scowling at us and then marched out of the tent, causing Emalyee and me to break out in laughter again.

After dressing, I followed Emalyee out of the tent and toward the dying embers of last night's fire. We had a quick breakfast and soon after, the campsite was packed up. All thirty guards were ready, and we were off again to some mysterious location *His Highness* wouldn't divulge to me. As we continued riding that morning, Emalyee and I sat side-by-side, talking about our lives, men, and making jokes. Talking with Emalyee during the journey helped me feel more at home. A smile crept across my face as I caught sight of my sister riding behind me a little ways, chatting away with Eryx.

The tip of my nose was beginning to burn from the brutal force of the sun, and my legs were cramping, muscles spasming in unimaginable ways from the second day of nonstop riding. Emalyee and I had been laughing about fashion sense and the crazy outfits girls wore to impress men—a topic relevant in both time periods. Even though I wasn't familiar with every outfit style in Verastarr, I could relate because every Friday night I watched my roommate dress up in impossible skirts and eccentric tops to attract her next hookup at the bar downtown. In the midst of our conversation, a soldier came riding up, "Commander Sébastien Capetian would like a word with you, miss." We both grew silent for a moment.

As I turned to Emalyee, we both began speaking at the same time. "Why does *Commander* Sébastien want to see you?"

Realization dawned on our faces that neither of us had any idea which of us the soldier happened to be speaking to. We both glanced at the soldier again, who was regarding us with an amused expression. "I believe the commander was referring to you, miss; something about unfinished business," he replied, directing his sentence to me.

Ah, so he thought that I would be interested in finishing last night's conversation with him even after I had asked him to drop it. Well, jokes on him, I guess. That wouldn't be happening.

"Please inform *His Highness* that I am currently engaged, and should he wish to speak with me, he may find another time to do so," I responded.

"Miss, I am under orders to bring you to him," the soldier pleaded. "Need I remind you that it was none other than Commander Sébastien Capetian, Prince of Verastarr, who took you in?"

I scoffed at his words, before shooting daggers back at him and reemphasizing, "Like I said, you can inform *His Highness* that I cannot merely be summoned like an animal, and if he wishes to speak with me, he may choose another time or get me himself."

The soldier began to ride off, and I turned my attention back to Emalyee, who in turn was looking at me with surprise and possibly pride. "Are you aware that you just turned down a direct order from the *Prince* of Verastarr?"

Laughing softly, I explained to her, "Yes, I am aware and he will possibly murder me for it. But, if he thinks he can just summon me whenever he wants, well, he is wrong. And I know what he wishes to speak with me about, and as I told him previously, I really have no desire to continue the conversation with him. If he has an issue with that, well, he can get over it."

Emalyee looked at me for a moment, before laughing softly and saying, "Void-damned. Sébastien has finally met his match with you. He could always stand to be taken down a bit."

Chapter Seven

VERASTARR

OUR LAUGHTER DIED DOWN as we noticed not one, but two destriers approaching us. We took in Dravyn's disapproving frown as they drew closer, as well as the amused glint in his eye. Then, I shifted my gaze to the left, toward Sébastien, cringing as I took in his steely, murderous look and the blatant anger pooling in those icy blue eyes.

Dravyn gave us a subtle nod as he rode up, while Sébastien just glared venomously at me, his mouth a taut line barely restraining the anger storming within him. Before I knew what was happening, he had my horse's reins in his hand and had spun around, heading back to the front of the line with me unwillingly in tow. Confused and outraged, I tried to jerk the reins to my own horse back to no avail. I turned to glance back at Emalyee, who shared an apologetic look with me while being sternly lectured by Dravyn.

As we approached the front lines, my outrage brewed, annoyance flaring up that Sébastien believed he could control me. I thought about the options I had, knowing what it was he wanted to speak to me about. I could tell him off for the arrogant act being displayed, or I could remain silent the entire time. After shifting through the benefits of each, I decided.

If he wants to play, I'll bite.

The silent game it was.

Sébastien fell into his spot leading the line, and I noticed him trying to calm himself down before he spoke. With his eyes closed and the subtle flare of his nostrils, he took a few steadying breaths, though I doubted it would work well for him. My gaze shifted, looking out into the browning grass fields, admiring the occasional trees and the birds flying about as he began to go off on his little rant that dripped authority.

"I thought I made myself clear back at the château that my word is law and I'm not to be undermined, under any circumstance. Was that not perfectly clear? I won't tolerate you withholding information from me."

Much to his displeasure, he was met solely with silence, as I didn't even acknowledge him. *Yes, I was aware my actions were slightly rude, but what does he expect me to do? Do whatever he says, anytime he says something? He might be a prince, but I don't think so.*

"Did you not hear me?"

Silence. Once again. The only sound filling the air was the low rumble of our horses' hooves on the dusty path and the distant mutterings of the men traveling behind us.

A laugh caught in my throat as I heard his frustrated growl beside me, but what I wasn't expecting was for him to yank my horse toward him, away from the line of soldiers and toward the forest. The horses walked according to his direction until we came to a clear meadow surrounded by large oak trees, where Sébastien stopped to dismount.

He lifted me down, but refused to let me go, as he trapped me between his body and the horse, towering over me and forcing me to tilt my head to meet his raging eyes. I attempted to move away from him, yet his steel grip kept me in place. The more I struggled, the tighter the hold became, until I found myself flush against his body, staring up at him, even as my body wished to betray me and sink into the warmth. With a defiant glare, I simply matched his gaze, once again not saying a thing.

"You can play this little game of yours for as long as you want. I just want you to keep this in mind: I'm stronger, more powerful, and have all the authority. You, on the other hand, have nothing to stand up against me with. So, if I were you, I would give in and accept the fact that I have the control here."

I scoffed at his demeaning speech before I gave up with my silent streak and began to respond. *"I'm stronger, more power-ful, and have all the authority,"* I sarcastically mocked. "Let me tell you something, you may be the Prince of Verastarr, but I am *not* some woman you can push around and dictate what I can or can't do. Did you want to tell me when I could breathe, too? How 'bout what I'm wearing—is that okay with you, *Your Highness*? I'm not like some of the women you are used to who can be bossed around or fall at your feet. Try to break me all you want, but I lived in a land where royalty was overrated, and I learned to fight for what I believe in."

Sébastien stared at me incredulously, venomous rage and surprise written over his face. He bent forward, his breath falling heavily across the bare expanse of my neck, dancing across my skin as he tucked a loose strand of hair behind my ear and muttered, "We shall see about that." A dark chuckle slipped from his freckled lips. His hands rested firmly on my waist, his fingers splayed over my middle as they encircled me, and he went to help me back up onto my horse.

"Capetian, Capetian! Enemies!" A younger soldier ran up yelling as he tried to speak through his heavy breathing. "Coming hard . . . so many . . . can't be overtaken."

I heard Sébastien shout something as my mind processed the soldiers fighting through the trees. I watched in shock as a burly, armed man charged straight toward us, his blackened metal sword raised dangerously overhead. I stood, frozen in my spot, unmoving, as the shouts and screams grew louder around me. I faintly heard Sébastien telling me to get down and stay put. Yet my mind flashed back to that fateful night long ago.

The ominous, dark gray creature filled the doorframe of our living room, his yellowish-gray teeth emerging as a snarl shook the walls. Seefer attacks had begun to frequent the Capital and lives were lost daily. The only way to destroy a Seefer was through magic, and those who came face to face with the beasts never breathed again. They hunted in packs, leaving only carnage in their tracks. The snarls crept closer through the darkness, and my mother's screams for us to hide were barely heard. Behind me, I felt Kateya's whimpers coursing through her body as the beast stalked closer, its target in mind. Cowered by the brick fireplace that was built into the hiding spot underground, I pressed Kateya inside until there was no further to go, my body in front of hers to keep her safe. I held the rusted fire poker shakily in front of my body as the beast moved in. The horror of the mangled beast still haunted my nightmares. Missing patches of blackened fur, matted with a crimson tinge, feral burnt orange eyes lighting up as a red mist swirled through them. Claws clacked across our tiled floors, as the Seefer crouched before rising onto its haunches, a shudder reverberating through its body as it pushed off toward its prey. Another sobbed scream flew through the air as I raised the fire poker in front of me.

"Cassandra!" A snarled shout snapped me back into the present, as I watched Sébastien fend off a soldier, an iron scent filling the air as crimson dripped from his sword.

Distantly, I heard shouts and yells, cries of pain mixed with the clashing of heavy metal swords. I ducked behind my horse, frantically searching to see if I could spot my sister, to see if find something to defend myself with, but there wasn't anything. The sound of metal came closer, and I glanced up to see Sébastien two meters away from me, fighting another man. I watched in fear and awe at their fighting. Parry, blow, duck, repeat. A movement I had memorized following the attack on our family. My father taught Kateya and me the basics for self-defense, and I continued the lessons early each morning with him. The sheer power of their blows and intricate detail of each movement was astonishing, yet I knew that even the slightest misstep could lead to serious injury. As I watched the scene unfold before me, I realized two more soldiers were approaching, and they weren't with Sébastien.

"Sébastien!" I shouted. "Another two are coming!"

I noticed him glance up as he parried a blow before assessing the situation.

"Get on your horse and ride hard; hide only when you find shelter." He grunted as he blocked yet another blow.

"I can't leave my sister." I shouted in reply, as I continued searching for a weapon to defend myself.

"Your sister is being protected by three of my best men.' He grunted as black mists rose from the ground, darting toward the incoming soldiers with rapid precision. "You, on the other hand, are in danger." He finished as his sword cut through the air, slicing through the man's jugular and I nearly yelped as his body crumpled to the ground.

"Now Cassandra." Sébastien's voice demanded as the two soldiers rushed upon us.

As much as I hated taking orders, I realized that my life depended on this since I had no form of protection. I quickly mounted the horse closest to me. A brief glance in Sébastien's direction showed more men charging for him. A dark mist stormed the ground surrounding him as a deadly growl pierced my ears. My mind raced as I stared at the form in front of me: that of a towering wolf. As I turned around toward the shelter of the trees, I realized I had no idea just how powerful Sébastien was, but he controlled mist and had the power to shapeshift.

I pushed hard in the direction of a dark forest. Eldroy took control and jumped over fallen trees, avoiding low branches. I rode, still too much in shock from the attack and the shift of magic that occurred. Magic and the powers that came with it were rarely seen in the East Engles. It was known that the royals from each land contained magic, yet following The Fall, the use of magic was rarely seen. As I looked for some form of shelter, I feared for my sister, Kateya, and what she might be going through. The thought was almost enough to force me back around toward the battleground.

I heard the sound of horses' hooves hitting the leaf-covered ground with strong force, shaking the forest floor. Not knowing whether the rider was a friend or an enemy, I realized hiding was paramount. A small alcove was formed by a tangle of tree branches and bushes, providing what I hoped would be a decent hiding spot out of view. As I approached the hidden cove, I threw myself off Eldroy and prayed that he would continue to run. The impact of the landing held me down as pain pierced my side. I hadn't been prepared for the force of the ground.

Even as I whimpered in pain, I crawled over to the alcove and pushed my way deep into the bushes, attempting to hide from view. Brambles and branches clawed at my exposed skin, leaving marks that burned. No sooner had I hidden than the sound of metal swords clashing violently in the forest surrounded me, making me regret not having a dagger for the third time today. I attempted to push myself back further in the alcove, yet the pain in my arm and my hip hindered me from moving more than a few feet. I sat there quiet as could be, slowly breathing, knowing that I was the prey. A memory of Mum flitted through my mind of a time before The Fall. A time when spirituality existed in our land, a time before fear was worshiped. She had whispered a prayer over the land as the Nordak grew stronger. It was a time before prayer to The God of our descendants was forbidden. As the memory left, a rushed prayer slipped my lips in a whisper.

Please keep Kateya safe and alive. I can't lose her, not like this. She doesn't deserve this. Neither of us do, but especially not her. Please. Oh please, let us survive.

Amen

The pain in my side had intensified, and I glanced down

to see blood slowly seeping out onto my red shirt, blending in as it darkened slightly. The faded brown leather pants I wore for travel were torn in various places, and I knew the rest of me must look just as disheveled. I figured at some point in my ride away from the battleground and the soldier chasing me, I must have cut myself on something in the forest, perhaps the large branch I flew past. The sounds of metal clashing angrily and shouts slowly began to fade around me as I realized that the fight must have been coming to an end. But was I in the clear or was I still prey?

My best option would be to stay hidden here for a little longer. The missing dagger thing was really biting me in the ass. If someone found me, I would basically be at their mercy. I just hoped Kateya was alright. If she wasn't, I didn't know what I would do. My mind wandered to what form of power or magic Sébastien had coursing through his veins if he could shift. *Was that still a power the royals at home held?*

"Cassandra!" I heard someone shout.

Should I answer them? I wondered. *What if they are enemies?* I thought and then reasoned with, *How in The Void would they know your name then?*

My internal struggle resolved; I shakily replied, "Here."

I heard footsteps marching around in the forest, leaves cracking underfoot, before a pair of onyx boots stopped close to my hiding spot. I heard a low chuckle before a deep voice broke through the silence. "Nice hiding place."

A sigh of relief rushed from my lips that it had been Dravyn who found me, and not the commander. I slowly, painfully crawled out of my cramped spot and allowed Dravyn to help me up. He looked at me, taking in my appearance, no doubt since I was covered in dirt and leaves with some scratches, and asked me if I was okay.

I glanced at him, slightly annoyed he was asking before muttering, "Of course I'm okay. I need to check on my sister, though. I need to know she's okay."

I began to walk slowly back to the group before I heard him say through chuckles, "Well, I'm going back to the others, but I will let them know where to find you."

I internally groaned as I realized I was, in fact, heading the wrong way. Before I turned toward Dravyn, I attempted to mask my pain. "Glad to know that a life-threatening attack isn't enough to kill your humor," I retorted.

"Well, you know, nothing like some violence to get the ladies in the mood."

A laugh slipped from me. "Don't let Emalyee hear you saying that. You'll find yourself out on your ass before you can say sorry."

Dravyn clutched at his heart, feigning a wounded groan as we walked into a clearing, and I watched as soldiers were walking around, preparing the horses, and checking for injuries. As I scanned the area, my gaze froze on Kateya as she found me at the same moment. A second passed before she ran over to me, throwing her arms around my neck as we gripped each other tightly. Thankful to both be alive.

Apparently, while they had been surrounded, most of the enemies had come after Sébastien, as they were targeting a powered royal. The soldiers who had been with her weren't as injured as the ones that had been closer to Sébastien. My thoughts briefly flew to Sébastien, wondering if he was okay. If he had been harmed in the attack. I dismissed the thought as quickly as it entered my mind, not wanting to care about him or his entitled ass. I had a plan, after all. Find my pendant, learn how to use it to bring us back to East Engles, and bury the necklace where no one can get ahold of the power ever.

Right?

Sébastien strode over toward us with a concerned expression when he noticed us walking into the clearing. Why he would be concerned was beyond me, though. His face and shirt had crimson spatters darkening the material, his leathers a matching design. I noticed the two friends step to the side a little and talk. I could tell by the expressions on Sébastien's face that whatever they were talking about wasn't promising, and both were hardened by the surprise attack. Dravyn shouted a command, and the soldiers began moving around and mounting up. Sébastien walked over to me then and informed me that I would be riding with him. I attempted to protest this new development; however, my argument was instantly shut down as he pointed out that I had let Eldroy run off while I hid for my life. Groaning, I followed him slowly over to his horse.

Warm, calloused hands encircled my waist as he lifted me up onto his destrier. My mouth tasted like metal, and I realized that I had bitten my lip hard, to the point of breaking the skin. I felt the horse I was atop of moving, and glanced back, barely processing that the commander had mounted the horse behind me. His tattooed forearms wrapped tightly around me as he motioned his horse forward. I gasped slightly in pain as the horse trotted along. I hadn't meant to gasp out loud. I didn't want anyone to focus on the fact that I was minorly injured, for it was nothing compared to the various injuries I'd accumulated over the years from training and Nordak attacks.

I felt Sébastien stiffen beside me before cautiously asking, "What's wrong, Cassandra?"

"Nothing," I replied quickly, too quickly, hoping he would drop the subject. But knowing that it was Sébastien I was talking about, meant that might never happen.

"Nothing, really?" he questioned, his voice dripping with sarcasm. "I highly doubt that. No one gasps from a casual horse trot."

"I'm sure many people might when forced to ride with you," I instantly retorted. "You are just too Void-damned arrogant to notice."

I felt his arms tighten around me as he struggled not to reply harshly, but my thoughts faded away as a wave of pain radiated through my body. I felt Sébastien turn his horse off course once again, his arms supporting my body as the wave of pain refused to subside.

Sébastien helped me down before demanding I explain to him what happened.

"It's nothing. Seriously. A small scratch. I don't know why you care; let's just keep going."

"A small scratch, huh? Do you often gasp from light scratches?"

"I told you. The pained noise you heard was a direct result of me having to endure a ride with you. That's all."

"Very well, let's go," he responded, his black leather gloves wrapping around me to lift me up.

My eyes briefly shut as pain radiated from the cut on the side as he gripped it. His hands moved off my body. I watched as his ice-blue eyes scanned my body in depth, narrowing in on the darkened crimson section of my shirt.

I remained frozen as his hand reached out, lightly pulling the fabric up at the source of the color change, sending slight shivers up my body as he pulled the fabric away. I could only watch his face as he inspected the cut, his eyes a flurry of emotion. His fingers traced gently along the outer edge of my wound, checking the severity before his gaze flicked back up to mine with a pained expression as he sternly said, "You should have told me," before stalking away.

The healer was over in an instant and bandaged up my cut and inspected where I fell. Both my hip and my wrist were now sporting large, blackish-blue bruises that were in no way attractive. Only after the healer assured Sébastien that I was alright and would survive did he allow everyone to proceed.

It had been two days since Sébastien deigned to speak to me. Not that I was complaining.

"How is your cut healing?" His words rolled off his tongue as he adjusted his grip on me.

"Fine, thank you," I replied as my eyes stared off in the distance to the mountain range, inching closer toward us. His silence grew into a thick fog hanging over our heads. Sighing, I questioned, "During the attack. You shifted. Is that a power all royals have?"

After a moment of silence, his voice cut through the fog. "Yes. Each land in Vanaiyer has a different power in addition to our magic. It's a power that only royals are born with. Here in Verastarr, royals are born with wolvyn blood coursing through them."

"Are royals the only ones with that sort of power?"

"Do you truly not know this? Every child is told stories of the shifting power and elemental magic roaming through our realm."

Annoyance reverberated through me. "No, I don't know. That's why I was asking, *Your Highness*."

Those ice-blue eyes flared with heat as he continued, "No, royals aren't the only ones with that sort of power in them, but they are the only ones born with it. Royals can spread their power to whoever they choose, although it is typically given with high consideration. For instance, my father chooses to share the wolvyn power with those in his council and high-ranking captains of the guard."

My thoughts flitted to The Fall, wondering how many wolvyn had been forced into hiding due to the powers they held. "How many wolvyn are there?" I questioned Sébastien.

"There's not an exact count. But I'd say there are roughly three hundred living in Nytestarr." He spoke with the ease of someone who grew up around magic and power. "There are others in the land, though, some unaccounted for. And some who have turned against the royals."

"How do you know if someone is a wolvyn?"

"The pack bond. While different from the mating bond, the pack bond can be felt in a wolvyn's soul. In simpler terms though"—his forearms wrapped tighter around my body as he pushed the sleeve of his left arm up, revealing an intricate tattoo—"every wolvyn is inked with this imprint as the power settles into them. My brother and I were born with ours, just as my father was."

Settling back against Sébastien's muscled form, I stared at the detailed markings on his forearm, watching the scattering of swirled ink crawl up his skin, tracing along corded veins, as I admired the intricate design. The likeness of a wolf—or wolvyn I should say—etched into the design, blended seamlessly. My eyes closed as I relaxed against his body, the canter of the horse mixed with scents of spice and pine lulling me to sleep.

The duration of our five-day horseback journey went smoothly, minus the one surprise attack. Emalyee and I grew close over our journey, laughing and talking, spending nearly the entire journey together. Kateya and I talked often as well. She had a new friend in Eryx and while she was worried about getting home, I watched my sister slowly begin to get lost in the day-to-day events and travel, focusing less on the fear of the circumstances.

I, on the other hand, was close to losing my sanity with the constant stream of thoughts chasing after me. The new knowledge regarding magic, powers, and the wolvyn sat at the forefront of my mind, making me wonder what type of magic was stored in the pendant I'd worn daily.

The further we traveled from the field where Kateya and I first appeared, the more alert and concerned I became. We couldn't afford not to find that pendant—I was positive that it held the answers to returning home. I avoided talking to Sébastien unless necessary. Which was just as well—he spoke solely in dark glares, grunts, and growls, while also refusing to let me out of his sight. I longed to be home in Estaire and have dinner with our parents or laugh at the bar with Aerilyn.

My thighs were exhausted from the constant riding, and the cut on my side was healing over as the bruises faded from black to a darkened purple. This was the state I found myself in on the last day of our journey as we began approaching a large, bustling city.

Chapter Eight

VERASTARR

LAVENDER AND LEMON VERBENA FLOATED in the air as we approached the outskirts of the city. It reminded me of the same scent that greeted us when we first arrived in Verastarr. As we entered the city, the worn dirt path we'd followed faded into a narrowed, onyx cobblestone road. People crowded the street, and the low rumble of noise was nothing compared to the street vendors. Merchants lined the sides of the streets, shouting off names of goods to be purchased. I was drawn in by the chaos of the merchants, the feeling exciting and familiar, reminding me slightly of the marketplace that I used to visit with my father on occasion.

The rush of people around me felt like the Capital in East Engles. Women out shopping, bright colored dresses, flowing pants, artists painting on the street corners. The moon rippled across the sky, hidden by hues of purple-blue clouds. The town was alive despite the time of day. I took in the lack of fear from everyone around me. At home, we rarely ventured outside after dusk. With the Seefers coming out to hunt and the lack of magic, it was best to stay inside. But here the people were alive, dancing and painting in the streets, the roads lit by moonlight.

I remember the last time I truly danced under the moonlight, carefree and at peace. It had been a few weeks prior to The Fall. Father brought us to the Engles Festival, and we stayed out all night dancing, shopping, and playing carnival games. I had been looking around at the festival vendors. Father would laugh at me occasionally, telling me that any pieces I found at jewelry vendors at the festival were not worth my time. We had jokingly bantered back and forth most of the night until I finally proved him wrong when I discovered a beautiful necklace. Father admitted his defeat at that moment. I think he just pretended to dislike festival jewelry because he would secretly purchase pieces for Mum.

That day played across my mind as we proceeded past the merchants calling out to us. I turned to look for my sister. She rode behind me, a far-off look in her eyes, and I knew she, too, remembered the last time we'd been this free—a time before our lives changed and dusk didn't instill fear. I could read the worry and concern in her eyes as we continued, and it hurt me even as I knew the same emotions were painted on my face the further we rode into town.

I looked forward again and was shocked by the view in front of me. A large Palace was right before my eyes. I immediately recognized it—who wouldn't? It was the exact Palace I was supposed to be at this week, just a few hundred years in the future. The Ny Palace. Which meant we were in Nytestarr, the Capital of Verastarr.

As we began approaching Ny Palace, I noticed that the streets were lined with people, all cheering for their prince. The streets became difficult to maneuver and soldiers began falling in alongside us, escorting us toward the Palace. Kateya glanced over at me, back at the Palace, and then returned to look at me as she slowly realized that we were actually going to be entering Ny Palace.

"Can you believe it, Cass?" Kateya nearly squealed with excitement shown across her face. "Do you think we will actually be allowed inside? Will we get to sleep in the Palace? What do you think the inside looks like?"

Laughing as my sister rambled on, I looked on with a matching level of anticipation. We had seen the outside of Ny Palace when we were younger, back when traveling between the lands was more acceptable. We had never entered the Palace, or met a real king before (though apparently we had met a real prince that I wasn't too fond of).

My curiosity grew as we entered through the Palace gates, the charcoal stone structure towering overhead. We passed by the outlines of gardens as we approached the front entrance. Taking in my surroundings, I could see black ivy crawling through the gardens, the night lilies in bloom. A flower everyone knew of but ceased to exist in our time, as it was said to make powers stronger. Sébastien dismounted before assisting me down and walking off to discuss something with a man I presumed held a high ranking in his guard.

The soldiers who traveled with us soon dispersed as well as the servants. I turned to speak to Emalyee, only to discover her walking away with Dravyn. Sighing, I watched as the commander returned, approaching Kateya and me.

"Let's go," he commanded before walking toward the grand entrance. Kateya and I followed Sébastien as we walked into Ny Palace.

Entering through the Palace doors, I stopped. Gawking at the inside, I took in the tapestries hanging from the walls, the grand walkway leading to the throne, and the stone walls towering high toward an arched ceiling. The Palace was various hues of black and charcoal interspersed with the occasional crimson accent, much like the crest colors I had seen at the château. A white movement in the corner caught my eye, and I noted two wolvyn lounging, watching our every movement. Sleek, white fur clung neatly to the muscular frames of what appeared to be wolves, only twice as large. Sharp claws protruded from their paws and their eyes glowed with a swirled mist as they watched us. I wondered how many shifters chose to live in their wolvyn forms.

Busy admiring the Palace, I hadn't realized that the others had continued walking, until Sébastien turned back my way. He interrupted my train of thought as he snapped, "Didn't anyone teach you any manners?"

I looked at him quizzically, confused and wondering why he was asking me that. "What?"

Muttering something, he took a deep, controlled breath. "Next time, have some respect when you walk into someone else's home and keep up rather than standing there, frozen in the doorway. Understand?"

I glared at him before shoving past him. "If you insist," rolled off my tongue. I hurriedly walked up to Kateya while making a mental note not to shove past Sébastien again. My shoulder was throbbing from the contact, which just angered me even more.

Approaching Kateya, I asked, "Do you think we are supposed to just wait here?

Shrugging her shoulders, she simply replied, "I'm not quite sure."

"Kat," I snapped at her, my anger from the commander's tone radiating from me to her. "I could've figured that one out myself. Thank you *ever* so much for your insight."

Her emerald eyes darted over to mine as she muttered, "What made you so uptight?"

"Uptight? Really?" I snipped back. "*I'm* the uptight one?"

"Who else?" she snarked, and our stare-down began, both of us glaring in sisterly fashion, daring the other to look away first and show a sign of submission.

A sarcastic cough sounded from a meter away, causing both of us to break our glares and turn toward the sound. Dravyn relaxed as he leaned casually against a column, looking amused at our competition.

His voice sounded through the room, a slight chuckle

laced in with his words. "As highly entertaining as this staring match has been, I was so fortunate as to be in the wrong place at the wrong time and have been sent to show you to your rooms. Tomorrow, you're to meet with His Royal Highness, the King of Verastarr."

His eyes flicked over to mine. "If it were me, I would be on my best behavior. The God only knows how Sébastien has managed to keep his cool around you, but the king . . . You don't become king for no reason, and he has more than earned the title."

I nodded in acknowledgment, slightly confused as to why we would be meeting with the king.

Pushing off the column, Dravyn mockingly bowed. "If you follow me, your humble servant will now escort you to your rooms." A laugh slipped from my sister's lips as a smile graced mine and we trailed behind Dravyn.

I slid down the closed door after saying goodnight to Kateya. After the past week, I was drained of energy. I stared into the room, not fully processing anything in my line of vision, as I crafted a list in my head of things that I needed to do. *Find the pendant. Research the powers and magic of the realm. Actually, first, get a dagger. Then, return home with Kateya.* I peeled myself off the floor slowly and crept over to the bed, barely pulling the covers over me before I let sleep claim me for the night.

Sunshine danced across my face all too soon as it pulled me from my dreamless sleep. I slowly shifted up, fully taking in my surroundings. The sheets and comforter on the bed were a light gray color with intricate detail sewn on the edges. The door to my right was made of a dark oak with an open arch above it. To my left was an alcove window, a small lounge bench underneath, the perfect place to cozy up and read if one had the time. From my window, I could spot the Sea of Avyz glimmering and reflecting the sun's rays. The Sea of Avyz bordered all five lands in Vanaiyer, reminding me of the times I spent back home by this very body of water.

The room was decorated in a simple style, a singular tapestry hung on the wall above the bed, and a few paintings were scattered across the remaining walls. Sheer, black curtains blew with the breeze by the alcove, and there was a dressing table and a door on the wall across from my bed.

Slipping out from the silken sheets, I padded over the chilled marble tiles to the door, giving the handle a slight twist. It clicked free, revealing an open, airy washroom. A tub rested in the center, a large opening in the wall lined by a columned barrier, providing a relaxing feel. I turned the valve, allowing the water to fill up the onyx stone tub as I stripped the layers of my clothing.

Wincing at the heat, I lowered my body in, allowing the heat to carry my thoughts away as I dunked my head beneath the rippling water. The scent of lavender greeted me as my head broke the surface. I grabbed the bar of soap and began scrubbing my skin as if I could scrub off the chaos of the past week. Examining my side, I noticed that the cut had almost fully healed, an angry pink line in its place. With a sigh, I leaned my head against the cool stone, closing my eyes as the scent of lavender permeated my skin.

A soft rapping broke me from my daze. *"Enter,"* I called. An elderly woman with streaks of gray weaved into her hair walked in.

"Ah, good morning, miss. I have laid out fresh clothing on the bed. You are expected in the main chamber shortly; please be ready." And with that, she turned on her heel and left.

Sighing, I pushed up and began to dress to meet the king, praying that he had a lighter spirit than that of his son.

My shirt slid against my skin as I walked in silence down the hall, my sister by my side, following the two guards in front of us. I could not help but attempt to determine the underlying reason why the king of all people would want to meet with us. I knew Sébastien doubted my story, and that he believed I meant no good, which made my concern rise with every step. My breathing was shaking as we approached the door. I continually glanced to my side, checking to make sure Kateya hadn't noticed my rising stress levels as we made our way down the hall.

Why would the king believe me when his son didn't remotely trust me? Was I walking my sister toward impending death?

My jumbled thoughts continued to assault me as we walked down the corridor toward the main chamber, the door looming the closer we got. I stared at the doors, silently begging myself not to go through with this. I knew Sébastien found us inconvenient, even if he played the role of kind host. But didn't he know? How could he not be aware that he was contributing to our punishment, that the moment we met the king we would most certainly be sent to the dungeons for how insane our story sounded? Or that we could be punished for the use of magic that was not ours to use.

The guard in front of me raised his hand, pounding on the door before I heard a commanding voice through the walls say, *"Enter,"* and the doors were pushed open.

I swallowed nervously, glancing once again to my right. Kateya's eyes met mine and we gave each other tight smiles as we slowly made our way through the door. Glancing around as we entered the chamber, I noticed that, unlike the majority of the Palace I had seen so far, this room was under-decorated. The walls were simple, stone blocks, with shelves of dusty books on one side, and a large chair and a couch in the center. My gaze locked on the three wolvyn in a dark corner of the chamber, recognizing the ice-blue eyes and black-gray fur of the largest wolvyn before scanning the rest of the room. I noted an older man by the large chair, his back to me in deep conversation. As Kateya and I walked into the room, a slight chill filled the air, and the silence flooded the space.

The three wolvyn shifted back, fully clothed, my jaw dropping slightly as I recognized the other two men, one being Dravyn, whose eyes caught mine and a silent grin spread across his face at my shock. Sébastien walked over past me as he approached his father, who had turned to assess us.

"This is Cassandra Dumont and her sister Kateya. They showed up just outside Nordak-controlled lands a week ago and have cost me five men already." His voice dripped ice as he introduced us.

My heart dropped at the tone, already knowing the direction of this conversation. Forcing my lips to turn up, I replied, "Pleasure to meet you, Your Majesty."

The king assessed us as a predator stalks his prey, and the air dropped another ten degrees. His eyes were a stormy blue-gray that spoke of danger with the same icy chill as his son's. I noted how similar the two appeared, both built for battle, hardened by life.

Taking a seat, he began to speak. "Welcome to my land. I have heard much about you. But first, how was the journey here? Was everything alright? No troubles, I hope?"

I regarded the man speaking, wondering what he actually knew of our journey over. If he knew of the attack or the arguments that took place. Whether he was looking for a serious response or was just using common courtesy and feigning interest. I simply replied, "The journey was fine, thank you."

He inclined his head with a slight nod, leading me to believe I had answered correctly before his attention turned to the others in the room. After speaking to the three other men for a few moments, he flicked his hand as a dismissal to them and directed them to show Kateya around the Palace grounds.

Standing there, I began to wonder why he had dismissed Kateya, yet hadn't dismissed me. I watched as his gaze went from me to the commander, who I noticed was still in the room. His voice cut through the air, commanding throughout the room as he dismissed Sébastien as well. My head snapped toward Sébastien, reveling in the shock radiating off him. I noticed the way Sébastien's jaw tightened in anger at being dismissed and his ice-blue eyes narrowed to slits, yet he held his tongue and stormed out of the room.

Frozen in my spot, I realized that it was now just me and the king. A bit of panic began to sink in as it hit me that he, this man in front of me, controlled this entire land, and suddenly, I began to wonder if I hadn't just traded one predator for an even worse one. He could punish me right now for the use of magic, the lost lives of Sébastien's men, withholding aspects of how we got here, and nobody would raise a finger against him.

As though he could sense my fear, he chuckled lightly before beginning, "It's a pleasure, Cassandra. Allow me to officially introduce myself. I am Adrastan Capetian, King of Verastarr and Alpha of the Wolvyn." I smiled politely at the introduction even as my insides shriveled up in fear. He continued. "My son, Sébastien, has informed me of the story you have shared with him. It would seem that you, my dear, have a great deal of explaining to do?"

At this, I nodded weakly, not knowing what else to say. "Am I correct in understanding that you believe it was magic which brought you to my land?"

I looked at him before replying. "Yes, as I told Sébastien, there must have been magic in my—"

The king held his hand up, stopping me. "Was this magic your magic, or was someone sending you here?" His stern voice demanded an answer.

"It just happened. I'm a mortal. I don't have any magic in me, and there was no one using magic on us. I told Sébastien, it was from the pendant on my necklace."

Those storm blue-gray eyes watched me with intent as he responded. "I have already heard the story from Sébastien. What I need to know is how. How was the magic activated? You claimed that you had this necklace for a long time. Is this the only time the necklace has done this? What did you say or do before it unleashed its power?"

I swallowed hard, my fingers pulling at a frayed string on my pants. My mind went back in time, back to the night of the attack. A time I had told no one of when my necklace had indeed released magic.

"And Cassandra." Adrastan's voice cut through the air like a knife. "I recommend not leaving anything out, as I have my ways of finding out the truth. Ways far less pleasant, which I will use if needed," he said, as his lip curled up.

Taking a breath, I calmed the shaking of my hands before I began. "The pendant. I often fidget with it and hold it against my neck. As I said goodbye to my sister that day, I remember holding it and wishing that I could just go back. I just wanted to go back, before the attacks, before The Fall, back to when our life was so much simpler. I remember thinking of this time when we were little that we had lived in Verastarr for a few years and how happy, how whole our family felt then. I was thinking back to those times." He tracked my every word and movement as I spoke.

"But to answer your question." I paused, making sure I could really do this. "No. That was not the first time that the pendant released magic. When I was younger. A pack of Seefers attacked our home. As a Seefer landed on me, its claws scratching down my side, I remember wishing over and over that they would leave, that all I wanted was for them to disappear. I couldn't let them get past me to my sister. No sooner had I wished than I felt a sharp heat on my chest and then an eerie chill slam through the house and the Seefers left. My family . . . we are the only ones I know that survived such an attack, but I never once told anyone about the chilled feeling I felt. As the years went on, I thought less and less about that day."

Adrastan stared at me in thought for a moment. "The necklace. Do you have it with you?"

I swallowed. "No."

"No?"

"No."

"Where is the necklace, then?"

"If I knew, you'd think the answer would have been yes—" I slapped my hand over my mouth. *Fuck. You can't talk to the literal king like that, Cass. Do you have a death wish?* "Sorry, I don't know where it is. It was ripped off the chain when it began burning me. When we woke up in a field shortly before we crossed paths with Sébastien, I couldn't find it. I've been trying ever since."

"Describe the necklace to me," he demanded.

"It was a red, rectangular pendant, maybe an inch and a half long. The pendant itself was a ruby-red color with swirls of gold and a few more intricate designs that looked as if they were trapped in it."

Adrastan stood up then, walking to the back wall lined with books. He searched for a few moments, pulling out a few books, putting them aside on the worn desk, before settling on a particularly ancient book. The seams threatened to fall apart, the pages yellowed with age. "Come," he commanded as he turned the pages while scanning each one. Settling on a page, he set the book down, his finger pointing down at the depicted sketch. "Is that the necklace?" he questioned.

Looking down at the book with surprise, I barely nodded my head. "I don't understand. Why? Why is there a sketch of my necklace in a book?"

Adrastan slumped slightly in his desk chair. "You're sure? There's no doubt in your mind?"

"Yes, sir. I'm positive. That sketch is of my pendant, down to the very swirls inside."

Adrastan muttered under his breath before releasing a heavy sigh. "I thought we had more time."

"More time? More time for what?" My voice raised an octave. "Why do you have a sketch of my pendant? It doesn't make any sense."

"Come, let's sit. I'm afraid I have much to fill you in on." Adrastan's voice was heavy as we moved to the couch. As I settled against the velvet material of the couch, he began. "At the beginning of my grandfather's reign, over 100 years ago, the Nordak lands began to get power hungry. They weren't satisfied with only having one power, they wanted them all."

"As you know, each land has its own power, but the King of Nordak at the time, wanted more. The four other lands, East Engles, Verastarr, Reggeon, and Avyon joined together, searching for a way to stop the Nordak from creating an imbalance of power throughout the realm. The four rulers, the Cordial, assembled in secret in the East Engles with their strongest power assessors. They presented three artifacts. Each of the rulers then gave some of their power and magic and forced it inside the artifacts. The power assessors then bound and banished the artifacts to the furthest corners of the realm."

He paused as I processed the history he had shared with me. "Once the four rulers returned home, one of the power assessors was captured by the Nordak. As it occurred, the King of the Nordak discovered the secret meeting and his fury was unstoppable."

"He tortured and destroyed the trapped power assessor until he learned of the three artifacts. The power he unleashed then was like none other. A power strong enough to anger The God, to cause all those with magic in their souls to quake in fear. It was then that Seefers first appeared to seek out the power hidden amongst the artifacts. The King of Nordak would stop at nothing to gain infinite power."

"A great power was cast across the land by the four rulers, a power that instantly killed the Cordial as they expelled their magic. Four deaths in exchange for a hope of a better future. In their place was a prophecy—a means of protection. The artifacts would not be found until they made their way into the hands of ones that were deserving. A power assessor was assigned to each artifact, who would travel the paths of time to ensure it made it to the right hands before accepting their fate and vanishing from the realm. The hands of those who would join to destroy the tainted magic of the Nordak."

I almost laughed because I knew one thing for sure. I was not qualified to destroy any dark magic. "I don't understand why my necklace would have been one of the artifacts . . . or why it would have been given to me," I pressed. My memory flitted back to that night, recalling the strange way the elderly woman had appeared before me, then how she had disappeared from my sight. I had assumed it was elemental magic, cloaking her in the night. Yet, what if it had been a power assessor, as the king described? One who vanished altogether once the artifact made it to my possession. *Void-damned. Why? Why did I have to be such a naïve young child and accept the damn pendant?*

"That necklace belonged to the first wolvyn alpha in our land and was passed down through generations. My grandfather sketched the artifact here in this journal so that future generations wouldn't forget it, even though it had been lost to us for the cause."

I sat in silence. Thoughts screaming in my mind, but not being able to escape. "What was the prophecy?"

Adrastan hesitated before replying, "The prophecy was written long ago. However, it has never been held in full by any one land, in an attempt to keep it from fulfillment." He then shared:

> *"The power of four melded in three,*
> *Scattered on winds of time,*
> *Forced by darkened powers to hide.*
>
> *Bonded through secrets and lies,*
> *A shattered acceptance,*
> *Destined to start the beginning of times."*

I stared at the king then, confusion plastered across my face. "I don't really see how that would have anything to do with me. I get that I accepted the pendant in my time. But I've got enough *power battles* going on back at home, there's no need for me to add any more brewing wars from other times to the list." I finished as I stood up and began walking toward the door.

A low growl was all the warning I got before I found myself pressed against the floor, a snarling wolvyn towering over me. Sharp claws pricked into my shoulders, bringing pinpricks of blood to the surface as they held me down. A dark growl shook through him, coursing over me in warning.

In an instant, the king shifted back, standing in front of me, as I lay frozen in place on the floor. "Don't test me, Cassandra. Don't mistake empathy for your circumstances with kindness."

My eyes blinked in shock as I slowly rose to my feet, my legs shaking as I sat back down. "I don't even have the necklace anymore. I'm not sure what you expect me to do."

Adrastan paced across the marbled floor in front of me, his black leather boots rhythmically thudding with each step. "If the pendant alone falls into the wrong hands, it will be useless. It was warded to only work when both the artifact and its owner are together. Which means that you will be the target if anyone discovers you are the owner of the first uncovered artifact."

"Will the pendant take my sister and me home?"

He sighed, sitting down across from me. "I couldn't tell you without seeing the pendant and the magic within. It's possible that it can send you both back, but we need to locate the pendant first."

Sucking in a shaky breath, I looked at him. "Why me? I have no ties to any magic or power. I didn't ask for this."

A chuckle escaped as he responded. "No one asks to play with fire—it just happens. Do you think I *asked* to be king? No. I watched a vicious magic take my father's life from him and was given this role at a young age. Do you think those before me *asked* to give up their lives to protect Vanaiyer? No, people don't ask for it; that doesn't change the fact that they could be born for this though. The God allows us each to have a hand in the path of our own destiny. It's merely up to you what you choose to do with yours."

Closing my eyes, I tried to stop the forming migraine as my mind hurt from the information, the shocking overload of news I had learned. Glancing back toward Adrastan, I questioned, "I could use some time to process this, if that's alright?"

He watched me for a moment before answering me. "Yes, I need to send out patrols to begin searching for the pendant." He paused briefly. "Cassandra, you need to understand—whatever time period you may be from, times are different here. Battles and attacks in all the lands have grown stronger as of late, and the Nordak presence has increased. My sons have been raised to command, toughened by battle and protective of their packs. I may be the king, but I won't interfere with Sébastien's decisions if you don't respect him and follow his lead."

I looked at him and nodded, understanding what he was trying to tell me, before heading out the door.

Chapter Nine

I WANDERED THROUGH THE HALLS, knowing what I needed. My mind wasn't going to just shut off on its own, and I desperately needed a few moments' reprieve following that conversation. I was rounding the corner, in search of a training yard that I presumed any Palace would have, when I bumped into a hard form, hands spreading across a body as the breath was knocked from my chest. Gasping for air, I glanced up to meet the twinkling eyes of Dravyn.

"Well, well, well." He laughed. "I didn't know we were that close yet. Should I tell Emalyee to make some space in our bed?"

"What can I say?" I joked back. "I just knew the moment I saw you that I had to have you."

"And where might you be off to this lovely day?"

I hesitated briefly. "Actually, I was looking for the training yard. I could use a distraction."

"And you thought that Sébastien would just let you wander into the training yard all on your own?"

"Well," I said, "what *His Highness* doesn't know won't kill him. I just—I need to clear my head, and a good sparring session usually helps. I used to spar at home with my father and Kateya and thought—well, I thought it would help."

Dravyn cocked his head to the side, assessing me for a moment. His dusty brown hair fell across his face, shadowing his gray eyes as he thought. "Fair enough. This could be fun. Let's go."

"Wait . . ." I looked at him as he began walking away. "You want me to spar against you?"

"I don't see anyone else volunteering . . . do you?"

"But you're the Captain of Sébastien's guard." I stuttered. "You're going to knock me flat on my ass. I was looking for a distraction, not humiliation."

"If you're not up to the challenge, that's fine by me. I can go see if there's some painting or local gossiping that you could do with the Palace ladies to clear your head instead?"

Sighing, I reluctantly followed him out toward the training yard.

As we stepped into the open air, the dull clanking of metal mixed with grunts met my ears. Dravyn stepped into a dirt packed ring, motioning me in. As I walked in, I pushed all thoughts out of my mind, focusing on my surroundings, assessing my opponent even as I walked toward the swords held on the side of the ring.

Picking up a medium-sized longsword, I tested the metal in my hand, feeling the weight before squaring up against Dravyn. We circled each other for a few moments before he lunged, his sword heading for my shoulder. I ducked to the left before swirling around to meet his blade. The shocked look plastered across his face proved he underestimated my skill. We parried, back and forth, side to side. My arms began to shake as sweat poured down my face, my clothing clinging to my body as we continued our dance. Strike, Parry, Duck, Block. Over and over we moved.

I felt my limbs shaking more under each block, muscles I hadn't used in the past week straining in protest. I blocked his blow, my arms trembling from the force, then struck back. Dravyn narrowly avoided a slice to his side, his balance causing him to stumble slightly.

A low laugh met my ears as a voice rang out over the ring. "Well, well. I was going to tell Emalyee to make sure she keeps tabs on her man. But from the looks of it, there might not be any man for her after this."

I heard a rumbled growl from Dravyn as I glanced toward the newcomer. I recognized him from earlier this morning as the man who had been speaking with the king when Kateya and I entered.

A blur of movement appeared in the corner of my eye as I saw metal flying toward me. I clumsily raised my arms to block, my limbs unprepared for the strike. I felt the blade nip my arm; a flash of crimson emerged followed by a sharp pain. Rearing back, I glared at Dravyn as I dropped my sword, my hand covering the shallow slice on my arm. "That was an unfair strike!"

"Last I checked, this is the sparring ring. And we were sparring. Never take your eyes off an opponent with a weapon." He flashed a smile as he spoke.

"Yeah, but someone stopped by. I wasn't paying attention."

"I fail to see how it's my fault you were more enamored with Kairon than our sparring match," he retorted.

"One might think you would be more concerned. He was attacking your manliness to begin with," I shot back.

Chuckling, he glanced over to Kairon. "Nice to see you, brother. Have you been introduced to Cassandra yet?"

"Not officially," Kairon replied. "Although, I have heard she's the reason for my brother's foul mood."

"Ah, yes. The big, bad commander has finally met his match." Dravyn looked over at me then. "Cassandra, meet Sébastien's older brother and heir to the throne."

Nodding my head in greeting, I answered, "I would greet

you properly, but I'm too busy trying not to bleed out, thanks to Dravyn."

Kairon hopped into the ring then, picking up a sword and tossing it between his hands. I watched him, noticing the similarities between him and his brother. The dusting of freckles they both sported across their cheeks, the same wavy hair just a shade lighter than his brother's, the similar tattoos across his arms.

"Ready for round two?" he prompted as Dravyn walked over to the edge and leaned against the fencing to watch.

"Why would I turn down the chance to lower the ego of the *heir* to the throne?" I replied saucily as I shook out my arms, preparing for my next round.

Kairon glanced over his shoulder toward Dravyn. "She's feisty, huh? I like her."

He struck. I raised my arms in defense, my muscles quaking in protest as I blocked, parried, and blocked again. We played on the edge, pushing each other and then backing off as we circled around each other like predators stalking their prey.

My steps weakened as we went back and forth, *strike, duck, spin, lunge.* The circle went on, my muscles weakening while Kairon seemed to be unfazed. I had just ducked his advance, spinning around to strike, when I felt the flat of his blade against the backs of my calves, knocking me to the ground.

The air rushed from my lungs as my body collided with the compact dirt, my blade knocked from my grasp. I felt the tip of his blade lightly against my neck as I froze in defeat.

"You put up a good fight." His words cut the air with a glint of victory. "But don't play with us wolvyn too long, or you might get bitten." He chuckled as he held his sword against my neck a moment longer, before lending a hand to help me up.

Standing up, I wiped the dust off my clothes as I replied, "Maybe I want to," before I hopped over the fence and walked back toward the Palace. My heart was lighter than it had been since arriving.

My wet hair clung to my back in strands as I reached for a plush towel, wringing the droplets out. My limbs protested my every movement following the sparring earlier. Having missed dinner due to unceremoniously passing out once I returned to my room, I threw on a pair of lightweight pants that flowed in the air with slits up my thighs and a black lace shirt that scooped down in the front. I exited my room in search of something to take away the hunger clawing at my insides, while wondering where my sister had been all day.

As I walked through the halls, I took in the canopied ceiling with skylights in each corridor, allowing the night sky to reflect on the marbled tiles under my feet. I heard Emalyee's laughter before I saw her rounding the corner.

"Cassandra!" she screeched. "You *must* come out into town with us!" A fit of giggles escaped her as she turned toward her man. "Right, Dravyn? Cassandra *must* come with us!"

My eyes collided with Dravyn's, then Kairon's, who was to his right, then to my sister and Eryx. Surprise glinted across my eyes at the attachment my sister was forming with the soldier, even as a smile tugged at my lips.

"A bit early to be drinking, isn't it?" I laughed.

Emalyee grabbed my hand as they approached in insistence. "Please come, Cass. Don't leave me alone with all these boys!" She pouted.

"*Boys,* you say," Dravyn responded to her, his words a slight slur. "I'll show you just how much of a man I am, since you clearly can't remember." His hand reached out, tugging her into his form in a possessive reminder.

My hand flew to my mouth, covering the laughter that

threatened to overflow. "My sincerest apologies for these two," Kairon said to me. "It appears as though some people rudely got into the good whiskey *without* me." He scowled. "Let's go. If I don't get a drink soon, I'm not going to be able to put up with you those two anymore and Eryx here will have to help me drag their Void-damned asses back home."

And then we were off, Emalyee dragging me along as she stumbled after Dravyn, Kateya laughing at my side.

The night air wrapped around my skin as we walked down the cobblestone road, the streetlamps dancing in the shadows as we made our way to a local pub. Emalyee practically skipped with glee through the door, and Dravyn claimed a bench in the corner of the pub and slid down, pulling Emalyee onto his lap. Smells of spilled alcohol and warm food wafted through the air, and the darkened atmosphere created a relaxed environment.

"I'll be over there." Kateya pointed toward where Eryx now sat, a few tables off with a few other men, presumably Palace soldiers based on their attire.

"You're leaving me?" I teased my sister. "Even when we traveled hundreds of years into the past, you still leave me alone at a bar."

"You aren't alone." She laughed as she began to step away. "You have them." Her finger pointed toward where Kairon sat down across from the couple.

"Fine," I whined teasingly at my younger sister. "Have *fun* with Eryx."

I turned toward the other three, sliding onto the worn bench beside Kairon, as a young boy approached the table, four malted whiskeys in hand.

The drinks were passed around, and the laughter began to

flow. I listened as Dravyn and Kairon recounted tales of their childhood, Emalyee interjecting every few sentences with a correction to their drunken childhood memories. Another round was brought and finished as the night stretched on. My brain began to haze slightly, a familiar slow buzz forming from the strong drinks. Dravyn stumbled up, in search of yet another round, when his voice filled the air. "Kode! I thought that was you."

I turned in my seat to see who he was talking to as two towering men approached our table. Kairon stood up, clasping each on the back as greetings were passed around. I sat silently in the corner, curiosity brimming at who the two new men were that the group seemed to be so close to.

"And who might this be?" the man Dravyn referred to as Kode inquired with a pointed look at me. I glanced at him, taking in his olive skin, piercing amber eyes, and shorter black hair slicked back, a few pieces falling forward. A loose, dark green shirt hung from his large muscled frame.

I stood then walking over to the group. "I'm Cassandra. And you are?"

"I'm Kodrayn, but call me Kode. And this here is Ryker," he answered in a husky voice as he nudged the man to his left.

"Ry," the other responded in greeting. As my gaze switched to him, I noted his light-colored hair and tanned skin crawling with tattoos contrasting with the white shirt fitted to his body.

"Sorry we're late to the party," Kode said as he slid onto the bench, the others following as another round was passed across the table. Glancing back at me, he drawled, "So, Cass. How do you fit into this picture?"

Laughing, I replied while sipping my drink. "I don't. I'm the tagalong Sébastien is reluctantly forced to have around."

"Ahhh. Speak of the devil, where is the big, bad wolf tonight?"

I felt the temperature drop before I saw him, his ice-cold

glare causing my blood to freeze. "Missing the party, it appears," he said, his voice cutting through the air.

"And you're late," Kode joked. "Good to see you again brother." Kodrayn stood to greet Sébastien.

"It's good to see you as well, brother." The two clasped hands, greeting each other with the same camaraderie as the others before Kode reclaimed his seat at the booth. Sébastien's eyes flicked around the table before landing firmly on me, taking me in from head to toe.

"Imagine my surprise," he bit out in a frustrated growl. "When my guards informed me that you left the Palace."

"Well . . . it's not like anyone said I couldn't. Plus, I was invited out, which means I didn't do anything wrong." I snapped toward the commander then downed the rest of my whiskey, embracing the sting down the back of my throat. "Should I have asked for your permission to leave, *Your Highness*?" The tension was thick in the air as those at the table watched the interaction, but I wasn't quite done.

I shifted in my seat, inching closer to Kairon, my blood tingling as I picked up his untouched drink, tracing my finger along the rim of the glass. "Do I need anyone else's permission, when I already had the permission of the *heir* to the throne?" I lifted the drink to my lips, smirking at him before I downed the drink in my hand. I knew the likelihood of waking with an angry hangover was high, but I wouldn't have had the courage to stand up to him without it.

Kairon and Kode chuckled at my words, even as the tension rose.

He moved in an instant. One moment he was standing at the edge of the table, the next his presence towered over me, yanking me up. "We're going," he said as he hauled me off, pausing to look toward his brother. "We'll talk about this later, *brother*," he finished before storming out, me trailing behind him by the arm.

We burst through the pub door, fresh air biting at my skin as he began walking toward the Palace.

"Was that truly necessary?" I snapped, a slight slur detectable in my voice. "We were just getting drinks."

Sébastien whirled, pressing me against a shop wall in seconds, his body pinning me beneath him, caging me in. My body hummed in response to his proximity, to the warmth and power radiating from him as the alcohol buzz edged me on.

"Don't think for a second you have any grounds on which to speak. Do you understand me?" Sébastien growled, his eyes commanding my gaze as he continued. "Do you have any idea of what your presence here, in this time, has started? The danger you have put yourself in? The danger you have put all my people in?" he spat out.

"You know what?" I bit back, the last two drinks rushing to my head and giving me liquid courage. "It's not like I asked for any of this. I was perfectly fine where I was back at home. I didn't ask to come here. To be transported through time due to some magical artifact. I didn't ask to get involved in whatever power struggle will most certainly come as a result. So stop." I poked him in the chest as I spoke. "Taking." *Poke.* "It." *Poke.* "Out." *Poke.* "On me." His hand caught mine as I attempted to poke him one last time, grasping it tightly. A fluttered gasp fell from my lips as he perfectly maneuvered his hold, snagging my second wrist as he lifted, locking them both above my head.

"Whether you asked for it or not, Cassandra, you were the one the Elders selected for the first artifact. And as such, you do not get to roam the city without my knowledge, without protection. It is too great a risk . . . for everyone . . . for you." The scent of forest pines and spice flooding my air flow as he pinned me in place, darkness misting around us.

I sucked in a breath as I held his gaze, feeling the heat from his body sinking into mine. Frozen in place, I felt the weight of his body surrounding me; muscled, thick thighs, pressing against me, holding me in place. I could feel his muscles rippled as he constrained himself, holding me secure. My mind briefly wandered, curious what it might feel like to be caged in like this by the commander for another reason.

"You know, commander." I broke the heated silence, still trapped in his grasp. "This is quite a position to find me in, should someone walk by."

I wiggled my hips, my body now pressing against his even more as his eyes flared briefly before narrowing in on me. The words continued to flow, my lips unfiltered from the whiskey. "Imagine if someone walked by, only to see their beloved commander, pinning me against the wall in the shadows of the—"

"You want to play, *princesse?* You want to play with the big, *bad* wolf, do you?" He breathed heavily in my ear. My heart raced as he spoke, heat slowly pooling as I tried clearing the images flashing through my mind. "I'm not afraid to bite, so I'd be careful what you ask for . . ." he finished, before stepping back, cool air rushing my heated skin as he yanked me with him through the darkness toward the Palace.

Chapter Ten

VERASTARR

I LAID awake in a foreign bed, my body tossing and turning —restless—despite the comfort of the feather mattress beneath my exhausted body and the lingering buzz from the pub. Internally, I was still battling with everything King Adrastan had told me earlier today. It felt like a torrent of chaos was crushing down on my life, my lungs gasping for breath. Sitting up on the bed, I let the blanket slide down, piling onto my lap as I gazed out the window. Moonlight spilt through the panes, dancing across the marbled flooring as clouds drifted across the night sky.

Slipping my toes out from under the warmth of my bed, I let them fall to the floor as I made my way to the bedroom door. Slowly, silently, I inched the door open, then walked down the empty corridor toward a partially hidden staircase I had noticed on my way in earlier that day. Following the spiral stairs, I felt a slight breeze begin to blow as I climbed higher, the pressure in my lungs lessening the higher I circled. Emerging at the top of the tower, I gently pushed the door open, leading out onto a parapet.

I walked along the outer wall, running my hand along the stone, the soft scraping of the roughened edges grating my fingertips as I let the night air surround me. A few guards stationed along the wall gave me disapproving looks; however, I blocked them out of my mind, instead focusing on the grounds surrounding the Palace. Even with darkness attempting to encase the night, the moon shone through, illuminating the Sea of Avyz and grass covered fields swaying in time with the breeze. I watched as the moon's light slowly made its way along the sea, drifting one way, then another, dancing on waves of black water. As though hypnotized by the light, I stood along the tower, watching time pass as the moon traveled across the sky.

Moments like these allowed me a chance to pretend that everything was right in the realm. That I wasn't part of a prophetic answer to a looming power war. That I was back home in my apartment, curled up with a good book and a cup of tea. Simply staring at the moonlight as it danced across the sea. I wallowed in the beauty, my mind drifting to happy memories that flitted on repeat.

"Is it a habit of yours to take strolls in the dead of night?" A warm, husky voice sounded from behind me.

Whirling around, surprised, I answered, "Is it a habit of yours to attempt to sneak up on me each time?"

I would recognize his voice anywhere. Even though I'd grown to despise the words that fell from those freckled lips, his voice was like the moonlight on the sea, both hypnotizing and enchanting, with darkness reflected underneath.

A dark chuckle filled the silence of the night as he gazed at me before replying, "That is what a predator does best, is it not?" His voice grew closer as warm breath crawled up my ear. He approached me, resting his hands against the ledge in front of me, his palms inches from mine. "Stealthily stalk our unsuspecting prey."

A scoff slipped from my throat. "If your aim is to threaten me or scare me into listening to you, that's not going to happen. I just needed some fresh air. I—I needed some time to process everything, and it's easier to breathe up here." I pushed off the stone wall, turning toward the doorway I came from, internally cursing myself for being somewhat open with him.

"Why are you out here?"

I froze, turning to stare at the man who continually interrupted my late night wanderings. With a sigh, I spoke truthfully, shocking myself. "The conversation with your father today was . . . Well, it wasn't one I was prepared for."

I don't know if it was the lingering effect of my drinks or the exhaustion, but I heard my own voice continue to ramble. "I don't know what I expected to hear, since this has all been, well somewhat a nightmare. But I hadn't been expecting a story of an ancient prophecy and magical artifacts. And I'm just trying to process it."

Sébastien stared at me for a moment, contemplative. "The prophecy has been in place for long before I was born. We just never imagined that it would come to fruition during our lifetime."

An owl cried in the otherwise silent night air as the two of us stared at each other, a momentary truce in our otherwise tense relationship.

"The war," Sébastien shared, "the one that started the prophecy, was known as the Great War. And it had the beginnings of one of the most horrific battles our realm would have seen, had the artifacts not come into play. You . . ." He paused. "Your arrival. It changes *everything*."

Red threatened the corners of my vision at the use of the nickname as I stared at Sébastien, breaking the truce. "For the love of The Void, stop calling me *'princesse.'* I don't know why you insist on it to begin with. I'm not royal. I have no powers. There's absolutely no reason to call me that."

"I'll call you what I like, *princesse*." The nickname rolled off his tongue in a teasing manner. "Every nickname has a purpose, does it not?

"And yours?" I prompted, intrigue thick in my voice, my anger diminishing for a brief moment as I thought to all the times his friends called him by his own nickname. "How did you get yours?"

"Well, I am the Commander of the Wolvyn Guard."

Scoffing, my voice caught the air. "If that's the truth, it's a bit lackluster. I was hoping for a bit more of a story than that."

"Well, maybe one day you will get it. Now, did I not make myself perfectly clear earlier? I'm not the type of man you want to play games with."

"I'm not playing games with you." The frustration bubbled back to the surface in an instant. "I told you I needed to air. I didn't leave the Palace. Or do you wish to confine me to my room too?" I snapped.

"Now," he drawled, a smirk snaking up his face, "wouldn't that be a sight to see? Yes, I could picture it." He paused, his eyes darkening. "You. Confined to your room." His voice lowered as he advanced toward me, my steps matching his as I backed up, only stopping as my back hit the staircase wall.

My heart pounded heavily as he towered over me, my head tilted back, meeting his gaze. "Not. A. Chance," I spat back even as part of my body involuntarily responded to his words.

He leaned down, one arm above my head holding him up, his face paused inches from me, ice-blue eyes piercing mine as they tracked my every movement. The air around me felt as though it dropped a few degrees, my breath coming quicker.

"We'll see about that, *princesse*," he purred into my ear. His fingers trailed up my side, drawing circles of heat across my skin as he moved them up along my ribs. My body burned beneath his touch; an ember sparked deep within me.

And then he was gone, chilled air settling in his place, leaving me staring at the Avyz, wondering what I had just gotten myself into.

My mind shifted through the day's events as my breathing returned to normal, putting pieces of information in folders in my mind as I planned a way out of this mess. My thoughts were rough, but I knew what needed to be done. Kateya and I needed to hold out until we found the pendant. If the king found it first, it was likely he would want me to help in the war that would brew once the power was discovered, and I couldn't let that happen. Once we had the necklace, Kateya and I could then use it to get home and this whole nightmare would be over. I just needed to play nice until we found it. If only it was that easy . . .

A constant, loud knocking on the barred wooden door woke me from my sleep. Mumbling some incoherent words, I stumbled out of the bed toward the never-ending knocking. Opening the door, Kateya rushed into my room, excited as ever.

"Oh good! You're awake. I thought I was going to have to burn down the door to wake you up. I haven't seen you all morning. But *ohmygosh*, Cass, I have so much to tell you. First . . ." My mind struggled to uncloud the words that rushed from my sister's mouth as I partially woke up. ". . . which is in two nights. So, of course, we will be going. I know the circumstances are kind of insane. But I mean, who actually gets to say they've been to a festival in an actual Palace?"

Only truly processing half of what she said, I half smiled and half grimaced while attempting to understand the continual shriek of words flooding my ears. "That's awesome, Kat. Sounds like you will have fun."

"Oh, you know I will! I thought perhaps you would want to know. Also, I have a date."

My heart froze for a moment as I snapped awake. "A date?

Kat. We have been here for less than two days. What do you mean, a date?"

"It's just a festival, Cass." Kateya sighed. "Look. I know we need to find that pendant quickly. And before you say it, I understand how bad the circumstances are. But just let me have this moment, okay? Eryx is *so* hot."

"Just be careful, okay? We don't know much about this land, these people, or what they might want from us."

"When haven't I been careful?" Kateya sarcastically sang, with a devious smirk as she skipped out of my room, leaving the door wide open, a smile pasted across her face.

I loved that she was happy, especially since everything that happened was shocking enough. I didn't know whether I should share all the things I had learned about the pendant yet with her or if I should just let my sister enjoy this ember of happiness before putting out the budding flame. Not even bothering to close the door, I dropped back into bed, sleep pulling me back under.

Once I had woken up a second time, I noted that the day had already half passed, the sun high in the sky, baking into my room. Hunger scratched at my insides, and I made my way to find some food, only to walk out the door and realize I had no clue where the kitchen was located.

Noticing a guard standing further down the corridor, I walked over to him and politely asked for directions toward the kitchen. I watched as he grimaced slightly before informing me that he was under orders not to let me wander around or leave my room.

Of course, I knew who those orders came from. *Sébastien.* Frustrated and slightly annoyed that he had the audacity to attempt to confine me to my room, I focused my attention on the guard in front of me, pouting slightly. "Sir, I believe you must have misunderstood me. All I asked for were the directions to the dining hall so that I might have a meal. I said nothing about wandering around. If you could simply escort me to the kitchen just for a bite to eat, it would be as if I never left, plus you would be there, and then nothing could go wrong." He simply stared down at me, pointing me back toward my prison-like chamber.

Sighing, I began to walk away as an idea formed in my mind. I was about to go through with it when I heard the strong voice of the king at the end of the corridor. "Cassandra, how are you faring this morning? I take it you have had enough time following our conversation yesterday?" His question left room for no other answers.

Turning, a smile made its way onto my face. "I'm doing perfect, Your Majesty. And yes, of course, more than enough time. Thank you," I replied, the lie dripping like honey from my lips. Because did he honestly expect me to be okay with life-altering news after one day?

His eyes narrowed at my reply before nodding his head once. "Very well. I have some matters to attend to before the Festival of Nightloc begins."

"Nightloc?" I questioned.

"Yes. Nightloc is a time-honored tradition in our land. A time when powers are most heightened. As such, we celebrate, holding a festival for all those with magic and power flowing through their veins. With magic at its strongest in two nights, it should be possible to send out a power call to locate the rough location of the pendant," he informed me.

Nodding at the news the king shared, I responded, "If you can send out a power call, does that mean that others may be able to as well?"

"Yes." The harsh tone of his voice took me by surprise. "All magic demands balance and the powers imbued into the artifacts may call to those with the same powers. The Nordak have been searching for the three artifacts since they were sent into the winds 100 years ago. Now, with the presence of the pendant on our land, others will be able to sense it, too. We must locate it before it falls into enemy hands."

"Your Majesty." A young man's voice rang out from a distance.

"I have matters to attend to," King Adrastan stated. "I look forward to your *willing* participation in putting this behind us, Cassandra." His piercing stare burned into me as he turned around.

I stood still for a moment, processing his underlying threat, before remembering my original dilemma. "Excuse m—" But at that moment a throat cleared from behind me.

"Miss, if you would return to the room, please."

Sighing, I walked back into my room.

My backup plan proved to be far easier than I anticipated. As it turns out, Sébastien posted guards by the door only. It took mere minutes to fashion a rope with the sheets from my bed. I secured the knot over the bathroom railing, thankful once again for the balcony-style layout of the bathroom. Climbing down the sheets brought back memories of Kateya and me when we were younger. As young girls, we had competed to outclimb each other on everything, and I found myself thankful for that skill.

Wandering through the garden, I let myself relax as I mapped my surroundings. According to the king, locating the necklace was probable. But the question was who would get to it first, and if the king's men did, how would I ensure I could get it without raising questions? I would play the part if it meant I could get my sister and myself home safely.

With the Festival of Nightloc approaching in two days, the

increase in guards and patrols was imminent, meaning my hands were tied to wait for the king's patrols to locate the necklace.

I wondered how Nightloc affected those with elemental magic and power. Did that mean their powers weakened over time? The king had described it as a night of power where those with magic in their blood were at their strongest. My distant thoughts were interrupted as I felt something warm and furry pummel into my legs and fall to the ground at my feet. Glancing down, I noted rusty red fur sprinkled with streaks of darker brown, tiny, pointed ears perked up as it looked around in confusion.

I heard a quiet rumble before a larger wolvyn appeared in front of me. My feet involuntarily moved back, as I watched the wolvyn shift before my eyes. In the wolvyn's place stood a woman a few years older than me, amber hair braided to the side and warm emerald eyes meeting mine. "I'm so sorry. I hope he didn't scare you." She rushed on to say, "We are still working on the running coordination of shifting, aren't we, Theo?"

The small wolvyn at my feet nodded its head in remorse as he padded over to his mother. "I'm Gea," she said in greeting.

Smiling, I replied, "Cassandra. And no worries, no harm done." I laughed.

She studied me for a moment before stating, "You're her, aren't you?" I stared at Gea, confused by her statement. "Sorry, I don't mean to be rude. It's just that most of the men have been sent off on patrols today for the king. My mate was sent off this morning. I heard rumors around the Palace about a woman losing something valuable to the king, and given that I haven't seen you around here before, I'm guessing you're the reason?"

"Um, yes," I replied, taken aback by her direct statement and unsure of what I was supposed to reply or how much I should share.

"Well, whatever it is that you lost. I hope for your sake it's found. You don't want to be around if the Capetians don't get their way," she replied before shifting, little Theo following along after her as I stood there wondering how my pendant had suddenly become the most sought-after object in the Vanaiyer realm.

Chapter Eleven

VERASTARR

EMALYEE APPROACHED Kateya and me following breakfast the next morning, informing us that we would need to be measured for dress alterations for the Festival of Nightloc happening the next night. Emalyee filled the two of us in on the details of the festival, gushing over the dancing that would take place that night while we stood with the seamstress being measured. She raved about the drinks, the dresses, and the men. As she spoke, I reminded her that she already had a man.

Emalyee laughed as she said, "Dravyn can use a good challenge every so often. It doesn't hurt to remind him he's not irreplaceable." She grinned.

"Emalyee," I scolded, as laughter chorused through the room from all three of us.

"*What?*" She smirked. "You have no room to speak. I saw you eyeing Kode and Ryker at the pub the other night. Speaking of which, we really all need to get together again."

"I was not," I swore, even as my mind raced back to the two towering men I had met last night. Even in the low lighting of the bar, they *had* been extremely well-built and dangerously attractive.

"You," my sister teased from beside me. "Eyeing up two men . . . how come I didn't meet them?"

"Well if you had managed to pry your eyes from your soldier, maybe you would have met them," Emalyee teased as she gave Kateya a pointed look.

"Point taken . . . but why would I want to pry my eyes off an attractive, chiseled soldier?' Kat joked back.

"What's the deal with those two?" I questioned. "They seem to know Dravyn and Sébastien well."

Emalyee nodded. "Well, as you already know, I tell stories far better than the guys. Years ago, five little princes met in the training yard here before a realm meeting. Those five little princes were inseparable. They grew up together, stole young girls' hearts together, and got into more trouble than one might believe. As time passed, the power struggles between the lands grew. Certain rulers wanted more power than others. Before all went to hell, those five princes formed a blood bond, swearing to be there for each other no matter what. To this day, they still all get together, wreaking havoc in the courts."

I stared at Emalyee in disbelief. "You're absolutely terrible at telling stories!"

"How?" she responded, feigning hurt.

"Five princes?" Kateya questioned.

"Blood bonds?" I added to the list of gaps in her story. "You have a lot more explaining to do."

"Oh, right. I keep forgetting that Sébastien hasn't shared much with you. He'll warm up to you eventually, I promise. Well, I think. I've never seen anyone push his limits quite like you seem to."

A burst of laughter split through my lips, the seamstress muttering for me to stay still while she finished. "Oh yes. I'm sure the big, bad wolf of Verastarr will warm up to me," I sarcastically responded. "Now spill, please."

"Well, you know Kairon is first in line for the throne of

Verastarr. And Sébastien follows him, although he's been raised to take over the King's Wolvyn Guard rather than rule the political side. Ryker, who you met the other night, is a faerie, the first in line for the throne of Reggeon. And Kodrayn, a vampry, is the King of Avyon—his father passed on two years ago. And then Dravyn was a syren in line for the throne for the East Engles, but his father was murdered when he was young, and his mother sent him here before she was forced into a marriage. As for the blood bon—"

"Wait," I cut in. "There's no way the two drunk, flirtatious men at the pub are *royals*?" Emalyee merely laughed as I continued, "And Dravyn? If he's a royal, how come he can shift to wolvyn form? Do syrens have the power to shift into lots of creatures? You *really* need to work on your storytelling."

"As I was *saying . . .*" she continued, ignoring my interjections to her story. "The five of them formed a blood bond . . . a brotherhood. It's an ancient magic rarely done anymore. It must be done with absolute dedication and love. They traveled to a cave hidden in a mountain range bordering Verastarr and Avyon where an Elder lives. They perform this ritual where their blood is mixed as their powers blend, then it's inked back in them. And that would be why they all have the same inkings across the left side of their chest. Those inkings are unlike their tattoos because they are bonded by magic to each other."

Shock was plastered across both mine and my sister's faces as the seamstress announced she was finished. "I don't know why I'm so shocked," I heard myself saying.

"As for Dravyn. That's his story to tell. You'll have to ask him if you want to know. *But,* I promise my backstory is nowhere near as complicated. I was merely the princess of Nordak—kidnapped at a young age and forced to live a life switching homes every year until I met Dravyn at the Festival of Nightloc three years ago," she finished.

Kateya squeaked in surprise. I stared, my mouth opening

to speak, with no words making their way out. Emalyee doubled over in laughter then. "You should see the looks on both of your faces. I'm only kidding." She paused, gasping for air. "My father is a high-ranking soldier of the Wolvyn Guard for the king. Although the part about meeting Dravyn at Nightloc is actually true—remind me to tell you that story sometime. It involved a good deal of wine, a chase through the courtyard, and ended with me stabbing him in the leg when he tried to move too fast," she finished with a grin.

My breathing returned as I glared at her. "I am never letting you tell me another story again. I feel bad for Dravyn and the stories he must have to endure on a daily basis," I shot back.

"I've got to run, but make sure you both make it to dinner tonight. I'm sure all five guys being together tonight will provide quite the entertainment."

We nodded as she turned and skipped off.

I walked through the gray corridors, following various sets of stairs as I avoided the wolvyn lounging around the Palace until I found a quiet room at the end of an unlit hallway. Opening the door, I let myself in, taking in the sincere peace that exuded from the sunlight streaming into the room, playing with the shadows. I walked the perimeter of the room before laying down, the cool tiles sending chills across my body. My mind turned over the information about blood bonds and princes while I stared at the intricate design of the wooden panels that held the ceiling in place high above my head.

How long I laid on the floor, letting a chill sink into my bones, I'm not quite sure. Something about the angelic serenity of a secluded room in a Palace allowed me to find a moment of peace and escape, something I hadn't felt enough of in my life lately. The stillness quieted the raging war of thoughts and fears brewing in me. A sharp yelp sounded from the doorway, and I pushed up, looking to see a wolvyn barreling through. The sound of boots thudding across the tiles followed behind the wolvyn. The fluffy, white wolvyn leapt behind me, using my body to shield itself as Kodrayn barged through the open door, skidding to an immediate stop at the sight of me on the floor, a wolvyn cowering behind me.

"Well done, Matteo. Finding a lady to use for protection, however, that won't help you join the ranks anytime soon. This game is far from over, that I promise you." The younger wolvyn scampered off happily.

Pushing off the ground, I wiped the dust from my pants as I looked over at Kodrayn, taking in his tousled onyx hair that was shorter on the sides with a slight curl on the top. "Do all wolvyn understand mortals?" I questioned.

"Yes," he responded as he leaned against the doorframe, his amber eyes glimmering as they reflected the sunlight. "Although I should not that I'm not a mortal, I'm a vampry."

"Ah, right." I murmured, recalling Emalyee's story.

"Wolvyn were once mortals, who now have shifting power in their blood. All wolvyn can understand mortals. Unfortunately, it doesn't go the other way around," he said with a laugh.

I nodded. "So," I drawl. "A king, huh? I think you missed that part of your introduction the other night," I teased.

He feigned shock. "Me? A king? Who would have thought."

I laughed. "Why are you and Ryker here?"

His face turned serious, his voice sharper as he spoke. "The Festival of Nightloc is held in a different land each year. The royals from every land come for the festival. It just so happens that Ry and I arrived before the others."

"You mean the King of Nordak will be here too?" I prompted. Kode nodded. His face was a mask as I reflected on the new information. "What happens at this festival that every ruler would come together despite the constant conflicts?"

A cold sensation I had begun to recognize brushed over me, chilling me to the bone as Kode opened his mouth to respond, "Every year—"

"Kode," an all too familiar voice broke through the air, interrupting Kodrayn's story. "Ryker is looking for you in the training yard, and why in The Void am I being asked who let the wolvyn in training play chase throughout the entire left wing of the Palace?"

Kodrayn turned, greeting Sébastien with a laugh before glancing back toward me. "And that's my cue. I'll see you later, Cass. Be sure to save me a dance tomorrow," he said with a wink. "And my sincere apologies for the game of chase." He apologized without an ounce of remorse toward his blood brother.

"Like hell she will," Sébastien growled as his friend left the room, chuckles rumbling in his wake. His eyes hit mine as he stalked toward me, a predatorial glint lying beneath the shadows.

Standing my ground, I watched his advance. "And just when my day was going so well, look who decided to show up." My voice glided through the air. "Is there something I can help you with?"

Sébastien came to a stop in front of me. "The festival tomorrow must go well. Not only will there be heightened tensions from all sides, but this missing artifact has also added lots of complications. I trust that you will be on your best behavior, correct?"

Scoffing, I met his gaze. "You truly think I don't understand the importance of tomorrow night? That necklace is my way home, the only way to see my family and friends again. The only way to get my life back. I will do whatever it takes to get it back, I guarantee you that."

"Just checking, *princesse*. After all, you have a tendency to sneak around, disobey orders, and infuriate those around you."

Laughing, I responded, "No, *Your Highness*. I don't infuriate those around me, I infuriate you. I do believe that all your friends found me quite charming the other night at the pub."

Sébastien pounced at the remark, backing me up against the stone wall, seething as he said, "I've made myself clear, have I not? I don't have time for games, not today. Certainly not tomorrow. I have enough to deal with and now I must spare guards to look for an ancient artifact that you miraculously managed to lose when you showed up. Do *not* test me."

"No one asked you to make a hero out of yourself and help me find the necklace," I responded with venom. "Just let my sister and I be on our way if we are such a nuisance to you. We will find the necklace and go home on our own without some dark and hardened prince controlling every moment of our lives."

He bent his head, looking me straight in the eye, his icy blue orbs glaring daggers into mine. "If it were up to me, you and this entire mess would have been dealt with. The only reason you are still here is by the order of my father and the fact that you alone can wield the power bonded to the pendant that you once wore."

"Why? Why is my pendant so important? Why does the king want it? Why is the entirety of Vanaiyer searching for it?" I cried in frustration.

Sébastien stilled for a moment, his eyes capturing mine. "Whoever holds the power in each pendant will hold more power than any current ruler. Find one artifact and they can start to take over Vanaiyer, find all three and there are no limits to the power they can wield."

"It's not like I knew what the pendant could do."

"Maybe. Maybe not. But either way, you brought the pendant back to this time. And now, it has become my problem to deal with," he snapped.

Glaring back, shaking slightly with rage on the inside, I rose to the challenge. "Then don't waste your royally precious time speaking to me. Go back to your marvelous commanding lifestyle," I mocked with a gesture of my hand. "How your friends manage to tolerate your constant brooding is eternally beyond me."

Sébastien stormed out of the room then, leaving me in a place that no longer felt like a safe haven, but echoed with hatred. I slid downward against the wall, burying my face in my knees as I relived the conversation I just had.

Picking myself up off the floor, I headed down the series of corridors and stairs to find Kateya, realizing that at some point soon, I needed to tell her everything I had learned regarding the pendant. How important it was and how much larger of a role it played than either of us thought.

Chapter Twelve

VERASTARR

PEEKING into Kateya's room from behind the partially cracked door, I admired how gorgeous my younger sister looked in her dress. She and a new friend she seemed to have made were getting ready for the festival. Parts of Kateya's wavy, blonde-brown hair were braided in intricate coils. She wore a navy-blue silk gown that hung low off her shoulders and flared out down to the ground. Kateya was breathtaking, and as I stood to get ready in my own room, I couldn't help but wish our mum could be there at this moment to see her, to see us.

I slowly walked the remainder of the way to my chamber and let a woman a few years older than me, who had introduced herself as Nyrai, help me prepare for the inevitable, inescapable events of tonight. Preparation flew by in a flurry of passing time and before I knew it, I was standing in front of a mirror, ready to go.

Looking at the reflection, I hardly recognized the girl in front of me. My light brown hair was set in waves cascading down my back, the lighter blonde-brown streaks braided down the sides, framing my face. My blueish eyes with specks of green sparkled, lined with charcoal black liner, and a rouge tint emphasized my lips. My gaze lowered, taking in the breathtaking deep crimson gown that fit my body. From the off-the-shoulder, sheer red sleeves draping down my arms to the lowered v-cut stopping below my breasts, the dress was stunning.

A night breeze drifted through the room, teasing the edges of my dress, making the slit down the left side of the dress crawl higher, exposing my hip. I stared in the mirror, looking at the exposed skin, my fingers tracing down the visible scar etched there. A reminder of that night from years ago, as claws had sunk into my shoulder and side, leaving three angry stripes across my skin.

I glanced over to Nyrai. "I look—this dress is just . . . wow." I breathed with a laugh.

"The dress fits you perfectly. You look stunning," she replied with a smile.

"Thank you for helping me. My hair would have been in chaos without your help."

As Nyrai left, I was hardly aware of the passing of time, instead, being encased in my own thoughts on how tonight would go. Sébastien came to collect me from the bedroom. He paused, caught off guard at the doorway, looking me up and down with a satisfied grin before the two of us walked gracefully in steely silence down toward the festival where I only imagined hundreds of citizens filled the halls. Kateya walked ahead of us, Eryx by her side as they chatted animatedly, my sister's laughter echoing throughout the hall.

We had nearly made it when Sébastien's father beckoned us aside toward a private corridor. Taking a single look at the pair of us, the king spoke, "Any disagreement between the two of you will be settled right away. I will not risk the importance of tonight with whatever anger the two of you are threatening to unleash on each other." And with that, he led us into a room in the corridor and locked us inside to settle our 'dispute.'

I turned toward Sébastien, glaring at him before walking off to a far corner of the room and settling down for what I presumed to be an extremely long, uncomfortable night. An hour or so passed in a deadly silence, neither of us giving in to speak to the other. Eventually, I couldn't take the silence anymore. I stopped my pacing, leaning against the wall as I addressed him. "Do you have anything to say? Or are we going to sit here in silence until we rot and die? Either is just fine with me, I just want to prepare for what sort of night I'm in for. I already told you that I have no intention of interfering with the festival. I'm aware of how important it is."

Sébastien gave a dark chuckle. "If I had anything to say, I doubt I would waste it on you, *princesse.*"

"What a surprise," I snarked. "And is there any particular reason you are in such a disparaging mood tonight, *Your Highness.* Or is it just my presence?"

I watched the commander sigh, running a hand through his thick hair as I looked at me, frustration still etched across his face. "A patrol group disappeared today," he admitted, stunning me silent. "We sent out three patrols to search for the artifact. Only two returned."

I stared, processing his frustration, the anger he felt toward me, was because he had men missing. Men who had only been gone because of my pendant.

"I'm sorry," I replied, at a loss for what else to say. "I know it doesn't mean much, but I'm sorry one of the patrols is missing."

Sébastien's eyes flashed in acceptance, his head nodding slightly as we stayed silent.

"Let's just get through the rest of the night without any other issues," he spoke, his voice harder. "Then I will worry about finding my men and *your* pendant."

My head snapped over to him at his words. *He wasn't possibly implying that they were missing because of me, could he be?* "Fine. I already told you I would be on my best behavior. Not to mention, you're the last person I would want to be stuck here with." I flashed my teeth in a sarcastic smile. "Now, Kode . . . he could be fun to be stuck in this room with. I bet I'd have a deliciously good time then. I did promise to save him a dance." Sébastien froze as I continued, "At least he seems to like me, unlike you. I wonder what he would be like—"

At that, Sébastien menacingly snarled, leaping from his chair, storming over to the wall I was leaning against. I chuckled at his anger. "I wouldn't have taken you for the type of man who gets jealous," I mocked, his eyes flashing in a slight rage. "Unless, of course, you're worried that any of your friends could give me a good time. But that shouldn't bother you, should it, *Your Highness*? I mean, after all, I'm just an 'infuriating' complication you have to deal with."

His body leaned into mine, and I felt his muscles ripple as his frustration coursed through him. His mouth was dangerously close to my ear, the scent of pine and spice flooding my airway. A scent embedding its way into my mind, the promise and allure of danger all in one.

"I can guarantee you, *princesse*. Kode will never be able to satisfy you the way you want to be. The way you *need* to be." His voice slid across me as his hand trailed painfully slow up the exposed expanse of skin from the slit of my dress.

My eyes hooked on those blue orbs as I bit my lip, excruciatingly aware of how high cut my dress was. That I was playing with fire. And not just with anyone, but with the man that seemed to hate me most in this land, and worse yet, I seemed to like it as his breath fanned across my neck in a sensual breeze. His fingers snaked across my bare leg, the temperature around us dropping as his hand inched higher and higher, taunting me. Daring me. My body involuntarily pushed into his, a hardness pressing against me as tension built around us. The air thick as his eyes pierced mine, entrapping my gaze with a force I couldn't deny.

The door opened wide, rattling across the room as the

wood hit the wall, and the king entered the room. "The festival will be starting now. I presume you have finished this dispute by now, correct?"

Sébastien answered, his eyes never leaving mine. "Finished? No, but we did begin to come close to settling things." Looking back and forth between father and son, I stood on the stone-cold floor waiting for King Adrastan Capetian to speak or leave.

Laughter sounded in the halls, and a head popped into view. "We can't be late to our own party now, can we, father?" Kairon's jovial voice sounded out. The three of us turning in greeting. King Adrastan nodded in agreement, turning to head out the door. I began to follow, but Sébastien grabbed my arm and tugged me against him, my back to his front as he leaned down to speak.

"We aren't finished here, *princesse*," he said huskily into my ear, heat coursing down my body at his words.

"On the contrary, you will find we are quite finished here, now and forever," I snapped back, frustrated that I allowed him to get close to me at all, at my body's involuntary attraction to him.

"We will see," he responded, a low chuckle slipping from those lips.

Scoffing, I yanked my wrist back, heading into the hallway. Kairon stood further down; Dravyn, Emalyee, and my sister by his side. "Finally," he joked. I made my way over to the group, a smile forced across my face.

As we walked into the Festival of Nightloc, my crimson red gown flowed in tandem with my steps, my leg exposed with each step as the air danced through my dress. I felt as though I was floating across glass, the low-cut gown drawing attention as I walked in the halls of the festival. Never had I felt as elegant as I did at this moment.

Taking in the hall, Kateya by my side, I noticed the magical décor throughout the room. While gowns of vibrant colors swayed to the heavenly music, lanterns floated up to the ceilings, lowering and then floating up once again. The skylights displayed scattered stars twinkling down while clouds cast small shadows across the moon.

"Our parents would love this," my sister said next to me as she admired the black mist floating around our feet. "I wish they were here."

"They would," I agreed. "Let's enjoy it for them. After tonight, we will hopefully be a step closer to returning home to them."

"You don't have to tell me twice." Kateya laughed as she skipped off toward her date, Eryx.

Kairon walked up to me then. "There's some time before the main event. Care to dance?"

"Do you have a death wish?" I questioned. "Your brother will kill you if he sees you dancing with me."

"My brother can piss off," Kairon said with a laugh. "I am the heir-apparent after all. Let's dance." I grabbed his outstretched hand, letting him lead me off toward the music.

"What exactly is the main event tonight?" I asked as he pulled me into his arms, sweeping me along to the steady rhythm playing around us.

"That is something that is better seen than explained. You'll just have to wait to see for yourself."

"Fine," I whined. "But if it's not as good as you make it seem, you better watch your back."

"Consider me warned." He laughed. "I've seen your skills. Not quite as good as mine, but certainly impressive for a *girl*," he teased me.

"Hey! Take that back. I held my own for quite some time," I quipped. As the music ended, a grip on my arm took me by surprise.

"Father wants you. The ceremony is starting soon," Sébastien stated in a non-negotiable tone as he looked at his brother.

"It's been a pleasure, Cass," Kairon joked as he turned to leave, Sébastien's grip tightening on my arm as his brother spoke. "I shall watch my back for the foreseeable future."

Sébastien began to turn, my arm following his motion. "I wasn't done dancing." He stopped in his tracks as I refused to move from the dancefloor, the next song starting up. With a muttered curse, Sébastien pulled me close to him, my body colliding with his as we began to ebb and flow with the crowd.

I glanced up in shock that he chose to dance with me, only to find his eyes already on me, watching me intensely. My body thrummed with delight as he began falling in line with those around us on the dance floor. The feel of Sébastien's hand on my lower back calling my focus onto him. "You dance?"

"Well, I am a prince," he said with slight disdain as he led us across the floor. "It comes with the territory."

"You say that like it's a bad thing," I said as he twirled me around to the rhythm of the music, a strong scent of pine and spice surrounding me, "What? If it doesn't involve battles or commands, is it not worth it?"

"I say it like a fact. There is a great deal that comes with the title of prince. Commander. Wolvyn."

"But there must also be a lot of good in return," I questioned, as he pulled me into his form, our bodies blending with the dance. "The people you can help, those that look to you for guidance. For protection." His eyes met mine with understanding as I continued, "You never did tell me the true story of how you got the nickname of 'big, bad wolf.'"

"I was twelve," he started, shocking me once again. "I had only just begun my official training in the Wolvyn Guard when a Seefer snuck onto the Palace grounds, cornering two of chefs' daughters who had been out playing in the gardens. I shifted and leapt in front of them, fighting off the Seefer. I managed to hold the beast off until the alarm sounded and more soldiers arrived. That's where I got this and the nickname." He pointed toward the faded scar that slashed across his eyebrow.

I stared in stunned silence, thinking back on my own Seefer encounter back home, the scars that still marred my skin. A common trait throughout the ages of time.

"You fended off a Seefer?" I murmured, my voice barely legible over the music.

"I had to." His voice was tight. "I wasn't about to let harm come to two of our own. It was the only choice I had, even at a young age."

I didn't say anything right away, knowing that the choice he made to fight for those two girls was the same one I made for my sister. And scars be damned, I'd make that decision over and over again, just as I'm sure he would. We spun me around once more, our dance a balance of footsteps and ease, as the music lulled me into the safety of his arms.

His eyes darkened as they caught on something in the distance; his lips pressed into a thinning line across his face before he spoke in a hardened tone. "Let's go."

"Wait, I wasn't done dancing."

"You're sorely mistaken if you thought I was giving you an option, *princesse.* Now, *let's go,*" he said as he turned on his heel, not giving me any other option but to follow. We rounded a corner, following the marbled hallway, passing festival goers. Rounding yet another corner, this one with less people, he opened a glass door that led out onto a terrace.

"What are we doing out here?" I demanded.

Sébastien turned on his heel, his face drawn tight, his knuckles going white. "I need you to wait here until I return. There is something that must be dealt with, and I need to know that you are safe."

"I don't understand why I wouldn't be safe *inside* the Palace. After all—"

"Cassandra." I froze, hearing my name fall from his lips. "*Please.* Just stay put for once."

I nodded as he turned and headed back, the door closing behind him and trapping the laughter inside. Sighing, I glanced around, taking in my surroundings. Black ivy crawled alongside the gray Palace walls. The terrace railings formed short columns that lined the space. The moon climbed higher through the night sky, an occasional star twinkling brighter than the rest.

If I had to wait alone, at least Sébastien deigned to drop me in a spot that was relaxing. I listened to the faded beat of the music as I leaned against the railing, breathing in the mixed scent of sea salt and pine branches. The breeze let the salty mist from the Avyz carry over to the Palace, coating the walls.

"There you are." A voice rang out from the doorway. I spun, recognizing the familiar grin of Ryker. "I have half a mind to kill Sébastien. *'She's on the terrace, just go get her.'* I have walked onto four terraces before this one. And that last one . . . *My eyes!* I will be scarred for life," he complained as I laughed.

"Better your eyes than mine." I chuckled in response. "Did Sébastien say why he left me out here?"

Ryker glanced at me. "Briefly. From what I gather, there's a higher Nordak presence than typical at the festival, and a few of the men spotted are ones whose movements we have been tracking."

"So, to solve the problem he just left me outside?"

"Look, darling. I don't know you well, other than our lovely encounter at the pub. I do know Sébastien, though, and if this was the move he needed to make, I would trust him without a doubt."

"So what? You were sent to babysit me? To ensure I stayed put like a *good girl*?" I scoffed sarcastically.

"I'd prefer the term keep company. But yes," he retorted.

"What did you do to get stuck with the job?"

"The festival will be starting shortly, and I was the disposable option."

Glancing over at him, I took in his all-black dress attire, the slicked-back, light colored hair, with a slight sun-bleached look. He looked to be no more than a few years older than me, and had an athletic build with muscles defined from agility rather than weights. The kind my roommate, Aerilyn, would rave about for days. I broke the silence. "What made the five of you make a blood bond?"

Ryker tensed, looking at me with such intensity my blood froze. "Who told you about that?"

"Um, Emalyee mentioned it the other day. I'm sorry. Forget I asked."

He sighed, running a hand through his hair as he stared out over the railing. "Well, you already know, no harm now, I suppose. When we were younger, there was a group of six of us who grew up together."

"Six?" I interrupted with a question.

"Yes. If you want to know, then let me tell the story. You're as bad as Dravyn."

"Continue," I quipped with a laugh.

"The sixth was the son of the current King of Nordak. During a particular festival one year, he sought us out, begging us to help him, claiming his father was after his life. Two of our fathers overheard, and they made the five of us swear not to interfere, that it wasn't our place. It wasn't our duty. That our duty was to each of our individual lands, not his. A few days later, his body washed up on the shores of his homeland. His father never even held a funeral. He simply lit his body, the ash carrying his soul off to The Void." A gasp fell from my lips as I glanced at Ryker.

"The next time the five of us gathered, we made the journey to form the bond. A brotherhood of sorts. Nothing we could do would bring him back—that decision would always be there to haunt us. So instead, we changed what we could, promising that we would be there for each other. We would put each other before our lands until our life's blood stopped pumping through our veins. We would always answer the call of a blood brother, no questions asked. And thus, the Brotherhood was formed. A tie between five princes of the Vanaiyer realm, a bond thicker than our duty to our lands. *Embers and Ash, even The Void won't hold . . .* "

I nodded in understanding. "A bond formed by friendship and pain, suffering and hope."

"Yes. But blood bonds were banned almost a hundred years ago. The shared power and binding of a blood bond is an ancient magic. One from the origins of our realm, one The God may not approve of, that connects us through all of time, *even* in The Void." A low rumbling cut Ryker off, and the terrace shook, causing me to stumble as it built.

"Is this supposed to happen?" I shouted over the noise.

"It's starting now. Welcome to the Festival of Nightloc," he said as the sky lit up. Brightened hues of color shot across the sky, leaving a trail of color behind, the colors swirling as they faded. The sky was filled with floating lines of purples, greens, and blues, fading, then growing brighter once again. They danced on for a few moments, lighting up the realm before they drifted down.

I turned to Ryker. "I've never seen anything like this before." I breathed as the colors fell, a warm sensation surrounding my body as the colors sank down around us and soaked into the ground.

"It's pure power. It can't be caught, harnessed, or stored. It just is."

"Where does it go?"

"No one knows. As a child, I had plenty of ideas. My mother's theory stuck with me throughout the years, though. She said that it was The God's way of reminding us that we are to use our powers and elemental magic for what is right. To remember that all the power we use has a cost, and that the magic we use belongs to one with more power than even the strongest of us. That it belongs to one that we all will answer to one day in The Void, so we should use it to be a light, to make a difference." I watched his gaze drift off as he spoke. Chuckling, he continued, "But I often think my mother told us that just so we would behave and not use our shifting powers to get into trouble."

Laughing, I responded, "I'm sure that must have worked extremely well."

"Come," he replied, leading me back toward the festival.

Chapter Thirteen

VERASTARR

LATER THAT NIGHT, after the festival, I lay cuddled in bed with Kateya, listening to her ramble on and tell me all about her magical night of dancing. It was in that moment, as I laid there, listening to my younger sister go on and on about the festival, the gown, the dancing, the rhythm of the music, that I realized something. I began to understand what I was missing. I had been so focused this past week on finding the missing pendant, the truth on the power it held, and getting us back to present day East Engles, that I had missed the adventure of attending a festival in a true Palace with my sister.

I turned on the bed, facing my sister. "Kateya?" I began. "The other day, I spoke with the king. He shared some information on the pendant, and I'm unsure what it means for our future." I recounted the story to her, sharing the powers contained in the pendant, the king's plans for it once it was located, the hope but uncertainty that it could take us home.

Kateya was silent for a moment, her soft, emerald eyes watching me. "We have to get a hold of the pendant first, don't we?" she asked quietly.

A heavy sigh fell from me as I looked over at her. "I think that's the only way. I'm afraid that if we don't get to it first, we will be forced to help participate in whatever power struggle is brewing, whatever war was paused when the artifacts were cast into time. And if that's the case, I'm not sure we will ever make it home."

"So, what's the plan?"

"I don't know, Kat. I don't know," I whispered. "Let's worry about it in the morning," I said as we both began to drift to sleep, curled up in each other, the sun starting to paint its way across the sky.

A hurried knock on the door shook us from our slumbered sleep, calling us back toward the present. *"Enter,"* I replied. I patiently waited for Nyrai to walk through as the door opened, yet to my surprise, it was not Nyrai who entered. Sébastien and Dravyn stepped in through the doorway as I hastily crawled out of bed, my nightgown clinging to my body, Kateya still buried in the covers. I held my breath, waiting for them to speak.

"We are sorry to intrude at such an hour, however we have received an estimated location of the pendant and we are preparing to ride shortly. I thought you would both wish to know that we will have this settled in a few days," Sébastien told me as he stood tensely inside the room, his large form filling the doorframe.

I nearly jumped from excitement as they shared the news before realizing this meant they held the upper hand if they were in possession of the necklace. "Thank you for letting us know. We can be prepared and ready to depart in as soon as twenty minutes, if that works for you?"

"You will not be coming," Sébastien said in a voice of steel before turning on his heel to leave.

Shaking off my shock and displeasure, I quickly stormed

down the corridor after the two men. "Sébastien, what exactly do you mean 'we won't be coming'? You just told me that you received word of my pendant, and now you will not let me come with you to retrieve it? It is *my* pendant, after all."

I was met with Sébastien's icy glare as he spun around on his heel to face me. "First of all, if I recall correctly, you losing the necklace is the reason we are in this mess to begin with."

Looking down, I swallowed the words bubbling up. "Secondly, no. Neither you nor your sister will be coming. The location of the necklace is not in a part of the land that is safe now; therefore, I will not be risking my men's lives or your own to protect you."

"Thanks for your truly *heartfelt* concern over my safety; however, I'm perfectly capable of taking care of myself. Just ask Dravyn. I'm sure he can attest that my self-defense is adequate."

Sébastien's head snapped toward his blood brother with venom. "I'm staying out of this one," Dravyn voiced with a grimace.

Annoyance washed over Sébastien's face, telling me my answer long before he spoke. "Have I not made myself clear? You and your sister will be remaining here in the Palace until we return with the pendant."

"Void-damn, Sébastien. I am perfectly capable of taking care of myself. I'm not *asking* for permission to come. I'm *telling* you I'm coming," I snarled back at him.

His eyes darkened, fury radiating within them as his look froze me in place, angry tendrils of black mist swirling up from the ground around us. "You will *remain* here in Ny Palace until we return with your pendant. Then you will do *whatever* is needed to fix this mess. Don't push me any further or you *will* find yourself chained in your room, unable to leave until my return. Have. I. Made. Myself. Clear?" He sneered.

Frustrated and feeling defeated, I stalked back toward my room, not giving him the satisfaction of a reply.

Surprised, I discovered that Kateya had followed me out of the room and heard the entire conversation that had taken place. "Who does he think he is, telling us we can't go along?" Kateya ranted. "Like we would let them get it first, just to hold it over our heads. I'm ready to go home, Cass. I say we just go anyway and get the pendant."

"I know," I agreed, frustration slowly ebbing off of me. "But maybe he's speaking the truth when he said it was dangerous. I don't want you getting hurt."

Kateya laughed. "I'm not five anymore, Cass. You don't have to always look after me."

"Ha. Ha," I mocked. "I'm still the older sister, and I will always want to put your safety above my own, Kat."

"Older by two years, Cass. Still, one of us needs to go, seeing as neither of them are going to want to give us back the pendant right away. And once it makes it to the king's hands, then we will be out of luck with no way home. If both of us don't go, then at least one of us should."

Grinning at her, I said, "That's exactly what I'm planning to do." I walked back into my room, throwing on a pair of black leathers in the closet and strapping the dagger I had swiped from the training yard the other day onto them.

Glancing over at Kateya, I said, "We both know that of the two of us, I have the best fighting and defense skills. If either of us is going, big sister comment aside, it will be me." Pulling my sister in for a hug, I whispered goodbye and snuck out of the room.

I slapped at another bug as it buzzed by. Sweat drenched my face as I pulled my hood back over it, disguising myself. *Why, oh why, had I decided to go along with this idea?* When Kateya and I had decided I would go, the logic had felt foolproof.

I had not counted on the fact that my riding experience was *still* lackluster, and that riding in disguise amongst a group of soldiers was harder than it seemed. I was constantly falling back to avoid conversations that would give away the fact I was not a man. The infrequent breaks proved difficult as well. We had been riding since dawn and I had yet to discover how far we planned to travel or where it was we were riding to.

A shouted command from up front led the men to begin turning off to the side of the path we had been riding, entering the forest. Tall pine trees covered the space, bushes and shrubs scraped across my ankles as they looked for a secluded area to take shelter for the night before dusk fell. There were roughly a fifty soldiers on horseback, several others in wolvyn form, which meant my hopes of remaining hidden for at least another day or two should be better than none, so long as I kept up my current game plan.

When tents were set up, I went straight to bed, exhausted from the day and desperately wishing to avoid the sight of any known guards who were traveling under Sébastien's command. I drifted off into an uncomfortable slumber, tossing and turning as I dreamed of home.

A chirping noise mixed with the loud crackle of the fire stirred me awake. Glancing around the makeshift camp, I observed the guards sprawled out on mats in every direction. I shakily rolled to my side and crept out of the circle of sleeping men, toward the comforting embrace of the sheltered trees that drew together. Softly, I padded along, dew-covered grass coating my bare feet as I made my way into the woods. An owl soared across the star-painted sky as I wandered further from the camp. When I finally found a spot a safe distance out of earshot, I relieved myself, wishing once for the luxury of a modern bathroom.

I decided to walk a bit further to clear my mind, and as the trees lessened, I stumbled upon a large lake, its grayish-black color calling me toward it. Leaning against the rough bark of a pine tree, I watched as the water lapped softly at the edge of the lake, an eerie silence settling in the air. I closed my eyes as I rested my head against the tree, breathing in the cool night air, when a low hiss caused my eyes to flash open.

The hiss grew louder as a dark figure crept its way toward me; fear building inside. My hand slowly felt along my leg, slipping the dagger I carried from its sheath as I rose to a standing position, my body rigid as I watched the darkness. The creature came into view as the moon reflected off its black coat, the panther lowering on its haunches, amber eyes tracking my form as it prepared to attack.

Lifting my dagger, I braced for impact, my limbs shaking slightly, knowing that I couldn't run. It was fight or be eaten, and I would sure as hell put up a fight. The panther launched through the air with a snarl, my body ducking to the side as my arm stretched out, nicking the underbelly of the beast. Warm liquid sprayed into my line of vision as I cut the creature, trailing down my arm while I held my ground.

It landed inches to my right, skidding slightly into the tree I had just been leaning against, as it missed my moving body. I squared off with it as it crept closer, baring its teeth as it viewed me like its next meal. Its razor sharp fangs glowed a yellow color as it began to circle me, trapping me with nowhere to go. Holding my ground, I tracked its movements, aware that I was its prey.

A menacing growl had us both freezing, the hair on the panther's neck rising at the sound. Its paws backed off as a larger figure stalked into view; the predator now prey. A dark snarl filled the air from behind me and the cat was scurrying away into the night, fleeing while it still had the chance. The only sound to be heard was the haunting breath of the unseen creature as it creeped closer to me undercover of darkness, a chill flowing through the air. I remained frozen in place, my dagger at the ready, praying I made it through the night.

Muscled arms wrapped around me from behind in a

crushing grip, pinning my arms to the side. The movement caused my dagger to be forced from my hand. My body shook slightly, fear coursing through me as I was held tightly, a firm hand clamped around my mouth. "Hold your tongue," a rough voice whispered in my ear. A voice I would recognize anywhere. Spinning me around, I came face to face with a furious Sébastien. "What are you doing here?" he snapped with venom once I looked him in the eye.

"I'm here to get my pendant back. Why else do you think I would be here? For fun?"

Sébastien regarded me carefully. "That's no way to speak to the person who just saved your life," he responded with a dark chuckle. "You shouldn't have wandered outside the camp. You would have been killed if I hadn't heard you sneak off."

"Would have? You're *that* certain I would have died?" I snarked back as I leaned against the rough bark of a pine tree, regarding Sébastien carefully as he paced in front of me, clearly angered and more than slightly enraged.

"I gave you one command . . . stay at the Palace, where it's safe. That's it. Was it *truly* that difficult for you to follow one simple command?"

Scoffing, I eyed him as I replied, "No . . ." before being interrupted as he questioned, "No?"

"I suppose, yes. I disagreed with your decision. You must understand, that pendant is my way home. My way to bring my sister to safety, back to our family, our friends, our *lives*. No matter what you say or do, I *will* defy you any time you say I can't do what needs to be done to escape this nightmare and bring my family back together." Sébastien watched me carefully as I spoke, his eyes narrowing before relaxing.

He reached out, his knuckles trailing up my neck before forcing my chin up so my eyes met with his. The fury was still visible as it stormed within them. His stern voice softened a touch as he spoke, "While I understand that, you disobeyed a direct order. An order that was placed for your safety. Your sister's safety. My men's safety. And this mission's safety. Your presence here puts more than just you in danger."

I blinked, looking up into his eyes. "I didn't intend to put others in danger. But I *can* take care of myself. I'm not helpless. I'm quite capable of defending and protecting myself."

A humorless laugh fell from those lips. "Need I remind you that you nearly became a meal minutes ago?"

I glared at Sébastien. "I would have done better if someone would provide me with weapons instead of treating me like an incompetent child unable to defend herself."

"Instead, you resorted to stealing daggers from my training yard, *hmmm, princesse?*"

I paused, shocked he was aware that I had stolen the dagger my first day at the Palace.

"Come now, *Cassandra*," he mocked, closing the space between us as my heart fluttered at the sound of my name on his tongue. "You didn't truly think that you could swipe a dagger from *my* training yard without my knowledge, did you?"

"I—well, I . . ." I stuttered, because *yes*. I had thought I had gotten away with it.

"One dagger," he taunted. "One is child's play. What had you hoped to accomplish other than drawing a little blood?" I watched his deep blue eyes as he spoke, the humor pooling in their depths seeing an entirely different side of Sébastien.

Suddenly, I realized how close he was to me. His face was mere inches from mine, and heat radiated off him from the proximity. His body was flush against mine, pinning me against the tree. I took in the small, silver scar across his brow; the scattering of freckles over those high, defined cheekbones that always made my stomach drop; the piece of wavy hair that fell across his eye. The night sounds of the forest faded out as my gaze focused on his lips, on the small freckles across them, wondering what they would feel like pressed against mine.

His arms caged me against the tree, rough bark scratching at my back as he tracked my every breath, heat building between us. I knew this would be a mistake. I knew I shouldn't be attracted to the one man orchestrating the chaos of my life. The man who thought he could control my actions. And yet. I threw caution to the wind like a fleeting thought as those firm lips came crashing down onto mine, taking what I freely offered.

My mouth parted at the welcome intrusion, the feel of his tongue against my lips a collision of power as we kissed. He pulled me in and demanded complete submission as he laid claim to my mouth, pulling soft whimpers from it as he explored. Heat rose within me as his hands roamed my body, his lips still commanding my focus as I melted into his firm hold.

I was drawn in, surrounded by the overwhelming scent of pine and spice, the feel of his hands weaving their way through my hair. The raw power and control radiating from him.

Time felt as if it faded into the background, the feel of rough bark replaced with dewy grass, as he lowered me to the ground. Dew drops dampened my clothing as Sébastien's form rested on top of me, covering every inch of mine with a welcome weight. The pressure of his lips against mine as his tongue claimed every corner of my mouth had a steady heat rising from within. His lips left mine, breaking the kiss, leaving me panting as they shifted their attention toward the side of my neck, biting and sucking.

A cool breeze fluttered across my skin as a tendril of black mist snaked across my skin, circling my wrists, holding my arms in place, with no chance of escape. My mind hardly focused on his action as his lips roamed over the expanse of exposed skin of my neck, kissing and sucking as my body arched into his, desire pulsing through me.

Every touch of his hands on my body, every flick of his tongue against my fevered skin drove me insane, hunger aflame within me. His lips crashed into mine once more, consuming me, dominating me, owning me.

A blinding pain seared across my right wrist, causing black spots to dance in my vision, a strangled cry of pain mixed with longing falling from my lips as he withdrew instantly.

A low curse followed as Sébastien recoiled and sat up on the grass next to me. I regarded Sébastien in a daze, my breath heaving as I focused back in on the present. He yanked the dagger from the ground, the blood rushing to my limbs as he freed them from the restraint, my wrist still coursing with pain.

I needed him to say something, anything really, or to leave so I could process what we had just done. That I had let the man who hated me, *who locked me in a cell*, kiss me like the realm was ending.

Another curse fell from his lips as I fixed the straps of my nightgown. Pushing off the ground to rest against the tree, my lips still tingled from his kiss while a faint itch of pain lingered. With a glance down my arm, I noticed a thin black line circling above my wrist, the inky substance flowing across my skin. "What the fuck?" I gasped, drawing my arm closer, analyzing my wrist further. "What is this?" I questioned as I threw my wrist out, looking over toward Sébastien.

Sébastien looked at me, the moonlight casting dancing shadows across his face. He sighed. "A bond."

I paused, wondering what in The Void he was referring to, my lack of wolvyn history clearly visible across my face.

"Wolvyn are like other creatures in nature, and as such, they mate. However, wolvyn are creatures of both power and elemental magic. Meaning that there's mating but there's also bonding."

"Bonding?" I questioned.

"Yes. For wolvyn, potential mates will bond over three phases. With each completed phase, a unique band is inked across the couple's skin. The bond *can* be broken during any one of the three phases, if the wolvyn chooses. However, once all three bands are formed, there is no turning back, and the wolvyn enter a bonding ritual, cementing the bond."

I stared at him in shock. "So . . . this band would imply that we completed a phase of a wolvyn bonding?"

He nodded in response; a tense look crossed his face.

"I'm not a wolvyn . . . I'm just a mortal. So how could I possibly be bonded to *you*?"

"I don't know." He groans as he rubs his hand through his dark hair, messing up the strands.

"How do we get rid of it?" I questioned angrily, staring at the glaring mark twisted around my wrist.

"There are only two ways. You can either eliminate the connection built for that phase. Or dark magic."

"Great," I muttered. "So, what exactly *are* the three different phases?" I asked as I tried to wrap my mind around the bonding concept.

Sébastien regarded me. "You know, for someone from the future. Your knowledge of our realm is shockingly lacking."

"Seriously? I wouldn't say that now is the time to debate my knowledge of wolvyn," I snapped.

Sighing, he began again. "There are three phases. They don't have to happen in any particular order, they just must all occur *genuinely*. The first phase most wolvyn experience is a physical connection. Inking typically appears once the pair have been intimate in some manner."

"That doesn't make sense," I countered in confusion. "We just kissed . . . like it was *just* a kiss."

"Well, bonds are tricky. If they appeared anytime a wolvyn acted on their urges, I would have been forced to utilize dark magic many times, starting a long time ago. Instead, the bond is ignited with mutual desire rather than lust. Both in the couple are required to have an overwhelming desire burning for the other to ignite the bond."

"*Okay* . . ." I said, conveniently ignoring the part about mutual desire, and jumping to how to get rid of it. "So to cancel the bond, we simply have to no longer desire each other? That seems easy enough." I coughed up a humorless laugh.

"Like I said, it's not that easy," he replied in a low tone, his head turning toward mine, a wave of onyx hair sweeping across his forehead, hiding the small scar across his eyebrow. "To cancel the forming bond, one of the two would have to desire someone else in the same manner and break the forming bond by engaging in an intimate action with the other wolvyn."

I groaned. "Because why make it easy? What are the two other phases?"

"Another is an emotional connection. This is founded on mutual trust, acceptance, and love. And the final connection is devotion. The terms of this phase are less clear. Devotion seems to be defined differently for each mated pair. But the consensus is that it takes a great act, similar to feelings of sacrificing one's life for the other."

"So, we should be fine. It seems *highly* unlikely that we would make it to the next phase, given your immense dislike for me. We just need to break the intimate connection, correct?" I questioned.

"Hopefully, yes. The longer the ink remains, however, the stronger the bond will begin to feel and the harder it becomes to remove."

We sat there for a time, the sounds of crickets filling the air, a slight breeze wrapped around me, surrounding me with its chilled embrace. He didn't speak anymore; he simply stood up, dusting the dirt from his black leathers, extended his large, calloused hand, and took my shaky one in his. He led me back toward the camp, the slight sting on my wrist a physical reminder of my stupid mistake of the night.

I laid in a makeshift tent, listening to the winds dance across the trees overhead, utterly confused. When did things become so complicated? What shifted between me and Sébastien? Would we be able to successfully break the forming bond? *Did I want to break the bond?* How had I allowed him to go that far with everything at stake?

As the morning sun crested the horizon, I watched as the men rose alongside it, already preparing for the day's journey. Inwardly groaning at the thought of another long day's ride, I pushed myself off the ground and folded up my tent. Grabbing some meat and bread from the cook, I sat on an old tree stump as I ate the meager breakfast, my gaze occasionally drifting down toward the black band the size of a bracelet flowing around my wrist.

I was well aware that whatever had transpired last night was an added complication to an increasingly complicated start. As I watched Sébastien direct his soldiers with a steely voice that dripped authority and anger, I knew that some of that raw emotion stemmed from my presence, as well as the new inking he sported on his tanned right wrist. Not wishing any of that directed at me, I slowly backed away toward the edge of the campsite, making myself invisible.

We began to ride once again. This time, however, I noted that there were multiple soldiers who stuck closer to my side as we rode out. I knew that Sébastien had ordered more of his men to remain near me for my safety.

While I thought this action of his was slightly unnecessary, seeing as I had been entirely safe without his protection yester-day, I let the matter go because it was better than him forcing some of his men to turn around with me in tow and escort me back to the Palace. No longer being forced to hide my identity gave me permission to relax a little and enjoy the journey.

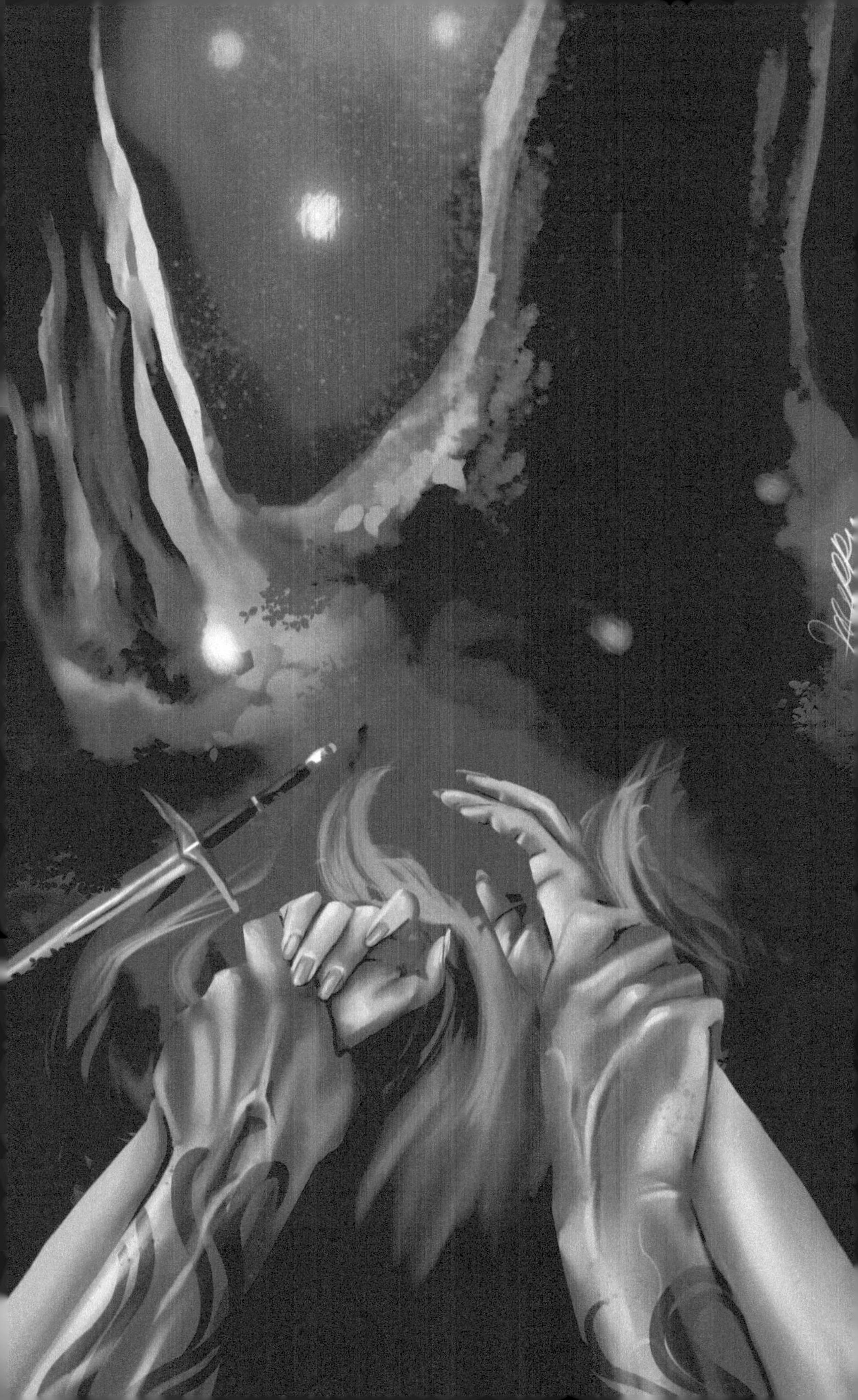

Chapter Fourteen

VERASTARR

A PATTERN FORMED for the continuation of the journey. Sébastien went the extra lengths and kept guards around me continuously for protection while we traveled. He hadn't once spoken to me since the night by the lake, and it made me slightly nervous that he didn't mention it. I knew we wouldn't be able to break the bond during the journey, but he could have at least provided the ideas he had for breaking it rather than ignoring me and pretending it didn't exist.

Every day we traveled, my hopes of seeing my home, getting the pendant, and returning home to the East Engles safely with Kateya increased. It felt as though finding the pendant would instantly return us to our normal lives, and even though I feared it wasn't true, I had to hold on to that hope. I couldn't even venture to think of what would happen if we couldn't locate the necklace and the worst case-scenario occurred. One that I didn't dare voice aloud for fear it would become our reality.

We had been riding for several days now. My thighs felt like liquid fire, my body ached from the constant trot, and I was not entirely certain how much longer I could hold out riding. I had hoped that over time, I would get used to it, but riding hard for ten hours a day every day wasn't helping my theory. I desperately wanted to give in, return to the safety of the Palace with Kateya, and yet that was not an option.

Glancing to my left, I was relieved to discover Dravyn rode close by, his dark brown hair tousled from riding. "How much further are we from the location the king gave us?" I half grumbled out.

A chuckle slipped as he said, "About half a day, maybe a little less. Think you'll survive?"

I shot him a joking glare, his hazel eyes meeting mine. "Yes, I'm sure I will survive," I retorted, even as my legs begged for a break.

"So . . ." He hesitated before going silent, a curious look pasted across his tanned face.

Glancing over, I prompted, "So?"

"It's just um, well . . ."

"Dravyn de Cauda is speechless. Never thought I would've seen the day," I teased him.

He let out a growl. "The inking on your wrist. When did that show up?"

"Oh." All joking vanished at the question. "The first night of the trip," I answered with honesty.

"Never thought I'd see the day." He threw my own words back at me with a laugh. "How'd you take the news?"

I was relieved to note the sincerity in his question. "Honestly, it still hasn't fully processed or made sense. Sébastien told me about how wolvyn bonds work. He says there is a way we can break it."

A slight *harrumph* sounded from one of the other soldiers riding in formation near me, followed by a sarcastic, "Good luck with that!"

My gaze flipped between the other soldier and Dravyn, both looking at each other with a look I couldn't quite decipher.

"What's that supposed to mean?" I questioned, concern creeping its way in.

"Technically, yes. A forming bond *can* be broken. Bonds are more complicated in real life, though. Not all wolvyn form bonds, and those who do are often destined to be together. The longer a forming bond remains, the more it sinks into the skin, solidifying the bond."

"I told Sébastien the other night. I'm not a wolvyn. So why would I even have this?" I gestured to my wrist, the black band a stark contrast to my fair skin.

"Bonds are made from primal magic," Dravyn responded thoughtfully. "It's possible the bond intertwined your power lines based on the magic from the pendant." He mused.

"Power lines?"

"Yes. How is it that you say you are from the future, yet you know shockingly little of your own history?"

"The Fall happened when I was younger," I recounted. "The Nordak grew strong enough to banish all elemental magic and shifting powers from the lands, haunting and harvesting from those who showed any sign of power. They destroyed all written records of power from Vanaiyer, forbidding anyone to speak of it."

"Void-damned." Dravyn sighs as he looks at me before explaining, "Power lines are the lines that each individual has in them if they possess a shifting power—such as shifting to a wolvyn form or any other form. It's possible that the primal magic of the bond could have connected to a power line in you due to the pendant."

I thought about his wording. "So, even though I'm a mortal, there may be a tie to power due to the pendant?"

"Possibly. I couldn't say for certain," he answered in honesty.

"But the bond can still be broken?"

"That remains to be seen. Sébastien is one of the most

powerful wolvyn in the realm. If anyone could break the bond, I would say it would be him."

I rode on in silence, the gravity of my situation rising. My horse trotted over toward the stream we approached to rest. I half rolled off, half flopped to the ground, too exhausted to care that my technique was not proper.

It wasn't until I was fully sprawled out in the billowing grass, eyes closed as I appreciated the steady, unmoving nature of the ground that I felt a strong gaze watching me. Pushing myself up onto my elbows, I recognized Sébastien regarding me from a distance, a slightly amused yet mocking smirk smeared across his devilishly handsome face that made my heart drop and heat fan my body. *Void-damn that man and his looks.*

Leaning back down, I closed my eyes and attempted to take a brief nap in preparation for the continuation of the journey. A continuation which occurred much sooner than I hoped as the command was being given to move on. I sat up, only to discover my horse had meandered away from me. Frantically, I jumped up in search of where it had wandered off to.

I felt a look of panic shadow my face as I searched around, not finding the horse anywhere in the vicinity. Sébastien sauntered over toward me, his destrier calmly following his lead. "Let's go," he demanded as he approached me, stretching out his hand.

Looking at him, I quietly muttered, "I can't find the horse I was riding."

A soft chuckle sprang from his lips. "I had one of my men take him. You appeared much too exhausted to be in proper riding shape. Now, let's go." He lifted me onto his destrier before mounting behind me.

"I would have been fine to continue riding," I lied through my teeth, my thighs burning even now.

"Fine as you may have been," Sébastien said with a laugh,

"I wasn't about to risk an injury had you fallen off your horse. It's clear you don't have much riding experience and are exhausted from riding full days. Just consider this me making sure my men don't fall behind due to having to pick up your body off the ground."

I felt Sébastien nudge his horse into a trot, my body thrown against his as he quickly caught up to the front of the lines and we were off with the rest of the men. Sébastien didn't speak to me as we rode on, and I made no effort to speak to him, simply grateful that I didn't have to concentrate on riding. Exhaustion tugged at my body. I was aware of his muscled arms wrapped around me as he guided us down the path, my body relaxing into his while his arms caged me in. The canter of the horse and faint scent of spice mixed with the heat of the sun bearing down on me lulled me to sleep as the exhaustion began to take me over.

I awoke a few hours later, nestled closely up against Sébastien's chest, his arm wrapped tightly around my waist, securing me to him. Shifting in his arms, I sat up, a prominent bulge notably pressing into my back, causing heat to course through my body as I shifted. I glanced around, taking note of the sun lowering in the sky and men scouting for a place to set up camp. "You snore slightly," he muttered in acknowledgement to me waking. My cheeks flushed at his comment, at the level of safety I must have felt from him in order to be be able to fall asleep on him.

"And you *clearly* liked riding with me in your arms," I shot back, not willing to let the embarrassment end with me.

A dark chuckle slipped his lips as a few shouts from across the group notified us that a location had been settled upon. His breath fanned my neck as he said huskily into my ear, "I never claimed I didn't, *princesse*. I quite enjoyed having you in my arms."

I heard Dravyn mention we were closing in on a small village that bordered the side of a mountainous terrain. I took in the rocky hills and towering peaks in the distance to my right, jagged formations scattered with protruding rocks as brambles scratched against my legs. I noticed the men slowed their pace as we neared, appearing more alert and wary than they had throughout the journey. We had been traveling through a darkened forest, brambles and thickets closing in on us as we stealthily drew toward the village.

Glancing toward Sébastien, I watched his face, attempting to read into the situation we were approaching. A flick of his hand, and Sébastien's men began to merge into a tight formation, cautious and prepared, on guard. We were approaching the edge of the darkened forest we had been traveling through for the past few hours when Sébastien signaled to halt. Some men began dismounting, shifting into their wolvyn forms, while others drew weapons, preparing for orders.

I regarded Sébastien as he scanned his men before motioning to five soldiers to approach as he ordered them, "You five and Cassandra shall remain here. The moss rocks over there should provide enough shelter. You will protect her at all costs and keep a close watch on her. I do not want her attempting to sneak off to assist us. Her life is in your hands and if she is in harm's way, you *will* answer to me. *Understand?*" The five men he hand-selected nodded gravely as they began to scout the area to secure its safety.

I was less than happy with the turn of events and was about to voice my thoughts on the matter when Sébastien glanced over at me with an icy look that silenced me instantly. He strode over, leading me further into the forest and away from his men, before he turned, forcing my gaze up to hold his. His frame towered over me as I looked up at him, noting how his eyes softened slightly at the sight of me, a wave of worry flashing across his chiseled face for the briefest of moments. "I realize that this situation doesn't please you. However, this village has recently been taken over by Nordak presence from what my scouts have informed me and is considered enemy territory. I *will* be taking the proper precautions. It will be risky enough for my men to ride in; I will not risk your safety as well."

I interjected, "Just because I'm a woman doesn't mean I don't know how to fight. You don't have to shelter me as if I'm incompetent."

Sébastien released a frustrated growl. "You're staying here because you are the key to that pendant. You are what they need to access the power harnessed inside. I don't doubt your fighting skills or your competence. But I will do everything in my power to ensure you are out of harm's way. That said, you will remain in hiding with my five most trusted men, and you will not come out until I, and I alone, am there. Do I make myself perfectly clear?"

I regarded Sébastien while he spoke, watching his nostrils flare, his eyes flashing with concern, *concern for my safety*, and while I knew his logic made perfect sense, I despised being told to stay put. My gaze met his piercing stare as I gave a brief nod and agreed to comply with his demands. He led me back to his men, and I watched as Sébastien took charge and discussed plans with his soldiers. I was aware that this would be risky, but hope welled in me at the increasing thought of being able to return home with Kateya soon.

As I watched, the men rode off out of the darkened forest, and I turned my attention toward the selected soldiers who had been charged with protecting me. Behind me was a cluster of trees with some larger moss-covered rocks in the surrounding area. One of the soldiers approached and escorted me over toward an oak tree near the center of the tree cluster.

The tree we had stopped in front of had a hollowed core, burrowing deep in the ground. He explained to me that I was to crawl inside the trunk and remain in the tree until Sébastien returned. Looking at him, I scoffed, "You want me to sit in an old tree trunk that has a hole in it for the next few hours, as though I am a young child playing in the forest? No thank you, I can stay out here with the five of you."

At this point, Sébastien's third-in-command, Geoffrey, approached. Painfully yanking my arm, he pulled me close as he held me against him, towering over me. He looked me straight in the eye as he growled. "Sébastien may listen to your pitiful excuses, but I will not. The hollowed tree is where you will be most protected, so that is where you will wait. No discussion, it's an order."

He hauled me over his shoulder like a sack of potatoes as he finished speaking and proceeded to unceremoniously dump me inside the hollowed base. I shrieked before a rough, darkened hand was placed over my mouth, ordering me to be silent.

I freaked slightly at being dumped in the base of an ancient tree. Thoughts flooded my mind. *What type of animals live here? What if I get bitten by a poisonous spider? Or a snake? How long do I have to be here? Why aren't they hiding?* A dark shadow scared me out of my thoughts as, to my horror, I discovered they'd placed one of the larger rocks at the base of the tree trunk. *Wonderful. Now I'm in the dark too. And what if no one ever finds me?* I sat like this for a time, trying to calm down, a prayer falling from my lips.

I awoke, unaware that I had let myself fall asleep to begin with, the smooth interior of the tree firm against my back. My concept of time had completely vanished and as I peered out from behind the moss-covered rock, I could slightly discern hints of golden hues peeking through the trees, indicating sunset. We had arrived mid-morning, which began to worry me, because it should not have taken that long to retrieve a pendant. Even though Sébastien had mentioned the village had recently been occupied by Nordak, I couldn't imagine what was taking that long.

As soon as these thoughts began to cross my mind, a shout sounded out from the forest. The shout was not the victoriously triumphant shout I had been waiting to hear since I'd been placed in hiding. It was a disgruntled, pained shout that rang with a warning of danger. The ground began to tremble under the hooves of battle stallions while metallic clashing filled the previous silence of the forest. I trembled and pressed myself further back into the hollowed tree for the first time since I'd been thrown in. I was grateful that I was relatively hidden as the sounds grew closer to my hiding place.

Groans and cries of pain filled the air as the fighting seemed to progress, covering more and more ground in the forest, the overwhelming stench of iron seeping into every pore of the tree trunk. I knew Sébastien had placed his five most trusted men in charge of protecting me, but I was not exactly sure where they were at the moment, the fighting not yet in front of me based on the sounds of it. I grasped the leather handle of the dagger attached to my side, holding it in front of me, even as my body flattened itself further into the shadows.

Suddenly, the stone that had been covering my hiding spot was pushed away with a grunt. Geoffrey peered down at me, sweat dripping from his curls. He urged with a heaving voice, "Go! Run! As fast as you can. Run far away and don't stop running until you hear nothing behind you!"

I looked at him, no doubt with questions written across my face. "Sébastien specifically said not to leave here until he himself told me it was okay. Are you certain? I think staying here might be a better idea." As the last word left my mouth, an angry shout came rushing toward him.

I watched as he shifted in front of me to fight off the attacker. His brown fur trembled with rage, a furious snarl released from within him as he mauled the soldier in front of me, blood splattering across his fur and dripping down his fanged teeth. I pushed myself back against the other side of the trunk hard, shocked as I watched him dash off, leaping onto another enemy, blood matting his fur as yet another soldier went down.

A foreign noise sounded from further up the tree. Then another. A whistle followed by a thud, like arrows hitting their target on the tree trunk. One struck the edge of the hollow, and I checked, praying to see the black and crimson color of the Capetians, but no, I was met with dark blue-ish gray feathers at the tip. I understood now that Sébastien's directions hadn't necessarily covered terms of an all-out battle happening where I was hidden.

I peeked out of the hollowed trunk and bit my lip hard to keep the bile from rising up. The scent of blood and death filled my nose as grunts, snarls, and cries of pain reached my ears. Bodies littered the forest ground, mauled into pieces. I searched the area, trying to find where to go. I heard orders being shouted to men on both sides throughout the forest, clangs of metal meeting metal, and a voice yelling, "Run! Run NOW! Fast and hard! Don't stop!" And I went, fleeing for my life as adrenaline coursed through my body, urging me on.

I ran toward an area in the forest that seemed clear of fighting. I could hear shouts and horses galloping in the distance as I made my way through the thickets. I pushed myself, willing my legs to carry me far away from this scene, branches slapping at my face and arms, arrows whizzing through the trees. The trees began thinning as I continued sprinting, my lungs heaving as I prayed that nobody was following me. That I would make it to safety. Branches and brambles clawed at me as I pushed my way out of the deepest parts of the forest, distancing myself as much as possible from the sounds of battle.

At this moment, I wished more than anything to be back

home in Estaire, cooking in the kitchen with Mum or laughing at the bar with my sister, yet here I was, running for my life. There were just a few scrawny oaks in front of me now, before I cleared the forest, so I pushed on. My lungs protested my movements as I began to break free of the forest, my head searching my surroundings for shelter.

The fighting still sounded as loud as before, indicating there was no end in sight. My feet stumbled over a grass-covered rock, forcing me to regain focus and continue sprinting. I had just passed the last line of trees, breaking free of the forest when sharp pain seared through my upper arm, causing me to fall to my knees. Spots bled into my vision as I curled over, a shout screaming from my lips as warmth flowed down my arm, coating my skin in crimson.

Glancing back at my arm, I saw the dark blue-gray fletching of an arrow protruding from my right tricep. The pain had me on the verge of collapsing. I tried touching the arrow embedded deep in my arm, knowing from what Father taught me growing up that it was best to break the shaft, so it was shorter in length, but not remove it without help.

No sooner had I grabbed the arrow than I began to black out, stars dancing in my vision. I quickly let go, the excruciating pain dying to a raging throb as I felt warm blood cascade down my arm.

A sharp shout caught my attention as I saw men clothed in charcoal armor moving through the trees in my direction. I knew I had been spotted. Whimpering, I pushed myself up, the arrow shooting another round of pain down my arm at the jarring movement. I began to sprint once again for my life. The forest had ended at the base of a rocky hill with no shelter in sight, the start to the mountains we had ridden along. I felt exhaustion overtake me as I began to run up the hill, pushing my legs with each step, my lungs burning as I pushed past the pain, my life dependent on making it up.

The rocks began to blend, forming jagged graveled

terrain. I kept moving upward, gravel falling downhill underneath my boots, my feet digging in with each step. I could hear the sounds of those chasing me and knew I couldn't stop. They were hunting, and I was the prey. I felt my foothold slip before I could cling to anything and next I knew, I was down and sliding. The sharp edges of jagged rock took slices of my skin as I slid down the hill a ways, gravel burying itself in my body. My face began to sting as small cuts appeared; my outfit shredded as I slid down. A cry of pain escaped my mouth as the arrow protruding from my arm hit the side of a large rock. The wooden shaft snapped while ripping my skin, my fight or flight response the only thing keeping me alive.

A small shelf of rock caught my eye as I slid past, and I reached out as I fell, clinging to it for everything I was worth. My nails were shredded as my movement slowed. Relieved I had stopped falling, I took a second to catch my breath. My body felt as though it was on fire, every part of it screaming for me to stop, to just give up. My blood painted the side of the hill, seeping into the gravel stones. Even my muscles protested at the thought of running up the hill again. I let myself forget, for a split second, that I was being chased by Nordak soldiers, that I was running for my life. Just for a second.

A dark chuckle brought me to my senses, as a deep voice fell over me, "What do we have here?" Turning my head, my gaze was met with a muscular, burly soldier, towering over me, covered in dark armor; a large sword in his hand with crimson still dripping down the blade. I scrambled, attempting to get up, to run away again. If I could only get away, this horrifyingly terrible reality might seem less real.

Attempting to push myself up to run, my arm buckling under the weight, I heard motion from the beast of a soldier near me. I pulled my left arm behind me, before launching it forward, the dagger I had been carrying flying toward my attacker. An enraged roar filled the air as I met my target.

I began willing my feet to move uphill, gravel once again sliding under my feet as I trudged upward. I only made it a few steps forward this time. My head was ripped back by a sharp yank on my hair, which brought me to my knees. He'd caught up to me. He gripped the short, jagged edge of the gray-blue feathered arrow protruding from my upper arm and shoved me back into the mountainside. I slammed into the rocky terrain face first, pain lighting my body on fire and rendering me useless.

My vision went black around the edges as I landed on the razor-sharp gravel. His hand didn't loosen its hold on the arrow, but instead increased in pressure, causing me to shout out in pain. Glancing down the hill, I could see dots of dark blue climbing the hilly terrain, dots of black and red right behind them while stars danced across my eyes, before I blacked out in pain, praying for a swift death.

Chapter Fifteen

VERASTARR

A SHARP PAIN throbbing in my side woke me, my mind fogged as my eyes shifted while I scanned my surroundings. Flashbacks of the battle flooded through my mind as fear spiked deep within me. I could make out dark bricks around me, my eyes adjusting to the lack of light, a growing chill fueled by darkness setting in and I knew . . . I'd been captured.

A whimper fell from my lips as I struggled to push my body up, yet was unable to. My hands were tied roughly behind my back, the rope digging into my skin, cutting off any feeling in my hands. I looked down, trying to make out my injuries in the darkness. I could feel the piercing throb in my upper arm and a fresh pain radiating from my side, every muscle in my body protesting even the slightest movement.

My clothes were stained with dried blood. *My blood.* I forced myself not to vomit as I glanced down at my legs, noting the gashes and cuts from the mountainside. I knew I was in bad shape—the constant haze of pain threatening my vision told me that. Tears sprung from my eyes as I attempted to move once again, agony igniting in new areas from my efforts.

I made out a metal barricade on one side of the grimy

cell, the dull drip of water in the distance, a chill already sunken into my body. I forced myself to breathe, regulating each breath with a steady in and out, knowing that I couldn't let my fear catch fire and spread. I needed a focused and logical mind to get myself out of this. A haunting clang from further down the darkness rang through the hall, a flicker of light approaching as I tried to crawl to the shadows. My teeth gritted in pained determination. If I could just blend into the shadows—

"Good. You're awake," a dark voice said from the other side of the rusted metal bars, his figure dimly visible.

"What do you want with me?" I spat.

"Aren't you a feisty one?" He chuckled sinisterly. "Get her out. He will want to see her."

"Who? *Who* will want to see me?" I forced out through clenched teeth as the door scratched open.

"You'd best just shut up, girl," he spat as he turned around, leaving the two younger men towering in front of the entrance of the cell, a malicious glint in their eyes.

I turned to the two men in front of me. They couldn't be much younger than me, yet angry scars marred their skin, their hardened faces looking me over with wrathful disdain.

"This is a mistake," I pleaded with them, tears welling in my eyes and threatening to spill over as the one to my left yanked my hair, jerking my head upward as he spit down at me in disgust.

"Get up," he snarled. His fist yanked my hair again, and a cry filled the room as I struggled to my feet, wounds opening at the forced motion, my body begging to stay still.

"Where are you taking me?" I cried as his hand clenched around my injured upper arm, his thumb digging into the laceration. My body nearly buckled under the harsh grip, fresh blood cascading from the wound in my arm as black spots danced in my line of vision.

His grasp tightened as he began to move. "Shut it, whore, and get moving."

I missed a step as I was pulled forward, not trusting my body to keep me up. The pain raged and my mind numbed with each step I took toward an uncertain future. The grimy halls and poorly lit corridors were a blur as I walked up a final set of stairs and found myself outside, the night air filled with bawdy shouts and lewd jokes from men in gray armor.

I tried to force the pain out, numbing myself inside, breathing in and out, as I took in my surroundings, looking for any way out. I realized this must have been the village that Sébastien and his men stormed. Wooden buildings lined the sides and the two guards tugged me roughly into the small square in the center of the village.

A sob built inside me as I witnessed the massacre in front of my eyes. I could spot the shadowed outlines of wolvyn scattered on the ground. Wolvyn who had fought and given their lives for my pendant. The smell of burnt flesh filled the air coming from the large bonfire roaring in the center of the square, as it lapped viciously at its victims. Fur pelts hung to dry close to the flames, dark liquid dripping from the hides. Bile rose as I realized the Nordak were skinning the wolvyn, tossing their remains with no care or burial.

We came to an abrupt stop in front of one of the buildings, my mind struggling to shut out the pain as I was brutally shoved through the doorway, exhaustion causing me to stumble, unable to break my fall as I crashed to the rough floor. My shoulders screamed in agony as I tried to push myself upright, my hands still bound behind me.

"You're dismissed," a cold voice said from across the room. The two men who led me here fled from the entrance, shutting me in an unknown room. "Come," the voice spoke again.

My body was hardly able to obey the command as I slowly limped across the room toward the voice. I stopped by the fireplace, lifting my gaze to meet the man before me. I studied the towering male in the dim light of the room. Long blond hair fell from his shoulders in an unkempt fashion, one side in tight braids against his skull. Tattoos crept up the side of his face. A long silver scar, a stark contrast against his cheek, met harsh green eyes aimed maliciously toward me.

"What do you want with me?" I bit out as the fire crackled beside us.

A slap burned across my cheek; his hand retracted before I could process the movement. A fresh twinge of pain was added to the other reminders of my living hell.

"Silence," he said as he toyed with a curved knife in his hands. "I will do the talking. You will only answer when asked a question. Do I make myself clear?"

I nodded, my cheek stinging as I glared at him.

"Good. Now. Who gave you the artifact?"

I looked at him in shock, refusing to open my mouth. If they had discovered the pendant first, that meant they needed me alive to use it, which meant he couldn't kill me.

His chuckle snaked its way through the room over my body. "We might need you alive to harness the powers bonded to the pendant, but that doesn't mean I need you in one piece. I just need you breathing." He looked over at me with a pointed stare, his eyes glinting at the threat. "So, I would start speaking if I were you."

"I found it in a fountain back home," I lied with a forced smile. It's not as if he would know the truth. I laughed in my mind. He walked up to me then, his foreboding presence towering over my body, and he grinned down at me.

"Perhaps." He paused. "I will start with a little introduction for you. My name is Lux Eldritch. I come from a long line of Eldritch, all in service to the King of Nordak. Do you know why that might be?" he prompted.

"No," I spat, not giving a damn.

"I thought not. For generations, those of Eldritch blood

have possessed a special power. The ability to pry into the minds of others, to probe and search, to grab the answers withheld from us."

My blood froze, my mind racing as I tried to push any thoughts out, emptying my brain. "How?" I whispered.

He smiled as his cold hands forced my chin up, my gaze holding his. "Would you like to answer the question the easy way? Or will I need to break you first?"

I took a shaky breath, trying to control my memories and thoughts. "Not sure why that matters to you. It was years ago," I pushed out, not giving him what he wanted to know.

"I asked you who gave you the artifact," he snarled.

My body shook at the fury in his voice, my limbs struggling to hold my weight. Yet I remained silent.

"Very well." He growled. "Have it your way." An invisible blast hit my skull, crushing me to the ground as the pressure built. His jaded eyes watched me with a sinful grin as I cried out. My brain felt like it was being held by frozen talons. My eyes squeezed shut as I struggled to empty my brain and the clack of claws scraped against the inside of my head. The pressure built as my brain felt like it would shatter, my thoughts moving in slow motion as he pried his way inside my mind. Tears streamed down my face as my scream of unparalleled terror filled the room.

The pressure was relieved for a moment. "Perhaps you would like to try that again?"

I mumbled an answer through a sob as the pressure diminished. The talons were still there, tracing their points along my brain. A reminder and a threat of who dominated who.

"I was given the artifact in Verastarr years ago by an elderly lady," my lips forced out through a body-wrenching sob.

"When did you first use the power within the pendant?" he interrogated, his breath crawling over my skin, my body begging to break away from his hold on me.

My mouth opened, then closed. I hesitated. "Why do you want to know?"

"I believe I made it clear I would be doing the questioning tonight. Not you," he said, the fire crackling and popping as he waited. The claws sank further into my mind, forcing the information that he wanted out.

"When I was younger, it protected me in an attack," I forced out.

"*Hmmm.*" He pondered as I realized that the Nordak didn't have as much knowledge regarding the hidden artifacts as they seemed to. My realization was confirmed as he spoke again. "And now you harness the power at will?"

I remained silent, knowing this was an answer I didn't want them knowing. A question that I myself wasn't sure of the answer to. My mouth formed a tight, unyielding line, my gaze meeting his with fierce determination.

An increased pain built on my injured arm as Eldritch gripped it right below the cut. The blade of his curved knife pressed in on the reopened wound, widening the gap as he twisted in with venom. Tears slipped down my face as I held my ground, my arm gushing as I lost blood.

"I. Won't," I muttered through clenched teeth. "Tell. You. You can't break me." Searing pain radiated from my arm as his invisible talons gripped my mind in a vicious grip. His power tightened around my mind, my vision going dark around the edges as I willingly welcomed the darkness. The escape.

My eyes began to crack open, groggily fluttering. My heart sank as I realized I was back in the grimy, dimly lit cell. I must have been laid on the floor after I passed out from the pain. Straw scratched at my face, my body stiff and pain ridden, as a wave of despair sunk into claws into me, threatening to reach the very depths of my soul. I fought against it, knowing I couldn't give up. I couldn't give in. I wouldn't fail my sister; I would get us home. I had to.

I ripped the battered hem of my torn up shirt, taking the strip of fabric and wrapping it around my upper arm that still trickled slowly, tightening it to stop the flow. Pushing myself up, thankful my hands had been unbound, my breath came in stuttered gasps and heaves. I tried to stand, grabbing the bricks and digging my worn nails in to pull my weight up, blood caked on my skin as I leaned against the cool wall.

I took a step forward, then another, forcing myself to move, to let my muscles acclimate; aware that if I stayed still, my body would give in. I was too close to breaking, so I took another step, and then another, shutting out the pain, the fear, the emotions that all bubbled beneath the surface, threatening to rush out.

The creaking of a door drew my attention, the loud scraping of metal against the floors, and I froze, praying that they weren't here for me. The click of boots halted a few steps before my cell door, my body releasing a breath as I sagged to the floor in relief.

The day faded into nightfall, repeating itself over again, with no one coming to visit. I could feel the energy draining from my soul, slowly, with each passing day. My body weakened as I starved for food, my lips cracking from dehydration. My injuries began to set in. The gash on my arm burned as I felt a fever creeping its way through me, hazing my mind so I couldn't tell the passing of time. I felt myself drifting in and out of fitful episodes of sleep, my body fighting to heal itself as I laid in an unmoving heap on the cool floor.

"Harder, Cassandra," my father urged as I picked myself off the ground, my body aching from the last blow he had delivered. It went like this every morning as the sun rose over our house. I met with Father in our backyard, picking up a training weapon and sparring with him. The first

few weeks I had fallen and collected more bruises than I had ever imagined possible. Mum had refused to let me out of the house for a week after I walked back inside for breakfast one morning speckled black and blue. Each week was a new skill, a new weapon, or a new stance. And each week I built up my strength, my determination, my resilience, as I sparred.

Pushing myself off the grass, I circled Father, watching his every step, the placement of his foot as he approached me. I studied him like a hawk, until I could memorize the moment before a person struck, the split second it took for the opposition to pounce. Today, however, my guard had been off, my attention straying to the upcoming dance at school later that night. Father got another jab in; my ribs protested the blunt end of the sword in his hand. We had been on swords for four weeks already, my arms trembling each time I used the sword, as I slowly built muscle to wield it better. "You've got to push, Cassandra. Swing the blade with all you have," Father reprimanded as we circled, swing, duck, and block on repeat in my mind. *"Do you think your attacker will pause when you feel weak?"*

"No," I gritted out as I struck again, my arms shaking as he blocked my advance.

"No. They won't. A predator will stop for nothing once they spot their prey. You can't let them see weakness. You can't stop, you can't give in because the moment you do, you've lost it all."

I surprised my father then, spinning around as I got a jab in, knocking him off his feet. "Like that, Father?" I giggled.

"Yes, just like that, Cassandra. Just like that," he finished as Mum called us in for breakfast.

A key turning in the rusty lock that kept me trapped in this hell stirred me from a fevered dream. My mind struggled to separate reality from my dreams as a guard entered the cell. He grabbed my arm and harshly pulled me up. My limbs were unable to support my weight as we moved through the metal doorway. My mind drifted to my sister, praying she was safe and out of harm's way. I wondered what had happened to Sébastien and Dravyn. I wondered if they would come for me, if he would find me. We entered a new building, my mind unable to process where I was being hauled to. The moment my arms were released, I sank like a weight to the floor, my surroundings a blur as I struggled to hold myself up.

The boots in my line of vision prompted me to tilt my head, and a sigh heaved from within me as I recognized the familiar blond hair of my nightmare reincarnated, Lux Eldritch. He squatted down beside me, his calloused, blood-stained hand reaching out, forcing my gaze up to meet his gaze. "Perhaps our feisty little she-wolf would like to try this again?" he spat as he watched me struggle for each breath.

Fever chills coursed through my body as he looked at me. His left hand opened in front of me, a red item falling from its grasps, before swinging in the air in front of me. A feeble gasp slipped out as I recognized the item in his hand. It would seem that the Nordak had indeed found my pendant. "How do you harness the power from the pendant?" he prompted, his fingers tightening around my neck, crushing my windpipe.

"The necklace," I forced out, my voice rasping from a lack of water and oxygen as I attempted to answer. "I have to be wearing the necklace in order for it to work." I had no idea if that was remotely true. But after what King Adrastan had told me about me being able to use the magic in the necklace, I hoped that if I had it, I could heal the wound on my arm, otherwise I would die soon. This fever was rapidly dragging me under. And if I healed myself, I would better my chances of escaping this Void-damned hellhole.

"You don't truly believe we would let you have the neck-lace, do you?" Eldritch mocked as he stood up, pacing the floor in front of me. His boots thudded in time on the wooden floor. A harrowing tune, counting the moments until I faced death's doorstep.

"If you want to access the powers tied within that pendant. Then yes. I will have to wear the necklace," I sarcastically forced out.

His hand shot out, his grip tightening around my neck, bound to leave nasty bruises should I ever make it out. The circulation to my brain was abruptly cut off. I gasped for air like a floundering fish, his fingers crushing my throat, holding me off the floor by my throat alone. "Do not take that tone with me, girl. Do you understand?" he questioned as I glared at him, my body fighting for air. His fingers loosened to a warning squeeze. "Do. You. Understand?"

I nodded as he released me from his grasp, my body collapsing back onto the floor, my lungs screaming for air as I drew a gulp in. My hand shakily rose to massage my neck.

"Foolish girl to believe that we would allow you to wear that necklace. That we would grant *you* access to the power inside. You are nothing. You will never get a taste of the power within this pendant," he said, his eyes gleaming in admiration at the stone in his hand.

I looked at him, wondering what he thought they could do. If King Adrastan was correct when he told me the history, only I was able to release the magic from inside that necklace. If they didn't let me use it, I failed to understand how they thought they could harness the power inside.

A harsh knock on the door interrupted my fever-induced pondering. "Enter," Eldritch commanded as he walked further from me. Hushed tones met my ear as the men who entered chatted. Unable to make out the conversation, I remained immobile on the floor, my body sinking inside itself even as I refused to give in. The footsteps began to retreat as the commander's voice cut through the air, chasing them. "Inform the men to pack up. We move out at dawn."

"Yes, sir," they quickly replied, their footsteps scurrying further away from their fearsome commander.

"And take her back to her cell. She's no use to us until we

are in front of him," he bit out. A guard hurried toward my body, hauling me up and out of the room as my legs collapsed underneath me, refusing to work.

"Move it." A harsh command sounded from my left as I was shoved forward out into the rain. I stumbled and failed to catch myself, vaguely feeling my body go down. Muddy water seeped into my battered clothing as I tried pushing myself up, tears slipping down my dirt-stained cheeks. A hand yanked me up by the hair, my scalp protesting the abuse as I was hauled unceremoniously to my feet.

The night air chilled my dampened clothes, and shivers shaking through my body used up all my remaining energy. The door locked behind me as I collapsed to the floor of the cell, straw sticking to my shirt as my body gave up.

Darkness crept in as dry sobs racked through me, my father's words echoing in the depths of my mind, encouraging me to continue pushing, to keep fighting, to not become prey.

Yet I allowed the darkness creeping its way in to swallow me whole, washing away the pain surrounding me as it lulled me away. I could feel my soul drifting away from me. Even the bond on my wrist, unwanted as it was, was fading off into the abyss, tendrils of ink slowly seeping away. I gave in to the darkness as the fever took over, apologizing to Kateya that I wasn't strong enough.

A growl sounded through the darkness; the snarls called to me from the depths, reaching out. My body felt as though it was floating through the waves, being tossed around in tranquility. "Cass!" a voice called out through the waves. "Cassandra, please." I heard the voice more clearly this time. "Cassandra! I need you to wake up, *princesse*. We need to get moving."

"Go away," I muttered to the blackness of my mind. "The

nickname is annoying enough in real life," I whispered. I heard metal scraping in the distance, and urgent whispered tones. Even as my mind chased the empty void that called me, a promise of escape from the pain was within my grasp; all I had to do was grab hold.

The smell of spice and pine flooded my fading senses as I felt myself floating through the air, a scent of safety, of home. A firm pressure secured me against a muscle form, the tight grasp shaking me slightly from my stupor. Panic coursed through my system as I struggled feebly against the hold on me, unable to even thrash, much less protect myself from my captor.

"Cassandra, stop," a vaguely familiar voice sounded quietly from above me. "I need you to relax, *princesse*. We will get you out of here. But please, stop fighting me." My body responded to the soothing voice breaking through the darkness of my mind, relaxing in the grip that carried me.

"You came for me." My words came out in a cracked, distant voice I hardly recognized as my own, as tears streamed down my cheeks. "I wasn't sure if you would. But you . . . you came." Relief flooded my systems as I felt calloused fingers brush across my face, wiping away my tears as the voice of the one man I'd recognize anywhere spoke again.

"Of course I came for you. I will always come for you Cassandra. *Always*." My heart hummed, even as my mind began to darken around the edges and I retreated back to The Void calling my name.

I heard voices around me as movement jostled my battered form. "We need to get her out of here. She needs to get to the healer immediately."

A hard voice spoke above me, "Ry. Get her out of here

and to a healer and don't you dare lose her or it will be *your* life you forfeit. Kode and I will finish this."

I felt myself float through the air, another set of hands grasping my body tightly, but with gentleness. "Glad to see you, darling." I heard a voice whisper above me. My mind tried to grasp at straws of reality, wondering if I was truly being rescued, attempting to claw my way out of the darkness wrapped tightly around my fading soul.

"Necklace," I forced out, expending the diminished energy found in my body.

"We're already one step ahead of you, *princesse*. Hold on just a little bit longer, you're going to be okay. I promise you that." Sébastien's voice sounded out in rushed, pained tones. "Go, Ry. Get her out of here and get her to the healer first. She won't make it much longer in that shape."

The hold on my body shifted as a low rumble came from behind me. *"Embers and Ash,"* came the voice of one blood brother.

"Even The Void won't hold . . ." the far off voices of two other members of the Brotherhood called back with resolve.

I felt Ryker push off, then heard the fading voice of Kode growling, "Let's give them hell," as we left. The wind wrapped around my shivering body as we made our way from the Nordak camp, my mind drifting in and out of consciousness. I struggled to discern whether I was in a fever-induced dream back in the dingy cell or if I was truly escaping the grasp of that Nordak commander. Faint whispers sounded in the wind as we moved further away from the dark village that held me captive. "Stay with us, darling. Keep fighting the edge. Don't give in to The Void yet. I'm not sure if any of us will be able to handle Sébastien's wrath if you do."

Chapter Sixteen

VERASTARR

I BEGAN to come to my senses, my surroundings a blur as I attempted to recall everything that had occurred. My body was crying out in pain, stings and cuts on fire; my right arm throbbed, threatening to drag me right back under into the blessed abyss. Memories flooded back as consciousness barreled into me; the cold cell, Eldritch's furious face, soldiers shoving me around, tossing me carelessly back into my cell. In an instant, the memories of the past few days threatened to push me over the edge. I felt sturdy arms around my body and began to lash out, knowing I needed to escape, that I couldn't give in. *I couldn't give up.*

I kicked and twisted, blocking out the pain as I threw my arms out with all my force, trying to knock out whoever had captured me. My captor's hold tightened as panic began to rise within me.

"Cassandra! Cassandra!" A voice urgently repeated. "Cassandra. It's okay. I've got you now. It's over. Please stop fighting me, *princesse*, you're safe now," soothed the husky voice I began to recognize in my panicked, pain-addled mind.

"Sébastien?" I questioned feebly, as I slowly opened my eyes more, trying to turn to get a glimpse of him, to see if I was truly safe, not just hallucinating from the pain. I noticed the edge of a makeshift bed pallet by my feet, the tint of a darkened fabric overhead—similar to the tents the soldiers often slept in on travels. Icy blue eyes collided with mine, commanding my attention.

"I'm right here, Cassandra. Don't move, please. The healer will be back in shortly. Just stay still," Sébastien told me as my body began to relax into his muscled form. I felt his chest rumble as though he were talking to someone, but I was too far gone, retreating into the little pain-free bubble in my mind, the darkness urging me to retreat. "Cassandra," his voice rumbled beneath me. "Cassandra! Stay with me. I need you to stay awake; do you understand? Open those gorgeous eyes, *princesse*."

"I-I don't . . . I don't know if I can. It hurts, everything hurts. I-I'm so tired," I muttered, my voice drowsy and raw as I spoke. I felt Sébastien shift slightly, causing me to cry out as fresh pain coursed through my body. "No, please no. Everything hurts," I cried. As he grunted, I felt him shift before adjusting me again slightly, the feel of his body warm behind mine, his eyes holding mine in place as I rested my head on his shoulder, fighting off the chills lingering in my body.

"Capetian," a voice shouted outside of his tent.

"Enter," Sébastien replied as the tent opened and an elderly man shoved his way through. "Cassandra," he said, concern laced in his voice, "the healer is here now. Everything will be okay. I just need you to stay with us. Stay with me. Can you do that for me?"

I vividly remember what happened following the healer entering the tent. The healer approached, glanced over my body, inspecting the damage done with worry in his gaze. He knelt, lifting my right arm and causing me to release a hiss of pain as he poked and prodded near the arrow wound festering on my arm. Rapid words left the healer's mouth, aimed more toward Sébastien than me. I was far too weary to follow the conversation, only catching fragments of sentences: "No infection;" "hold down;" "sew."

I felt Sébastien shift before noticing that two other men had entered the tent.

"Darling." A familiar voice hovered in the air as a towering male with light colored hair passed through the tent entrance, a low growl rumbling from beneath me at the use of the nickname. "How nice of you to grace the land of the living once again. I did so appreciate the dead weight on my flight, but we can argue over that later." Ryker finished with a laugh, his eyes dancing with amusement.

"Good to see you alive again, Cass. Don't know what the Sébastien over here would have done if you didn't make it out of there in one piece." Kode chuckled in a friendly greeting as he ran his hand through his tousled black hair.

The three of them rotated me on Sébastien's makeshift bed, angling me so my right arm was accessible. I was unsure as to exactly what was happening, however, I felt a strong pressure on my ankles and lower back, as if I was being held down. My head jerked upward in concern.

"What do you think you're doing?" I demanded, my voice fading even as I spoke.

Sébastien sighed deeply from behind me, his solid form still supporting the majority of my weight. "Cassandra." He paused, noticeably. "Cassandra, I need you to listen to me. The healer must stitch up the wound on your arm. I won't lie to you, it is going to be painful, so I need you to try to focus on me. Understood?"

I tilted my head to glance at him through a daze. "You're telling me." I paused as I struggled to breathe, my ribs still painfully sore, whether from falling or being tossed around, I was unsure. "In a time full of magic and power, where people can shift to wolvyn, fly in the air, I think . . . and bind magic to a necklace. You have no solution for stitching up skin that isn't painful?"

Kode laughed in the background as Sébastien answered, "Unfortunately, no. It's believed that The God meant for even those with powers to be subjected to the effects of this realm. A reminder to us that we aren't immortal as He is. That we may still feel pain, sorrow, and loss and should cherish the life lines within our souls."

I glanced up at him. "Power with morals . . . how novel," I muttered as his chest rumbled, a soft smile appearing on his freckled lips.

"The healer is ready. I need you to stay awake, if possible. I know the pain is immense, but you've been teetering on the edge of The Void since we rescued you and I'm worried that if you slip again, it will be too much. Understand?"

I could hear the pain and anguish behind Sébastien's voice as he spoke to me.

"I'm not going to die on you now," I murmured as I met his gaze. "Not after I just escaped, at least."

A look of terror briefly flashed across Sébastien's face at my words, but his lip tilted up. "Just as long as you understand. I'm commanding you not to die on me."

"Yes." A chuckle slipped from my lips. "I understand, *Your Highness*. No dying on you," I answered as I looked at Sébastien, my mind slowly tuning out my surroundings. I saw Sébastien's lips moving, but no longer heard what he was saying.

I didn't know what to expect, until I saw a form of a thin needle in Sébastien's healer's hand, aimed toward me. I'd had stitches before when I was younger. Kateya and I had been playing around, climbing the trees in our backyard, and I had fallen, resulting in a gash in my knee that had required a few stitches. But that felt different. Mum and Father were there to comfort me. I had been taken to the hospital, they numbed my knee, and afterward we had gone as a family to get ice cream.

This experience, this was the complete opposite. Unrecognizable screams sounded from my lips as the needle was pushed through my flesh over and over again. Without completely realizing it, I began to attempt to retreat to the lingering darkness in my mind once again, hoping that it would provide some form of comfort. I screamed again. Tears streamed down my face.

I heard them talking, but couldn't process the words. My arm felt like it was on fire, like nothing I had ever felt before; a shock of burning pain seared through me relentlessly. I felt the comforting weight of being held down as that black tunnel began to swallow me up once again, and I let it. Retreating once again, letting it take away the pain.

I awoke slowly. My eyes shifted, trying to discern what had happened, where I was. A dull ache spread through me, and I rolled to my side ever so slightly. I was in a tent. Groaning from the effort, I pushed myself up into a sitting position, my head spinning from the not so sudden movement. I glanced down, shocked to find that I was wearing a lightweight crimson tunic. Grimacing, I noticed the small cuts and larger gashes that slowly began appearing on my skin as my eyes focused. I could tell that it was bad. Tilting my right arm, I attempted to look toward where the arrow had been, but all that was visible was a rough cloth bandage wrapped tightly around where I presumed the stitches were. I knew they would scar. Memories of Lux Eldritch carving his knife in the wound haunted my mind.

A deep groan escaped my lips as I pushed myself up

from where I had been sleeping. I knew I was in a bad condition. I knew I had been rescued. I even knew that I needed to focus on recovering. But even with all of that. I had to get answers.

What had happened?? Did they find the pendant? Did we get it back? Could I get it into my possession? I mean, it couldn't possibly be missing still, could it . . .

"You're awake," a voice said from the corner, my neck snapping in the direction as my eyes clashed with Kode's amber ones.

"It would appear so. What happened?"

"Oh. You know. Women. Can't quite deal with the pain from stitching, I guess. You blacked right out," he said with a chuckle.

"Ha. Ha," I retorted at his mocking. "Seriously though, Kode. What happened?"

"Sébastien sent word to us following the attack. Ry and I came to the rescue, of course. It took some planning, but we were able to break through the Nordak village border."

"Do you always answer each other's call for aid?" I questioned, interrupting him.

"Yes," Kodrayn answered. "It's part of our blood bond, our pact as a Brotherhood. We will always answer the call of another blood brother. We will place that call above our duties to our own lands, our own people."

"Always?" I prompted.

"Always," he confirmed. "That's why our pact holds true. *Embers and Ash, even The Void won't hold.*" He paused before continuing. "Not even death can keep us from answering a blood brother's call."

I nodded, realizing that their bond, their Brotherhood, held more weight than most in their land were likely aware of. An alliance that could alter the course of tides in a war. "What happened next?"

"Sébastien used his wolvyn form to hide in the shadows.

As you may or may not remember, once Sébastien found you, Ry flew you out while we went in search of Eldritch."

"Is he dead?" I questioned.

Kode looked at me, his face a mask as he spoke, "Cassandra, I do hope you realize, Sébastien will take the lives of any man who touches you—who brings you harm. Eldritch never stood a chance, not against him. And his journey to The Void was one of prolonged suffering for the state we found you in."

"How did you know where I was?" I questioned. "Did you find the necklace?"

He sighed. "Cass, there is a great deal you don't know and don't need to know. The Brotherhood has had eyes on that camp since they first captured the village."

"Why not take them out then?"

"Because," he said then sighed, rubbing his neck as he looked at me. "This emerging war is bigger than that. If we don't play our hand right, we won't make it through in one piece."

I nodded. "And the necklace?"

"Yes. We got that too," Kode responded as he pushed off the ground, walking out of the tent, the flap of fabric flowing in his wake.

Stumbling toward the tent entrance, wincing as I went, I pushed open the flap to go find Sébastien. That man owed me answers and a pendant. No sooner had I opened the flap and taken a few steps out into the afternoon air than a soldier on the other side proclaimed, "Miss?" shocked as could be. "What are you doing out here? That's no way for you to recover. You should go lay back down and rest."

Grimacing from the effort, I replied, "Well, I'm awake now. And I wish to speak to Sébastien. I have questions to which I would like answers."

"I'm afraid you can't do that, miss. Sébastien placed strict orders that you must remain here in his tent, recovering and protected," the soldier sternly replied, standing his ground, a little agitated that I was being so demanding.

"The Void-damned man and his need to command and protect is getting to be too much. I want to know where my pendant is, and I desperately want to get away from this terrible—" A strong hand clamped over my mouth before I could finish my sentence.

"Now, that's no way for you to be speaking to my men, is it now, Cassandra?" A voice snaked in my ear as I whirled to meet Sébastien, glaring at me with a gaze so cold, I'm sure it would have made all of East Engles freeze over. Before I could protest, I was lifted into his arms and carried back into the tent.

I deserved answers. Yes, I was aware that I was injured. But couldn't these men stop thinking about that for one minute and provide me answers? I know how to take care of myself, injured or not. Opening my mouth to speak, a furious Sébastien shot daggers at me, his blue eyes iced over as though daring me to do it. His look prompted me to remain silent, my mouth closing, just as it had opened, silently. He paced in front of me then, and if I thought a speaking Sébastien had been terrifying, a silent, broodingly pissed Sébastien was worse. I was certain of it.

Finally, he stopped pacing. He just stood off to the side of the tent, staring me down. Once again, I opened my mouth to speak, but his hand raised up. "No, Cassandra. Save it. I don't want to hear your excuses right now. I understand you want answers regarding your pendant. However, that is no way to talk to my men, or anyone in a position of authority over you, or charged with your protection."

Once again, I attempted to speak. How could he just ignore me and not let me voice my opinion? Trying to speak seemed to only make him angrier, though. He stalked up to me, his eyes storming with a hint of pain swirling deep within them. "Do you have any idea what it was like?" he demanded as pain laced his voice, his breath brushing over me. "Any idea how it felt to see you bloodied and bruised, tortured and on the brink of death when we found you? What it felt like to know that we might lose you? That *I* might lose you?"

I inhaled a breath as deep as my bruised lungs would allow. *Did he . . . ? No. It's not possible. Commander Sébastien Capetian certainly didn't have feelings for me, right? That's just the emotion of me on death's bed talking.*

"We have limited time to make our next move. I expect full cooperation from you. Need I remind you that your sister is still being *safely* protected at the Palace?"

I froze at the subtle threat regarding Kateya. "Cooperation for what?"

He sighed as he leaned against the column supporting the tent. "When we entered the town to retrieve the pendant, we found the Nordak had been expecting us. They were prepared for our arrival, and we were ambushed. Not only were you captured, but we also lost thirty wolvyn in the ambush."

A gasp fell from my lips. "I had no idea it was that many," I whispered, stunned at the amount even as my mind vaguely remembered the savage funeral they had received.

Sébastien grimaced as he continued, "We set up camp a distance from the village, sending patrols to scout the village. I knew that their attention to capturing you alive indicated they had discovered the location of the pendant and secured it before we arrived. The entire ambush was a trap, a way to lure you, the key, to their camp." I listened as he kept speaking. "The Brotherhood was called—"

I interrupted. "About that. Ryker can fly? How did no one tell me about this?"

Sébastien looked at me. "Your knowledge of the lands in our realm is shockingly scarce. How is it that you still know next to nothing regarding Vanaiyer?"

I scoffed. "Thanks. Your ability to share that same knowledge seems just as scarce, if you ask me."

"Fair enough. And yet, you hardly seem to know anything power-related or history related at all."

Sighing, I responded. "There was an attack. We now call it The Fall. It forced those with elemental magic and shifting powers into hiding if they hadn't already been sought out and murdered. No one speaks of magic anymore. No one uses it. Everyone lives in fear of mentioning it, even as a joke. Almost all knowledge or records of elemental magic and powers were burned or destroyed. I grew up in a land where no one used magic for anything. Ever. We all lived in fear daily of where the Seefers might strike next, even as we try to go on with our normal lives. At least here, in the past, you can level the playing field. You have a way to fight back against the Nordak," I said with a heavy sigh. "We don't. Especially those of us who were always mortal."

Sorrow crossed his face as he shook his head. "I'm sorry. When we sort this out, I will show you the books in the library on Vanaiyer, if you want to learn more."

I glanced at him, surprise flitting across my face at the kind gesture. "I would love that, thank you. So, reinforcements were called?"

"Yes. Ry and Kode aided the call and brought men. The combination of multiple powers strengthened our forces. We got word of their plans to depart for Nordak lands and knew we had to strike."

"And you safely got the pendant back?"

"Yes. The pendant has been secured. We brought along a magic assessor to analyze the powers held within the pendant." He grimaced as he finished his statement. "Unfortunately, he was less than helpful on the matter, as the magic contains a trace of primal power within it. Therefore, we head out tomorrow for the Barree Rise."

"The Barree Rise?" I prompted.

"The Barree Rise is a mountain range that spans the border of Verastarr and Avyon. Located deep within the range is the cave where we formed our brotherhood bond. It is there that we should find the answers we seek regarding the pendant."

"You expect us to find answers in an old cave?" I questioned.

"Yes. It's not just any cave. In this cave resides one of the oldest magic assessors in our realm. One of the assessors who assisted in the creation of the three artifacts. An Elder."

I stared at him then. "What makes you so sure that he will want to help us break the bond that releases the power?"

Sébastien looked at me, his eyes churning with a mix of emotions as he answered, "We have you. And you, *princesse*, whether you like it or not, are the beginning of the end of this coming war."

"And what if I don't want to be a part of this?"

Sorrow flitted across his eyes as he leaned in, his breath caressing me and sending heat to my center even as his voice sent chills of warning. "Unfortunately, you don't have a choice in the matter. No one has much of a choice in regard to this prophecy written long before our time." My eyes darted toward the tent entrance, thoughts of fleeing running through my mind. "And you know as well as I do that running from your destiny isn't an option. Whether you want to admit it or not, our paths were written in the stars before we were ever born." He looked at me with a mix of sadness and authority. "You may want to rest up. We leave in a few hours for the Rise."

I groaned, my heart heavy as I laid back down, knowing that I needed the rest to heal.

Chapter Seventeen

IT WAS STILL dark as we left. There was a smaller crowd of us heading toward the Barree Rise, the rest returned back toward the château. My bones ached as I rode. I glanced around at my traveling companions to see who joined us on our journey. Sébastien took up the lead. I recognized Kodrayn, Ryker, and Dravyn. I also noted Geoffrey, three wolvyn, and a few others I didn't recognize. I wondered what the determining factor had been in deciding who traveled with us to the mystery cave. Were they all sworn to secrecy? Did they have binding loyalties to the Brotherhood?

While my fever had disappeared, the pain in my arm and side lingered, and small cuts scattered across my skin remained; a constant reminder of what I had recently endured. Dravyn rode up to my side.

"Are you doing alright with everything?" Dravyn questioned, his voice laced with gentleness.

I paused briefly, reflecting on his question.

Was I doing alright? I honestly hadn't even stopped to think about that. Perhaps I knew, if I did, it would be too much. It would all be too much.

I nodded. "I'm doing as well as expected, I guess. It helps not to think about everything."

He regarded me, the early morning light glimmering across his face as the sun rose. "Fair enough. Sometimes, though, it helps to free your thoughts, too. Burying them deep within you will only cause them to fester and grow."

"Perhaps." I sighed. "But I'd rather not relive getting captured and kept in a grimy prison cell underground, now or ever."

We rode in silence for some time, and the landscape slowly changed as we traveled further west. I broke the silence an hour later. "What do you know about the powers from the different lands?"

"What do you want to know?" Dravyn answered with sincerity.

"Everything," I responded. "For example, does each land have different powers? How do the powers work? And why does everyone differentiate between shifting powers and elemental magic—doesn't everyone have both?"

"It's a good thing that we have plenty of time." He laughed softly and then paused to reflect. "Each land has a different shifting power. That way, no one person can have too much power, *even though that hasn't stopped rulers from trying to blend powers for centuries.*"

I listened intently to every word as he continued, "Five lands, each with a different power: wolvyn, vamprys, syrens, faeries, and gryffins. Only the rulers of the land and children they bear while in power will gain access to the power to shift at birth."

I stared at Dravyn in shock. "So, rulers of every land can shift?"

"Yes," he replied. "As you may have noticed, Verastarr is home to the wolvyn. They can shift into supernatural wolf form, and they often travel in packs. Ry, as you noticed, can fly, since he is a faerie, as is his family back in Reggeon. Kode is a vampry and—"

"I hope you're only sharing good things about me now," Kode joked as he sidled up next to us, his muscled frame towering over me even on horseback.

I looked at Kode. "We'll see. Dravyn was telling me about the different powers in the lands."

"Ah," he joked with Dravyn. "Well, carry on, teacher."

"As I was saying, before being interrupted"—he shot a look over at Kode, causing me to laugh at the friendship—"Vamprys, like Kode, have fangs, with the ability to draw blood from others—"

I interrupted then. "You have fangs? Like sharp pointy teeth *fangs*?" I questioned Kode with shock.

He threw me a dimpled smile then, his amber eyes flashing as two fangs peeked through his lips while I stared in awe.

"Would you both stop interrupting," Dravyn grumbled as we laughed. "And finally, gryffins are for the Nordak, shifting into a beast that's part lion, part eagle."

"And each ruler can give this power to others?" I inquired.

"Yes, but it's not quite the same. Because it is gifted, rather than a power they are born with, it cannot be passed down through the generations," he confirmed. "Rulers tend to only give power to those with loyal blood, and those gifted have to pledge to protect the gifting ruler's territory. If broken, the power vanishes immediately, and with it, the person who was gifted is destroyed."

My jaw dropped as he finished. "You're saying that if a person breaks that pledge, they die?"

"The pledge taken is serious," Kode clarified. "It's not a free gift. Those who accept the pledge understand there is a payment, so to speak. It all goes back to the fact that there is a balance required so that the power in the realm doesn't overtake all and destroy us in the process."

I stared at Kode, then looked over at Dravyn before questioning. "Emalyee told me you were from the East Engles. How can you shift to a wolvyn, then?"

I noticed Kode fall silent to my left as Dravyn's body tensed, his eyes distant.

"The East Engles, as you know, is a land of water and sea, beaches and salt air, and the syrens, of course. When I left the land, I could only stay hidden for so long before I was hunted for the powers I was born with. I pledged my loyalty to King Adrastan, giving up my syren abilities for wolvyn abilities." My eyes filled with sorrow for him as he continued. "While a great sacrifice, it preserved my life, and meant that I would no longer be hunted. I found a pack, a family."

"What about elemental magic?"

"Magic is more common. Others can be born with magic or develop it over time. Magic can range from healing magic to low level natural magic," Dravyn answered.

"Natural magic?"

"Fire, water, wind. In other words, magic which stems from the elements of nature," Dravyn replied.

"It's the rulers, though, those born with power coursing through their blood, that control the most powerful forms of magic. A magic that works together with their powers," Kode added.

"Like Sébastien," I prompted, eager to show I understood. "When he calls a dark mist up from the ground?"

"Precisely," Dravyn confirmed. "A magic like that is not just an elemental magic—it is larger, more controlling."

"Emalyee mentioned that things such as a blood bond require ancient magic. How does that tie into shifting powers and elemental magic?"

Both men fell silent then, glancing at the other before Kode answered. "It doesn't. Ancient, primal magic is rarely used anymore. The consequences are higher, the stakes greater, and the magic runs deeper."

"Why use it then?"

"Sometimes, the risks are necessary for a greater good," Kode concluded.

"The Elder we are visiting is one of the last two remaining magic assessors with ancient magic," Dravyn added.

"What happened to the other?" I asked, curiosity building.

"He was captured years ago by the Nordak King," Dravyn said.

"Why?"

"The king wished to merge powers," Dravyn shared. "Despite all the warnings, he sought a way to combine them. When his magic assessors failed to merge powers, he turned to the Elders. He captured the first one he encountered, forcing the others into hiding. He sought the magic to merge the powers between himself and a pureblood wolvyn."

"Was he successful?" I interrupted.

"Depends on what you define as success. Did he merge powers? No. But something new was created. A mix between a wolvyn and a gryffin." Kode snorted while Dravyn continued. "However, ancient magic has consequences. This new creature, while stronger, appeared sickly, with darkened fur missing in patches, taloned claws, and sharpened fangs, and was unable to shift to mortal form."

"You're not saying . . ." I looked between Dravyn and Kode as I swallowed.

Dravyn nodded in confirmation of my suspicion. "This was the creation of the Seefers, an uncontrollable species linked to the Nordak King."

I fell silent, thinking about the history of the creatures who had ravaged my home, attacked my family, killed our friends. The creature who left scars across my body and nightmares when I closed my eyes at night. A whistle came from up ahead, and my attention returned to focus on our journey as Dravyn and Kode left my side, heading toward the call.

We had been traveling west for five days. My thighs slowly grew used to the constant riding, and the gash on my arm was healing, although I pushed the knowledge that the stitches would need to come out to the back of my mind. The travels had been complication free, not a soul in sight as we approached the mountain range. The weather had begun to shift as we grew closer to the Barree Rise. The temperatures dropped, the sun disappearing from the sky, replaced with ominous gray clouds. I shivered, pulling my cloak tighter around my body as we approached the base of the mountain range.

My horse pulled to a stop as Sébastien and his men discussed the course we would be taking. I looked up at the mountain range; rocky peaks, barren of any life, were all I could see. A singular pathway wound through the range, hardly visible over the onslaught of snow. I noticed the white caps at the top of the mountains showing the further change in temperature we would be traveling through. I wondered how well the horses traveled through the mountains. Had someone carved paths on the sides of the slopes long ago?

A shout grabbed my attention. "We must make it to the tunnel by nightfall, otherwise we will be exposed to extreme elements. I don't need to remind anyone why this range is so barren. We stop for nothing. Push hard and best of luck," Sébastien voiced to the men traveling with us. I noticed a few men who had traveled with us dismount, tying up their horses before shifting into their wolvyn form.

I stared at the range in wonder, curious what was so unnatural about the mountains we were about to enter. Sébastien rode up to me, his dark hair mused from the wind. "You're still healing from the attack and your riding has improved some over the past weeks, but not nearly enough to take on the Rise," he started before I interrupted.

"Gee. Thanks. Way to simultaneously compliment and knock a girl down."

His gaze met mine, a set determination across his features. "You'll be riding with me. I won't risk you falling down the slope of a mountain because you can't control your mare, or withstand the effects of the Rise."

"What is so concerning about these mountains?" I asked.

Sébastien looked at me, his ice-blue eyes holding my gaze as he spoke. "There's a reason people don't often seek out the Elder. The Barree Rise is a place few seek to enter, surrounded by primal magic and wards to protect it. Those with power can withstand some of the supernatural effects. Even so, we have never made this journey without losing someone."

I stared at him in surprise, wondering why these men would willingly make this journey once, let alone multiple times. "Never?"

"Never." His voice held firm, a hint of sorrow in the tone.

"Why aren't you shifting into wolvyn form then?" I questioned as I glanced around us at most of the men who had shifted.

"Last I checked, being mortal, you don't have any magical abilities. Which would make you the most vulnerable in our group. So . . ." Sébastien paused. "I'll be riding with you. The Whisperers are hard enough to withstand in shifted form."

"Whisper—" I didn't even finish my sentence before Sébastien ordered those with us into formation.

I followed him over to his horse, trusting that if he told the truth, I would most likely be safest with him.

The winds whipped around the jagged peaks as we continued passing through the rise. My body shivered as the temperatures continued to plummet, snow flurries beginning to flitter past as we pushed on. I sank further into Sébastien, drawing on the warmth radiating from his body. Looking around, gray met my eye as far as I could see. The slopes were painted with a dark ink, and the clouds hovered low around us, my fingers itching to reach out and grasp them. A jolt from the horse set off the sounds of rocks falling below us, my body rigid as we continued.

"How much further is the tunnel we are headed toward?" I asked between chattering teeth.

"Not too much further," he replied, the tendrils of his breath warming my skin. "We will rest in the tunnel for the night and should reach the Elder by tomorrow evening." His arms shifted, pulling his cloak tighter around both of us, encasing us in warmth, as a flash of inked skin sent a reminder of the ink that had appeared on my own.

"Do you think that we will get an answer about making the bond disappear as well?" I questioned earnestly.

"It is possible. Bonding is an ancient magic. Primal magic tends to play by its own rules. There is a reason it has been banned from common use. It requires a balance in all manners, even answers. The Elder tends to provide answers when it intrigues him and when the balance allows."

I paused for a moment, soaking in what he had said. "Have you visited the Elder often?" I prompted, curious to learn more about the man who chose to live alone in the mountains.

"A few times, yes. Once for the Brotherhood. Another journey or two with my father, each journey just as dangerous as the one before. It matters not how many times you travel the Rise, the risk is ever present."

"Why risk it then? Are the answers the Elder provides truly worth the sacrifice? The lives lost?"

"Well . . ." He paused for just a moment. "Sometimes the risk of the journey is worth the answers." An eerie ringing filled the air as he spoke. A piercing ring, with the whispers of despair and hope singing along with it. A faint whispered pleading reached my ears; a weakened voice sounded as though it were crying out for help. "Cassandra, whatever happens, do not listen to what you hear. Do you understand me?" Sébastien voiced through gritted teeth, his arm forcing the air from my lungs as his grip around my middle tightened, holding me firm against him.

The voice grew, the hair on my body rising as I forced out, "What is that?"

The hardened edge in his voice threw me off as he spoke, "No one knows. Folklore says it's the sound of those lost to the search of the power craze. Those who brave these mountains for answers, only to lose themselves to the magic they seek, bound to roam the Barree in search of more. Always in search of more. They call to those on the same journey, luring them into their deaths. Another soul to search for eternity."

I took in a sharp breath at the thought as he finished. "We call them the Barree Whisperers."

I closed my eyes and buried my face into the side of his chest, breathing in the smell of spice and pine, letting it calm me as I shut out the noise around me, focusing instead on the steady heartbeat beneath my head. *Thump. Thump. Thump. Thump.* It relaxed my mind as the Whisperers carried on around me, their eerie song of longing piercing the air as the chill continued to set in around me.

"We're approaching the tunnel entrance." His warm voice rumbled next to me as I peeked out from beneath the cloak surrounding me. A slim gap, hidden off to the side of the slope, began to stand out, slightly darker than the remaining rock around us. I felt the instant chill surrounding me as Sébastien gracefully leapt down, assisting me off the horse as the men around me did the same.

I watched as the wolvyn approached the crevasse in the rock, the darkness swallowing them as they disappeared inside. The only sound filling the air was the faint whistle of the arctic wind as it passed by. A tussle of rust-red fur popped out a few moments later and then men began moving, leading the horses through as we walked inside the mountain.

I stopped a few steps in. Darkness shadowed the walls, dancing by the crack in the mountain wall. A match was lit, and a flicker of light came to life, casting a warm hue across the space. Letting my feet carry me across the stone, my eyes wandered over the inside of the mountain. The rough outside edges of the stone were a harsh contrast to the smooth feel of the interior against my fingertips. Stalactites hung overhead, the firelight dancing off the tips, casting a subtle design on the stone beneath my feet.

I drew in a breath at the sheer beauty found within a barren range of mountains. Glancing around, I noted the entrance formed a circular enclosure, two paths carved into the walls, the tunnels continuing to unknown depths. The ever-present chill cascaded along my body as I made my way back toward the center of the action. The men traveling with us started a fire as pallets were set up close to emerging warmth.

"That's not enough. I refuse to bring less than seven." Kode's voice sounded far away from the fire as I turned my attention toward the huddle of men, eavesdropping on their conversation.

"You know we can't bring that many. The Elder won't allow it," Sébastien retorted.

"Fine. But one of the four of us stays here."

A sigh sounded, then a collective pause. "I'll stay," Ry

volunteered. "I can't shift in the tunnels. Plus, if someone gets drawn in by the Whisperers and attempts to throw themselves off the Void-damned edge, I can catch them before they meet an untimely death."

The group nodded. "It's settled then," Sébastien decided. "The three of us and Cassandra."

Dravyn nodded as Kode grumbled, "At least put it on record that I recommended seven or more when this plan goes to shit."

"I'll write it in my diary tonight," Dravyn said with a chuckle as he clapped Kode on the shoulder and walked in my direction toward the fire.

Chapter Eighteen

VERASTARR

THE LITTLE CRACKLE and pop of the fire stirred me as I lay snuggled on a pallet on the cave floor. Warmth had continued to escape me throughout the night, my teeth chattering as I had slowly inched closer to the flames. I awoke a few feet from the fire; the dying embers glowed, their light fading across the stone.

As the remaining embers faded, I sat up, glancing around as the men around me began to rise, preparing for the next phase of the journey. Travel rations were passed around as the group huddled around the relit fire, discussing plans.

"You know the drill." Sébastien's voice traveled over the now roaring fire as it radiated warmth. "A small number will make the journey the remaining distance. The others will remain here, protecting the sole entrance to the tunnel system. No one enters, no one leaves until we return. Stay in your shifted forms as much as possible to fend off the unnatural beings on the Rise."

The supplies were divided amongst the men, and the four of us continuing through the tunnels, packed the necessary equipment and prepared to journey to the heart of the Barree. I stared at the entrance to the cave. My gaze switched rapidly between the outside realm and the tunnels leading to my unknown future.

"It's not as daunting as it appears," Sébastien said as he handed me a pack to carry.

"It is when whatever lies within those tunnels holds the answers to my entire future," I replied, my voice hoarse as I stared at the tunnels carved into the walls. "What do the symbols mean? The ones above each of the tunnels?" I prompted.

"They aren't words exactly. The symbols shift for each person who enters the cave. They depict what the person seeks and what the person unknowingly desires," Sébastien explained as he gave a once over on his pack a final time.

"How do you know which path to choose? They're just symbols." I was still a bit confused.

"You don't. You let your heart listen to the call and follow that course."

"What call? What happens when you travel in a group, like we are? How do you know who should choose?"

"It depends. When we came for the blood bond, we were all searching for the same thing, so we were called to the same tunnel. Some come with others and split, venturing into the tunnels alone."

I stared at the two tunnels side by side, wondering where each one led. "What if you choose wrong?"

"For some, you simply don't find what you're searching for. For others, you don't find your way out," he finished.

"Ready?" a voice asked from nearby the tunnels. Sébastien and I made our way over toward the others as they finished speaking with Ryker.

"Best of luck," Ry responded, clasping each of his brothers on the back before heading back toward the camp. I looked around at Sébastien, Dravyn, and Kode before staring at the tunnels in front of us.

"Well, *princesse*. Which way are we going?" Sébastien asked lightly, as though he were asking what I wanted to drink.

"Sorry, what?" I choked out. "Why would I know?"

"The pendant belongs to you," he answered, as if that explained everything. "It will tell you which way to go." He reached into his pocket and said, "Turn around."

I slowly turned around, as I felt him come up behind me, his nearness causing small shivers to rush along my skin. His arms circled in front of me, placing the lost pendant around my neck. His fingers brushed against the nape of my neck as he clasped the necklace into place.

"It's simple," he whispered, his breath playing alongside my neck. "Close your eyes and just listen."

My lashes fluttered as my eyes closed. My fingers grasped the familiar weight of the pendant against my skin once again, and I rested in the silence, listening to my heart. I felt Sébastien firmly behind me, the air dropping in temperature as I closed my fingers around the pendant, shutting out my surroundings. A feeling of warmth spread to my right, brushing along my arm as it wrapped itself up my right side and my eyes flew open.

"The right tunnel," I whispered in awe. The others grabbed the torches and made their way toward the entrance of the right tunnel, yet I remained. Frozen in place.

"What if I'm wrong?" I turned toward Sébastien, my mind second guessing itself.

"You felt something, didn't you?" he prompted.

"Yes?"

"Then you're not wrong. This tunnel is built around magic, and magic," he said as he gestured to the pendant, "calls to magic."

I nodded, accepting his answer as I took my first step into the unknown, onto the path that would give me—*us*—answers.

The chills faded as we ventured further into the tunnels, my skin warming as the temperature rose. A soft drip of water trickling down and the sound of our boots were the only noises heard. We walked in a single-file line, the tunnels closing in the further we traveled. The torch light flickered on the smoothly carved stone as we entered the heart of the range. Each time the tunnel split, I stood in front of the paths, searching for that feeling, the call of magic to magic.

"It's no wonder so many people don't make it out of these mountains," I muttered as I stood at yet another split in our journey. Once again, I waited to feel a call to one direction or the other. "The only way I feel the magic is through my pendant. I have no other power. Other mortals would be insane to venture into the tunnels."

Behind me, Kode chuckled slightly and Dravyn responded with a humorous remark as the warm feeling crawled up my skin once again. "We go left," I said as I began to walk into the darkness, the torches flickering behind me. My hand trailed along the stone as I followed the tunnel in, leading the way while praying we approached our destination soon.

A low whisper floated past with each step, growing slightly louder. "Do you hear that?" I hesitantly asked, glancing behind me, noting that Dravyn and Kode had already taken defensive positions.

"The whispers. They keep getting louder," I continued, the whispers growing in strength as I ventured further in. A sharp wind whipped through the tunnel, and soon after, an icy blast swirled around us carrying even more whispers, as our torch blew out with the force and engulfed us in darkness. The gust began to circle again, the whispers crying out for help as the wind grabbed onto us. I began to feel confused, torn as a snarl filled the air, ricocheting off the tunnel walls, the men traveling with me shouting as the whispers screamed.

"Run. Now. And don't listen," one of the guys shouted behind me. I didn't need to hear the command a second time, and I took off, pushing my feet as I sprinted. My boots hit the stone as I ran away, the thud of heavy boots and wind closing in behind me. My foot collided with something on the ground with a sickening crunch, sending me flying, just as a heavy weight collided into my skin, barreling me down into the stone. I crashed to the floor, a cracking noise surrounding me. Then a familiar feel of fur brushed my skin and above me, Sébastien towered in wolvyn form, snarling into the winds that were tormenting us. His form hovered above me, unwavering until the winds began to withdraw.

My breath came in heaving bursts as Dravyn approached, relighting the torch we had brought with us. As the spark flickered to life, a strangled scream left my throat. A scattered pile of yellowed, cracked bones mixed with fresh ones laid on the ground surrounding me, causing me to scramble away, my back pressed against the cold stone wall as I struggled to breathe.

"W-what was that?" I forced out between breaths, my voice wobbling slightly in fear.

"That," Kode answered as he rejoined the group, "was the reason I voted to bring more people along."

"The more precise answer," Sébastien took over as he dusted off his clothes back in his mortal form, "is that those were The Barree Whisperers."

"*Wait, what?*" I said on an exhale. "I thought they only existed *outside* the mountain?" I stared at him, still glued to the side of the tunnel, unmoving.

"These are the whispers of travelers lost in the tunnels. But only the whispers of travelers with unsure hearts. They are the pleas for help from those who ventured down these tunnels in search of their heart's desires with impure intentions. Lost amongst the tunnels, they fade into the walls, haunting those who enter after them."

"So, you're saying there are more of them?" I whispered as a chill shook through me right to my heart.

"Perhaps," Sébastien responded. "It is unknown how many Whisperers roam these tunnels in search of travelers. So, we should keep moving; best to not let them track us here."

Sébastien took a torch and reached his hand down to help me up. Grasping his hand tightly, I shakily stood up to follow, grimacing as I took in the remains of bones littering the tunnel floor more and more the deeper into the dark unknown we pressed.

We resumed walking in silence, not a word spoken by any of the three men. "Question." I broke the silence. "If the Barree Whisperers are winds, why are they so dangerous that we need to keep moving?"

"They get in your head," Dravyn said. "The whispers you hear are only the beginning. They latch on to your mind, filling your head with the perfect nightmare concocted just for you, driving you so insane the only outcome is death. The visions will feel as if it's a reality that can only be escaped through pain, torment, or the end of your existence."

"They're that powerful?"

"They're the forsaken souls of those driven to madness by the item they searched for," Kode said. "They haunt these tunnels, attempting to stop others from the answers they seek, just as they were stopped."

I looked at the three of them in turn. "And none of you thought to mention that to me when we started out?"

"Would it have made much of a difference?" Kode forced a chuckle.

"I would have been more prepared or alert," I hissed back. A warm burst of heat radiated from my necklace, and I cried out in surprise. My gasp filled the tunnel. Out of pure habit, my hand flew to my chest to grab the pendant. All three men turned toward me, concern stamped on their faces and weapons drawn.

"My necklace," I said as my voice filled with urgency. "It's growing hotter. The last time it did this, it brought Kat and me here."

"We must be close. The Elder can sense the ancient magic flowing through your pendant and is calling it to him," Sébastien replied as we came to a larger opening in the tunnels. "Which direction makes the necklace grow warmer?"

I turned in a circle slowly, feeling the temperature shift on the stone around my neck, walking and arranging my path as the stone grew hotter to the touch.

Pain began to radiate from my chest as I walked between scattered rock formations inside the opening. "I think I'm getting closer," I voiced, wincing in discomfort, the necklace beginning to burn slightly against my chest. My steps were careful as I followed the temperature changes, stepping over rocks and crevasses.

A stabbing flood of heat burst through the necklace, and a cry of pain filled the tunnel. I stepped over a rock; the ground began to rumble and split, causing me to stumble down. The shouts of Sébastien, Dravyn, and Kode fell behind as I stumbled down a slope, small pebbles and rocks scratching my skin.

Chapter Nineteen

VERASTARR

ANGRY VOICES WOKE ME UP. The throbbing in my head rendered me useless as I lay on the hard ground, wondering what had happened. My mind strove to clear the pounding in my skull as my hearing came into focus.

"You could have killed her. Was that a risk you truly felt necessary to take?" Sébastien's voice came through loud and clear, as did his harsh tones.

"No need for such dramatics," an elderly voice wheezed in. "All's well that ends well, *is it not?*"

My eyes cracked open and were met with a dimly lit cavern. Light seemed to simply illuminate the space, radiating from no source. An elderly man stood in the distance with Sébastien pacing in front of him, as Dravyn and Kode leaned against one wall, their arms crossed in obvious distrust. Three predators with murder in their eyes intently focused on an unconcerned, wrinkled, silver-haired man in front of me. The pounding in my head throbbed, the scratches on my skin beaded with droplets of blood as I shifted slightly.

"Ah, you're awake, dear," the elderly man said as his head snapped in my direction. I met deep purple eyes as I sat up, my fingers touching a slight gash on my head that slowly oozed crimson. "I believe we have much to discuss—you and I." He glided off through a door carved into the wall of the cavern.

Sébastien rushed to my side, offering his hand as I rose from the ground; blood rushed to my head with the effort and increased the throbbing. My breath hitched as his fingers lightly trailed the cut along my temple, ensuring that I was alright, "We'll see what he has to say," he whispered urgently, with an air of stern authority. "He may come off like a fragile elderly man. But he's a powerful magic assessor with the ability to wield primal magic and remain hidden from most for over a hundred years. He's not to be trusted."

I met Sébastien's gaze. "If he's not to be trusted, why are we here?"

"The Elder will give us the answers we seek. His word itself can be trusted. It's the methods taken to get those answers that can't be. One doesn't survive for over a hundred years without being deceptive. He works in deals and trades, all in exchange for answers. We must watch our words with him."

I nodded as we walked through the door the Elder had vanished through moments before, a low hum floating across the air as we entered. I took in the room we had stepped into. Glass jars lined shelves hollowed into the rock itself. A fireplace was carved into the stone, where blue flames danced in the air, then vanished. Two chairs sat beside the fireplace, a worn rug underfoot. A desk was off to one side, scattered with yellow-brown scrolls of paper. Books were stacked precariously on the desk, others formed an unorganized pile by one desk leg. The room was dimly lit on its own, just like the one we had just been in. The flames from the fireplace danced in shadows across the walls of the room.

The Elder looked up from a chair by the fire, his gaze shifting from me to Sébastien by my side. "Cassandra, come. Sit, my dear." He gestured to the seat across from him and then he looked at the man standing only a few feet from me. "She will return to you shortly, Sébastien. You can see yourself out now."

My gaze snapped from the Elder to Sébastien and back again, uncomfortable with the immediate dismissal. Sébastien's form tensed beside me, a familiar chill filling the space around me, black mist circling around us feet as he stared down the Elder.

"Put your magic away, *son*, and wait outside. It's of no use here; you would do well to remember that." His voice cut through the room, his eyes staring at Sébastien.

I watched as Sébastien took a menacing step forward, standing tall as he spoke. "I don't care what ancient magic flows through these mountains. Hurt her or fail to give her back in one piece and you will be wishing it was you who had been captured one hundred years ago." He turned stiffly, heading out the door.

I approached the chair he had indicated with uncertainty, studying him for a moment, the flames casting shadows across his wrinkled face. His deep purple eyes swirled with silver that matched his long hair as his gaze held mine. *Eyes that I had only seen one other time in my life . . . twelve years ago . . . the night before my family left Verastarr.*

"I've anticipated this day for many years, my dear," he said thoughtfully. "You have many questions, I presume?"

Swallowing, I nodded my head. "Yes. I'm hoping you have the answers I'm looking for, but first, why should I trust you?"

He chuckled lightly. "Cautious. I respect that, dear." His gaze met mine as he continued, "I was there that fateful day, years ago, when the three artifacts were created. The day they were sent to be scattered on winds around the realm. And I *knew* I would be here the day the winds brought those artifacts back and the war would begin. I, dear, am the power assessor who was tasked with guiding the path of those who destiny chose. I have nothing to gain, for my life begins to end as the three artifacts return to me."

I watched him. "I'm sorry. How could you have *known* you would still be alive? I was told that the artifacts were sent to be hidden; it doesn't seem like the rulers anticipated them being found for a very long time."

"They didn't. But all magic requires a balance. When the artifacts were sent on through time, an anchor was linked to ensure each artifact would make it back into the hands it was meant to find."

"It's not possible to know who the artifacts would make it to." I scoffed at his words. "You just sent them out into the realm—what did you expect?"

Light, raspy chuckles filled the room. "Well, of course we didn't know *who* they would go to. But we did know that they would reach people who meet certain qualifications. It's destiny, dear. You can't escape it."

"I don't intend to escape anything. I simply intend to use the pendant to bring my sister and me back home to our family."

"The necklace"—he gestured to it where it hung heavily on my neck—"doesn't work quite how you are hoping. It's not a magical lamp granting you wishes. It's a bond of power waiting to be released."

"What do you mean, waiting to be released?"

"When the artifacts were bound with the power of the four rulers," he began, "the magic used to send them through time created a seal. Only the individuals destined to find them would be able to open the seal, and then harness and embrace the power in the artifacts. By accepting their destinies, they would gain access to the power bound to the artifact."

My fingers picked nervously at the hem of my shirt. "What do you mean by accepting their destinies? And why can I not simply use the pendant to bring myself home? It brought me here; it should be able to bring me back."

The Elder sighed, his fingers combed the short-trimmed silver beard absently. "The artifact presents two options to the chosen individual. It's how the magic was cast. Call it a failsafe to ensure that only those selected could access the powers within. You can accept the power within the pendant by either accepting a destiny to help stop the power war brewing between the lands, or you can reject the power, and the pendant will transport you back to your home, scattering itself along the wind as it searches for another with similar characteristics."

"That seems simple enough. How does one make that decision to reject the power?"

"You must shatter the pendant at one of the sacred locations on a day when the moon is not visible." He paused, sorrow crossing his face as he looked at me. "I must warn you though, Cassandra." He pointed to my neck. "The artifact, if you choose to reject the powers within, will only send one person home."

My head snapped up, my eyes searching his as I processed what he had just said. "What do you mean by one person?" My voice rose an octave. "Tell me you're not serious! How is that even possible? It brought us both here."

"The power inside is meant to be bound to one person. Each artifact links to a separate individual, though all entwined, they are separate. If you chose to reject that power, it would send one person back. A balance. One brought—bonded through secrets and lies. One who could return."

"Sure. I've been told that part of the prophecy. *But it brought two.* So, it must return two. If The God is so focused on the balance of magic, then it will return us both."

Sighing, he continued, "The God created the realm and gifted us with magic and power. We are incapable of fighting against the balance. Here." He extended his hand. "Let me look at the necklace again. I can try to search within the bond to see."

I hesitated briefly, remembering what Sébastien had said about trusting him, but I thought it was worth the risk. I reached behind my neck, undoing the clasp as I handed the pendant over to him gently. His chilled fingers grazed mine as he took possession of the necklace. I watched as he rose and glided over to his desk, and heard the soft turning of pages with the occasional crackle-pop of the fire as he searched.

Finally, the pages stopped turning, and I watched as he lifted the pendant in front of him, holding it by the chain. It started swinging slightly on its own as he held it in the air, swaying back and forth. His lips began moving slightly, with no sound falling from them. The hum continued growing, the pendant slowly defying gravity, floating up as he released the chain from his grasp. The fire flickered to my side, the invisible dim lighting dipping darker before resuming its normal brightness as the pendant fell back with the force of gravity, his hand snaking out to catch the chain, swinging from side to side as it settled in his hold.

"What did you do?" I whispered as he re-approached, handing the pendant back to me.

"It's not possible," he replied simply.

"What do you mean, it's not possible?"

"I searched through the bonded power." He paused, then questioned, "Have you seen what power looks like when it's alive?"

"No. In my time, the power has disappeared. Those who held it were either hunted and killed or forced into hiding."

His eyes saddened as I spoke. "Living power, dear, has its own heartline. A line that can be found within each individual containing power. A storyline. A start when it first began flowing through its destined end." I nodded in understanding as he continued, "The line is solid for parts that are lived through, yet hazier in the future. I was able to search within the powered bonded to the artifact. Though you haven't accepted the power, the heartline is attached to you, the chosen owner of the artifact."

"How does that tell you it wouldn't be able to bring both my sister and me home?"

"The line begins with one, stretching across the space of power. A second line is entwined for a brief period, before continuing in a single span. It entwines once more, but the remaining line is a singular heartline."

I thought about his words, thinking of the two instances that the heartline was entwined as it hit me. "You said the line entwined at two points?"

"Yes."

"Were they both solid or hazed?"

A frown marred his face as he answered, "They were both solid. Instances of the past. The heartline doesn't indicate any further entwined moments, meaning that only one can travel through the void of time back to your present day."

I looked down as I thought. "But how would that even be —" I cut myself off, realizing the answer before I even began. The necklace had only utilized magic twice in my life, both times with Kateya there with me. A soft "oh" fell from my lips.

"The pendant has used its magic once before, hasn't it?" he prompted.

"Yes, when we were younger. It saved us from a Seefer attack at our home. The future is always uncertain; I don't understand why the power line couldn't be entwined again in the future."

"It's all a game of balance, dear. It must be balanced to evolve properly."

Tears welled in my eyes as I looked at him; his figure wobbled as they threatened to spill over. "There must be something else that can be done." My breath was shaking as I spoke. "Something? Anything at all. My sister and I need to be able to get home together."

"I'm afraid there's nothing that can be done."

I looked at him, angry tears rolling down my cheeks. "You're over a hundred years old and live in a mountain filled with banned primal magic. Yet you're saying *nothing* can be done?" I shouted at him in fury.

The ground beneath me shook, pebbles falling from cracks in the room as the Elder rose in front of me, his face a mask of anger. "Don't you dare raise your voice at me. You do not know what you're asking. Have you not encountered the Barree Whispers on your journey here? Been attacked by Seefers? Ancient magic comes at a deep cost, a cost that you do not wish to pay. Terrible things happen to people all the time, people who don't deserve it. The God always gives us choices in life. What do you plan to do with yours? The right choice is never the easiest, but you already know that, don't you?"

I sucked in a breath as I stared back at him. The pounding on the other side of the door alerted me that Sébastien and the others had felt the power displayed. "She's my sister. I won't have her trapped here forever. I won't do that to her."

The pounding continued as the Elder took his seat once again. "She doesn't have to remain here forever. As I said, power is a focus on balance. If you choose to reject the power bond within, it shall send you home, trapping your sister here for the remainder of her life in return to maintain the balance of power used."

"I won't do that to her," I interrupted. "She deserves more than that. She deserves to live."

"If, however, you choose to accept the power within the necklace, the power will accept you in turn. It should return your sister home, a restoration of balance in the release of the power. Again, that is the hope. The magic never should have brought two in the first place, so I can make no guarantee."

I looked at him with tear-stained cheeks. "It's me or my sister, isn't it?" I whispered back sadly. "It will keep one of us, no matter what I choose."

"A balance restored, yes."

I stood, pacing slowly as I attempted to steady my breathing. Panic threatened to overflow as I realized that it was either me or my sister. All this searching, hoping, and for what? It wouldn't bring both of us home. "We didn't ask for this, you know. Neither of us asked to be brought back in time. To be dragged into the middle of an impending war."

"No one asks for their destiny—it's a path given to us by The God. One we must each choose to embrace or not. And once you make that choice, you must live with it, make the most of the choice, and stand strong in your decision. I must ask, though. Is it truly so bad to remain here? I saw the forming of a wolvyn bond inked on your skin. Would love not be a reason to stay?"

"Love?" I laughed. "Love is what I have for my sister. My parents. My friends. All in the future. This band marks a moment of weakness. A moment of passion. Not love," I bit out.

"An unwanted bond then." He paused as he watched me pace, my boots digging into the rug with each step. "Consider this my token of goodwill, then. The ink in each band of the bond sets after a certain period. Roughly two weeks, occasionally a little longer, following its appearance on the skin. Yours appears to be rapidly running out of time before it's set."

My pacing stopped as I turned toward him. "What happens if it sets? It can still be broken, right?"

"Yes, Cassandra. It can still be broken. But like all magic—"

"Yes, I know. All magic requires a balance. What the hell is the balance for that, then?"

"The bonded ink remains—a lingering bond even once it's broken. A lingering connection to each other, even when the other has moved on."

"Well, of course." I laughed. "I'm beginning to learn that

nothing is quite as simple as it seems when it comes to your answers."

"Not all answers sought are answers the heart desires. You have much to think about, I imagine. We shall speak more tomorrow. If you follow that tunnel there, it will lead to a room for you to rest."

My gaze followed his gesture as a tunnel revealed itself along the side of the wall. "Thank you for your answers," I weakly replied as I walked in the direction of the tunnel. My mind reeled from the overload of information I had been given.

Chapter Twenty

VERASTARR

A TRICKLE of water tickled my ears as I entered the room, leaving the tunnel behind me. Staring down at my arms, a reflection of blue light coming down from the ceiling of the cave shimmered across my skin. Laying my back against the wall for support, I sank to the ground, feeling unexpected heat rising from the stones beneath me. Sitting against the wall with my knees raised, I hunched over and let the tears fall.

Sobs racked through me as the desolation rose. I couldn't believe it. I refused to accept it. I just wanted to wake up from this bad dream, to escape the nightmare of a situation I found myself in. I didn't know how long I sat there. The warm ground beneath me did nothing to stop the arctic dagger that had plunged into my chest, my veins running cold as my heart shattered.

I didn't want to choose. I shouldn't have to choose. Kateya and I both *deserved* to go home; neither of us asked to be wrapped up in this mess. And my sister, she had her whole life laid out for her still.

Hell, so did I. A life which seemed so far away right now. Friends who I hadn't thought about in weeks. My parents, who had to be worried sick for us. The tears continued, staining my cheeks, my body shaking as I let out my frustrations, my fears, and the overwhelming sorrow found in my heart.

At some point, the tears began to dry, my heart numbed as I sat motionless on the floor, time wasting away aimlessly. A warm hand on my shoulder startled me. I gazed up and met the icy blue eyes I'd grown so familiar with.

"Come with me." Sébastien stretched out his arm. I hesitated, staring at his extended hand in silence, before slowly reaching out, allowing him to pull me from my numbed state.

I let Sébastien pull me up and lead me through a maze of tunnels, the dimmed, blue light continuing to flicker across my skin. My mind was blank, void of feeling. He stopped short in a foggy room where a warm mist rested heavily on my skin. I nearly crashed into his unmoving form.

"Where are we?" I asked him as I looked around the space in surprise. It was an enclosed circular cave with various grooves and crevasses formed throughout the ground and walls. The ceiling was covered with the same deep blue luminescence as the other rooms I had entered, casting deep shadows and blue tones through the cave. A large willow tree grew out of the stone under the mountain, its branches stretching high as it filled the space. The hanging branches were an iridescent color shimmering on the water below as they swayed slightly. The willow sat beside a deep pool, steam wafting up from the silver-colored water.

"The Reflection Pool," he answered softly. "Or at least that's what we called it when we first found it."

"I find it hard to imagine five boys finding this and giving it such a romantic name like the Reflection Pool." A hint of a smile crossed my lips for the briefest of seconds.

"Yes, well, unfortunately, we let Kairon be in charge of naming this cave," Sébastien replied.

I walked over to the edge of the pool, my hand trailing along the smooth bark of the willow tree on the edge. The iridescent branches seemed to be reaching out toward me as I lowered myself down. I dipped my toes into the water, causing ripples. Leaning back against the tree, I lowered my legs into the water and enjoyed the warm heat surrounding my ankles, then my calves.

"Why did you bring me here?" I asked as Sébastien lowered himself beside me, his shoulder gently brushing against mine as he settled in.

"My father brought me to the Barree Rise when I was fifteen." His eyes misted as he remembered. "My mother had fallen ill after barely surviving a Seefer attack while she visited a neighboring village. My younger sister was mauled to death by a Seefer in the attack. She was only five years old." He paused for a moment, and I stopped breathing, sorrow building within me as I waited for him to continue. "My father was determined to do everything in his power to save my mother and bring my sister back. He couldn't accept the fate dealt to them." He shook his head.

"Including ancient magic?" I prompted.

"Yes." He sighed. "My father bartered with the Elder for quite some time. But I knew." His tone held remorse, sorrow as he spoke.

"I knew the moment we left the Palace that I wouldn't see my mother again." He looked down at his hands and then at me. "I watched my father plead for any magic or power that would help my mother survive and bring my sister back. He was driven to the brink of insanity from the grief. And the Elder, well, he offered the only thing he could. He cast a strand of ancient magic on my father, one to ease the grief he felt. Not just the grief, but the blame and guilt he carried after the attack."

I looked into Sébastien's eyes as he spoke. I understood that far-off look on his face. "I sat right here while my father spoke to the Elder. I sat here wondering how my father could have allowed my mother to go to the neighboring village that day. I resented him for allowing her to take my sister with her. He was the king, after all. He should have been more concerned for her safety." His voice rose in frustration. "He had to have known that the Seefers were a threat when he gave my mother permission to go."

He looked directly at me. "I had so much anger and hatred toward my father over their deaths. And as we left to head home, my hatred grew. I just couldn't understand how he could dare move on. Dare to escape the pain. The sorrow. The constant guilt—with magic. By the time we made it back to the Palace, my mother had passed on. And my father simply carried on as if nothing had changed. As if their deaths didn't matter in the least."

"I'm so sorry," I whispered, surprised at his confession.

"On my next journey here, I asked the Elder why he took away my father's pain," Sébastien admitted as he sat up tall, looking into the Reflection Pond. "The Elder responded it was because a strong ruler must lead with confidence and control. That a guilt-ridden ruler, one with emotions and sorrow. One who felt pain and admitted it, wouldn't be able to rule the land and remain in control."

"Your father's pain wasn't removed for his benefit, was it?"

He shook his head and laughed darkly. "No. No, it wasn't. I learned then that any choice, decision, or answer given on this damn mountain is for a bigger story, a future intent and *never* for personal gain." We sat in silence as he finished sharing, reflecting on the past. On what we had each gone through to get to this moment.

"I'm going to lose my sister," I whispered through the tears as I stared at the ripples in the water.

"I know," Sébastien replied slowly. "I'm sorry."

"This was never supposed to happen. I was supposed to get the pendant back and wish us back home, away from all of this," I admitted, gesturing to the cave surrounding. "There wasn't supposed to be a choice. It wasn't supposed to be one or the other going home."

"There's always a choice," Sébastien's voice flowed over me as I struggled to breathe through the pain rising inside. My feet swirled through the warm water before I spoke.

"It just doesn't mean there's always a good choice. I'm going to send her home." My voice wavered as I said it aloud for the first time. Tears fell, dropping into the pool below me, swallowed up by the silver liquid. "At least then I know she will be safe, back with our parents, her friends. She can have a normal life. The life she always wanted, even if I'm not there." I sighed. "I don't want her to know the truth yet. It's selfish, I know. But I want the last few days with my sister not to be filled with sadness. If she knows, she will try to change my mind. But there's no changing destiny, right?" I forced a chuckle. "A wise man once told me you can only embrace it."

He looked over at me, regarding me for a moment before he spoke. "Would it be so terrible to remain here, in this time?"

I held his gaze, unsure how to reply. "It's . . . It's not that it would be *so* terrible. It's just—" I paused. "It's just that I'm losing everything over a prophecy I never asked to be a part of. I'm losing my home, my family, my friends. My whole life."

"Lifes can be rebuilt. Homes remade," he said slowly as the water rippled beside us. "I know it's not what you want to hear. And nothing will make the choice you have to make any easier. But just know that if you choose to stay, you will always have a place in Verastarr."

"And what sort of life would that be?" I questioned him. "A life forced to be the answer to a prophecy written long before me. A life where you control what I do because of the power in the artifact. A life where—"

He cut me off then. "It can be whatever type of life you want, *princesse*."

I fell silent for a moment, reflecting on his words before I stood up and walked away from Sébastien, making my way toward the other side of the pool. I stopped by the ledge, pulling my shirt off and shimmying out of my leather pants, letting them fall to the floor as I stepped down the ledge. My eyes held Sébastien's as I let the warm water surround my skin. "Now, if you don't mind. I'm going to lie here for a while and try to forget everything."

"I think you misheard me, *princesse*," Sébastien said with a slight growl, his eyes flashing into slits, as his wolvyn side rose to the surface, tracking my every movement as my exposed figure waded deeper into the pool. "I said we called this the Reflection Pool. *Not* the Forgetting Pool."

"Well, right now," I said, as I lowered myself fully into the silver-touched water, "I *need* to forget. I need to forget about the pendant, about traveling back in time, about *you*. Because the alternative is remembering. And right now, I don't want to remember. I don't want to remember that when we make it back, I have to say goodbye to my sister forever. That I will have to stay here forever. That I will never see my family again. So, *Your Highness*, I plan to forget for a few moments," I said as I sank under the water. I felt warmth surround me like a hug as the water wrapped around me, bubbles drifting up as I slowly sank lower, the air escaping my lungs, before giving a kick and drifting up. I broke through the surface as I flipped and floated on my back, half submerged.

The water rippled unceremoniously over my exposed flesh, causing me to push up to avoid sinking under, treading water slightly as I refocused my gaze, locking onto the dark form wading toward me.

"What do you think you're doing?" I snapped as my body floated further away, heat flushing my chest from Sébastien's daunting presence. Black mist snaked up his naked torso, hugging his inked chest before expanding across the surface of the pool. Tendrils reached out, teasing my neck, causing shivers to course across my slick skin. His muscles rippled as the water collided with him, coating his skin while he approached. I watched as his eyes flashed between slits, his wolvyn side on the hunt. His abs contracted, shadows highlighting the deep lines of muscles as he struggled to keep his wolvyn form under control.

"If I recall correctly, you said you planned to just *forget* for a few moments, did you not?" His husky voice glided over to me, his movements still advancing.

"Alone," I retorted. "I planned to forget on my own." My back hit the warm stone, stopping my continual retreat as the slippery surface blocked me from putting any more distance between our bodies.

"*Well, princesse,*" he said with a slight growl, halting inches from my body, his breath warming my skin. "Your first mistake was not specifying that prior to removing every article of clothing in front of me."

I scoffed as he spoke, even as a slight heat began to build, betraying me. My body begged to be touched. To be his.

"And *your* first mistake was thinking you were invited to join me," I snapped and slowly drew my leg back slightly as his advance halted inches from my form. I waited, my gaze flickering up to his, watching for his next move. My breath slowed as mist began swirling around us, dancing across my shoulders as it closed us in. Sébastien towered over me, his eyes flashing as he stared down at me, desire written across his features.

"I don't recall *needing* permission to join," he retorted with a smirk as he leaned in, whispering into my ear. "After all, this is my land." His fingers snaked down my neck as he finished speaking, a slight chill remaining behind as his fingers lowered beneath the surface of the water.

My mind began to fog, the mist surrounding us like a cool embrace against the onslaught of heat roaring within me as Sébastien's fingers traced lower. I knew I shouldn't let him continue if we wanted to have a solid chance to break the forming bond. Only I struggled to find the words to stop him as his fingers traced circles across my thighs. Opening my mouth, I began to protest half-heartedly, only to be interrupted by Sébastien as his lips covered mine, trapping my words. The kiss was consuming and demanding, taking from me what I willingly gave while driving me to want more. To want more of him.

A moan fell from my lips as his tongue pushed into a deeper exploration, his fingers reaching my center, stroking circles to match the claiming pressure on my lips. He broke the kiss with a grin, my body missing the heat as he put the slightest amount of distance between us, his fingers slowing down, barely relieving the ache between my thighs.

"Don't think about protesting again, *princesse*. You want to forget what you've learned today. Fine," Sébastien growled. "You want to pretend this is all a bad nightmare. Go right ahead. But let me guarantee you this," he whispered against my lips, tilting my chin up to meet his narrowed gaze. "When I'm finished with you, there will be no forgetting me. Not in the past. The present. *Or* the future. I will forever be a part of you . . . of your memories." His fingers slid over my skin before tracing back down beneath the water's surface.

"How can you be so sure of that?" I half muttered in response, his fingers pausing at my question, and he pulled back, creating space between our bodies.

"How?" he asked, as he slowly looked at me, his fingers tracing up my thighs, drawing steady circles as his gaze captured mine; entrancing me. "Because——" his voice paused.

His fingers, rough against the softness of my thighs, distracted my thoughts as he pulled my body off the wall, and my legs wrapped around his trimmed waist, clinging to him. At his mercy, I let him guide me through the water, my mind hazy as tendrils of black mist surrounded us, a darkened chill that kissed my skin as his heated touch lit a flame within.

"I'll linger in the back of your mind." He nibbled against

my neck. "A constant presence, just as you have been in mine, since the very first moment we crossed paths."

Fingers traced up my center then, circling as he thrust a finger into me, my body tightening in response. The pressure began to build as tendrils of black mist danced above the water's surface, tracing across my bare skin. My fingernails dug into the cords of muscle in his back, my hips moving to match each thrust of his hand as water sloshed around us, coating our skin.

"Fuck," I moaned into his shoulder as he pushed me flat against the stone wall, shifting my weight. His fingers began to move in a steady motion, the slight tracing across my center causing me to arch into his solid form.

"Breathtaking," he muttered as his black mist swirled across my exposed breasts, sending heated chills through me as they heightened every sensation in my body. "You are stunningly . . . murderously . . . breathtaking like this."

My nails left half moons across his inked skin as the water sloshed around us while his fingers picked up tempo. My walls tightened as his firm build pinned me against him. "Sébastien," I cried out as my teeth bit into his shoulder, marking him. Laying a claim to him. "Oh fuck—" I cried out right before he withdrew his fingers. A whimpered groan of frustration left my pouted lips as I stared at him. "Why'd you stop?" I questioned, my mind fogged, my breath unsteady as I met the storm of uncertainty ragging within his eyes.

"I can't—I won't go any further . . . not yet. Not until you're certain. And if you keep that up any longer, *princesse*. I won't be able to control myself," he replied through gritted teeth, his breath slightly ragged, as he withdrew, the chilled air gaping between us.

"Certain of what?" I questioned in frustration, a silent plea in my voice for him to finish what he started.

"About your choice to remain here, in this time," Sébastien stated simply, as if that resolved my burning need.

I stared at him, shock and disbelief blending with desire across my face as he held my gaze, his eyes tracing over every inch of my skin with barely constrained resistance.

"Going any further, could strengthen the bond between us, making it near impossible to break easily," he continued. "And I don't plan to start something I won't finish. If we go any further . . . I plan to ruin you to the point that no other man would ever compare to me. You'll be *mine*, and mine alone," he said in response, a growl deep in his throat.

My breath caught in my throat at his words, at his promise of what would happen if I stayed . . . if I chose him.

"Have a good night, Cassandra." He turned his back toward me and exited the pool.

I closed my eyes, wondering what on Vanaiyer just happened between us. Taking a deep breath, I began willing away the thoughts and fears darting across my mind. I pushed away thoughts of never seeing my parents again. Of never seeing Aerilyn or our apartment. Of never going back to my job. Of having to say goodbye to my sister. Of the bond with Sébastien. I just floated. My mind was blank as I stared at the blue-speckled ceiling, wisps of the willow tree dancing as I floated by. Round and round I floated, letting the water drown my thoughts and emotions. I tried to embrace the peace by shutting the realm away for a few moments.

When I raised my head up to swim over to the ledge, I realized I was all alone, a smile forming across my face, grateful that Sébastien trusted me enough to leave me to myself. Pushing myself up the ledge, I climbed out of the pool. Silver droplets fell from my body as I threw my shirt back on.

I walked back toward the trunk of the willow tree and laid down, the stone warm on my back as I stared up at the iridescent branches hanging above me. They swayed slightly, lulling me to sleep with their peaceful dance, at ease in the land they grew in.

A noise woke me the next morning, as I stirred, my body protesting the stone underneath that I had used as a bed. I sat up, glancing around as I awoke, the memories from yesterday rushing back in a torrent as my mind came alive. I groaned slightly as I pushed off the ground, padding over to retrieve my pants and slip them on.

I left the cave, following the noise through the tunnels in search of the others. I began to wonder if I would ever find them when voices to the left of the tunnel split notified me of the direction. The early morning laughter mixed with the subtle clanking of dishes grew as I turned into the room, the faces of three shirtless men greeting me.

"You're awake. Finally," a cheery Dravyn said.

"Wondered where you ran off to yesterday," Kode said by way of greeting. Sébastien nodded his head in a good morning to me as I approached.

"Breakfast?" I inquired, looking between the three. "Did you leave me any food?" I leaned against the carved-out counter, swiping a slice of orange from the plate as I looked between the three as they laughed. "Well, mission accomplished, we have met with the Elder. So, are we leaving soon?"

"We have a few other things to discuss while we're here. We'll leave later this afternoon," Sébastien responded.

I nodded at his response as I took another slice of fruit, before turning on my heels and heading back in the direction I came from. I wandered the tunnels, attempting to retrace my steps from yesterday, back to the study I had been in.

"Looking for something?" A raspy voice carried through the dimmed tunnels ahead of me.

"Actually, I was hoping you might have some more information on my pendant." I approached the Elder. His eyes watched me as though trying to see into my soul.

"Ah. Unfortunately, I do not have much on that," he replied with a sigh.

"I thought you were there when it was created? Shouldn't that give you some sort of special insight into it?"

"My dear, it doesn't work like that. All magic paves its own course. No one knows how the powers in the artifact will work. Will they blend together? Will they war against each other? Will only one be dominant? We do not know these things for sure, we can only speculate," he said, resuming his walk through the tunnels, and I followed him.

"There's nothing you can give me? I'm just supposed to blindly accept whatever is inside of this pendant?" I asked in frustration, gesturing to the pendant resting around my neck.

"I wish I could be of more assistance, my dear," he answered as the flick of a knob opened the door in front of us, leading into the same room I had been searching for. "I do, however, have something else you may borrow which may be of assistance to you."

I followed him inside the study, the door closing behind me with a thud as I padded in and watched him rummage through the clutter of books around his desk.

"Ah, here it is," he said proudly as he picked up a worn, crimson-colored book with black edges and handed it to me.

"*A History of Vanaiyer Sacred Bonds*?" I read the title out. "How will this help me?"

"The book in your hands is one of the oldest archives, documenting the process of bonding, mates, and fated bonds in our realm. It may be of use to you considering your unique circumstance as a mortal forming a bond with a wolvyn," he replied with a slight gesture to the lingering inked ring floating on the surface of my wrist. A sharp knock drew my attention, and I looked up from the book.

"Off you go." He showed me to the door. "It appears my services are once again needed."

The door opened to reveal Sébastien standing on the

other side, a tight expression on his face. His glance strayed from me, to the Elder, then back again. "You agreed on no bargains. I will hold you to that," Sébastien growled. His words directed to the Elder as his gaze held mine. Pushing past Sébastien, I muttered thanks for the book, wandering off to begin reading.

I settled down beside the willow, the calming ripples of the pool relaxing me as I stared at the book held between my hands, wondering if I truly wanted to know what lay inside. I opened the pages, my eyes scanning over the text as I immersed myself in the content, absorbing all the information I could.

"Find anything interesting?" Dravyn prompted as he approached me from the entrance of the cave.

"You'd be surprised," I responded. "I've never been told any of this information on bonding before, or mates. It doesn't exist back home. I'm honestly shocked by the amount of information that has just disappeared after The Fall."

"Bonds are sacred, especially wolvyn bonds. They form a unique connection, like no other. It's no wonder the Nordak sought to wipe out all those with powers and bonds."

"Why are wolvyn bonds more unique than the others? I haven't read that far, I guess." I laid my head against the smooth bark of the tree, looking up at Dravyn.

"Ah." He lowered himself to the ground, lounging in front of me. "In wolvyn bonds, a special connection is formed following the final phase of the bond. One that allows communication with the other."

"You're not serious, are you?" I asked, giving him a pointed look. "I can already communicate with Sébastien, granted it doesn't often go well." My thoughts drifted back to last night, as he had sat with me sharing about his childhood. "I'm not seeing how that's so special."

"Would you just let me finish without interrupting?" he

teased with a laugh and gave his best pouty face. "Just once, for me."

"Fine, fine. Do go on," I mocked as I tossed a small willow branch that was laying by my feet in Dravyn's direction.

"As I was saying, the communication is internal. When two wolvyn bond, the bond blends with the heartlines connecting them and they can share thoughts with each other."

Intrigued, I questioned, "How is that different from the pack bond?"

"So much to learn," he replied with a *tsk*. "The pack bond is one all wolvyn share—a united call. If Sébastien were to make a call, all wolvyn would feel it and respond, but the bond the two of you have, if it progresses, would allow you to communicate thoughts to each other without speaking."

"Fuck no." I sat up, staring at Dravyn as he laughed. "I don't need him to have the ability to hear my thoughts."

"Give it time; it grows on you. Look at Emalyee and I."

"What about you two?"

"Well, I have been gone for nearly two weeks. Yet I can still tell her that I'm safe; I can pass on messages that need to be relayed in a quick manner."

"That's how you called for help so quickly, isn't it? When we were in the village. You were able to tell Emalyee to get Kode and Ry, weren't you?"

"And she's learning," Dravyn teased. Approaching footsteps drew our attention as Kode popped his head through the door.

"We're heading out, and we got lucky he's in a good mood. He said he would stop the tunnels from shifting."

"I'm sorry, what?"

Both of them stared at me in silent shock before Kode spoke up. "Please tell me you realized the tunnels were shifting as we traveled through them."

"Is this the reaction you expect from someone who knows

something?" I replied sarcastically. "What do you mean, the tunnels *move?*"

"It's a magical, abandoned mountain range. We nearly froze to death. We were chased by whispering spirits of lost souls. And yet, the fact that the tunnels shift shocks you?" Dravyn responded this time.

I glared at both of them slightly before muttering, "Well, yes. I didn't expect that, okay."

We stood at the entrance to the cave that I had tumbled into yesterday. Sébastien finished his conversation with the Elder off to the side as Kode and Dravyn began climbing back up the slope.

"It was a pleasure to meet you, my dear." The Elder walked up to me as Sébastien headed to the base of the slope. "You will do well to remember that all power comes with a balance, especially when it comes to yours. A unique position to be in, use that position well."

I nodded and took in his appearance one last time as I thanked him for the answers he had given me before walking over to Sébastien, climbing up the slope, and back into the tunnels.

Chapter Twenty-One

VERASTARR

THE ELDER HAD REMAINED true to his word. The tunnels formed one singular path back toward the entrance, where the remainder of our group was camped out. I couldn't help but wonder as we made our way back what our original plan had been once we left the Elder. Would my necklace have led us out if we were no longer seeking the Elder? Had they just planned to wander through the tunnels until we eventually made our way back? My heart felt hollow as we worked our way closer to the outside. Each step forward I made was one step closer to saying goodbye to Kateya. One step closer which every bone in my body begged me not to take.

The journey back took hardly over an hour and before I knew it, I could hear the wind whistling its way through the outer cracks of the Barree Rise. I knew the journey back to the château was bound to be exhausting, but I was grateful to be out of the heart of the Barree Rise, even as the chilled air bit into my skin once again.

As we entered the outer shelter inside the peak, Sébastien, Kode, and Dravyn split off, speaking with others who had made the journey with us, before the three of them and Ry grouped off. I heard their hushed, yet urgent tones as they spoke and argued with each other while I stood by the cackling fire, unsure of what I should be doing at the moment. Eventually, I sat myself down, inching closer to the fire to draw any warmth possible, my teeth already chattering as I shook, unprepared for the gusty breezes making their way inside the mountain ledge.

We prepared to head out the next morning, although I was still unsure of whether we were going directly to the Palace or if we would stop at the château first. I heard the signs of Sébastien's men packing up the camp as I laid on the stone ground, shivering in place, the dying embers of the fire failing to push any heat in my direction.

Pushing off the ground, I began to get dressed, adding the few spare layers I could find in any attempt to stay warm when we exited the cave. As we brought the horses outside with the last remains of our supplies, I took a deep breath, telling myself not to let the cold get to me as I stepped out into the arctic weather. Snow flurries whipped across my lashes as the forces of nature brewed around us.

"What a lovely day for a ride," Kode joked, the humor fading as we were bombarded with a strong gust of wind, the horses growing restless as the gust urged them closer to the edge.

"Are we sure this is the best idea?" I was concerned about the gray clouds overhead, which were traveling with shocking speed.

"We don't have much of a choice," Sébastien answered from behind me. "We can't afford to stay on the Barree much longer; we're running out of food, and we are more of a target on our way down."

"More of a target?" I prompted.

"On our way to the Elder, the Barree Whisperers wanted to distract us from our journey. Now that we have our answers, they will simply be vengeful."

"What exactly do you mean when you say they will be vengeful?"

He glanced at me as we walked over to the horses. "Very few make it this far through the Rise, much less get the answers they are searching for. The Whisperers tend to grow resentful and full of hatred toward those who found what they never could."

"Vengeful how?"

"Death. They seek death," Dravyn said as he looked up from securing his saddle.

"They will try to kill anyone who exits the Rise; they don't want anyone to leave with hope, since they themselves couldn't find it," Sébastien added.

"Yet you continue to make the journey?" I wondered if they all had a death wish.

"You can't let the fear of death dictate how you live," Sébastien told me as he helped me up onto the horse before he slid up behind me.

The men began to head down the winding trail as snow flurries cut painfully into our faces, my lips numbed as icy gusts threatened to push us over the narrow ledge. My body remained pressed tightly into Sébastien's, the heat between us barely enough to stop the chattering of my teeth as we trudged along. The only sounds came from the howling of the wind mixing with the shivering of the group.

We traveled like this in silence for a few hours. I mulled over the news from the past day, the realization that I would be sending my sister off, the impending war brewing on the horizon, and the knowledge that my life had been forever changed. As the horse carefully made its way down, the snow caked on my eyelashes, the cold wind freezing my hair, and I mourned the loss of my parents who I would never see again. My career that had only just started, but was everything I had worked for. My friendships, my home, modern appliances. My mind processed that I would never turn on a TV show to binge watch again. I would never walk into a coffee shop or go to the mall. And my sister, who I would have to send home, whose life would forever be altered, wouldn't be able to share with anyone what had happened these past few weeks without endangering herself under the Nordak control due to our apparent use of magic.

A shout sounded from ahead as we were halfway down, causing everyone to stop in their tracks on high alert. I felt a familiar eerie silence creeping past us and watched as the men around me began shifting into wolvyn. Sébastien swiftly leapt down from behind me, a blast of cool air hitting my back as he grabbed me.

"Get down and stay silent. Cover your ears and don't make any sudden movements. Do you understand?" he whispered sternly as I curled low on the ground, nodding in response as icy snow bit into my cheek. My hands pressed tightly against my head, muting the sounds of the wind howling in the distance. Sébastien shifted. His towering wolvyn form stood in front of me, his black and gray fur shaking slightly, teeth bared as his eyes traced the path around us.

I glanced around, noticing the wolvyn traveling with us had shifted closer toward Sébastien in a tight formation as they held their ground against an invisible threat. I heard the faint whispers growing louder as they approached, the noise bleeding through my hands calling to me even as I tried to block out the tune. Sébastien's snarls mixed with the Whisperers', yet they prevailed.

A low moaning came first, heightening in volume before passing over us. "Cassandra." I faintly heard my name being called. "Cassandra!" The voice rang out more clearly, a voice I recognized. But it wasn't possible, because Kateya wasn't here, right? "Cass, help me, please."

I pushed up from the ground slightly as I opened my eyes, my gaze searching the path as my sister's pleas filled the air. I saw the others around me. Some glancing around frantically, others sobbing or screaming, a slew of chaos scattered across the sides of the Rise as the whispers filled the thin air. Sébastien snarled toward his men, struggling to get them under control as the Whisperers ran rampant.

"Cass, please. I tried to follow you to get the pendant, but I got lost. Help me, please," the voice sobbed through the air in front of me. I started to stand, to search the path to ensure my sister wasn't here. Because she couldn't be, or could she? *Were the Whisperers getting to me?*

Her sobs flooded through the chilled air as I stood up, taking a step forward and another. The snow soaked my clothing, freezing me to the bone as the terrified voice of my sister drew me in.

"Cass," the voice whispered as I approached the side of the mountain, snow tumbling down the ledge as I peered below for my sister, whose screamed sobs were all I could hear. Just as I nearly confirmed I was going crazy, that Kateya couldn't possibly be here with me, an icy blast blew into me, my balance toppled as I teetered on the ledge of the slope, snow cascaded down below me, my footing slipped on the icy slope as a scream fell from my lips.

A dark form collided into my side, knocking the wind from me as I flew with force away from the edge, landing roughly in the snow. My head snapped up in a daze as I turned in horror to see Sébastien clawing frantically where I had just been. His hind legs were hanging, his front paws grasping for traction against the icy terrain. "Sébastien!" came a strangled scream that was lost in the wind as I tried to move to help him.

The winds continued blasting in full force around us, whipping us around with each gust, and my eyes stung as snow blinded me. My hands grasped for him as his claws slipped, his wolvyn form flailing over the edge, swallowed by the snow storm. Time seemed to slow, to pause briefly as his wolvyn form hovered in the air, before continuing his fall.

Another scream fled my lips as I looked around in the remnants of chaos from the Whisperers for help, a plea repeatedly falling off my lips to those too far from me. A small part of me broke as I watched his shadowed form fall out of view, my voice hoarse as I screamed by the edge of the mountain, my heart hurting as I realized what he had done. That he was lost forever, that his soul, like those before him, would forever wander these mountains. Haunting those who came ahead.

A searing pain tore through my right wrist as two more forms launched themselves over the edge of the Rise, their bodies hidden in the snow. I felt myself collapse into the snowbank, chills soaking into me as pain flooded my senses.

Heavy tears rolled from my eyes as I thought about Sébastien pushing me out of the way, saving me, even though it cost him everything. A sorrow I hadn't expected to feel for him coursed through me, even as a part of me wondered why he chose to save me. Why he would sacrifice himself for me?

"Cassandra." Dravyn's voice broke through the pain as he grasped my shoulders, shaking me. "What happened? Are you hurt?" Concern flooded his voice as he held me up. I could see the remaining soldiers rushing around, gathering the scattered horses, shouts and commands flooding through the air as chaos ensued.

My gaze met his as I responded in sobs, "Sébastien"—*sob*—"fell over"—*sob*—"saving me"—*sob*. "He's gone. It's all my fault."

Dravyn sighed as he knelt in the snow in front of me. "I know, Cass. We know. He sent out a pack call as he slid. Ryker and one other faerie took off over the edge right after he fell over. They're searching for him now."

"Searching for him? Didn't you hear the part where I said he fell? I don't see how they could find him in a snowstorm this intense with the Whisperers still here," I cried through blurry eyes and sobbing breaths. My heart felt numb, empty as

I replayed the scene of him falling over the edge over and over again in my mind.

"They'll do their best to find him." He sighed, a note of worry in his tone.

"Why aren't you more concerned about this?" I half shouted at him, still in shock. "Sébastien *fell* . . . over the edge of a Void-damned mountain."

"Cassandra," Dravyn replied, a bite in his tongue I hadn't heard from him before. "I need you to listen to me. We are doing all we can to find him right now. We all knew the cost of this trip. *Sébastien* knew the cost." Dravyn shifted his focus and gestured toward my wrist that I had been holding due to the pain. "What happened?"

"I'm not sure," I responded as I looked from my arm to him. "A searing pain hit my wrist as Sébastien fell. The only other time I felt that was when the bond formed." I stopped in my tracks as I looked back to my arm, trying to push the layers up. "Does the bond vanish when a wolvyn dies?" I questioned.

"Each bond is different, it's hard to say. Some vanish, others have had their inkings long after their mate passes on."

I stared at my arm after pushing up the layers, goose-bumps forming as my bare skin was exposed to the elements. Another black line, identical to the first, was imprinted on my wrist slightly higher up. "What?" I voiced aloud in shock.

"He triggered another phase of the bond as he fell," Dravyn took in my wrist and the look of confusion on my face as he stared at the second inked line drifting across my skin.

"It appears so," I said and let out a shaky breath, my eyes glued to the newest inking on my skin. Dravyn stood up in front of me as I continued to assess the ink decorating my arm, tears still slowly marring my cheeks.

"Round everything up," Dravyn's clear command cut through the chaos and unease of the scattered group. "We need to get moving. We can't stay still much longer, or the

Whisperers will be back. Let's go. *Now*." His stern voice sent the men spinning into action, not giving them time to process the madness that had occurred. Not giving any of us time to process that we were missing at least three men. That a prince of Verastarr had just thrown himself over the side of a mountain to save me.

I stood up, my legs shaky as I stayed away from the ledge. Dravyn assisted me onto his horse before the now smaller group began to move down the Barree Rise once again.

"How did that happen?" I forced out shakily as we resumed our journey, now five men short. "I mean, I know that the voices were the Barree Whisperers, but how did they affect us like that? It didn't happen last time, in the tunnels."

"*That* would be the Barree Whisperers revenge version. They have a way of getting into each individual mind, crafting a whispered voice that calls only to them, luring them to the edge."

"You're saying each person hears something different?" It never occurred to me that the others hadn't heard Kat's voice like I did.

"Yes. They mimic the person who means the most to you, preying on your emotions to drive you to the edge. It's easier to resist in your shifted form because there is more power to combat it, but it still affects each person deeply, haunting and taunting them."

"What about Ryker? What will he do if he finds Sébastien's body?" I asked, my voice cracking slightly. I was still in shock that Sébastien had pushed me away from the edge, sacrificing his chance of survival for me. Shocked that I had so easily been led to the edge. It's like I had known in the back of my mind that the voice was not truly my sister's, but I had been powerless to do anything other than listen to the voice crying out for me.

"Ryker will meet us at the base of the Rise, with or without Sébastien. But we can't stay here. They will return, again and again, until there's no one left—no souls remaining to bring to The Void's doorstep. We must get off the Rise. Sébastien would do the same. Everyone who agrees to this journey knows the risks, the rules, and accepts them. They make their peace with The God before they set off," he finished, a hint of sadness lacing his voice.

"What happens if he . . . if he doesn't find—" I couldn't finish the sentence.

"We'll deal with that then." Dravyn's voice bit out, a hardened edge to his tone. "For now, we have to make it off the Void-damned Rise."

"He shouldn't have saved me," I bit out as I stared off into the distance, the snow-capped peaks seeming so peaceful from far away, a stark contrast to the hell they created.

Dravyn remained silent for a few moments. "Maybe not, but that's the choice he made."

"Who else did you lose?"

"Two other wolvyn went over the edge. They were younger," he said with a sigh. "This was their first outing."

I remained silent for the remainder of the trip down, sorrow radiating from deep within me for the amount of souls I had witnessed lost to The Void since my arrival in the past. Guilt welled in me that Sébastien had pushed me out of the way and sacrificed himself for me. That he would give himself over to The Void so I might live another day. The thought that it would have been better if he hadn't saved me crossed my mind again before I quickly pushed it away.

The snow had slowly stopped falling; only an occasional flurry brushed across my tear-streaked cheeks as we reached the bottom of the Rise without any further issues.

"We'll set up camp once we break away from the Rise." Dravyn's direction broke the silence as we rode out of the Rise, and the temperatures rose as we left the abandoned range.

Chapter Twenty-Two

VERASTARR

THE OCCASIONAL CRACKLE from the fire was the only sound in the night air as the heat spread throughout the camp, thawing our frozen bodies. The typically jovial group of men was made solemn by the loss of three of their own. The air hung thick around us, filled with their silent grief.

I glanced over to Dravyn from across the fire as the others began making their way toward tents for the night. "What happens now?"

"We wait. Ryker knows the drill. He has one full day to search, then we must keep moving back toward the château." Dravyn looked over at me, the firelight casting dark shadows across his face.

"One day?" My voice nearly squeaked in shock. "One day doesn't seem nearly long enough when you're looking for an actual *person*."

"It's often all the time we can spare to afford," he responded, somewhat brashly, even as it was laced with worry.

"Even for a prince?" I questioned, still in shock. Back home, search parties could last for days, weeks. One day didn't seem like nearly enough time.

"I don't know what it's like in your time," he replied over

the crackle of the fire. "But here, one day is longer than most get."

I stayed silent for a moment, mulling over my thoughts. "Is it always like this?"

"The journey across the Rise? Yes. Life in Verastarr? No." Dravyn sighed.

"Why would any one of these men volunteer to go into the Barree Rise if they knew this is what they would encounter?" Sadness coated my voice as I looked at Dravyn, my heart breaking for the lives lost all over a stupid pendant. It felt like their deaths were my fault, and I once again wished I'd never accepted the pendant all those years ago. The lives lost, the sacrifices that had been made and would have to be made, didn't seem worth a singular piece of jewelry.

"That necklace you're wearing. That pendant." He gestured toward my neck. "To everyone here tonight, it represents hope. A promise of a future where they don't have to be filled with worry for their family and friends. A future without the looming threats of attacks and ambushes from the Nordak. These men here would sacrifice *everything* for a chance at a future of peace."

I tossed and turned on my bedroll long into the night—my mind continually replaying the last few seconds before Sébastien fell over the edge of the Rise. Tears welled in the corners of my eyes; lingering, but never falling as my mind kept struggling to grasp what had happened. I eventually fell asleep beside the fire that night, my sadness and sorrow building within me at the loss of Sébastien and the two wolvyn. The guilt that I survived was an ever-present weight. When I awoke, the campsite was still asleep, snores filled the air, and an occasional bird sang its morning song. I was only partially looking forward to returning to the château. The thought of no longer waking up on rough surfaces, with new aches in my bones was a welcome thought, yet still marred by the fact that we were returning with less people than we had started the journey with, and far less people if you counted those who fell during the ambush when I had been captured.

I rose quietly, padding across the camp toward the trees. Out of earshot from the camp, I stretched, changing into traveling leathers, the fresher onyx-colored pants growing on me as I strapped my dagger on my upper thigh. I glanced at the side of my arm, studying the lingering injury intently. My fingers trailed along the healing stitches that I knew would be ready to come out in a few days. An event that I was dreading. As much as I hated the lingering reminder the scar would forever leave on my skin, I knew that I was on the fortunate side. I was returning. I had made it out of this journey *alive*, which was more than many could say.

A twig cracked to my left, my body tensed at the intruding noise as my hand flew to my side, gripping the handle of the blade. My back flattened against the rough bark of the pine tree as I looked through the morning light, praying there was no danger lurking close by.

Another snap had my head twisting to the side, dagger drawn and at the ready as I waited for the intruder to show themselves.

"Wandering away from camp, once again, *princesse?*" A velvety-soft voice whispered from behind me.

My heart stopped beating in my chest, my pulse racing as I spun around in disbelief.

"Your—You—I—" Tears welled in my eyes, blurring my vision as I struggled to speak, to utter a coherent thought as I stared at the man in front of me. My dagger slipped from my grasp as it hit the grass with a thud. "I watched you fall! How are you—how did you—you're here."

"You can't get rid of me that easily," he said in a teasing

voice, contradictory to every emotion welling inside me. "It almost appears as if you were afraid I died. As if you *missed* me."

"I don't understand," I stuttered as I took in his appearance. Dirt-stained cheeks, small cuts in his clothing, and that one swoop of hair that hung over his right eye slightly. "How did you survive?" I questioned, still in denial that he was truly standing inches from me.

"Well, my saving you from throwing yourself off the ledge triggered another phase of the bond. It suspended me mid-fall as I shifted back and the bond inked itself across my skin, miraculously giving Ry enough time to show up and interrupt my plunge to a sudden and painful death," he casually replied as though his encounter with death was a daily occurrence.

I stared at him briefly, wondering how he could speak so easily about *falling* off a mountain. "I'm sorry, suspended you in the air?"

He leaned against a thin tree trunk nearby, his eyes devouring me in the early morning light as he answered, a calm voice to the stark pitch mine had taken. "Wolvyn bonds involve magic, as I'm sure you have come to realize by now. When the bond inks, it's as though a pause happens. Only momentarily, but it happens, nonetheless."

"Wait," I voiced, realizing I had felt that pause. Only I thought time had been slowing as I witnessed him plummet to his death, not because it was the bond.

"You felt it too, didn't you?" he answered and my head nodded in agreement.

I approached him slowly, as though any sudden movement would cause the image of him to vanish like he had on the edge of the mountain. Once my initial shock melted away, a slight spike of anger boiled up within me, tipping against my lips. "I can't believe you!" I snapped when I was within his reach. "Are you insane? You practically threw yourself off the edge of a mountain."

"One that you were more than willing to walk off, if I remember correctly," he said with a slight glint in his eye. "I was simply doing you a favor by saving your life."

"While appreciated, I don't quite understand how sacrificing your own life is considered a fair solution to that predicament," I retorted. "You quite literally threw yourself off the edge of a mountain for me. And also cemented the next phase of our bond." I waved my newly marked wrist in front of his face.

His hand whipped out, grabbing my arm mid-wave as he gave a tug, yanking me toward his body. The pressure remained on my arm, sending tingles down my body as his eyes took on a dark glint. "You'll find I'm more than willing to sacrifice a great deal for you, *princesse*. And the new ink looks good on you." His mouth curled as he spoke, his eyes flashing as his fingers traced the edge of the bonded mark.

Heat built within me, as I stared at him, my mind overwhelmed as I tried to process everything. "Just so you know, I still haven't made a decision yet about, well . . . just no decisions have been made."

"Who said anything about any decisions needing to be made yet," he drawled, pulling my arm so I was flush against his chest as he leaned down, his breath spreading across my bare skin.

My mind went back to the night at the Rise, to the feel of his hands on me and his lips hungrily claiming mine, when all I had wanted was to taste every part of him, to drown in his touch.

We traveled for three straight days. The attitude as we traveled switched from joking laughter to sorrow for the lost men, to high alert, depending on the time of day. My muscles had begun to grow used to riding, although I still envied those in our party who could take to the air and avoid the constant cantering of the horses.

I spent most of the journey processing the news from the Elder as I still struggled to accept the path I had to choose. Because how does one choose between themself and their sibling?

Even though I knew deep down that when we returned to the city, I would choose my sister over myself without a second of doubt, a heavy blanket of sadness cloaked me. I would be sacrificing my career, my family, the friendships I had built, my entire life. And all for what? An ancient prophecy? A desperate last effort founded in the past. It just didn't feel fair, although what in life is fair to begin with?

Near the end of the third day, I started to recognize where we were heading. The large, looming gates of Château Comptal came into view. "Sébastien." My voice faltered as I spoke, confused as to why we were not heading back to Ny Palace. "Why haven't we returned to Ny Palace? Kateya is still there. I—Well, I just assumed we would return for her . . ."

His grip around the reins tightened as a low rumble came from behind me in response. "We can't go back yet."

"Why not?" I persisted.

A disgruntled sigh filled the dusk air. "There's been unrest in a few areas surrounding the château following the ambush at the village that must be dealt with. There's also the matter of your necklace."

My head twisted to meet his gaze. "What about my necklace?" I questioned, unsure why it was a matter to be dealt with.

"Releasing the power within the necklace is the easy part," he responded with a low chuckle. "Controlling the magic that's released . . . that's another story." A long pause filled the air before he spoke again—his tone tainted with a hardened bite. "You were, and still are, an easy target with that necklace around your neck." The stitched injury twinged at the reminder of how easy a target I had been, as his deep voice rumbled on. "Those who sought to control the power in your necklace through force will still seek that power even once it's been released. If they can control you, then they control the magic that will be tied to you."

"Then I won't let them control me," I retorted with determination.

"Controlling magic isn't easy," he responded with a loaded sigh. "Those who receive powers and elemental magic train for years to understand the force flowing through their veins. To be one with the power rather than enduring the continual fight within. We don't have that time. As soon as the magic is released, you will be both safer and more in danger than before."

My eyes met Sébastien's with a fierce determination. "Well, *Your Highness*," I replied sarcastically. "I don't plan on dying or getting captured anytime soon, again."

A harsh chuckle slipped from those freckled lips as he held my gaze. "Come now. Don't get too cocky. Let's just see if you survive training first."

I was so exhausted that I hardly processed being assisted off the horse or being escorted to a room on one of the higher stories in the château when we arrived. A slight smile reached the corners of my mouth as Rosalie hurried into the room, and for once, I was grateful for her help as she assisted me in removing the grime-covered leathers I had plastered to my legs the past few days and getting into fresh clean clothes. Sleep pulled me under immediately, my body beyond exhausted from what I endured in the past weeks.

I woke to the soft sounds of trickling water and a lavender

scent wafting across the room. I noticed Rosalie drawing a bath, and again, a slight smile spread across my lips at the normality, yet luxury, of a bath. Noticing I was awake, she assisted me in getting in; then, after some convincing on my part, she left me to myself. I sunk deeper into the marbled tub, letting the water rise higher, surrounding me in a liquid cocoon as steam billowed through the room. After scrubbing my hair with lemon-scented shampoo until my scalp burned, I leaned back into the bubbles as the sweet smell permeated the air.

My mind drifted over everything, from the pendant scalding my skin back at the airport to being kidnapped and attacked, to discovering that both Kateya and I couldn't return home together. It felt like my worst nightmare. Giving up everything, losing my sister to the future, never getting to embrace my parents, or party with my best friend. A small part of me wondered about the life I could have here, though. Whether I would be happy. If I could get used to this life. Choosing not to subject Kateya to this fate meant choosing this destiny for myself, and I couldn't help hearing Aerilyn's voice in the back of my head.

A smile crept across my face as I thought of her discussing the options with me. I already knew my man-crazed best friend would be screaming at me. *So what, you have to stay here? Have you not seen him?? You have a towering, possessive alpha male, who is a literal prince, bonded to you. Also, did I mention the magic? And the men here? Why not stay?* Groaning at myself and my imaginary conversation, I pushed myself out of the tub, realizing I desperately needed some socialization.

I reached for a plush towel draped on the counter, the thick material soaking up the droplets of water cascading down my body. I dressed and wandered down the staircase toward the château courtyard.

Not necessarily sure if I was allowed to leave my room, I took the risk, figuring that the garden was still part of the castle, so I should be alright. I desperately wished for the company of Kateya or Emalyee. I wanted to be able to laugh and make jokes with them, anything to help to forget the numbing heartache I felt.

I wandered the gardens, walking on the soft dirt as dried leaves crunched beneath my feet, and arched trees made a canopy above me. It was calming and peaceful here, with a slight chilled breeze blowing gently through my hair. I hadn't heard the footsteps approaching behind me until they fell in line with mine, matching my pace. Yet I didn't need to look over to know who was intruding on my walk. The chill in the air that made you wish to disappear, mixed with pine and spice, gave him away.

"I don't recall granting you permission to wander the castle grounds, seeing as the Nordak attacks have increased. However, I will let it slide for now." His deep voice sounded from the side, a slight tease to it mixed with sincerity.

I took a good look at Sébastien, his dark, wavy hair flowing down in curls framing his face. "I figured that château grounds had to be safe enough."

I could see the tense set of his jaw and the rigid way he walked—upright and carrying a heavy weight due to the latest attacks. He gave orders, but he certainly didn't like taking orders, I knew that. But the Nordak attacks were growing closer to us. To me. The concern was etched into his face.

We walked along in a comfortable silence, taking in the fresh air and the way the birds chirped softly as we continued. Looking over, I noticed him relaxing, his muscles unclenched, and his lips not drawn as tight. "I had no idea," I started, pausing to see if he would stop me. When he didn't, I continued. "About the ambush, I mean. I wouldn't have wanted you to go had I known there would be an attack. And I am truly grateful for your help. I may not always show it or act like it, but I do appreciate both you and your father's assistance in finding the pendant. And I'm sorry your men were injured because of it."

He looked over at me, regarding me with those deep blue eyes that spoke volumes before saying, "I know you didn't have any idea." His usually authoritative voice was somewhat softer, smoother than when he usually spoke to me. "If you had, you wouldn't have snuck along on the journey."

"Did you know?" I questioned. "About the rules linked to the pendant, I mean."

"That only one of you would be able to go back? No," he responded, his voice colder than before. "It wouldn't have mattered. Your life was altered the moment you accepted the pendant. From the moment on, your life was in fate's hands. And your fate became ours to control."

I stopped and met his hardened gaze with one of my own. A snarky reply was on the tip of my tongue, but the words froze as I realized it didn't matter. It didn't matter what fate's plans had been, or what his plans or his father's had been. I wasn't going back. I *couldn't* go back. But that didn't mean I would let someone else control the rest of my life. "I want to learn to fight against those with magic," I voiced. "You said it yourself, that I will have an even larger target on my back once I shatter this pendant."

Sébastien looked down at me, a smile curling upward across his mouth, making my stomach flutter. "It's about time, *princesse*. We will begin training tomorrow."

"We?" I prompted.

A low chuckle surrounded me, and I felt fingers tilting my chin up to meet his strong gaze. The touch of his fingers sent a rush through my body, fanning a flame of desire. "But of course, Cassandra. Who else did you think would train you?"

My mind flashed to a multitude of men I would have chosen to help me train before I would have asked Sébastien.

"What? Are you afraid to get your ass handed to you?" he

taunted in my ear, a shiver coursing through me, fear clashing with determination.

"Not at all," I replied, not one to back down from a challenge. "Just wasn't aware you thought so highly of yourself," I jabbed back.

A chuckle emerged from his lips, those icy orbs darkening into slits as his face inched closer to mine than I wanted, the murderous look in those eyes sending another pang of heat straight through me, the need to feel him on me stronger than before. "Don't tempt me." He breathed into the remaining space between our lips.

I opened my mouth to respond, but the words never came. His lips crashed down on mine, firm and commanding as they pried mine apart, forcing entry into my mouth and taking what he wanted. I fell into him, lost in the moment, my hands tangling in his wavy hair. His arm wrapped around my waist, pinning me up against his solid mass. The outline of his corded muscles against my body, his fingers snaking their way through my hair before giving a sharp tug. My head snapped back from his hold on my hair, my throat exposed as his lips moved on from mine, leaving them longing for another taste.

His lips feathered their way down the column of my neck before I felt his teeth sink in. A sharp burst of pain mixed with the subtle scent of iron flooded my senses as I realized he broke the skin. His tongue soothed over the abused area in a circle, causing a heated moan to escape my lips as he licked up my neck before he pulled away, leaving me gasping for air as I met his darkened gaze.

"You bit me," I forced out as my common sense decided to return to my body.

Sébastien growled at me before turning away. He left me there, still staring at him in shock. He'd almost rounded the wall of the garden when I finally processed that he'd left me there, gaping at him like a fish out of water.

"Sébastien!" I called, running after him. "Sébastien

Capetian," I said again when I stopped right in front of him, blocking his escape. "What in The Void! You bit me." His eyes narrowed as I yelled at him, but I didn't realize until I felt my arm being yanked and I found myself pinned up against the stone wall of the garden, Sébastien's form looming over mine as he growled, his voice dancing over my exposed neck, over the spot he'd just bitten.

"And I'd do it again in a heartbeat, *princesse*. I'm doing my Void-damned best to fight the pull on the bond. To wait until you've made your decision." He growled as he held me against the wall, his body pressing into mine, his muscles rippling with restraint. "And you certainly didn't seem to mind a moment ago as you were moaning with my tongue on your neck, now did you?"

I matched his gaze, a fire raging inside me at both his retort and the feel of his body pinning mine, as my skin bristled.

"Capetian." A stiff voice broke our standoff from the entrance of the garden.

Sébastien pulled away from me slightly, "What is it, Geoffrey?" I recognized the name as he rounded the corner of the garden toward us. It belonged to his third-in-command, the soldier who had tossed me into the tree and journeyed with us following my rescue. I felt Sébastien shift, his body shielding mine slightly as Geoffrey approached, speaking rapidly. When I felt every muscle in Sébastien's body tense, concern swept over me. I hadn't been paying close attention to what had transpired in the conversation, but when Geoffrey turned to take his leave, Sébastien focused his attention back toward me. I could feel something was off.

"Sébastien? Why was Geoffrey concerned?" I questioned.

"It's nothing, Cassandra. Nothing you need to concern yourself over." I opened my mouth to speak, but his stern voice emphasized, "I mean it, Cassandra. I can see the curiosity laced in your eyes, and right now is not the time. So, leave it be, before I have to make you. Understood?"

I groaned internally, but I didn't say anything as he took my hand and led me back toward the entrance of the garden.

There was a sense of urgency bustling around the courtyard this time. Soldiers and wolvyn rushed all over the place, and when I glanced at Sébastien, I noticed his eyes scanning the surroundings like a hawk watching its prey. He led me into the château, his feet moving swiftly as I was half dragged along behind him. We rounded a turn, went up three flights of stairs, and two more turns later, he was pushing a large wooden door open swiftly. "Cassandra. You will remain *here*. Under no circumstances will you leave this room. And I mean no circumstances. There is an opening here," he said, gesturing toward the window. "Stay away from it for your own safety and the safety of those under my watch as well. I will be back shortly. *Understand?*"

Nodding, I replied, "Yes, I understand. I will stay here away from the window. I won't break my word." With a steeled look into my eyes, he left, locking the door from the outside, trapping me in while leaving me to wonder how he thought I would leave if he was locking me in.

I wasn't exactly sure what was going on, but I knew it wasn't good from the number of soldiers I had seen in the courtyard. I assumed there would be some sort of fight if that many soldiers were getting ready.

Looking around, I could tell that this room was larger than the one I was staying in. There was a bed centered against one wall, and two iron swords and a shield hung above it. The lingering scent of pine and spice told me who's room he'd brought me to. *His room.*

To my side was a table with a few books stacked on it. Unsure of what I should do, I wandered over to the desk, looking over the titles of the books. The titles were foreign to me, all related to war tactics and history. I settled on a book that appeared to cover the history of Vanaiyer, eager to put the time to use, learning as much as I could of the history of my own realm. A history that had been taken from me long ago.

Picking up the book, I softly turned the pages. Walking over to the bed in the center, I propped myself up and began to read, not entirely sure what else there was to do while I waited for the door to be unlocked.

I'm not sure how long I read for, but the sunlight had begun to fade, and I lit the bedside candle, reading and researching into the evening as dusk settled over the château.

Chapter Twenty-Three

VERASTARR

A SHUFFLING NOISE woke me from an unexpected slumber. Glancing up, I wondered when I had fallen asleep. Sunlight was no longer peering through the window as Sébastien's shadow dominated the dark room. I stared at him, slightly confused for a moment while I fully awoke. He simply returned my gaze, his exhausted eyes lighting up briefly with a flicker of amusement at my confusion. "I see you made use of my personal collection of books," Sébastien stated as he broke the silence. I grinned sheepishly at the comment.

"I hope you don't mind. I was unsure of what else to do since you *locked* me in your room," I replied. I hadn't meant for him to catch me reading his book collection. But I also hadn't meant to fall asleep.

Laughing, he responded, "No, I don't mind at all. I actually find it truly fascinating that you would choose to read history books. I brought some bread and cheese up for you, figured you might be hungry."

I was shocked he had thought of that. I realized I had hardly had anything to eat all day since I had slept so late, and a pang of hunger rumbled low in my belly. "Thank you."

Sébastien smiled subtly in acknowledgement of my thanks

as I took in his appearance. His wavy hair stuck in clingy strands to the nape of his neck. Dirt and sweat streaked across his face, and the moonlight highlighted the crimson splatters painted over his body. I knew what had happened, but I wasn't going to ask him about it. So, I sat there, eating the bread and cheese he had brought up, hoping he would mention something.

His movements across the room were deathly quiet as I ate and matched his silence, returning to the book I was reading. I soaked in words flowing from the page as I learned more of the history of my homeland, of our entire realm, wishing that books such as these hadn't been banned in my time.

Glancing up after a few pages, I noticed he had stripped down; his battle-worn leathers had been removed and a low hanging pair of pants replaced them. My heated gaze traveled up his body, taking in his firm, muscular chest, the tattoos that snaked across his skin, and the smaller silver lines of faded scars as he used a washbowl to rinse the grime off his tanned skin. He must have felt the intensity of my half drooling gaze on his form, as he sent a little smirk my way and leaned against the wall to watch me back.

I couldn't take his silence any longer and it just slipped out of my mouth. "So today, what happened?"

"What do you mean, what happened? Are you referring to us in the garden?" he softly rumbled. "Or why my men and I rushed off like that?"

I felt my cheeks heat, blushing as I recalled all the events of the day. *I had been so focused on where he had gone off to that I couldn't believe I had nearly forgotten what had happened in the garden earlier that day.* I glanced up at him, remembering he had asked a question. "As much as I would love to know what the hell you were thinking in the garden. My question was about why you rushed off," I replied. "I'm assuming there was another attack?"

Sébastien regarded me for a moment before responding.

"Now that the Nordak Captains are aware we are in possession of the first of the prophesied items, they will stop at nothing to get their hands on you. Only a fool would attempt to enter the château, though. It won't be long until the Nordak receive the message we left for them."

My gasp rang out harshly against the silence of the night. I hadn't considered that the men who had captured me would directly attack the château or attempt to. Looking at his face, I could see the weight of leadership that he bore constantly, the hardened lines around his eyes, the concern for his people, his land. The authoritative power he had could aid many in Verastarr, yet it was a hard burden to carry.

"I see. I'm sorry that this necklace has caused the deaths of so many," I voiced as I stared out the window at the dark night sky, not a star in sight.

And then he was there, tilting up my chin so that our gazes collided. Tears burned at the corners of my eyes as I processed how many good men had died in the last few weeks, all because of this stupid necklace.

"The deaths of those men are not your burden to carry. They knew what their oath of loyalty could entail. Do you understand me, Cassandra?" Sébastien demanded.

I nodded in reply as I held in the tears threatening to slip down my cheeks. Before I lost all of my courage, I asked, "What about this?" I gestured to the lines inked across my wrist, a daily reminder of the connection forming between us.

Sébastien's eyes gazed deep into mine as a weighty sigh fell from his lips, drawing my attention toward them briefly. "I'm not sure." His hesitation snapped my gaze back to his, and the unexpected response shocked me. "Breaking the bond grows harder as each line is formed, forging a connection deep within our very souls, binding us together. Not only that, but the concept of breaking the bond when you were returning to the future held a different weight than it does now."

"What do you mean?" I asked.

"Breaking a bond isn't cut and dry. Nothing is when dealing with magic and fate." He sighed heavily. "You returning to your time meant that a broken bond wouldn't have been discernible to those around you. Here, if we choose to break the bond, not only will it be excruciating, but it will also tarnish your reputation forever, making it near impossible for you to find another mate."

"Why?"

"Because I'm a prince of Verastarr. The Wolvyn Commander. There are people who already know we have begun bonding, and if we break the bond, others may perceive it as you not being good enough as a mate for a prince."

I stared at him in the dim light of the room as the realization of the implications of what he was saying set in. I may not know much about being bonded, but I was two phases into being bonded to him. *A fucking prince.* Rejecting a bond with him would be a glaring red flag to any man who crossed my path. A red flag that screamed I wasn't good enough for a future king. *Void-damn.*

"What do you suggest we do about the bond then, *Your Highness*?" I snarked back.

I don't know Cass . . . but if I have it my way there won't be another man on either side of The Void that could touch you the way I have," he said in response, a growl deep in his throat. He approached the oak door and opened it, signaling that the conversation had ended.

My body thrummed in response to the claim he made as I looked at him with slightly narrowed eyes. I was frustrated that he didn't have a complete answer. Frustrated even more that my body's response to his statement betrayed me. His face formed a knowing smirk, as though he knew my body felt the pull of his claim over me. Rising from the bed, I walked through the open door without a word, dragging the last shred of my dignity behind me as I returned to my room.

My arm throbbed as I laced up a pair of charcoal practice leathers before heading toward the drill pit. The stitches in my upper arm had been removed earlier that morning, and the healer cleared me for training before he left my room. An angry red scar left in its place, a reminder of how weak I'd been. How easily I'd been captured. And I resolved that I would never feel that way again. I prepared to head to the training pit, figuring that if I was going to begin training, I may as well start now.

Sharp commands mixed with heavy grunts and clashing swords sounded through the sweat-permeated air as I approached the pit. Stopping at the railing by the first sparring ring, I paused, taking in the hustle around me, watching the soldiers practice with precision and unmatched strength. To my right, I noted a separate ring where two wolvyn circled each other, their fangs on display as they prowled before launching through the air to attack.

"Quite impressive, isn't it?" Dravyn snuck up on me from behind. Whirling on my heel, I focused on the Captain of the Guard.

"Yes, I've never seen fighting quite like that."

Motioning for me to follow, Dravyn explained, "We train all wolvyn to be skilled fighters in both forms. The advantage of shifting between forms can be the difference between surviving or not. Besides, if one can't control their shift under duress, they're an easy target to be picked off by the Seefers." Entering a ring, Dravyn looked back at me, and a practice sword flew through the air toward my face. "I don't have all day."

Narrowly avoiding the tip, I caught the handle with a grunt as I entered the ring. "A little warning would've been nice."

"What?" Dravyn taunted as we began to circle each other, eyes tracking the others' subtle movements, waiting for the moment to pounce. "You think you're going to get a warning mid-battle?" he continued mockingly as he mimicked an enemy. "Fair warning, my lady. I'm about to beat the shit out of you, striking on your left first."

"Ha. Ha," I deadpanned. "You're just so funny." He struck then, catching me off guard as I ducked, air whooshing by on my left side. My arms weakened as I blocked the blow, the clash of metal vibrating through my arms. A dull twinge of pain shot through my upper right arm after having my stitches removed, yet I pushed through.

"I even warned you." He chuckled as anger rose up within me. Block, parry, duck, strike. We continued on until mid-morning. Dravyn paused every so often to instruct me on a new technique or more solid stance to hold my ground. My limbs protested more with each block, my body barely managing to duck. I tracked his movements, anticipating his next strike. Side-stepping his advance, I rounded on my heel, my blade cutting through the air toward his unprotected blind spot. My muscles tensed as I anticipated hitting my mark, only to find my equilibrium pulling me down from the force of my swing as I swiped through thin air. A low growl sounded to my side as I lost my footing and collided with the dust.

My skin was coated in a fine sheen of sweat, my arms screaming for reprieve as I looked up from the ground toward the shifting wolvyn in front of me. "Same time tomorrow. Except we will be going over the anticipated use of magic mid-fight." Dravyn spoke with a winning grin.

"Unfair." I groaned, dusting off my training leathers, knowing I should have anticipated his move, yet still unused to the use of magic in a drill pit. Standing up, my gaze collided with icy blue eyes as I took in Sébastien's form one ring over. His gaze held mine, even as he blocked an advance from the other man in the ring, his muscles rippling as he countered the attack, bringing the offender to the ground before clasping hands and exiting the ring.

His gaze was like a magnetic force field, pulling me in. I toyed with the inside of my lower lip as he approached me. My heartbeat increased just watching how his tousled hair clung to his skin, his corded muscles on full display.

"Your blocks and advances seem to be improving," Sébastien stated.

"Thanks," I replied, toying with the sword in my palm as he stopped in front of me. "Dravyn said we would work on anticipating shifts tomorrow."

Sébastien ran his hand through his hair, tousling the strands as he responded. "That's the easy part—the challenge is how to strike after the shift."

"Easy?" I nearly screeched from shock. "That's the easy part?!"

A low chuckle caused my insides to flutter. "Shifts can be anticipated," Sébastien shared. "All power has a tell; once you can discern each tell, the shifts aren't as unexpected. The challenge is how to best strike your opponent following their shift so that you get the upper hand."

Nodding slowly as understanding dawned on me. "What are the tells?"

"One thing at a time, *princesse*. Tomorrow you will train your stance and form with Dravyn and shift attacks with me."

I groaned in response. "I think I would much prefer to have Dravyn beat the shit out of me, rather than both of you."

"You never train with just one person. Every tell is unique, different. Training with one person alone will limit your capabilities in a fight."

I sighed, knowing that his words held truth, but not looking forward to the beating I was about to undergo.

"Before we start power blocking techniques, you have a few years of catching up to do. Follow me." Sébastien turned on his heel and grabbed a shirt from the railing by the ring. Tugging it over his body, he hid the exposed tattooed skin which had been threatening to permanently distract me.

Following Sébastien through the grounds, then up a spiral staircase on the far wing of the château, I wondered how I would ever manage to learn my way around the place with how directionally challenged I was. The staircase that we took led to a series of hallways, and finally to a small wooden door that was barely discernible along the wall. Sébastien opened the door, motioning for me to enter before him.

I gasped as I entered the room. It was smaller in size in comparison to others. A circular room lined with stone bricks indicated that we had entered part of a tower. This room felt cooler than a majority of the rooms here, possibly because it was more hidden in the château.

Immediately, I fell in love with the atmosphere. The wall was covered from floor to ceiling with various texts and books. There was a large window off to one side allowing sunlight to stream in, as well as a warm breeze that played with the fabric on its sides. Glancing behind me as the door shut, I regarded Sébastien. "I have never seen this large of a collection of books in one location before." Libraries had long since been banned in the Archives in Estaire following The Fall. Books of any form were rare to happen across and far less likely to contain knowledge on our realm.

Chuckling, he replied, "My father is the King of Verastarr. In his travels and journeys, he always makes an attempt to collect books and manuscripts. He keeps his most prized books at the library in Ny Palace; this one here was built through love. My mother had a passion for literature and my father, while a tough warrior, always brought a new book back from each journey for my mother until she passed." Walking to a row of stacked books by the window, Sébastien pulled a few from the shelves.

"These contain the history of Vanaiyer as well as the

creation of power through the five lands. Before you can attempt to control the magic released from your pendant, you need to comprehend not just the history of the magic that will flow through your veins, but also the essence of it. After training with Dravyn and I daily, you're welcome to come here and use the library to study."

"Thank you," I replied, sincerity laced in my tone at the gift he was offering. "When will you get word on how soon I can return to see my sister? She has not been told about what we discovered on the Barree Rise, correct?"

"No. My father thought it best for you to be there to inform her," he replied and then sighed.

"Your father already knows about everything we discovered with the Elder?" Shock flooded through my words.

"Yes," Sébastien answered, as though I had asked the stupidest question.

"That just seems so quick. How did you send men back to Ny Palace that fast?"

A low laugh floated by. "The bond, *Cass.* Wolvyn bonds provide the ability to communicate from far distances, remember." A trait of wolvyn I had most certainly forgotten about, as I still struggled to learn about the history of my own realm. He glanced back over his shoulder as he exited, and his voice carried, "Emalyee enjoys the books to the bottom right of the window. Something tells me you will, too." He sauntered out of the room with a devilish grin that left me strangely muted.

I wander around the open space, my fingers trailing across the spines as I took in the sheer number of books all within one place. My excitement was tangible. I walked each section of the room slowly, noting the organization of the space, the titles. My journalism instincts took over, the need to research, to absorb as much knowledge as I could. I began to collect books, eager to begin learning everything I possibly could. I collected titles focused on the Great War, on shifting powers and elemental magic. I even stacked up titles related to mating bonds in wolvyn and how they were formed. A laugh formed in my throat as I turned back toward the chair I'd selected, noting my pile of books had grown to nearly twenty, but I couldn't stop collecting titles of interest. I wanted, *needed*, to learn everything I could about Vanaiyer.

I finally knelt down by the window, a blush spreading over my cheeks as I realized Sébastien was correct in his assumption that I would enjoy the same books Emalyee had collected. Grabbing an eye-catching title to read later that evening in my room for fun, I settled down in the oversize chair by the window, picking up a book I'd selected on the magic of the five lands and began absorbing every inch of knowledge I could as the warm breeze danced across my bare skin.

The week went by in a similar fashion; sparring with Dravyn and Sébastien in the training pit took up my mornings, leaving me exhausted with shaking limbs. The bruises and cuts from unanticipated turns and shifts began to amount across my skin.

My afternoons were spent curled up by the window in the library, pouring over history books, researching and taking as many notes as I could. I soaked up information on Vanaiyer and the origins of magic amongst the realm, astonished at how much of my own history had been hidden from me as I grew up.

I finished the last chapter of *Wolvyn: A Bond Through Time*, and my muscles screamed in protest as I pushed myself off of the faded, ruby red velvet couch I had been occupying the past week. Making my way over to the window ledge, I paused, leaning against its worn, wooden frame as dusk rolled in like a sky on fire. Breathing in the lavender-scented air, I closed my eyes, relaxing myself as I practiced my breathing routine, a habit Aerilyn had forced me to partake in with her each night.

"Just trust me, Cass. I learned about the technique in yoga class. It's supposed to help us stay young and beautiful."

I simply stared at my best friend then before keeling over in laughter. "Yoga class? You mean the 2 p.m. class you show up to once a week for college credit? I call bullshit!"

But still, the breathing exercise became routine, each night at dusk. Of course, we tended to follow it up with a large glass of wine . . . or three, which I'm convinced negated any effects we may have received from the exercise.

Reopening my eyes, I lingered around the bookshelves, taking my time as I searched for a new book to read that night. When I was younger, my mother used to read to us every night, and as I got older, reading became my escape, a way to journey into a new reality, an adventure I longed for. After The Fall, a majority of the books I had grown up with were confiscated, hidden away, much like everything else that was good in our realm. Deciding on a worn romance book, I settled back down, snuggling into the couch as I was whisked away to a far-off island, a welcoming spring breeze fluttering by as time escaped me.

"Reading something good, *princesse*?" a husky voice interrupted, drawing me from my escape, back to reality. A slight rosy hue crept across my cheeks as I realized I hadn't even heard Sébastien enter the library. Dark shadows crept across his face as night rolled in. My eyes traced his body, noting his unbuttoned black shirt, the outline of his tattoos tracing down his chest visible, catching my eye for a moment too long.

"What makes you think that, *Your Highness*?" I sassily tossed back.

"Just a lucky guess," he retorted with a devilish grin.

I knew I was playing with fire, yet I couldn't resist as the words flowed freely from my lips. "It's a nice escape, you know? Reading about men who actually know how to please a woman—who take control," I taunted, watching as Sébastien tensed, his body vibrating against the challenge I was putting out in the air. "It's not like I find that here."

In a flash, he was there. A snarl formed as he gripped my head, tilting it up to meet his fiery gaze. "Really, now?" he growled as his grip on my hair tightened, a pained gasp escaping my lips as I met his heated gaze. "Tell me then," he bit out. "What happens next in your book?"

Looking up at him through my lashes, I swallowed before shakily replying, "I wouldn't know. I was interrupted," I sassed back as my body trembled under his grip.

Tension built in my stomach as I glanced over Sébastien, taking him in. The tousled hair that hung just below his eye; the floating black ink contrasting his tanned skin; the dark tendrils of mist that radiated around his body. My eyes roaming over the onyx shirt that hung loosely, the black training leathers formed around muscular thighs, before I sharply sucked in air at the outline in them. I envisioned leaning forward, tracing—

A low growl fell from Sébastien, his hold tightening in my hair. "What. Happens. Next?" he demanded. My mushed brain paused to process what he was asking about before remembering the book.

"Well, in the book she was a-about t-to—" I stuttered, "and then she w-would—" I couldn't finish the sentence as my gaze roamed over his chest, unable to meet his eyes.

"I don't have all night, *princesse*," he warned as his grip on my hair tugged, forcing me to stand—to meet his darkened gaze. I froze, my mind on overdrive as my eyes clashed with his, while he cupped my neck. His free hand wrapped around mine, guiding my hand with his own as it moved closer to his form.

"Perhaps, showing me would be easier, *hmmm*?" he asked. Heat rushed to my cheeks at the thought—my body alight as anticipation rushed over me, allowing him to guide my hand over his body. The feel of his bare chest hot beneath my touch, muscles rippling firmly beneath my fingers as he guided my hand lower.

The door burst open without any warning, bouncing off the wall with force. "Well, well . . ." Dravyn smirked as he entered the room. "Isn't this a fun little surprise." He looked between Sébastien and me, as I yanked my hand back, pulling out of Sébastien's grip.

"I thought I made myself clear that I was not to be disturbed," Sébastien snarled, not even looking at his second-in-command. "Get *the fuck* out."

"Much as I would love to *get out*. Unfortunately, you are needed, right away. If that part wasn't clear."

Sébastien growled as he looked at his friend. "This had better be good, *Dravyn*." As he followed his second-in-command out the door, leaving me wondering what might have happened between us and what *was* currently happening that needed his attention so desperately.

Chapter Twenty-Four

VERASTARR

SHOUTS and the clanking of armor coming from the outer courtyards drew me from my sleep early the next morning. Glancing out the small window in the room, I first noticed the sun had not fully risen, a faint red hue tinting the skyline, but then I saw a sight that I had never seen before in my life. A few hundred armor-clad soldiers were cantering in on horses. Panic rose in my chest as I wondered what was happening. I hurriedly threw on the first pair of training leathers and shirt I could find, braiding my wavy hair to give it some sort of styled appearance before rushing out of my room toward the courtyard. Freezing halfway down the corridor, I whipped around, racing back toward my room. My hands grasping for the dagger I kept under my pillow at night. Once my trustworthy blade was secured around my leg, I headed back out the door in a blur. I did not stop running until I reached the courtyard, scanning through the sea of men for either Sébastien or Dravyn, hoping one of them could inform me of what was happening.

Dravyn saw me standing by the edge of the courtyard. The look of discontent and fury was clear in his eyes, even from across the courtyard. Stalking over in my direction, he demanded to know why I was by the courtyard.

"Well. It's not like a few hundred men moving around is exactly silent, now, is it? All the shouting and metal clashing together woke me up, so I figured I would come find out what's going on. Glad to see neither you nor Sébastien gave any thought to filling me in," I deadpanned, frustrated at his reaction.

"Follow me," Dravyn responded. "Now!" He grabbed my arm with a firm grip, leading me away from the courtyard whilst I protested. "If Sébastien catches you out here right now, he will be furious."

Once we were a good distance from the organized chaos flooding across the courtyard, Dravyn stopped as we stood in a darkened hallway, the shadows hiding our forms. "It would be best for you to learn not to wander into a courtyard whenever you hear shouts. I swear, you will be the death of me," he said in a disgruntled voice as I laughed.

"Have you not met Emalyee?" I teased. "She's just as *unruly* as I am. Looks like you might as well prepare for an early death."

Dravyn shook his head, glaring at me as he turned his back and stomped off down the hallway. I contemplated leaving; however, I also wished to know what was happening.

A shiver began to creep across my bare arms as the chill from the dampened hallway sunk in, and I debated getting the hell out of this walkway before I saw the flame of a torch. Sébastien approached me, looking displeased to have been pulled away from his tasks. His black leathers hugged his muscles, and his hair was disheveled, a few strands hanging over his eye and resting on pronounced cheekbones, causing my heart rate to increase.

"Cassandra," his gravelly voice began, frustration ebbing from him. "Imagine the thrill I received when I had to have the Captain of my Guard inform me that you are wandering around the courtyard in the middle of battle preparations. Still no learning curve?"

"I was correct then in my assumptions that the shouts from the courtyard were due to an upcoming battle," I retorted, ignoring his insult in an attempt to stop him from berating me further.

A sigh fell from his lips, yet he responded, "Yes. You were correct. The Nordak have launched new attacks on surrounding villages. They are growing anxious the longer that pendant is in our possession." He gestured to the heavy weight hanging from my neck. "My father has sent a few hundred soldiers to fight alongside us. It seems that a warning message during the last ambush was not enough." His eyes darkened, a glint of fire surfacing, and a shiver coursed through my body from the fury swarming in his eyes rather than the cold this time.

"What's the plan, then?"

Low chuckles echoed through the corridor. "The plan," he paused. "Is for you to make it back to Ny Palace and shatter the damn necklace open."

I opened my mouth to respond, yet Sébastien stopped me. "This is not up for discussion, Cassandra." My name rolled off his tongue like a curse, and I knew he was pissed. "You may have been training with Dravyn the past week and have some skills with a blade, but you will not be riding into the center of the battle with us with that around your neck. Shattering the magic within the pendant will give us a few days' time head start on the Nordak before they set their Seefers onto our borders in search of the power."

"Fine," I replied in annoyance. "It would still be nice if you thought I could handle myself in a fight."

Stepping closer, Sébastien's eyes captured mine. "There's no doubt you could handle yourself in a fight, *princesse*," he said as his muscular body drew closer to mine. "But I won't be bringing you into a fight with an additional target on your back."

"Additional?" I questioned.

Sighing deeply, he replied, "*Yes*. The pendant around your neck is the glaring target." His fingers grabbed my arm with ease, pulling my wrist up to eye level as his thumb traced around the ink under my skin. "This would be the additional target. A bond to a prince is leverage for any who capture you."

He bent his head down, hardly giving me time to process his words before his lips met mine again in a sweet clash. Time felt as though it had stopped. The scent of pine and spice flooded over me while his arms wrapped around my body, holding me close as he deepened the kiss. His lips danced across mine, his tongue sought entrance. A soft whimper escaped me as his teeth caught my bottom lip, toying with it as he pinned me against the stone wall, a damp chill coursing through me in contrast to the inferno rising inside. At that moment, my life felt complete, as though, for the first time since ending up in Verastarr, everything would be okay.

He broke the kiss, leaving me breathless as I gazed deeply into his eyes. Sébastien remained silent for a moment before clearing his husky voice and saying, "I'm sorry. I just . . . as much as I would prefer to continue drawing sounds like that from you, I must return and oversee the final battle preparations. Geoffrey will ensure you return safely back to my father's Palace in Nytestarr."

"Wait," I breathed, my mind still focused on the feel of his lips on mine. "You're not coming with me?"

An apologetic smile flashed across his lips. "Attached to traveling with me?" he teased. "I plan to return to Nytestarr after the battle and traveling without me will make you less of a target."

A somber sigh fell from my lips as I realized what returning to Ny Palace meant. I whispered, still entranced by the feel of his lips on mine and the proximity of our bodies. "What's the likelihood that the Nordak anticipate us splitting to travel back to Ny Palace?"

"Possible, but not probable. You will be traveling with a small group of men. The Nordak would be expecting us to either keep you here or send a large force with you. They won't be expecting a few soldiers on a journey home," he replied before walking away to finalize battle plans with his men.

Rosalie was in my room when I returned, anxiously awaiting my arrival to assist me in gathering my belongings for the journey. Since we returned to Château Comptal, Sébastien had ensured I was provided with any clothing I desired. I had taken great joy in conversing with Rosalie during my stay and it saddened me that I had to leave her behind. She had become a friend to me in the short time I had stayed at the château, yet she reminded me that should the battle go well, I would hopefully be returning to the château. I continued packing the necessary items, ensuring a few daggers were included as a feeling of unease spread over me, flashbacks to our previous journey a reminder to be prepared.

A knock resounded on my door just as we gathered the last of my belongings. "Cassandra?" a voice sounded from behind the door, and I immediately knew who it belonged to as the door opened.

"So much for giving a girl time to get ready," I sassed, turning to Sébastien, my heart rate rising as I took in the man before me, clad in lightweight armor.

"Geoffrey and the other six men are ready to go. You will be traveling off the main path. If anything happens and the group is separated, ride hard to the north. I know you want to see Kateya again but, Cassandra," Sébastien said with authority, "if you're caught, they won't play nice this time around. Be smart and stay alert."

I followed behind him as we left the room and made our way to the back entrance of the château. I wondered what lay ahead, praying that I made it back to Ny Palace safely to at least be able to say goodbye to my sister one last time.

I had been so deep in thought while following Sébastien to the courtyard that I failed to notice he had stopped until I walked directly into him, nearly falling from the shock. Glancing up quickly, an embarrassed blush spread across my cheeks as Sébastien's mouth formed into an amused grin. "Lost in thought?" he teased. "Might I be so lucky as to believe it was I who distracted your thoughts?" His smirk led me to believe he was confident in his suggestion.

"Only in your dreams would I be lost in thought over you," I replied, smirking back as I taunted him.

"You wound me," he threw back, pretending to be stabbed by my words.

Stopping by the back gates, where the seven men were waiting to escort me to my uncertain future, Sébastien tenderly wrapped a lightweight cloak over my shoulders, fastening the clasp under my neck. His fingers tilted my chin up as our eyes collided.

"Be smart, *princesse*," he said again, the words rolled off his tongue most endearingly as his gaze held mine. "Stay hidden when you can and if anyone ambushes you, give them hell. Don't go down without a fight."

I nod in understanding as he backed away. "Give them hell, too, *Your Highness*," I tossed back, my smirk growing as I continued, even as I battled a growing sense of sadness welling within me. "If you can, that is."

His dark chuckle filled the air as he walked away, readying

for a battle of his own. My stomach clenched as nerves jittered inside of me while I mounted my horse, kicking his side into action, leaving the safety of the château behind.

Chapter Twenty-Five

VERASTARR

THE JOURNEY back to Ny Palace seemed to pass slowly. As the hours carried on, my anticipation of seeing Kateya again built. I longed to see my sister, and I missed the constant chatter and jokes between us. I had even begun to miss long talks and late-night bar adventures with Emalyee. Yet each step on the journey toward Ny Palace was one step closer to saying goodbye to my sister, my best friend, my entire life.

Thoughts of Sébastien's safety flashed briefly across my mind throughout the trip. The long, heat-filled days riding horseback allowed my mind to wander to thoughts of him. I knew he and his men had the numbers and the strength to eliminate the Nordak threat close to the château. Yet, something just felt off; as if we were missing part of the picture, and I couldn't quite figure it out. Shattering the pendant hanging from my neck meant enacting the first part of the prophecy King Adrastan had spoken of. That meant there were still two items scattered across time, destined to shape someone else's path, just as this Void-damned necklace had done for me.

Our previous journey into Nytestarr had come with an attack as we traveled. I admitted to myself then that I found it odd we encountered no troubles in our travels, no surprise attacks. We hadn't seen a single soul as we traveled. Surely, with the Nordak attacking more and the upcoming battle, there would have been more activity than we saw throughout the journey.

Thoughts of the ambush that happened when I left, and the looming sense of danger fled from my mind as Nytestarr came into view on the horizon. Excitement welled in me at the thought of reuniting with my sister. I was still unsure of how I should best share with Kateya the news the Elder had given me back at the Rise. How does one tell their built-in best friend that they will never see them again? How does one tell their younger sister that they were ambushed, attacked, and kidnapped? The new scars on my body were a constant reminder of that week. I did not wish for my sister to know the full story. We had gone through much already; but maybe she should know.

Entering into Nytestarr this time felt different. The market vendors that once flocked the streets were no longer bustling around the crowded streets shouting of goods to purchase. Only a few people were out and the majority of them were women. I realized then why so few people wandered the once packed streets. Sébastien had not shared how large this battle against invading Nordak would truly be. It appeared that many men loyal to King Adrastan and Verastarr had left to join the attack against the Nordak. I could not stop myself from worrying over Sébastien, Dravyn, and the many other men who would be fighting for the king and Verastarr. How long would this fight truly go on? Or was this merely the start of something larger than all of us?

I had just been assisted off of my horse when I spotted Kateya from across the courtyard. My heart raced as I quickly sprinted toward her, crashing into a hug as the two of us collided. We stayed still, clinging to each other for far too long before an "Ahem" sounded behind us. Turning, we discovered King Adrastan standing and watching our reunion.

"I am thrilled that you have finally returned *safely*. I am sure you wish to have some time to speak with your sister after so long apart. We will speak soon in my study," he said with an air of finality.

"Yes, Your Majesty," I replied with a nod of acknowledgement.

It was at that moment that I noticed Kateya looking at me, her eyes swimming with questions. "Did our plan work? Did you get the necklace back? Did they notice?"

Shit. The plan. That all seems like a lifetime ago. "Kateya," I whispered; my voice hardly seemed to work at that point. "Let's catch up inside?"

The look in her eyes as she nodded told me she understood that the news was not what she had been praying for all these weeks. As she led the way toward the room she had been staying in, I wondered what life had been like for her here in the weeks that I had been away. Had she made new friends? Had she been happy? Making our way through the grand halls of Ny Palace, we casually chatted, filling each other in on what we had been doing for the past weeks. We carefully danced around the subject of the once missing necklace, of any hardship or struggle, until we arrived at Kateya's room and had some privacy to talk alone.

"Well?" she questioned. "*Please* tell me we can finally get out of this Void-damn place."

"Kateya," I replied, my heart breaking as I stared at her next to me on the bed. "I. Well. I, or we really, found the necklace. Just . . ." The words fell out of my mouth, feeling empty.

"Just what, Cass?" my sister asked, a frown creased her forehead as she watched me closely.

"Well . . ." And then I gave her a recap, starting with sneaking off to follow the group, then the attack and being kidnapped, and ending on the journey to the Barree Rise. "Getting the necklace back was pointless for us. The magic would have never allowed both of us to return home." My voice caught in my throat as I spoke to my sister.

"There's got to be another option, Cass. We will find one, I know we will. It won't end like this. I won't let it. The God wouldn't let it end like this for us, I know it." Her voice wavered as a sob slipped out.

"Kat." I sighed as I drew her in for a hug. My arms wrapped around her in a silent embrace, knowing that words wouldn't fix this. Nothing could fix this. "If I don't release the magic in the pendant, we will both be hunted for the rest of our lives. I don't want that for you—for us. This has to be done."

She looked at me then, her cheeks puffed, and tear stained. "I can't lose you, Cass. I can't. This will kill Mum and Father."

"You won't. I promise, Kat, you won't lose me. I don't have another option. *We* don't have another option. It was my stupid necklace that got us into this mess. And I'm going to get you back home."

"We'll find a way." She sobbed as hope ebbed away. "There must be something."

"Short of finding the other artifacts," I scoffed softly. "I can't think of any other way to get us both back home."

A maid knocked on my sister's door then, informing me that I was to meet with His Majesty immediately. Only once Kateya assured me that she would be alright did I leave her room to go meet with King Adrastan. In my mind, I had a list of questions that I wish to discuss with him. I was unsure if he had the answers I was hoping to find, but I knew I needed to at least try.

I stopped in front of the closed doors. The same wooden doors I had stopped in front of weeks ago when I had first learned of the prophecy surrounding my necklace. Taking a deep breath, I squared my shoulders and entered, the dark ambience of the room filling the empty void in my chest as I stared at the King of Verastarr.

"Come." His deep voice broke the silence as he turned.

I followed King Adrastan through two dark oak doors into a smaller room off to the side. This room was entirely secluded, with not a window in sight. The empty expanse of walls matched the lack of furniture found in the space, which was decorated only by a desk and a settee next to a wall of dust-coated books. After his gesture, I sat down on the settee and looked at him expectantly, wondering why he wished to speak with me.

Adrastan paced across the darkened marble tiles, the heel of his boots scuffing across as the silence grew between us. I opened my mouth to break the silence, yet closed it again. My fingers scratched at the side of my riding leathers as he continued to pace.

A heavy sigh escaped the king as he pinched the bridge of his nose before looking over in my direction. "While there is much to be discussed in regard to the ordeal and lengths taken to retrieve the necklace. I do wish to say that I am sorry for the situation that you and your sister find yourselves in, Cassandra." I dipped my head slightly. "The Nordak attacks shall only continue until they possess the power within the necklace. It's merely a matter of time before the Seefers grow in numbers too large and a breach occurs."

"What's so special about this necklace?" I snarked as frustration rose within me. "I get that it's part of the prophecy, but why do they want it so bad? It's not like they don't have their own magic."

His pacing once again paused as he stopped to stare at me. A gaze that had me withering from the intensity. "Those pieces of the prophecy," he began, as his voice commanded silence, "they were bonded by the rulers of the four lands of Vanaiyer. Four of the most powerful people to exist in the realm. That necklace around your neck doesn't contain just any magic. It contains the elemental magic and shifting powers of four rulers of Vanaiyer. When you break open that necklace, shattering the magic bonding it together, you release the power of all four rulers."

"Wait, *what?*" I sputtered as I met his gaze, a mixture of shock and horror plastered across my face.

"Releasing that magic must be done. But it will make you the most powerful and targeted individual in all of Vanaiyer as soon as the power is released."

"No," I shrieked, jumping up from my seat. "No. I don't want that. I didn't want the fucking power when it was only *one* ruler's magic within. There's no way in hell I'm going to release the power in it with even more magic inside. No. Not happening." I began to head toward the door in a rush.

"Cassandra," King Adrastan bellowed from across the room—an arctic chill freezing me to the bone, holding me in place as darkness swirled around me. "Perhaps you didn't understand me clearly the first time." He snarled in my face as he came into view. Angry mist whirled around us as he spoke. "You *will* release the magic found inside that pendant or you will be signing a death warrant for both you and your sister. Is that what you want?" He paused for a moment. My mouth opened to reply before I shut it with force, my teeth grinding into each other as I remained silent.

"Your only chance at survival is to release the magic and learn to embrace and control it quickly. Leaving the pendant in one piece opens you to attack. The Nordak will come. They will want the power of the other four lands and will use you, torture you however they must in order to harness that power.

Now I asked you, is that what you want, Cassandra?" he hissed.

My eyes burned with fury, even as I processed the weight of his words. "Just because I don't want that," I snapped, "doesn't mean I fucking want *this* either." I scream, raising my arms as I yank at the pendant secured around my neck, ripping the chain off to wave it in front of his face.

His face turned murderous then as his arm flew out to stop mine mid-air. "When? *When* did you get these?" he yelled in an arctic tone. His eyes flashed as they narrowed in on the ink wrapped around my right wrist. My forming bond.

"I-I . . . um . . ." I stuttered.

"When." His tone cut through the room as his grip tightened, crushing around my forearm.

"The first appeared not long after we left to search for the necklace," I spit out through the pain. "The second on the way back down from the Barree Rise."

"To whom?" His eyes held mine, frozen in place as his voice dropped. "Do you not understand the circumstance you have found yourself in? Of course not. You. A mere mortal. Play with the primal powers by beginning a bond with a wolvyn before you have even shattered the pendant?" he continued reprimanding me. "I said. To. Whom?"

Wincing, I swallowed before looking down, suddenly admiring the intricate design of the floor beneath my feet as I attempted to regulate my breathing. "Sébastien," I whispered, my voice barely reaching my own ears.

A low growl rumbled from in front of me as I forced my gaze to meet his. "We will discuss this"—he gestured to the marks on my arm in frustration—"at another time. You have the night to say your goodbyes. Tomorrow, that pendant is to be broken. Go," he snarled as he released my arm.

I stared, my feet immobile as I processed his words. *Tomorrow.*

"Now." His iced command hit me and I hurriedly turned to flee the room.

Chapter Twenty-Six

VERASTARR

I RAISED the glass back up to my lips, wincing as the amber liquid burned down my throat. Emalyee had dragged us out tonight and while I wasn't in much of a party mood, I had to admit if we had stayed in, Kateya and I would be a bawling mess of tears. This way at least, we got to make one last cheerful memory together before she goes home. *One last.* I tossed back the rest of my whiskey at the thought. Tonight was going to be a long night.

The music picked up, and I watched as a younger man I had seen before reached for my sister's hand, tugging her up as they swayed to the rhythm. She seemed happy. Carefree. The sight of that made me smile. Turning to Emalyee, I questioned, "How were things in the past few weeks? Was my sister okay?"

Sipping the remainder of her drink, she responded, "We kept her busy. She was worried for a while, and I think she always felt like something was wrong, but she kept busy. Eryx," she said as she gestured to the man dancing next to her, "kept her occupied. He didn't give her enough free time to sit alone with her thoughts."

Nodding, I admitted, sadly, "I wish I could freeze tonight

on repeat. I'm dreading everything that comes with tomorrow. I don't want to give up my sister, she's my best friend. But who would I be if I sentenced her to this? It's not her choice and she doesn't deserve that."

"And you do?" she retorted back.

Sighing, the reply fell empty from my mouth. "It's not like I have a choice. You should have seen the king's reaction when he saw this." I gestured to my wrist, the black inkings stark against my lighter skin.

"That bad?"

"I wanted to shrivel up and die on the spot."

"Well," she said, patting my arm, "one impossible thing at a time. Let's survive tomorrow first. Then we can deal with that." She pointed at my wrist.

"Ladies . . ." a slurred voice called out beside us. "I come bearing drinks. And more drinks." Kairon chuckled as he sat himself down next to us, his dark hair flopped over his eyes as he glanced at us. "Stop with your pity party and get in the mood, Cass. The night is still young." He slid our drinks down the table.

Laughing, we caught the drinks, sipping them as we glanced around. "Always good to see you, too." I chuckled in response.

The music picked up, drawing a crowd as the notes flowed lightly across the bar. Pushing up from her seat, Emalyee gestured to us both. "Let's go. We're dancing."

I stood up, finishing off the rest of my drink, liquid courage rising within me as we took to the dance floor, letting the music carry us away. We left our worries at the door as the music droned on and the night blurred by. We danced, twisted, and laughed to the beat as a warm spring breeze flew in from the open windows. Kairon and Eryx ensured we all had drinks in our hands as we danced with the crowd, swaying to the music that lifted our moods. We only left when the moon had risen high in the night sky, the bar closing after last call, as we drunkenly stumbled our way back to Ny Palace, with Kairon singing the entire way.

Feeling foggy from the drinks, I settled myself into bed and felt the dip of the mattress as Kat followed my lead, settling in beside me. As I was about to close my eyes, I heard my sister whisper my name.

"Cass," the whisper beside me increased in volume.

"Yeah?" I questioned as I rolled over on the bed, my mind still hazy as my sister looked at me.

"I don't want this night to end." She sighed as a tear dripped down her face, her glistening eyes meeting mine in the moonlight. "I can't do this without you."

Tears welled in my own eyes as her image blurred in front of me. I reached out to grab her hand in mine. "I know, Kat, I know. Someone has to go back to our parents, though. And I can't make you stay here. I *won't* let you stay here. It's going to be okay, you know."

"Will it?" she whispered in frustration. "Will it be okay?"

It has to be. I nodded in reply as I stared across the bed at my sister, snuggled in the comforter, looking at me.

"I'm glad we went out tonight," she said with a cheerful sigh. "I've missed this—us going out, hanging out like we used to back in Estaire."

"I've missed this too," I said with a smile. *It felt like ages ago since we had been this young and carefree.*

"So," she whispered. "How's the brooding commander? At least tell me he's good in bed. He's got to be, right?"

"Kat!" I gasped, a chuckle escaping my lips. "What on Vanaiyer? You can't be serious right now. Why would you think I slept with him?!"

"*Well,*" she teased. "I'm not wrong, am I?"

I laughed as I looked at my sister. "Only partially right."

"I knew it!" she shrieked. "Grumpy asshole or not. You can't deny he's hot. And the way he looks at you . . ." She rambles on about his body.

I smiled as I thought about the brooding wolvyn I'd begun to bond with. My thoughts drifted back to the night he protected me back at the lake when I wandered off while traveling and to the night at the Barree Rise and how open and honest he had been with me.

"*Cass!*" Kateya's voice pulled me from my thoughts.

"Sorry, what?" I distractedly asked.

"Do you think he's the one?" my romance-loving sister prompted again in a dreamy voice.

Laughing, I responded. "I don't know, Kat." My voice sombered for a moment. "But I think . . . I think I may be starting to fall for him."

"I knew it!" she shrieked with excitement.

Teasing her in response I questioned, "*So*, tell me about the guy. Eryx, right? Is *he* the one?"

"Maybe," she sighed. "Or at least he could have been if we were born in a different time." She let out a strangled laugh as a wave of happiness spread across her face at the mention of his name. She talked about her time here without me, gushing over Eryx, the brown-haired soldier in the Wolvyn Guard. Telling me about the late nights at the bars, sneaking around Ny Palace security with Eryx, stumbling home drunk and happy as the sun rose in the mornings.

I smiled as I listened to her talk, realizing that her time here had been much like it would have been in the future: happy. Filled with laughter and late-night adventures.

We talked late into the night, whispering as we caught up and teasing each other before falling asleep curled up in bed together.

I slowly woke up, my head pounding as I lay next to my sister, watching her snore softly beside me with her hair splayed out across the pillow. I smiled as I began to settle back down in an attempt to ignore the throbbing headache I had drunk myself into, when a weight settled back into my chest, and I bolted upright in bed. A groan slipped from my lips from the sudden movement, my head pounding as I remembered what today was.

No. No. No. Can't we just rewind a day? I just got my sister back; I don't know if I can do this. I don't want to say goodbye to her so soon.

I slowly slid out of bed, walking over to the bathroom as I stumbled in the still dark room. Cracking open the door, I slipped inside, careful not to wake my sister, who was sure to have it worse than I did this morning. I splashed cold water on my face as I attempted to wake myself up, unsure who I should blame more for the deathly hungover feeling I had.

Last night was fun. And I will forever be grateful for one last happy memory of spending time with Kateya. It certainly would have made my life easier to deal with today had I not been massively hungover, though. I slipped onto the bathroom balcony, sinking down against the stone columns as I stared out over the city, my thoughts darkening to match the weather. Storm clouds rolled in, the sky an ominous, angry gray color as the temperature dropped.

A fitting mood for the day, I thought bitterly as tears streamed down my face. I had to be strong for my sister, but right now . . . right now, I didn't have to.

Kateya and I stood in silence in an enclosed room in the far west corridor of Ny Palace. The room had its own entrance, in order to be as detached as possible from the remainder of the building. Kairon had told us the night before that this room was the training room. For centuries, the future leaders of Verastarr had come here to learn how to control the power flowing through them, and I now understood why.

Glancing around the space, I noted that there were no windows, no furniture—it was a room devoid of character in order to practice one's emerging powers without causing harm. The blank stone walls created a forlorn look as a chill settled into them. An onyx marble dais stood tall in the center, the singular item in the room. The air in the room felt powerful, yet empty, as though awaiting something spectacular, while torchlight flickered back and forth in the shadowed corners of the space.

Kateya's hand slipped into mine as we looked around, taking in the last place we would ever see each other. Tears welled in my eyes as I forced them back, knowing I needed to concentrate on the task. Needed to be strong for my sister.

"Ladies." King Adrastan broke the silence as he walked in, his face emotionless, and his presence filling the room. "Breaking the magic within the pendant is fairly simple. The magic within can only be called out through the chosen individual with a spelled artifact in a sacred room." He gestured to the space around us, indicating that this chamber had been deemed sacred for the use of magic.

He pulled out a dagger, its charcoal gray blade shimmering with a wicked point at the tip as he rested the blade on the dais. "Holding the dagger with both hands, you will begin to wish just as you did back in the East Engles. Only this time, you will be wishing to send your sister back. You *must* continue repeating the wish aloud and in your heart, as you bring the dagger down through the center of the necklace with as much force as possible, effectively shattering it."

I nodded solemnly as I listened to his instructions. "What happens once the necklace is shattered?"

"When the dagger breaks through the magic inside, it should release the power within and be received by you," he said sternly, as his steeled eyes met mine. "From that point on, you are on borrowed time until you learn to control the power given to you."

I understood. From the moment that necklace shattered, my life would never be what it was. Although, if we were being fair, my life already wasn't what it used to be, I thought as I stared at the dagger resting in the center of the room, an ominous glint catching my eye as I watched it.

Kairon rushed in, the force of his entrance causing the doors to bounce off the wall, closing on their own.

"Yes, son?" Adrastan inquired as Kairon hurriedly crossed the expanse of the room, whispering in low, urgent tones to the king. The two spoke rapidly back and forth, their voices rose as the conversation carried on.

Kateya nudged me as we stood in place. "I wonder what's going on?" she whispered.

"Nothing they would tell us about," I said with a sarcastic scoff. "Secrets seem to constantly appear here."

"Very well." The clipped tone snapped us from our whispers. "Take one hundred men to the east, heading toward the border. Only attack if need be; we need to lure them in with comfort to wipe them out entirely," the king finished, dismissing his eldest son.

Kairon nodded as he turned to exit the room. A small smile of acknowledgement graced his lips as he passed us, the doors falling into place with his departure.

"It seems time isn't in our favor; we must get this finished quickly," Adrastan said, directing his attention back toward the task at hand.

I stared at the king, curiosity rising in me. "What changed?

Why is it so important that we shatter this necklace so soon?" I questioned with suspicion.

"That necklace," he replied in a level tone, "once shattered, will send out a beacon—a flare of magic—notifying the others that the power has been opened. Each of the rulers will feel it and they will know it's been released. The search for the remaining two artifacts will be on, and with the Seefers encroaching on our borders presently, your safety is at a higher risk." He looked between my sister and I. "You have five minutes to say your goodbyes, then we move on with the plan." He left the room, leaving us alone in stunned silence.

"I can't do this, Cass." My sister's wrecked voice hit me like a brick. "I don't want to say goodbye."

"I don't either, Kat. I don't want to lose you."

We held onto each other, tears streaming as our broken sobs filled the air, a gutting song echoed off the walls.

"I'm going to find it," she whispered between sobs.

I froze, confused for a moment. "Find what, Kat?"

"The next piece. The next artifact. I can't lose you forever, Cass. I'm going to come back," she finished with a sniffle as she wiped wet tears from her cheeks. "I promise."

I smiled sadly at my younger sister. "Kat," I said, my voice thick with pained emotion. "I love you. I want more than anything to not have to say goodbye forever. But you can't go off searching for the next artifact for the remainder of your life. You've seen how insane this entire nightmare has been. There's a war on the horizon. I want you to be safe, Kat. Home and safe. Living life to the fullest. Going out, partying, getting your dream job, falling in love. Not searching for an artifact to send you back into the past with war brewing and death surrounding you."

"I can't live without you," she cried, gripping me tighter, hot tears cascading down her cheeks as she stared up at me. "I refuse to. I will find it, Cass. I have to."

My heart felt like it had been gutted in two. How on

Vanaiyer am I supposed to put on a brave face as my sister clings to me like her life depends on it? I prayed to The God that this would work, that my sister would make it home safely so she could have a normal life.

This is what's best for her. Neither of us asked for this, but at least she has the chance to go home, to live out her life in peace. "We're going to be okay. I promise, Kat," I whispered as I hugged her back with everything in me. "No matter where we are, we always have each other. That's what sisters are for, after all."

The door opened as King Adrastan reentered the room. His face was a blank canvas, as though he was indifferent to the heartbreaking scene about to occur before him. "Let's begin." His words cut through the air.

Kateya slowly stepped away. Both of us wiped tears from our faces as I made my way over to the center of the room. My fingers shook as I moved my hair to the side, my arms reaching behind to unclasp the necklace. They fumbled a bit before the clasp finally sprung free and I held the necklace in front of me, watching the pendant swing from side to side.

I stared at the chain of the necklace as it hung from my hands, a childhood keepsake of my time before The Fall. The magic that protected us from the Seefer attack in our house. The same magic that brought us here to our nightmares. The reason I was kidnapped and tortured. The reason I met Sébastien. The reason my life would never be the same. Looking at it brought me back to the happiness of my childhood. I had so much love for this necklace, once upon a time.

Yet as I watched it swing in front of me, I only felt hatred. A deep loathing for what it cost me. Kateya stopped in front of me, as though sensing the inner turmoil building, her hands wrapped around mine as we lowered the necklace to the dais.

"You've got this, Cass. I will always love you," she whispered.

Staring at her with tears in my eyes, I nodded as I watched

my sister walk away. "I will always love you, too, Kat. I love you so much." My hands trembled as I picked up the dagger that laid next to the pendant. A low vibration bounced within its blade, as though magic was calling to magic.

The dagger felt heavy in my hands, as I lifted my gaze, first to Adrastan who watched on with a blank expression, waiting, then to Kateya who nodded in encouragement through a sad smile, then down to the necklace, the ruby-red glint of the stone sparkling in front of me.

I raised my hands up, staring at the pendant as I pushed away my sadness. I couldn't mess this up for her. Kateya had one chance to go home, to have a normal life, free of this war. I had to get it right. My lips echoed the wish deep in my heart for my sister to get home, back to our time, over and over as my arms slammed down with force. My gaze held my sister's the entire time.

The tip of the dagger collided with the pendant, a sharp pain going through my body at the force as I drove the dagger all the way through. My eyes met Kateya's as the pendant broke, shattering and bursting into minuscule pieces that flew across the room. An arctic chill sunk in, the force causing us to stumble back as I fell to the ground. Sharp pain hit my body as a piece of the shattered glass sliced across my skin, blood beginning to well.

Black mist suddenly appeared, swirling out from where the pendant had been shattered. The mist picked up speed as it twisted and moved around the room, circling around my sister and me. The feeling was all too similar to what had landed us here in the first place.

I watched in horror as the mist wrapped tightly around my sister. Shards from the pendant circled her as more thick mist rolled into the room from every direction. The temperature rapidly dropped as the mist encased my sister fully, and the wind howled around us, stealing my screams for her. I could no longer see my sister and my heart shattered like the pendant as the truth hit. She was gone. Back to the present. And I . . . I was trapped back in time.

The mist circled upward into an ominous cloud of darkness that funneled above me. Shattered pieces of the pendant continued to batter against my skin as the winds sucked the air from the room with such force the torches flickered before they died out. The room fell to darkness as the mist began descending rapidly toward me.

A sharp blast slammed into me, drawing the breath from my lungs as I doubled over, struggling to breathe. A chill sunk deep into me, flowing into my veins as I lost control of my body. My vision darkened at the edges as I drowned under the overwhelming wave of power that whipped into me. I could feel my body giving out, losing the fight to the forces, but I wouldn't let it kill me.

Darkness enclosed me, my body frozen, my mind racing as I knew what I needed to do as darkness overtook me. I would rise from beneath the shatter.

Chapter Twenty-Seven

THE THROBBING in my temple grew as my mind began to stir, the cool stone floor pressing against my cheek. Pain pricked from various parts of my body. My eyelids felt heavy, fluttering as they struggled and refused to open. Murmured voices reached my ears as I struggled to wrap my mind around what had happened.

"No. That's not what was agreed upon, *son*." A snarled voice broke through the haze clouding my brain.

"I don't give a *damn*. Do you hear me? Fuck your plan. She's mine," Sébastien's voice growled in return.

Me, I realized. They were talking about me. And that's when it hit me.

The reason I was knocked out came flooding back, a cry threatening to force its way from my lips. *The necklace. My sister. The pain.* My body felt as though it was on fire, heightened to new levels of sensation. I felt my blood pumping through my body, a slight vibration rumbling from deep within my being.

My limbs refused to cooperate, to provide even the slightest movement to indicate I had awoken. I concentrated on cracking my eyes open, my view of the two men arguing angled from my position on the floor. I felt as though I had been drugged. My body floated on a new level. The throb in my head threatened to take me back to the darkness, as I struggled to focus back on the conversation occurring across the room.

"She won't be able to handle that amount of power. Even the strongest rulers take years to master the power flowing through their veins. And Cassandra . . . she has the power of four rulers coursing through her."

"She will learn to handle it. In order to survive, she must, and we *will* help her. It's not a matter of discussion, *Father*," Sébastien snarled, his anger radiating from him. I noticed his appearance, his black leathers were stained with crimson splatters and dirt coated his clothing as he paced in front of his father, frustration evident in his icy gaze.

"You must break the bond between the two of you. Her power will kill her. She's a moving target. A weakness."

"*A weakness?*" Sébastien scoffed at his father in disgust. "She is many things. But never a weakness. She will burn the realm down with the power inside her. And I, *Father*, will be standing right by her side, clearing the way for her."

"Don't do this, son," Adrastan demanded. "We have come too far for you to be distracted by a simple *girl*. You've formed bonds plenty in the past and broken even more. It's time to stop playing games; we have a war to face, and we don't have the resources to worry about a bonded girl with fresh power who won't be able to control what's flowing through her."

"*ENOUGH!*" Sébastien roars, shifting mid-snarl into his wolvyn form as he launched himself at his father. Fangs displayed, the two circle each other, pelts shaking as they track each other's movements. I watched in awe as I realized that Sébastien was mid-spar with his father over me. *Because of our bond. Because of his claim over me.* A slight smile graced my lips as I realized this man would go to war to protect me, to defend me. And I would trust him to keep his word, knowing he would destroy any who stood in my path.

The words *"And I,* Father, *will be standing right by her side, clearing the way for her,"* ran through my head as I stared at the wolvyn across the room, grateful that he believed in me enough to defend me, thankful he was mine whether I had thought I wanted him to be or not.

A burning pain seared my arm as I lay on the floor, still recouping, my body refusing to listen. I watched as the circling came to a halt, and an icy blue gaze met mine from where I lay on the stone floor, unmoving as he dipped his head in acknowledgement toward me.

Sébastien's form shifted back to mortal in an instant, his father seconds after.

"I've had enough of this child's play. Do you understand what needs to be done?" His father, the King of Verastarr, seethed.

A cold smirk graced those freckled lips as Sébastien broke eye contact, turning to meet his father. "Yes, *Father.* I am *perfectly* clear on what must be done." His gaze swept to mine, cold and calculating as he carried on. "It would seem Cassandra and I will be traveling to Caperdov to complete the bonding ritual. Isn't that right, *princesse?*" he finished as he rolled his battered sleeve up his forearm, his arms flexing with the movement as he brandished a newly inked line above the other two.

I watched as his father's eyes widened, taking in the newly marked design, *a recently marked design.* "Well, well," he drawled as he crept slowly over to me, my limbs struggling to push myself up to a slouched sitting position. Pain in my arm and side radiated as I met the king's steeled gaze. "It would seem congratulations are in order. Welcome to the Capetian family, *my dear,"* he sneered as he turned and walked out of the room my entire life had been altered in.

Sébastien grimaced as he stood over me, extending his arm. The ink danced across his skin taunting us as I placed my smaller hand in his rough, calloused one. I noted the blood smears streaked across his tan, freckled skin. My legs shook as I stood, dizziness spiraling around my body as my head throbbed from the movement, pain searing over my body.

"You've got this." His voice broke through the pain, stern with an undertone of warmth. "Pick up the pieces and rise above them. That's all you can do now."

My gaze met his as my vision blurred with tears. Nodding, I righted myself and took a step forward to leave. Only my body wasn't on board with the motion, and I felt myself falling before firm arms wrapped themselves around my waist, bracing my fall as he lifted me and pulled me against his chest.

"Let's get you cleaned up, *princesse*." Sébastien's low voice wrapped around me as he helped me pick up the pieces of my heart and walked out of the room with me in his arms.

"Speak to me. What's going on in that pretty little head of yours?" Sébastien's voice rumbled. I sat perched on the edge of his bathroom counter, the water running beside us as he washed the blood from his chest.

Steam billowed around us as I locked eyes with Sébastien. "You stood up for me," I whispered, my voice barely discernible over the cascading water. "Against your father. Why?"

That cocky smirk appeared again as he spoke. "I told you, *Cassandra*. You're *mine*. How many times do I need to say that before you understand?"

"What happens next?" I questioned, gesturing to the fresh ink marring my skin.

"Now, we travel to Caperdov," he said with a glance to me, water dripping down the hard planes of his stomach, catching my eye. "The power flowing in you will start to awaken and when it does, it will be a beacon to those of like power. We are playing with fire, using borrowed time to travel."

"Why the rush?"

"Once your power comes alive, you will be a moving target. You're not trained to use your powers. You, unfortunately, have limited knowledge regarding them, and your fighting skills, while slowly improving, are no match for a trained military leader. Traveling prior to learning to control your power would mean guaranteed death."

"That I understand," I replied in a flat tone. "That still doesn't explain why we need to do the bonding ritual so soon."

He sighed as his reply carried over the water. "Once all three aspects of a wolvyn bond become apparent, there is a limited time for the bond to be accepted or broken. If it's not broken or accepted in that time frame, the ancient magic decides to self-destruct, essentially killing the bonded pair from the inside out. First stripping them of all power, then shutting the power host down."

A shocked gasp flew from my lips as he continued. "It's likely that the Nordak captain who captured you noticed the beginning of the bond. If we can't accept the bond for any reason, we will be quite painfully killed. Capturing us is the easiest way to eliminate our chances of performing the ritual. The second in line for the throne of Verastarr and the most powerful female in Vanaiyer dead, without completing the bond."

"How much time?" I questioned.

"Three days. Four maximum." His voice sunk into the air, the heated steam doing nothing to stop the arctic chill freezing my blood.

"*Three* days? *Three*?!" I shrieked.

His low chuckle filled the air as the water turned off.

"This isn't a laughing matter, *Sébastien*," I snapped as I

crossed my arms in front of my chest and glared at him. "Nothing about this is."

"Get some rest, *princesse*. We leave early tomorrow to ride to Caperdov." Watching as he turned to enter his room, I rolled my eyes before I hopped off the counter. My body protested slightly at the movement, enough for me to know that tomorrow's travels would hurt. *I missed traveling by car.* That would have been nice. A dry laugh escaped as I headed to my bedroom.

I lay there, staring blankly at the ceiling, watching the shadowed outlines flicker slightly across the space. Nobody told me how much it hurt—being alone. My insides twisted at the thought, my mind flickering to Kateya, praying that she made it back to our parents safely, that our parents were safe.

The sting in my eyes returned as I fought to hold back tears. I never got to say goodbye to my parents, to hear *I love you* one last time. My mind could barely process the fact that my entire family, my life, my existence wouldn't even happen for many years. *Centuries even.*

Eventually, the shadows faded away and the tears dried across my cheeks as a knock sounded on the door, reminding me to get ready. With a deep sigh, I rose from my bed. Padding over to the bathroom mirror, I barely recognized the reflection.

Sunken rings lay beneath my eyes, their dark purple hue highlighted the sorrow resonating within my soul. My usually vibrant blonde highlights were a dull gold swallowed by the brown of my hair. Tiny cuts and gashes speckled my arms and cheeks, with a yellowish bruise on my collarbone. *Breathe, Cass. Pick up the pieces and rise above. You've got to. Otherwise . . . you're toast in three fucking days.*

Lacing up the worn riding leathers in my closet, I stared at myself once again. The onyx color contrasted with my fair skin, and I strapped the dagger to my side. *I can do this,* I muttered to myself. *We could do this.* My mind drifted back to the night in the cave back on the Barree Rise, then the library in the château. Heat drifted down as I recalled his mouth on mine, his fingers roaming over my body, and a soft moan slipped into the air. *Well, there's certainly that.* I smirked as I secured the second blade in place on my body before exiting the room.

Sébastien stood to the side of the courtyard stables, securing the reins of the horse we would be taking as I approached behind the group.

"Take the back route to Caperdov," Kairon stated with authority. "We located ten Seefers to the west. You should be clear if you follow the coastline."

Sébastien nodded in agreement, his father remaining silent in their exchange.

"Any word from the south? My men cleared the group out three nights ago. However, I can't guarantee that it was the only camp."

"It's been silent so far. We've got men on watch surrounding the château borders. They'd be idiots to attempt an attack this far north," Kairon replied.

"Idiots with the entire realm to gain." Adrastan's stern voice joined the conversation. His eyes met Sébastien's as he continued, "The Nordak will stop at nothing now. The power is released. The pair of you the target. Ride hard and stay out of sight when possible. You know the ritual must be completed prior to high point tonight. A lucky guess would venture that her magic will activate with the ritual. Be alert and be gone by sunrise."

I approached as the men said their goodbyes, mounting the horse before Sébastien swung into place behind me, his body hard against mine as he took the reins.

Chapter Twenty-Eight

VERASTARR

WE RODE UNDETECTED and undisturbed during the day, often riding through darkened pine forests that hugged the coastline, our movements blending in with the shadows. Dusk crept upon us as we approached our destination, the occasional song of a bird the only sound echoing in the forest. My eyes widened in awe as we approached a grassy field. The breeze flowed gently through the blades of grass, hues of purple drifting along from the flowers scattering them. I noticed a small spring to one side, its silver water bubbling as it lapped at the surrounding stone.

Sébastien gave a slight pull on the reins, slowing our motion as we stopped in front of the field. I stared at the towering stone structure in front of us. The top nearly matched the height of the pine trees we had traveled through all day. Oval in shape, the stone was covered front and back with markings inked on its surface, intricate detailing and lines, some matching the lines we had on our own wrists.

Sébastien broke our silence as we dismounted. "I will go into detail soon, but for now, copy my movements and repeat after me."

I nodded with confusion, yet I did what he asked as I

followed closely behind his every step. His movements stopped in front of the stone as he looked over at me before lifting his palms and placing them against the surface. Hesitating for a moment, I glanced between him and the stone before lifting my palms and copying the motion.

Shock flooded through me—the stone was hot to the touch, vibrating beneath my palms. *Magic,* I realized. The hum of power radiating through the stone drew me in, my mind hazing slightly as I forced myself to listen to the words flowing from Sébastien's lips, repeating them. I looked around us, as the words fell from our lips, the sky darkening above us, the winds whipping in a circular motion around the grassy opening, the gales picking up as the towering stone glowed brightly through the darkened expanse. The markings on the stone began to glow, sunset hues drifting off the stone into the air surrounding us.

A sharp pain in my wrist caused me to glance down. The same red-orange hue of glow leaked from the ink around my wrist. I watched the particles of ink stretch off my skin, drifting over to him. Sébastien's hand reached out, and the glowing ink flowed up from our wrists, floating and twining together as our palms joined. The ink danced in the air, twisting as it entwined before floating its way through to the stone, entering it as the vibration grew louder, rumbling the ground beneath us.

"Now!" Sébastien's voice commanded as he took a step forward, yanking me along with him. His free arm reached out to the stone as he pushed his arm through the space, his body was swallowed as he walked *through* the stone.

What on Vanaiyer is happening?!

My mind panicked as I felt his grip on my hand pulling me through the stone with force before I had time to process what was happening.

Slamming into his chest, I froze. My head whipped around, panicked, yet everything appeared normal. We stood in the same grassy field, with the same flowers, with the same silver spring, but something was off. I just couldn't place what it was. Pushing off Sébastien's chest, I glared at him. "What the *fuck* was that?"

His low chuckle filled the air as his gaze met mine. "That, *princesse*, was the beginning of the bonding ritual." He began walking, assuming I would follow him. I stayed firmly in place, as I looked around with confusion, cataloging each detail while I scanned the area.

The sky was dark, yet no longer with a stormy vengeance brewing. It was a clear night sky, the dark blue hues peaceful with stars scattering the space. The winds had died down, and the field was alive with the songs of forest creatures. Any glow from the stone had disappeared, the vibrations and humming noise vanished without a trace.

"If you would just follow me, I told you I would explain." The disgruntled rumble came from across the field. Sighing, I took off after him.

"You know," I snapped back. "If you just told me what was happening to begin with, it would save me from being confused." I was annoyed that he hadn't kept me in the loop. "It's my life too. Might have been nice to know we started the bonding process."

Glancing over his shoulder, he replied with a devilish smirk, "Where would the fun be in that?"

I stopped as I stared at the entrance to a cave. A cave I could have sworn wasn't here when we first arrived. "Okay, I *know* this wasn't here. What's going on? How is the land changing?"

Sébastien's gaze clashed with mine as he leaned against the side of the cave, gesturing for me to sit down. The warmth of the stone seeped through me as I regarded him. "You might have noticed. We took no guards, no extra protection, the bare minimum when traveling here." I nodded as I stared at him. I had thought it was odd that with all the concern over the Nordak, we traveled alone.

"Caperdov is a sacred place of magic. From the outside, it appears just as you saw it, a grass field with a small spring. To enter as we did, you must have completed the three phases of wolvyn bonding. When we placed our hands on the Stone of Dov, the ink bled through, the magic of this place drawing it out and accepting it. By stepping through, we have accepted that we are bonded."

"Wait," I growled. "That's what we were doing?! I thought it had to be night for us to accept the bond?" I questioned. "Don't you think I at least deserved to know that?"

Sébastien drew closer, his muscled frame towering over mine. "Would that have changed the outcome, *princesse*?"

I opened my mouth, then closed it again. This was a discussion for later. I needed more answers first.

"When a bonded couple enters into the Caperdov, a seal of magic is spread across the place. In truth, this is the safest place for you to be as your powers awaken. The seal created by the magic is impenetrable by outside forces."

"There's no guarantee that the power will awaken while we're here," I replied as I held Sébastien's gaze.

"No," he simply replied. "But my father predicts that the power channeled into you will awaken here, the call of the surrounding magic and the bond calling it out. When it does, you will need to be prepared. The power in that pendant will be unlike any power in the realm—a combination of four of the Vanaiyer lands. I won't be able to teach you how to harness each of the powers, but I will be able to teach you to use your wolvyn power once it comes through from the power release."

I stayed silent, processing his words. It was a lot to take in, the bond, the new power I supposedly gained, the fact that I would no longer be a mortal, the death wishes people had for me now, especially considering my sister just left the day before. *I mean, give a girl a break.* "So, what now?"

"This cave leads deep underground. If we follow this path, it will take us to the Lyte Dov, which is where the bonding ritual is cemented."

Staring into the darkened opening further inside the cave, a chill radiated from its depths as I gestured toward the looming entrance. "Well then, after you, *Your Highness.*"

The tunnels we had been trekking through began to grow lighter, the chilled air evaporating as I followed Sébastien to a stop inside a hollowed-out room. Glancing around, I saw the expanse was bare, no furniture or objects in place, as though it was a deserted room. The stone walls and flooring were covered with dark, blueish black ink that seemed alive as it moved across the expanse. I could feel the same low hum and vibrations rising from the stone. A sound I had begun to recognize occurred when larger amounts of magic were dispelled. Rounded walls funneled up, circling higher to an open point. The jagged opening provided a full display of the night sky, the moon almost directly overhead as the twinkle of the stars glowed brightly, bouncing off the stone.

"What is this place?" I said in awe as I took in our surroundings.

"Welcome to Lyte Dov." Sébastien's voice echoed across the stone as he spoke. "The most sacred and powerful place in all of Verastarr. The power held in this one room outmatches even the power of the four rulers that you have received."

A gasp fell from my lips as I circled the room, feeling the power rolling throughout the space. "With so much power, why have the Nordak not attempted to break through the barriers for its power?"

Sébastien's ice-blue eyes darkened as his gaze met mine. "This is the most well-kept secret in Verastarr," he stated with an air of smug pride. "Even if they knew of Caperdov, it can only be accessed by wolvyn. *Fully bonded Wolvyn.* The pair must enter willingly and the power within would expel any additional people who attempt to cross the threshold."

"I'm not wolvyn, though," I stated with slight confusion.

"You may not be wolvyn yet, but the wolvyn power was given to you when you shattered the pendant. Don't underestimate the strength of primal magic. Caperdov can feel the power in you, enough to accept that you will be wolvyn."

"Who controls the magic found here?" I questioned as I gestured broadly to the room we were standing in.

Sébastien chuckled as he watched me. "No one. The magic found here is primal magic. Its very existence stems from the beginning of times. It was always just meant to be. A force of its own to recon with."

I nodded in understanding as I stood near the center of the cave and further questioned, "What happens next?"

He walked slowly toward me, his eyes tracing my every movement as his motion halted, his body inches from mine. "Next, *princesse*, we let the bond cement."

I held Sébastien's gaze, the intensity of the moment building. My lips yearned to feel the firm pressure of his, and my thoughts wandered as his gaze swallowed mine, heat flooding through me. He reached out with his hand, the ink coming alive across his tanned skin as the moon reflected off it. "Are you ready to dance with destiny?"

Sucking in a deep breath of air, I gingerly placed my palm within his extended one, trusting him fully with my life and my future. His fingers entwined with mine as he shifted our palms, holding them in the center of the room. I held Sébastien's gaze as the moon rose, fitting perfectly in the cave opening.

The temperature dropped rapidly, shivers coursing

through my body as goosebumps scattered my skin. I gasped as I noticed the ink from the top of the cave begin to come alive, a bluish white light filling it as though the moon had cried tears that leaked into the ink. Slowly, the glow began to sink in, trickling down the walls. The intricate designs carved throughout the cave now beamed like the moon as the glow descended, swallowing more of the room.

Sébastien and I stood in silenced awe as we watched the glow of power approach us, covering every inch of stone, before snaking up our bodies, illuminating the inkings across our own skin. The moment both our wrists were entirely filled, glowing with a bluish hue, a familiar pain seared across our wrists. A pain I had begun to recognize as part of the bonding process. A warm gust of wind blew across the cave, warming our chilled skin as it swept across the glowed inkings, picking them up.

The whirlwind grew stronger, Sébastien's hand tightening its hold on mine as the gusts blew around us, the ink removing itself from the wall, dancing around us as it flew in circles. The humming increased as the ground shook below us, vibrating with the power flowing from it. Moonlight flooded in the cave. With every second the moon appeared closer than it should, the wind whipping by us. The glowing ink rose, transcending high above our heads, building and building.

As though time froze, the wind stopped. The glowing marks were held in place near the mouth of the opening, and the only sounds heard were the ragged breaths slipping from our lips as I glanced up in confusion. The pain dissolved from my wrist; in its place, thin linework connected the three designs, trapping and bonding them together.

My skin began to increase in temperature, unbearable heat coursing through me. I watched as my skin started to glow, a low gold color radiating from me, boiling my insides. I glanced at Sébastien, noting his skin was untouched. Suddenly, time unfroze. The wind descended in a sharp downward spiral. The gusts of wind whipped around us with increased intensity.

"Don't let go!" Sébastien's voice snapped through the air. "The bond is almost completed, but your magic is trying to break through." His words faded as the wind carried them away. My eyes widened in shock as I realized what was happening before snapping up as the onslaught of glowing ink rushed down, some markings dancing around us. My skin climbed in temperature, golden cracks emerging on the surface as though the power was threatening to break through from inside me.

As if it had a mind of its own, the wind twisted faster, funneling the inkings into a spear as they hurled down toward our entwined wrists. Like arctic ice blasts, the black ink pelted into our entwined hold and seeped in. The pinpricks of pain were indiscernible compared to the raging heat of the power struggling to break free from my body. My skin glowed brighter as the power from the bonding ritual assaulted us, our stances weakening as the wind tormented on. My grip slipped from Sébastien's as we continued to be battered, my body exhausted from the war it raged against the power coming through.

The ground rumbled as a bright flash flew through the room, throwing us to the ground, my head cracking against the stone. The blue glow of ancient ink vanished, leaving behind empty stone walls without a trace of ink on their rough surfaces. The wind silenced as my skin burst with a golden glow, my body alight with a raging fire of heat as the power surfaced within me, taking hold. Abruptly, my vision went dark.

Chapter Twenty-Nine

VERASTARR

THE OVERWHELMING SOUND of a low vibrating hum drew me from the dark pit I was in, the sound clashing with the throbbing on the side of my head as I stirred, cracking my eyes open to see where I was. My eyes met with Sébastien's icy blue ones as I recognized that he must have carried me out of the tunnels.

"Welcome back, *princesse*." He chuckled from where he stood in the spring to my side, silver droplets rolling down his taut body as he ran his fingers through his wet hair before giving it a shake. The ripple of his muscles drew me in with every movement as he held my gaze captive in his.

My heart rate increased as I stared at him, his gaze burning to the depths of my soul, marking me as his, taunting me. Remembering his words, a slow "Thanks" rolled from my lips as I pushed off the ground, struggling to ignore the heightened senses in my body, a result of the awakened power within me.

Pushing my hair to the side, I slowly tugged the riding leathers from my body, freeing me of the restraint, planning to join him in the bubbling spring. A smirk crossed my lips as I watched his gaze trace down the outline of my curves beneath my shirt. The crackle-pop of a fire hit my ears, causing me to pause. My head snapped toward the direction of the sound as I tuned in the noise of the fire I couldn't see.

"The fire you're hearing is past the forest, right alongside the coastline," he answered my unspoken question as he emerged from the spring, water dripping from his chest down his onyx-colored pants that hugged his build. My gaze caught on the hard outline in his pants.

"The c-coastline?" I stammered, my attention divided as I struggled to focus on his words.

"Yes, the coastline. While mortal hearing is subpar at best, wolvyn hearing is quite impeccable," he teased.

"It would seem so," I replied as I began to process the fact that I was no longer mortal. I was a wolvyn. A *bonded* wolvyn. And yet, I was also more. The power of four lands coursed through my veins now.

My body heated as he stopped in front of me, his sturdy frame towering over me, the calloused pad of his thumb tracing across my bottom lip, trailing down to tilt my chin up. He held my gaze to his.

Are you ready to play, princesse? the low voice husked in my head, and my eyes widened as a dark smirk tugged on his unmoving lips. *What?* he taunted me for my sudden confusion.

"W-what? How did you do that?" I demanded, shocked I could hear his voice so clearly in my mind.

"Wolvyn can communicate with each other only in their wolvyn form. Bonded couples can communicate through the bond in any form. Didn't you read about bonded powers?"

I stared at him. *Of course, I did. He knows that answer. That didn't mean I knew how to do it or expected it to sound just like talking aloud,* I sarcastically thought as I formulated a response.

A low chuckle sounded. *Careful there, princesse. You might want to put up a few barriers, I can hear all your thoughts.*

Asshole, I thought loudly in my mind, glaring at him in frustration as I raised my foot and slammed it down on his.

His laugh grew as he tugged me closer, our bodies pressed against each other as his breath snaked across the expanse of skin on my neck, trailing up before stopping at my ear. "Seems like you're ready to fight now, *princesse*."

I scoffed at his remark, even as my body longed to feel his fingers across my skin. His breath sent delightful shivers that danced over my body.

"From the moment you shattered that necklace, you became prey." He growled, his eyes flashing to slits as his wolvyn form rose to the surface, fierce and protective, *of me*. "There will be people who want your power, your connection to the throne, your soul. They will hunt you to every end. You must learn to move undetected, cover your tracks, and fight back when least expected."

Scoffing, I retorted, "I have no interest in being anyone's *prey*."

"Let's see what you've learned then. How well can you control the power flowing through you? Can you use it to mask your scent, your location? How well can the prey stay hidden when their life depends on it?"

My narrowed eyes met his, the challenge rising through the air. "I don't know how to use my power," I snapped, frustrated because he knew this.

"You've read the books on the history of magic. It's not the same as actual practice, but you know it's a matter of how your mind controls what's already flowing through your veins. You're running out of time, *Cassandra*. You've already been marked. The predators are on the hunt. And your soul is the target."

"And you?" I questioned.

"*Princesse*." His voice floated past my ear. "You have been my prey since the moment you arrived. And I . . . I am the *big, bad* wolf." His dark snarl shook my body, my physical response to his claim a direct contrast to the fear instilled as he spoke. "I will chase you to the ends of the realm. You will *never* escape me. *You're mine.*" His gaze held mine, his grip firm around my waist, digging into me before he released me.

A singular phrase floated across my mind as he smirked with a devilish look in his ice-blue eyes, stepping back. *You've got five minutes, Cassandra, and when I find you, I won't hold back. You're mine.* My heart dropped as my body hummed with delight. *Run,* he whispered. And the hunt was on.

My breath came in shallow pants as I pressed deeper into the cool stone. I blended into the darkness as I forged my way through the cave tunnels, weaving my way through the different paths. My ears tuned in to my surroundings, picking up every minuscule detail. The wolvyn hearing was the only thing coming to me naturally as I shifted through the noises I heard, tracing them back and finding their origins. Past the steady drip of water I passed earlier, past the wind cutting through the tunnel entrance. *Fuck.* Sébastien's light breathing sounded in my ears, mixed with the slight rustle of leaves. The echo indicated he knew I was in the tunnels and soon he would be, too.

I've got your scent, princesse. Don't tell me that's the best you can do. The taunt rumbled across my mind.

Fuck off, I snapped back in my mind, the dark chuckle rumbled back. I struggled to breathe, my body thrumming at the challenge, the adrenaline, the fear, even as I froze in silence, praying he couldn't hear me. My mind flew back to his comment about power being controlled through thoughts. It was about wanting an outcome in your mind. It was worth a shot.

Taking a deep breath, I cleared my mind, tuning out the noise, the fear, and focusing on one thought alone: Becoming invisible like a wolvyn.

I breathed. *In. Shift. Out. Shift. In. Shift. Out.* Nothing. The sounds flooded back in. I could hear his footsteps making up distance in the tunnels. *Come on, Cass. You can shift. You have to. All wolvyn can. Now you're one of them.*

I tried again, breathing deep as I focused on my outcome. *In. Shift. Out. Shift. In. Shift. Out.* A rippled tremor shot through my body, tearing into the depths of my soul. My senses heightened, my eyesight stronger in the darkness. My body screamed internally as my bones felt like they were being broken at once. I collapsed on the stone floor with a thud, my eyes connecting with a clawed paw in front of me. *Void-damned,* I thought as I realized that it actually worked. I had embraced the magic, controlling it to work for me. I was a wolvyn.

It's about time, princesse. The hunt is on. His voice vibrated through my mind, fear urging me to dart away. I rose on shaky haunches, processing the light silver coat of fur I could see on my forelegs. My eyes adjusted to the darkness of the tunnel, my vision picking up on the fine details I hadn't previously been able to see.

I slunk into the shadows, the concept of walking on four legs a strange sensation as I wove my way deeper into the tunnels. Losing track of the turns made, I began to feel disoriented. The click of paws scraping across stone still met my ears at every turn, a low howl from somewhere in the tunnels froze my heartbeat as I forced my legs to move faster, further, my strides lengthened as I raced through the paths striving to move undetected.

It was as though I could sense him gaining distance with each stride I took, and an imaginary taunt echoed in my ears. He encroached on me step by step as my muscles burned while I pushed forward. Rounding a corner, a flash of gray fur caught my eye as I skidded, unintentionally sliding out of control down a separate corridor of the tunnel, my legs collapsing from under me as I tumbled into a room. My focus on my form slipped as I shifted back to two legs, landing on my back at a dead end.

Limbs burned as the stone ground scraped against bare skin, and a metallic scent surrounded me as I pushed up onto my forearms. I was momentarily stunned by the space I found myself in. Smooth stone adorned the walls of the space, as balls of light floated midair, providing a glowing orange ambience dancing on the walls. A spring bubbled up on the far side of the room, a flat surface carved into the stone beside the spring. A lone string of flowers sprouted up from the crack in the ground, stretching toward the water source.

Ignoring the protest of my muscles, I pushed up rapidly, remembering why I had fallen to begin with. I darted up, my head snapping toward the entrance I had crashed through. Only to be met with a dark, ice-blue hunger.

The glint in his eyes reflected his anticipated win. Sébastien's form filled the archway as he leaned against the stone, arms crossed over his chest, his muscles straining against the seams of his shirt. "Like I said, *princesse*, you will never escape me."

Glancing around, I realized he blocked the singular entrance, and his presence filled the air. The scent of pine and spice wafted closer as he slowly stalked toward me, dominance dripping from him. I matched each of his steps forward with one of my own backward. Until my back met warmed stone, thrill coursing through me as he continued his approach, his eyes tracing over every inch of my body. A predator stalking his prey.

I held my breath as Sébastien stopped inches from me, a dark chuckle slipped from his lips as his thumb reached out, tracing my bottom lip before trailing his fingers down the column of my throat. "Might as well give up and accept defeat." His husky voice reached my ears sending shivers down my skin, while his fingers traced over my shirt, across my collarbone, before drifting lower.

I stared at Sébastien through lowered lashes, my body on fire from his touch. *"Defeat?"* I scoffed. "Never. You just got lucky this round, *Your Highness,*" I retorted with a smirk.

His fingers traced the rise of my breast, the intensity building as a familiar black mist began to trace up my ankles, kissing the inside of my legs as it made its way up.

"Lucky?" He grinned. "Luck had nothing to do with it, *mate.*" My breath hitched as his fingers continued tantalizing my body. His free hand traced over my other breast, trailing up before tightening in a chokehold around my neck, angling my lips toward his as they crushed over mine. Claiming me. Consuming me—his *mate.* I sunk into the kiss, his lips roaming over mine as his tongue probed, seeking entrance, forcing itself in, ravaging me.

My fingers dug into his chest with building urgency, my airway restricted as he held me pinned against the wall, my lungs begging for air as my body begged to be his. Blackened mist swirled around us, dancing on my skin, setting it alight as it teased across me when he broke the kiss.

"I've wanted you from the moment I laid eyes on you, Cassandra." He snarled into my ear as desire built. "And every moment since. You are always and will always be the center of my realm." I nodded with a smile as I watched his eyes flash. *My mate.*

"And you, the center of mine." I whispered back.

One hand captured my arms with force, drawing them up above my head, pinning them against the wall as tendrils of mist wrapped around them, holding them firmly in place. His eyes switched to slits and back again, his wolvyn side rising to the surface.

Our kiss grew frantic then, my teeth drawing his bottom lip between them, biting with pressure as a deep growl vibrated through him. His hands grasped my shirt, a firm yank tearing the material down the center. A sharp gasp fell from my lips as cool air hit my flesh. His eyes flashed into slits as they roamed over my exposed skin before his lips came crashing back down on mine.

I squirmed, desire aflame as Sébastien dragged his fingers along the sensitive flesh on my thighs, his eyes tracing my face, my body, as his fingers roamed up, drifting over the scar on my side. I tensed as he traced along the silver lines marring my skin. "Beautiful," he murmured, as I ducked my head. "You," he growled as he tilted my chin to meet his gaze, "are so utterly divine. Breathtakingly beautiful."

My body arched into his touch, a low moan filling the air as he slid his fingers inside me, stretching me. His thumb danced circles around my center in tandem with the thrust of his fingers, a deep need building in me as he worked me higher and higher.

"Sébastien," I moaned breathlessly against his neck as my nails dug into his back, my body beginning to shake as I marked his inked skin.

"*Fuck, princesse,*" he rasped back. "I never want to stop hearing my name fall from your lips like that."

The pressure built as his fingers worked back and forth, hitting that spot inside me with repeated precision. His hand circled my neck, cutting my air flow as I struggled to breathe, his fingers relentless in their pursuit. I surrendered to him as he controlled my pleasure, my pain, the air I breathed.

Spots danced in my vision as his ice-blue gaze held mine, dark hair brushing over his freckled cheekbones as he growled, "*You're mine, princesse.*"

As he thrust in deep and pushed me to the edge of oblivion, it was his name on my lips when I went over the edge.

My eyes fluttered open as Sébastien removed his fingers, his eyes holding mine as he raised them to his mouth. "You taste delicious." His grip still held me firmly against the stone wall as his lips claimed mine. Sweeping over them as he nipped my bottom lip. I leaned into him, the pressure of his lips on mine, guiding me as emotion rose to the surface. "I told you not to play unless you want to be bitten," he warned as his mouth feathered kisses down my neck before clamping down.

"Sébastien," I moaned out his name, as a sharp burst of heat fanned while he licked the area.

"Was that a complaint, *princesse,* or a challenge?" He smirked as his hands wrapped around my waist, holding me up against the wall as my legs instinctively wrapped around his sculpted form, hands tangled in his hair.

My eyes widened at the sheer size I felt at my entrance. His eyes were alight as his hold tightened around me before thrusting in with force, building a rhythm as he moved. The unrelenting pounding of him inside me as we came together again and again. Black mist cloaked us in darkness, trailing along my exposed flesh as our moans blended together. Sébastien devoured me with his lips, branding me with his kiss before he sank his teeth back into my neck as he thrusted.

My back arched to meet his rhythm and my body writhed as his lips continued to trace down my neck, leaving behind bruising marks as he nibbled and bit, sinking his teeth into my flesh.

He slightly shifted, using his thighs to urge my legs further apart where they were wrapped around him. The wall scratched at my back as my fingers clawed at his hair, tightening around strands of onyx as he continued—power building around us.

My mind hazed over, my body on fire as the words fell from my lips before I even processed what I said. "I love you," I whispered, truth flowing from the words as power rose to the surface of my skin, glowing gold as my body throbbed, the intensity too much to bear.

His eyes flared as he held my gaze, emotion swirling in gaze. "I love you too, *Cassandra.*" The words fell from his lips as he thrust deeper, his thumb sweeping over my center, pleasure erupting from me. "And I vow to protect you—from the stars to across The Void—there's no corner of the realm you could go that I wouldn't hunt you down in." His control snapped, thrusting hard before stilling, following me over the edge with a roar. His eyes closed as his grip on me loosened slightly.

My eyes glazed as I stared at him, a sated grin on my face as he lifted me off the stone wall. Corded muscles in his back tightened as his arms came around me and his hands tightened their grasp on me, holding me close to him as he turned us around, walking slowly toward the edge of the bubbling spring.

My thighs protested as he waded into the spring, the heated water a relaxing sensation on my overly sensitive skin as he held me close. Silver droplets danced across our bodies, washing off the sheen of sweat coating us. Affection drifted across my face as I stared into his eyes, the silver of the spring reflecting in them.

"You're mine, *princesse*. Yesterday. Today. And tomorrow . . . there's no forgetting me now," he growled softly against my ear.

Chapter Thirty

VERASTARR

"CASSANDRA!" A muffled shout sounded in the distance as I attempted to curl back into my dreams. "CASSANDRA!" The call grew more urgent, and a firm pressure on my shoulder shook me awake. My eyes fluttered open in confusion.

"Sébastien?" I muttered softly, my voice a hoarse whisper as I struggled to pull myself from my sleep.

"We've got to go. Now." His voice broke through my sleep hazed brain.

"W-wait. What?" I questioned as I sat up, looking around. I had been asleep on the raised stone slab; the bubbling spring lulled us to sleep late last night.

"*Now*, Cass," he voiced, leaving no option but to obey, as he stretched out his hand, tugging me up as he led the way out of the stone room.

"Sébastien," I demanded as I dug my heels into the stone, forcing him to look at me. "What the hell is going on?"

His eyes took on a haunted shadow as he spoke. "I shifted to check in with Dravyn. A system we put in place when traveling years ago after he was ambushed on patrol. The Nordak launched an attack on Nytestarr." He growled as he stormed through the tunnels back to the entrance. "Should have killed every last bloody bastard when I had the chance." His voice echoed, and I hurried after him.

"How many?"

"The Nordak presence had been dwindling prior to the first artifact reappearing," he stated. "However, Kairon has had growing concerns for the Seefer population."

"How so?" I questioned, my legs protesting as I half-jogged to keep up with his brisk pace.

"He thinks that our attention has been too focused on the Nordak. That they have been planting Seefers on our grounds every time they sneak a new guard through our borders."

I nodded, realizing how simple it would have been. The Nordak land, as empty as it was in appearance, teemed with gryffins. The ease of access they would have had, soaring overhead, undetectable until they landed? It made perfect sense, the perfect strike plan.

"Void-damned," he growled as we emerged into the darkness. The sun's touch was a few hours away as the night air haunted us. "We will travel fastest on foot, undetected."

"Fastest?" I wondered aloud, failing to see how he thought traveling on foot was faster than by the horse we traveled in on.

"Yes. Shifting will ensure we can sneak up on any intruders without being noticed. The longer you can stay shifted, the better."

"No pressure there," I snapped, praying I would even be able to stay shifted that long. "How long will it take us to get to Nytestarr once we shift?"

"Uninterrupted? Three hours. Follow my lead and stay close on my trail," Sébastien commanded as we approached the stone that we had first stepped through hours before. His calloused hand grabbed mine, turning to face me, and those icy blue orbs pierced mine. "Shift as soon as you cross over and stay low. Remember to keep your walls up. In wolvyn form, anyone can hear your thoughts if you don't have your barrier in place and are thinking strongly enough."

"Wait. How do I hold up a barrier?"

"Imagine building a wall with your mind. A fortress that only a few can enter into. Seal it tightly in the depths of your mind, then few will be able to hear your thoughts." His palm rose, resting on the stone as the ink came alive within it. "Ready or not, *princesse*, you've got to do this."

Nodding, I raised my palm, the familiar heat seeping through the stone's connection as Sébastien pushed his way through, his hand tugging mine along. *In. Shift. Out. Shift. In.* I breathed as I emerged on the other side. *Shift.*

A familiar sear of pain split through me as power encased my body, shifting into a silver-furred wolvyn, smaller in size compared to Sébastien's towering wolvyn form. His black and gray coat rippled as he beckoned for me to follow. Relief coursed through me as realization dawned that I had successfully shifted yet again.

We took off under the cover of night, wandering through the underbrush of the forest. The deadly silence that surrounded the forest felt like an omen for the morning to come. There wasn't a creature alive in the woods as we raced through the forest, paws colliding with the dirt with every stride. My mind drifted to building a barrier as I followed Sébastien, trusting his lead through the forest.

Visualizing a brick, I laid it in my mind, lining a second one next to it. Slowly, I built up an imaginary wall, the bricks growing in strength as they stacked up inside my head, trapping my wandering thoughts inside.

You need to reinforce your barrier with another layer, a low voice floated across my mind.

Wait, how am I still hearing you? What's the point of building a wall if you can still get in? I answered back as we continued running, my legs burning from the motion, still not used to my wolvyn form. The coastline was to our left as we forged on.

Well, princesse. *First of all, your wall is getting there, but still weak. Your thoughts are slipping through for others to hear. Secondly, I am the captain of the king's army and his son. My levels of power and experience sneaking through mental barriers is extensive; it must be. And lastly* . . . He paused, chuckling as he spoke. *We are bonded. Mates, in wolvyn form, have constant streams of communication that flow.*

Oh, I responded. *That would have been nice to know.*

Where would the fun have been in that? His chuckle warmed me even as we ran head first toward danger. *Keep building that wall.*

I continued adding imaginary bricks in my mind, testing the strength of my mental barrier as time sped by. Brushes and brambles snagged on my coat, getting caught in my fur as we moved undetected. The empty void of the forest filled me with apprehension with each step closer to the city we took.

A blood-curdling scream of pain pierced my mind, my limbs pausing mid-stride as a second scream followed the first one. The words engraved in my mind as a female voice echoed in my head. *NOOO! Dustin! Don't you leave me.*

Sébastien's steps faltered as we pressed forward with caution.

What just happened? I forced out toward Sébastien through my mind.

That—he sighed—*that would be the sound of a wolvyn losing their mate. Her mental barriers fell as her mate was murdered in front of her. Even the strongest wolvyn lose control of their barriers in moments of weakness and pain.*

My heart was heavy as I realized what we had just witnessed through the wolvyn bond. A glimpse of the horror we were running straight toward. Of a wolvyn who had lost her mate. The broken scream played on repeat in my mind.

Sébastien's stride slowed as we approached the outskirts of Nytestarr, our bodies pressed low against the ground as we crept along. The sun rose as we moved in, painting the sky in an amber glow that contrasted the darkness that still lingered, hanging low in the morning light.

Stay close to my side until we make it inside the Palace. Your best chance of survival and disguise will be in wolvyn form. Do whatever you can to stay in that form. Fight with your fangs and claws.

My heart hammered in my chest, nerves rattling around within me as we crept through the shadows of back alleys. Gone was the lavender and lemon verbena scent I had begun to associate with Nytesstarr. In its place, an all too familiar metallic scent coated the air as we moved, crimson staining the paved stones as we carried on.

Breathing deep, *in* then *out* repeatedly, I let the darkness slip inside me, my emotions buried in the back of my mind as I focused on the task ahead of us. Survival.

Sébastien's form crouched in front of mine, tensing as his coat shook slightly. Pressing my body to a crouch behind him, I waited, my muscles coiling as I prepared for what he saw. An empty trill filled the air, a Seefer running into view. Its ragged form charged toward us as Sébastien launched through the air, his fangs latching into the Seefer's thick neck, crimson spewing as he held on. Claws raked down the beast's body.

I froze momentarily. My mind screamed at me to run the other way, to escape this nightmare, as scenes flashed through my mind of the Seefers attacking my childhood home, claws raking into my skin back then.

Shaking myself free of the past, I snuck up from the side and pounced. My claws extended from my paws, finding traction down the battered coat of the Seefer, shredding as they raked down its body.

My head snapped to my left; I could hear far out in the distance a loud trill from two more Seefers approaching. Their amber fangs dripped yellow venom as they leered toward us.

The Seefer Sébastien fought collapsed to the ground in a motionless heap as the next two struck. A violent dance of fangs, claws, and snarls ensued as the two of us faced off against the Seefers. I launched through the air, my claws driving into the Seefer in front of me, my fangs sinking into the beast's leg as I thrashed my head back and forth rapidly. Iron coated the insides of my mouth as the Seefer snarled, ripping itself from my grip, mounting a counterattack. Claws raked past my belly as I dodged the attack, circling the beast.

Screams echoed in the back of my mind, momentarily distracting me, as other wolvyn lost control of their own mental barriers, pain radiating within the united wolvyn bond as we all felt their emotion.

Sébastien's pained snarl sounded to my right as I struck again, my fangs connecting with the exposed flesh of the Seefer's neck. I tore through the skin, blood coating my fur, matting it down as I thrashed back and forth, feeling the life drain from the creature. My eyes met Sébastien's dark gaze, blood staining our coats as he stood over his kill, anger and power coursing through the air.

We need to go, NOW. The Seefers are just a distraction. Since they've already broken through the main gates, the Nordak will go straight for the Palace.

I nodded as my limbs pushed on. Adrenaline coursed through my body as we veered to the right, staying out of sight as we weaved through the narrow streets of the city. Cobblestone pavers were underfoot as we advanced toward the Palace before slowing our approach as a hardly noticeable outline of a door came into view. I watched as black mist rose around Sébastien, twisting and hovering over the seams of the doors, pushing it forcefully open a crack.

Checking our surroundings to ensure we were undetected, Sébastien entered through the door as I followed behind, close on his heels. The door latched shut instantly with a heavy thud, darkness swallowing us before our eyes adjusted to the shadowed hallway. Cool, damp air seeped into my fur as our paws padded along the rough flooring.

What is this place? I prompted through our bond as we made our way through the tunnels.

This was the old escape route. Long before my father was king, these tunnels were used to evacuate the wolvyn ruling family if the Palace ever came under attack. My brother and I discovered these tunnels when we were boys playing hide and seek throughout the maze before our father caught us and forbade us from playing in them.

We hurriedly strode through the tunnels, praying that they remained silent from the sounds of battle. I noticed the tunnels began to weave in an upward trajectory, the incline growing steep as we carried on.

West wing! Dravyn's voice flooded through my mind in a shout. Sébastien's ears perked up as he froze before spinning, his legs launching into a sprint. *Three corridors down. Throne room. The floor is teeming with fucking gryffins.* Dravyn's voice once again rang through our minds.

My legs scrambled to keep up with Sébastien's sprint. Snarled growls grew louder as we approached a dead end. The noises down the connected wolvyn bond echoing in pained groans. *Whatever you do,* Sébastien threw down our bond into my mind, *stick close to me or Dravyn. Do whatever it takes to stay in wolvyn form. The Nordak don't know you can shift yet—use that to your advantage. Stay under their radar as much as possible.*

He skidded to a stop at the end of the hallway, turning to face me. His eyes darkened with vengeance and fury. He was prepared for the battle ahead. I stopped beside him, hardening myself as I struggled to keep the nerves building in my stomach down. My heart was beating out of my chest as I wished I could escape this day.

His head lowered, nudging the side of mine with his nose before he crouched down, springing on the door as it burst open.

Light flooded in, movement coming in flashes as a look of

horror smeared across my face. Large, golden creatures with the bodies of lions, feathered wings stemming from their sides, were locked into battle with the wolvyn. Dark red painted the walls and coated the floors of the open room, leaking out into the hallway. Cries and groans filled the air as weapons clashed, metal clanging throughout the space. Wolvyn and gryffins alike shifted back and forth between forms as they circled, sparred, and attacked. The outdoor terrace was swarmed with creatures charging in, claws raised as they chased their targets. I spotted the king on the terrace, taking on two gryffins. Sébastien's brother stood beside him as they circled the attackers.

Dravyn's wolvyn form roared over a fallen gryffin, blood dripping from his mouth as his gaze met ours. *Move!* Sébastien shouted in my mind, my gaze snapping into a defensive mode as I processed the man charging toward me, shifting as he leapt through the air. Sébastien launched himself at the gryffin, meeting him midair. Claws battled as they fell to the ground, fighting for dominance.

I didn't have time to see the outcome before another Nordak was on me, sword raised as he swung, aiming for my head. Swooping low, I dodged the blow, snarling as I countered the attack, fangs bared, wishing I could shift and face off with a sword rather than my claws. I leapt over the man, his bulky frame twisting as my claws raked the side of his body, the movement of my jump dragging them over him, through the armor he wore. His scream echoed beside me as he fell, clutching at his back, unable to stop the flow of blood gushing out of him as he collapsed.

Turning on my heels, I searched out Sébastien or Dravyn. Catching sight of Dravyn's dusty red-brown coat close by, I raced to his side, throwing myself at the second Nordak that charged toward him, claws out as I fought the man off. His dagger caught my side as we struggled for power, rolling on the floor, his form shifting to a gryffin mid-roll. He pinned me under him as his larger weight trapped me. *Sébastien*! I cried down our bond as I fought against the onslaught of claws trying to sink into my fur.

A snarl filled the air as black fur flew into view, and the weight lifted from me as the wolvyn finished off the gryffin. I panted heavily, my sides burning as I lowered my head in gratitude toward the wolvyn who saved me.

Stay with Kairon, Sébastien demanded from across the room, locked in a spar with a Nordak soldier. I realized that the black-furred wolvyn who had saved me was Kairon, as he nudged my side, forcing me to get up. The sharp trill call of the Seefers added to the chaos as the first of the mangled creatures leapt toward us, razored claws outstretched as Kairon and I circled the beast.

Our attacks were coordinated as we struck, claws unleashed, shredding into the Seefer. The echoed screams from down the wolvyn bond in my head faded to the background as a battle induced haze filled the void. The only task at hand was eliminating the Nordak and Seefers flooding into the room.

Blood coated me, my limbs growing weaker with each strike as I grappled for mental control over my power, my ability to hold my wolvyn form. My body was drained as I struggled. My eyes caught Dravyn and Sébastien on the far side of the room, in mortal form, as they defeated beast after beast. Their bodies were coated in a sheen of sweat and blood. Determination and rage were set in stone across their faces. The King of Verastarr battled three gryffins on the terrace, wielding magic unlike any I had seen as he faced the onslaught.

A sharp nudge to my side drew me from my assessment. Four Seefers closed in on Kairon and me as they backed us into a corner. Their shrill snarls haunted my soul as we stared down our attackers. The far right one tore through the air toward me, as two leapt toward Kairon. I prepared for the strike, claws outstretched as I clashed with the Seefer. Its amber fangs sunk into my back as we grappled for dominance. I thrashed on the ground, my claws scraping for any traction.

My fangs connected with the beast's neck, and I saw Kairon shifting back and forth as he delivered blow after blow to the two attacking him. The weight of the Seefer was crushing me as I drained life from it, my limbs protesting as I struggled to push the creature off.

Another Seefer rushed after me, my body pinned beneath the weight of the dead Seefer. With a final push against the unmoving beast, the last of my mental control on my wolvyn form slipped as I freed myself.

I froze in shock, my form shifting back to mortal as the Seefer drew in. My body instantly weakened as I looked around for a weapon, defenseless against the onslaught. My eyes caught on a dagger to my right, and I threw myself in that direction, fingers slipping as they closed over the handle.

I rose, twisting my body so the hilt of the dagger was in front of me, the blade connecting with my target as I held it above my body. Time moved in slow motion as I felt claws scratch my skin, fangs lowering toward my neck, as I fought off the Seefer, twisting the dagger deep within it. It wasn't enough. I kicked my legs feebly, my body pinned beneath the weight of the beast. I heard a roar in the distance, shattering across the room.

Out of the corner of my eye, I saw black fur dart forward. Gryffins closed in as my mortal form was now recognizable. And I became their prey. The weight lifted from me as Kairon barreled into the Seefer. He drew it away from me as he crashed into two gryffins. I took in a sharp breath, searching for a weapon, as Kairon battled three attackers.

"CATCH!" someone yelled to my left, a sword hurling through the air as I stretched out my hand, the hilt slamming into my palm as I wrapped my fingers securely around the weapon. A Nordak soldier rushed toward me, blade raised overhead as he swung in my direction. My arms weakened with each block as I defended, incapable of striking; my strength diminishing as I was backed into a wall.

My grip slipped on the handle as I blocked another strike, the sword flying from my grasp as I found the tip of his sword pressing against my neck. Pain built as he dug the tip in, breaking the skin, blood running down me.

"You're coming with me," the Nordak snarled venomously, his beefy hand tightening around my neck, forcing me in front of him like a rag doll. My legs shot back in an attempt to escape. "Not today," he growled as his blade dug into my neck, pushing me forward.

Sébastien! I screamed down our bond. Horror flashed through his eyes as they collided with mine across the room. I watched as he thrust his sword through the heart of a gryffin and yanked the blade free as he charged toward me.

Black fur crashed into my side as Kairon knocked me down. My attacker snarled as he lost his grip on me and shifted. Golden wings flapped as he dove toward Sébastien's brother.

I could only watch as the two collided; fangs and claws cutting through flesh as the gryffin struggled to remain in the air, Kairon battling for control. Blood soaked the ground as the two ripped into each other, snarled growls filling the air. I searched for a weapon, anything to help, as a high yelp cut through the air, my eyes snapping back to Kairon as I watched his form fall, landing on the stone with a *thud*.

A scream ripped itself from my throat, my voice hoarse as I threw myself over Kairon's wolvyn form, my hands shaking at the lack of response as I screamed for help. His blood coated my hands as I tried to stop it from flowing out of his mauled neck. The phrase *"Embers and Ash, even The Void won't hold"* flashed through my mind down the universal wolvyn bond as I felt his soul leave his body. Then the gryffin swooped back down, talons angled toward me.

A roar cascaded from the terrace, sweeping over the room as a powerful, primal blast of magic struck. Freezing black mist shot from the king's body. His form rose up into the air as sharp bands of power shot from him, coursing throughout the room as he expelled all the power he had within his body.

The temperature dropped as the power struck. Cries of pain radiated through the Palace as the king used the last remaining power, drawing from his own life force to vanquish the enemy, while I looked on in shock. Gryffins and Seefers alike dropped to the floor, blackened blood flooding the stone of the throne room.

"NOOOO!" Sébastien's voice roared as he sprinted toward the terrace. Distraught fear radiated down my bond from him as he pushed forward. The temperature was below freezing as my body clung to Kairon's wolvyn form on the ground by me, watching as angry black strands wrapped around the remaining attackers, sucking the life from them, vanquishing the Nordak presence from the room immediately.

The mist withdrew with just as much force, recoiling as it reached the king. His body was pelted as the strands of power sucked back into his flesh, his body arching back, his soul being claimed by The Void, before falling to the ground in a lifeless heap.

Sébastien fell to his knees, his roar of rage and pain echoing through the room. I felt his dark promise of revenge as he stared at the lifeless form of his father—the fallen King of Verastarr.

Chapter Thirty-One

VERASTARR

SOMBER SILENCE STRETCHED across the room in the moments following. Heads lowered in respect as Sébastien kneeled on the ground by his father's fallen form. Pain radiated through our bond in sharp bursts from him. I watched as the Wolvyn Commander, Prince of Verastarr—my mate—lost his entire family in the span of minutes.

Pushing upward, preparing to get up, I felt a tug holding me down in place. My blurry gaze turned as my eyes collided with Dravyn's. His head shook as he motioned for me to wait. So I stayed, my heart breaking as the man I had fallen for suffered, my heart calling out for him as I sat on the cold floor. A wave of anguish wrapped around the room for the souls that had gone to The Void, as we who survived were left to pick up the bitter remains.

Sébastien rose slowly, his body tense as he turned to look over the wolvyn who remained. I watched my mate, his body worn from hours of fighting, with blood splattered over him, and a few deep gashes slowly dripping crimson down his skin. His ice-blue eyes set, hardened, hiding emotion as he looked over his remaining guard, radiating authority and power amidst trial and pain.

His jaw locked into place as he rose to his full height. Sounds of movement rose from around me, my gaze shifting over the room as I watched in awe. One by one, men and wolvyn alike lowered themselves, kneeling before Sébastien as they pledged themselves to him. Sébastien met each one of their gazes, acknowledging them with a nod of his head.

Dravyn moved from my side, crossing the battleground of a throne room, as he walked toward the throne. Picking up an onyx crown, he stepped in front of Sébastien, kneeling down as he held the symbol out. The air was silent as Sébastien stared between his brother and father's fallen forms, before nodding once at his closest friend, accepting the crown. The weight of Verastarr now rested on his shoulders.

"Their deaths will be avenged," Sébastien growled as he looked on at his people. "The Nordak have drawn their last breath, and I don't plan to stop until we burn every last one."

A united howl sounded from the wolvyn in the room, rising as they accepted their new leader—the head of their pack.

Sébastien Capetian.

King of Verastarr.

The next few days following the attack were filled with chaos. Sébastien focused on restructuring the Verastarr Guard, preparing for the impending war as arrangements were made for those who had lost their lives in the attack.

I walked into the breakfast room, my black pants with the slitted sides flowing freely, a sharp contrast to the tight shirt that hugged my figure. My injuries were healing, though my magic and disconnection with my wolvyn form were still a struggle to control following the battle. Sharp laughter caught my ear as I glanced up. The familiar faces of Dravyn as well as Kodrayn and Ryker greeted me.

"Well, if it isn't our favorite little troublemaker," Ryker jibed at me as I took a seat beside Dravyn. The two of them had shown up shortly after the attack, battle ready as they helped Sébastien deal with the aftermath of the ambush, picking up the pieces and helping him to rebuild from the rubble.

"Morning to you as well," I retorted as I sipped a cup of tea, watching the men around me chat. The group seemed at ease, even as I sensed an underlying current of tension. "Where's Sébastien?" I questioned, turning toward Dravyn.

His gaze flicked from mine to Kode, then Ry, before finally dragging his eyes back to mine. "Busy," he replied.

"Busy with what?" I prompted.

"Last we saw him, he was wrapping up some things in the war room," Kode replied in.

"Since when?" I questioned the three of them. "I left well past midnight last night. How long has he been there?"

Dravyn hesitated briefly before speaking. "All night. The three of us left only hours ago." I stood up then, slamming my chair against the table, dishes rattling as the three men looked at me. The stitches in my side from the latest attack strained from the sudden movement.

"What is wrong with you three?" I snapped, glaring at the group. "You claim to be his best friends, *his blood brothers*, yet you let him stay in that room all night, once again. Some friends you are." I paused as I met each of their eyes.

I stormed out of the breakfast room as quickly as I'd entered, quickly making my way to the war room, to my mate.

I found him in the same chair I'd left him in, slumped against the handles as he analyzed map after map, planning, strategizing.

You shouldn't be here still, I voiced down the bond. *You need rest.*

Not until this is over. I won't rest until this has been made right, he shot back, his voice exhausted.

I sighed as I walked up behind my mate, leaning against the back of his chair, my arms wrapping around the tightly corded muscles of his chest. My fingers danced across his skin as I eased the tension from him, a low moan of relief falling from his freckled lips.

Even kings need rest, Sébastien.

I didn't stop running my fingers over his skin as his head fell back slightly, the weight of Verastarr heavy on his shoulders.

You need rest.

"My father always knew war was inescapable." Sébastien's voice fell flat in the silence. "Even before you showed up with the first artifact. Your arrival just sped up the timeline. The Nordak have been pushing boundaries, testing limits over the years. And we haven't done a Void-damned thing about it. Until now."

"You've decided what must be done then?" I questioned, bracing myself for the answer I knew was coming.

"Dathrian lit the fuse with his ambush. A line has been drawn and it must be answered." Sébastien resolved. "I will be declaring war. Tonight."

"WHAT?!" I shrieked, my voice raising two octaves as my fingers gripped his skin. I knew the answer had been coming, but I was still unprepared. Not yet ready for what a life of war would look like.

"Ryker and I will be supporting Sébastien in his declaration of attack, allying with Verastarr," Kodrayn's voice sounded from the doorway on the war room then. My head snapped up as I realized that the rest of the Brotherhood had arrived.

"And you're positive this is the only course of action?" I questioned Sébastien, but it was Ryker who answered.

"It's what must be done," he stated, and his voice hardened as he stared at me. "After they brutally murdered *our* blood brother. After they took the lives of far too many. It's the only option we have, we must fight and avenge their deaths . . . *Embers and Ash.*"

"This war has been brewing for decades." Sébastien's voice rumbled beneath my palms as he spoke. "With one artifact already having emerged, the other two won't be far behind. War is coming, whether we want it or not. It's just a matter of time until it lands on our doorstep."

I stared between all four men, the Brotherhood, noting the seriousness in their eyes, the set determination radiating from each of them. They were doing this.

"What about the East Engles?" I questioned, knowing that neither Ryker nor Kode were the rulers there. That left one land unmentioned.

Dravyn's jaw ticked as I asked the question. "They only look out for themselves," he said. "If the Nordak haven't already gotten to them, they will soon. Both of their lands combined have a higher population than ours. Our best hope is to intercept the other two artifacts before they do. All of Vanaiyer will be looking for the next two."

My heart grew heavy, praying that my sister didn't go looking for the next one. That she stayed in the present, far removed from this impending nightmare that we were fast approaching.

I smoothed my hands over the sleeves of the wine-colored satin gown. Rosalie tightening the black ties across the back of the dress as I stared at my reflection in the mirror. Black lace was intricately woven along the neckline, accenting the wine color. The slits on each side of my hip trailed up, exposing my legs. My reflection stared back at me, a woman I hardly recognized. The hard set of my face, the sorrow in my eyes mixed with fear for the future.

Tonight, Sébastien would accept his role of ruler over Verastarr officially. His first act, a declaration of war against Nordak, backed by Reggeon and Avyon; allies, as we burned the realm for justice. For revenge.

Strapping a dagger to the inside of my thigh, I walked out the door. My feet led me toward the throne room. A room I hadn't stepped foot in since we had lost Adrastan and Kairon, along with forty other wolvyn. My lungs tightened as I thought of entering the room, visions haunting me from that day. From all that had been lost.

I nodded to the guards on either side of the towering doors, as I stopped, waiting for them to be opened, to face a future I had never imagined. A destiny I had never dreamed I would have chosen.

A warm breeze fluttered across my skin, my dress dancing as the doors pulled open, my legs trembled as I stepped forward, entering the room. My eyes met Sébastien's across the space. Black leathers hugged his thick thighs, matching the black shirt he wore, the sleeves rolled up a notch or two, the top button undone, exposing his tattooed skin peeking through. A low heat built in my core as I walked across the space toward him. My king. My mate.

My Queen, he purred down the bond. The change of nick-name sent a spike of arousal coursing through me as I held his gaze, alight with desire. I stopped in front of him, my breath catching as he tilted my chin to meet his eyes.

"You're positive this is what you want to do?" I questioned softly.

His body tensed as his gaze tracked mine. "It's the only option. They took my father and my brother from me. In return, I will take everything from them. They have hunted our realm for far too long."

I nodded in understanding. The darkness the Nordak cast

as a shadow over Vanaiyer needed to be brought down. A darkness that had snuffed the light from my own time. One that had ruled through terror for far too long.

Leaning up on my tiptoes, I clashed my lips against his, inhaling the scent of pine and spice. The scent of my new home. His tongue pushed, seeking entrance as I lost myself in the feel of him. The desperation and speed at which our kiss escalated made it feel like there was no tomorrow. Tomorrow a war would be brewing, and the thought made my heart crack; the uncertainty made my very being ache. But today. Today I had him.

His hand wrapped around my neck, holding my head up as he gained better access, heat rushing through me as my body pressed against his, our lips dancing. He broke the kiss, lust blazing in his eyes as he stared down at me.

"I've known you would be mine since I first laid eyes on you," he said, his finger tracing the bond inked on my wrist. "Mine. For eternity. Because from the moment we met, our paths were intertwined. We will pick up the shattered pieces of our hearts—of the hearts of our people. And we will put them back together piece by piece. We will rise from within the embers and we will restore this realm." Strength and determination set across his face, his eyes dark as he stared out over the terrace, over the lands of Verastarr, our home. Our future.

I smiled as he finished, my hand entwining with his as we both took a deep breath, walking out onto the terrace. Out to accept our destiny. The future of Vanaiyer lay in our hands as we joined Kodrayn and Ryker. Preparing to set the realm on fire. Tomorrow. Tomorrow would be the start of a new beginning—war.

Spice Rack

If you wish to be aware of any chapters that contain explicit, on-page intimate scenes, please review the following list.

- Chapter 20 - one short scene
- Chapter 29 - one longer scene

Acknowledgments

I would like to thank my family for encouraging me to write and always believing in me. For always pushing me to write whatever came to mind, and who believed in this story throughout the years and its many changes until it finally reached this point.

My dad, who first encouraged me to pick up a pen and become an author.

My mom, who listened to more phone calls than I can count about my story ramblings and how to become a published author.

My brother, who said he would be one of the first people to buy my book.

And my sister—my constant reading buddy, partner in crime, drill sergeant, and the inspiration behind the character, Kateya. Thanks for always pushing me to be the woman I have become.

My husband, for constantly pushing me to write even when I would rather curl up on my couch and get lost in a good book. The man who reminds me that my story deserves to be shared no matter what.

My alpha reader, Donna. Thanks for reading through all the grammatical changes, the millions of plot changes, and for constantly begging for updates, chapter by chapter.

My lovely beta readers and booksta friends, Ashley and LeeAnn. Your feedback, thoughts, and sidebar comments as you read gave me quite a few laughs while I edited.

My developmental editor, Taylor. Thank you for making this book what it is and providing lots of comical comments throughout the editing process so I didn't get buried under the amount of time spent editing.

My late night lifesaver and copy/line editor, Caitlin, who gave me advice when thought bubbles constantly arose right before huge deadlines and helped me hash out final details to make this story what it is.

My proofreader, Brittany, for making sure my book baby was perfect and ready to go out into the world!

And most importantly, God, for giving me an imaginative mind filled with words to put on paper, a wonderful life, and salvation through His son.

About the Author

T.A. Reilly is an author of NA fantasy romance with equal levels of adventure, time travel, and romance mixed in. Reading came naturally to her at a young age, and the words began flowing shortly after that. She has traveled all over the world from a young age and is constantly counting down the days until her next trip! After graduating with a master's in Professional Communications, she decided to pursue her life-long dream . . . bringing time travel to life on paper. Currently, she calls Florida home. In her free time, she loves rewatching *FRIENDS*, going to the beach, and staying up too late, lost in a good book.

Connect with her on Instagram and TikTok as @tareillybooks

Did you enjoy reading *Beneath the Shatter*? Read the second book in the series, *Within the Embers*!

Books by T.A. Reilly

Scattered Destinies Series

Beneath the Shatter

Within the Embers

Above the Shadows

Book 4 (TBA)

Aurelian Guild Series

Solis Falling

Connect with T.A. Reilly

Ready to travel back to Vanaiyer? Read *Within the Embers* today!

If you enjoyed reading *Beneath the Shatter*, please consider leaving a review or star rating on Goodreads, Amazon, or any other platform you use. Your support for my novel means so much to me, and taking a few minutes to drop a review to let others readers know how much you liked BTS is appreciated!

Don't forget to subscribe to my newsletter to stay in the know about all my upcoming releases, teasers, exclusive content, and secret projects!

Where to Connect with T.A.:

Instagram - @tareillybooks

TikTok - @tareillybooks

FB Group - Ember's and Ash Reader's Group

Goodreads - T.A. Reilly

Amazon - T.A. Reilly

Pinterest - T.A. Reilly

Buy Signed Copies:

www.tareillybooks.com

9 798987 537015